Emily Barr has been writing columns and travel pieces for the *Observer* and the *Guardian* for several years. Her first novel, *Backpack*, was critically acclaimed and won the WH Smith New Talent Award 2002. She lives in Sussex with her husband and son.

Praise for *Backpack*:

'The emotional ups and downs of a Marian Keyes novel, and none of the annoying travellers of Alex Garland's *The Beach*. Fantastic' *Company*

'You won't want to stop reading' *Best*

'An assured debut, honest, sharply observed, funny and sad' *List*

Also by Emily Barr

Backpack

BAGGAGE

Emily Barr

R
review

First published in 2002
by REVIEW

This edition published in 2002
by REVIEW

An imprint of Headline Book Publishing

10 9 8 7 6 5 4

ISBN 0 7472 6677 8

Printed and bound in Great Britain by
Clays Ltd, St Ives plc

HEADLINE BOOK PUBLISHING
A division of Hodder Headline
338 Euston Road
LONDON NW1 3BH

www.reviewbooks.co.uk
www.hodderheadline.com

For James and Gabriel

chapter one

'I didn't say I wasn't pleased.'

Tony is being utterly calm and reasonable, yet everything he says, and everything he does, infuriates me. Until recently, I would have flown into a rage at this point, and rushed at him with my fists flying. I haven't done that for a couple of years. This is partly because I'm learning to control my emotions, but it's mainly because he is so much bigger and stronger than I am that my behaviour just used to make me look stupid. He would reach out and pluck my wrists from the air, and hold them in front of me until I stopped struggling. That's the trouble with being married to someone who works outdoors, in the quarries, for a living.

Married life has not been the contented haze I'd vaguely expected. Tony was not the first person who asked me to marry him. My neighbour's cousin got in first, when I lived in Bombay. Perhaps I should have accepted. I could, at least, have had a fair fight with Sanjay. I don't think I've recently reminded Tony, as I do from time to time, that, like Barbara Cartland's, my hand has been sought before.

'I should have married that guy in India,' I say, trying to wound with words instead of fists. 'He would have been delighted. He would have loved a baby.'

'Maybe you're right,' says Tony, smiling infuriatingly. 'But he would only have loved a boy. It's too late now, isn't it? It looks like you're stuck with me, and with my baby. What will you do if it turns out to be a Mini-Me?'

'Give it up for adoption.'

He shrugs, and turns back to the television. He is watching some cricket match. I glance at the screen, and feel an irate nostalgia for

1

the days when cricketers used to wear white. Today, half of them are in blue, and the others are in some disgusting green and yellow concoctions.

'They're in their pyjamas,' I tell him. 'They look stupid.' He doesn't react. I pick up the remote control, and switch both the television and the radio off. My husband, for reasons of his own, prefers to watch the cricket accompanied by the radio commentary, thus using up all our lines of communication from the outside world save the telephone. I'm sure that, sooner or later, he will discover a pitch-cam, or a changing-rooms-cam and monopolise the computer and phone line as well.

'Lina, love,' he says calmly. 'What did you do that for?'

I pick up the coffee mug and the empty beer can that are by his feet. He messes up the house just to annoy me.

'Why do you think? I've just told you I'm pregnant, and you're not even pleased. You didn't even look away from the telly,' I remind him, straightening the sofa cushions with my free hand. 'Other people's husbands make them lie down, and they bring them drinks and fruit and, I don't know, chocolate. They do not fucking say, oh, right, good, without even taking their eyes off the fucking cricket.'

I never swear, normally. I used to, but I don't any more. Swearing is a sure sign that I'm losing control. I am good at controlling the big things, and crap with the details.

'But I *am* pleased. I said I was.'

'You're not pleased *enough*. This is by far the most important day of our married life. We're having a baby, for Christ's sake. We've been trying for two years. We didn't even think we could have children of our own. I've known I'm pregnant for ten minutes now, and I'm beginning to wish I hadn't even bothered to find out.'

'Don't get upset. You're pleased really. You know it's only your hormones.'

I stand up and kick his shin. He doesn't even flinch, so I kick him again, harder, and leave. I walk out and slam the door behind me. I know he's smiling to himself, and switching the radio commentary back on. He isn't bothered at all. I dump his debris in the kitchen, and make a loud and pointed exit through the front door, into the desert.

I am not usually like this. Tony, equally, isn't normally such an arse.

We do, however, have our moments, and they usually happen when Red, our adopted son, is out of the house. Today he is down the road, playing Nintendos with his friend Eric. This means that he, too, will come back in a strange mood, because Eric's mother recently died of cancer, and it is gradually dawning on Red that the same thing could, theoretically, happen to me. Until now, I don't think he's ever thought of me as mortal. He doesn't like me to have so much as a headache. These days, he's unwilling to let me out of his sight. It probably doesn't help that, this year, I'm his class teacher. We see each other all day, every day. He's hardly going to fail to notice my pregnancy symptoms.

I wonder what it'll be like having a baby in the house. Sometimes I feel that I've got two babies already. I suppose a third won't make much difference. Red deals with worry by clinging to me in a manner more suited to a three-year-old than a big grown-up boy of ten. Tony does the opposite, and sulks, turning towards any form of armchair sport. For my part, I invariably end up giving the house a good spring clean and myself a good scrubbing. I have been called obsessive. I am frequently pronounced sad by the men in the house. Beth, my best friend, and my other friend, Nina, Eric's mother, now scattered to the desert winds, used to tease me ceaselessly.

'You must have been a joy as a child,' Beth said lightly a couple of weeks ago as we shared a bottle of wine at the bar. Her comment was provoked by the way I'd taken a clean handkerchief from my pocket and wiped our glasses before I'd let her pour it. I was surprised. We were there to drink to Nina, exactly a month after she died in the hospital in Adelaide. We weren't there to talk about my obsessive compulsion. I never speak about my childhood, and Beth knows that.

'What do you mean?' I demanded.

'You know. Just, like, you must have been the only thirteen-year-old in history who spontaneously irons and folds her clothes, who colour codes her wardrobe. I bet you did the dishes before anyone noticed they were dirty. Christ, you do the dishes when they're still clean. You were probably the one yelling at your parents to stop treating the house like a hotel.' She laughed, her perfect teeth glistening. Beth is the personification of the eternal Australian feminine. Her hair is naturally blonde and hangs silkily down her back. Her smile is wide,

3

her skin flawless and freckled. She, too, moved to Craggy Rock for love, but, unlike me, she has now left, due to hate.

When she caught my eye, her laughter stopped abruptly. I raised my eyebrows gently, and composed my face into my 'I don't want to talk about it' expression. Then I took a large slug of wine.

'Sorry,' she said quietly. Nobody in the world except me knows exactly what went on when I lived in England, but they know that my parents died suddenly, that I have no other family. They know that I don't talk about my life before I came back to Australia. From time to time, friends have suggested that I should have therapy, that my complete avoidance of the issue cannot be healthy, but I always laugh it off.

To show Beth that she shouldn't feel bad, I said, 'I wasn't always like this, you know. I was a messy teenager along with the rest of them. I wouldn't have dreamed of questioning the cleanliness of a glass in a pub. It's OK. Honestly.' And it was. I am comfortable with myself, with my life, now. I am not touchy, like I used to be. I am perfectly all right.

Now Nina has died and Beth has left. The three of us used to drink together and laugh together and keep each other sane in this weird place. Suddenly, I'm on my own, with two men.

I hope this baby's a girl.

It's a little bit cold outside, but I can't go back in to fetch a fleece. That would send the wrong signals to Tony and provoke a super-cilious smile. Instead, I will go for a brisk walk, and then I'll return home. I will work off my tension by mopping and disinfecting the kitchen floor. Then I'll let Tony give me a ball by ball analysis of the cricket, and then, perhaps, he might manage to express a genuine enthusiasm for the prospect of fatherhood. Either that, or he will ask me to have an abortion. I wonder whether we're dysfunctional, or whether all marriages are like this. I have no idea.

I thought he'd be pleased. When I stood in the bathroom and watched the big blue line appear on the pregnancy test, I gasped and forgot to breathe out again for at least a minute. I bit my hand. I looked again. I compared it with the picture on the box, although I knew perfectly well that two lines meant a positive. Then I couldn't stop myself laughing out loud. We had done it, after all. We were fertile. We were having a baby, at last.

Sometimes I hate Tony. Normally, I love him. He supports me and adores me. I feel comfortable with him in a way I never thought I'd feel comfortable with anyone. Occasionally, however, something tests our relationship, and I really need him. That's when he lets me down.

I start stomping up the road, trying to let go of my anger and to concentrate, instead, on my womb. Marital strife cannot be good for even as tiny an embryo as this one. After a deep breath of dusty air, I feel slightly better. I look around. Even though we've been living in this desolate outpost of humanity in the Australian Outback for nearly three years, I am still surprised when I step out of the door. Part of me will always believe that I live in a small town in Devon. For a few seconds, I allow myself to imagine what would happen if I returned to Kingsbridge now. The repercussions do not bear thinking about. Instead, we live in a dugout house, cut into an artificial hillside, on the very edge of a town you won't have heard of. It is named, with that peculiar Australian literalness that I am growing to appreciate, Craggy Rock. Sure enough, the place is full of rocks, and there is a certain degree of cragginess to every one of them. Our road, like almost all the other roads here, is stony and dusty. If you turn right, you pass the house where Eric's father now struggles, alone, to get Eric and his brother to school in the morning and to bed at night. Then there's Alky Bob's home, and the empty house, before you end up in the town centre, where such amenities as a cafe, three 'restaurants' (kebabs, pizzas, or pies), the town hall, the supermarket, the shop, and the backpackers' hostel-cum-internet cafe await your attention. Tempting as this is, it's hardly Oxford Street. I turn left instead, and walk out into the desert.

It is winter. The whole of the town is glowing red. This is my favourite time of day, and my favourite time of the year. I love the desert winters. I love the fact that I can often wear jeans and a fleece, socks, and even, if I'm pushing my luck, a jacket. I take a deep breath of clean air, close my eyes, and let it out again.

The earth in the town, and for miles around it, ranges from sandy yellow to the deepest red. When a desert storm whips itself up, the dust gets everywhere. It comes in under the door and around the window panes, ridiculing the care I take to plug the gaps. It gets in the drawers where my clothes are, and it drives me mad. It makes me realise why people believe in God. It is a powerful force which, reason suggests, cannot spring from nowhere, and die back to nothing, at random. Yet, apparently, that is what happens. It seems like a peculiar torment devised specifically for me. I think I've devoted my years in Craggy to a futile attempt to tame the desert. I am the female Sisyphus of our age. When I stop and think about it, there is nothing unique in this. Immediately, I feel less lonely. The modern world is full of individual lives devoted to, for example, the sorting out of pieces of paper. Millions of men and women spend all day filing things away, only to come to work the next morning and find an in-tray that has refilled itself. This goes on day after day, week after week, year after year. Just because my obsession is with dust and neatness, that doesn't make my quest any more futile than anyone else's. At least, as a teacher, I get to see results in my professional life, even when that result is not particularly welcome; for example when a girl who has imbibed my own brand of wisdom-with-English-Literature for three years leaves school at the age of sixteen and promptly steals my best friend's husband.

A month after we arrived here, Tony and I got married. We did it mainly to please his mother, who was already bewildered and grudgingly pleased that a nice English girl such as myself had not only taken her younger son in hand, but had actively persuaded him to move back to his hometown.

'You're sure you know what you're letting yourself in for, love?' she used to ask me, eyes narrowed and, presumably, trying to work out my hidden agenda. I'm glad Tony's not particularly rich, or she would never have let me, or any other woman, anywhere near him.

'Of course I am, Margot,' I'd tell her. My accent, though softened by five years in Australia, has always sounded particularly regal next to hers. 'I love it out here. The middle of nowhere.'

'You may call it the middle of nowhere, love, but to us who were born and bred here, it's not to be dismissed so lightly.'

Tony became so enraged by Margot's mistrust that he proposed to me, on the grounds that it would shut her up. I accepted, partly for the same reason. Some part of me was also caught up in the romance of a spontaneous Outback wedding. The elements didn't let me down. To this day, I have never seen worse dust.

The wind had been raging for fifty hours by the time I needed to leave for the town hall, and I was in despair. On Margot's insistence, I was wearing white, though both Tony and I had drawn the line at a religious ceremony. We paid good money for the registrar to fly in from Coober Pedy, and we got married in the shack which is the town hall. Had I put aside my scruples, of course, we could have had the cool elegance of a ceremony in the underground church, and, looking back, I wish we had.

Margot, Nina, Beth, Red and I stood at the window in Margot's house, which is a proper, air-conditioned bungalow, denoting her status in the community. We watched the devils of dust blowing up and down the street. Rubbish hurried by at roof height. The street was empty. Nobody was out. The town hall was round the corner, but if I attempted to walk it in my finery, I would arrive as an orange scarecrow. It was hardly every girl's childhood dream. I couldn't contain my angst. I half wanted to laugh. This could only happen in Craggy.

'I can't go out in this,' I muttered between gritted teeth. I was wearing a floor-length silk dress, cut on the bias, with a cowl neck. I'd been all the way to Adelaide to have it made, reasoning that this was, if all went well, the only chance I'd get. My imminent mother-in-law had tried to make me wear an ugly necklace she'd worn on her own wedding day, but I refused, on the grounds that I always wore my dead mother's fairy necklace. Even she couldn't argue with that. 'I'm wearing ivory, for Christ's sake! This is my wedding day. It's meant to be the happiest fucking day of my life.'

Margot took my arm in her iron grip. 'Noeline! There's no need for that sort of bloody language,' she cautioned. 'We'll see you right.'

'How can you? How can any of you? We should have stayed in bloody Sydney! I wish I was getting married there. I should have married the Indian . . .'

I tailed off at that point, realising I might have overstepped the mark.

When I burst into the town hall, a single-roomed establishment, I was wearing cut-off denim shorts and a baggy T-shirt, with one of Margot's tea towels knotted round my head. Tony was there already, chatting idly to Pete, his brother and best man. I could read the

7

confusion on his face. For a few seconds, he genuinely believed this was the wedding outfit I'd hidden from him for weeks.

My whole bridal party, apart from Red who is too short, stood in a protective screen around me while I changed. Shortly afterwards, I pledged myself to Tony for life.

I don't regret it. Perhaps, occasionally, I regret it, but hardly ever. I had no alternative; and it's worked out more happily than I ever dared imagine.

Today, the air is still and the storms are hundreds of miles away. The sun is huge on the horizon as I amble towards it, away from civilisation. When I arrived here, I would have laughed in the face of anyone who implied that Craggy Rock was, in any way, civilised, but it only took one trip into the surrounding area to change my perspective.

Even a few moments' walk from home makes the town look different. I look over my shoulder. From here, it is a settlement in the wide expanse of arid land which is barely habitable by humans or any other animal, save those conditioned for desert life, like lizards. It is a miraculous place. I love living in the middle of the panorama of earth. It keeps my life in perspective. I think of the cluster of cells inside me that must, even now, be dividing and multiplying and forming itself into something approximating a fish, if not yet a human. It will, I hope, grow and grow. I will swell and bulge and moan and groan and finally produce an independent human being from within me. There is something disconcertingly reminiscent of *Alien* about the whole process.

Tony will get used to the idea. We've been trying for long enough. He should be used to it already. Yet I am shocked myself.

There is a small hill fifteen minutes' walk from the house. It is the remnants of an old mining quarry which has been disused for years. I stroll up it, wondering whether, by the time summer has been and almost gone, I will be able to huff and puff my way to the summit, or whether I'll be stuck on the sofa monopolising the television, or looking up baby websites on the internet. I hope the pregnancy is straightforward. Already, and despite Tony's lack of enthusiasm for the whole project, I feel a little smug. I am special. I am growing a baby. You can't do anything better than that. The air is cool, and the whole of the desert is glowing. From here, I can see for, perhaps, one hundred miles in every direction. Craggy Rock looks insignificant. It begins and then, straightaway, it ends, and the desert stretches for miles beyond it.

I was initially disappointed that this desert didn't look like the Saharan cliché. There are no rippling dunes around here. There are stones and rocks, and instead of sand, we have pervasive, inescapable dust. I have, however, come to appreciate it. More than anything, I love its size. I love the fact that, unless you fly in one of the expensive little planes, it takes a day to get anywhere. I love the fact that there is no natural water supply, that the water has to come in on lorries.

Opals are the only reason the settlement exists, and they are capricious, occasionally making someone rich for life, but more often losing him (for it is invariably a him) his savings, and nudging him into a life of abject alcoholism. Tony is good with opals. We have a handsome, and secret, sum in the bank thanks to a couple of judicious finds he's made.

At the top of the hill, I watch the sun slipping away over the red earth. I look back towards the town, and see it flaming in the late afternoon light. I bite back all my ambivalence. I am happy.

As I walk towards home, I imagine myself with an alternative life. I am a lost traveller, staggering through the desert. I am about to die from dehydration. When I see the town, I dismiss it as a mirage. As I get closer, however, it doesn't shimmer and disappear, but becomes more concrete. My heart begins to lift. Then I am suddenly walking between doors and windows cut into artificial hillsides. I even pass a person, and give her a tentative smile. She spoils my fantasy by responding with a cheery, 'G'day Lina! How are you doing?'

'Hi, Nora,' I say. Nora runs the motel. 'Good, thanks. You?'

By the time I get home I am overcome with amazement at the fact that I live in a house, here, in the desert. I know everyone in the settlement. I have a key to the door, although I rarely use it as we hardly ever lock it. My life seems fantastically improbable.

An hour after I get home, Tony begins to accept the inevitable fact that he must be kind to me, as I am expecting his child. I'm going to have to get him accustomed to the idea in the next few months. I am almost tempted to confide in Margot (and thus in all our neighbours), just so she can bully him into niceness.

He steps over the threshold of the kitchen, onto my territory, and, as a goodwill gesture, he carries a glass and a crumby plate over to the sink, gives them a cursory rinse, dries them, and puts them away. Both he and Red are trained to do this, though it rarely happens. I am on my hands and knees, attacking a particularly tenacious stain on one of the tiles, and I watch him from the corner of my eye. The stain seems to be jam with some mystery glue-like ingredient added on top. I put my sponge back into the hot disinfectant, squeeze it out, and wait for him to say something.

'Do you think you should be doing that?' he asks, after a pause. 'I mean, in your condition.'

'No one's going to do it for me,' I point out.

'But, like, we can live with a dirty patch on the floor, or whatever it is.' He stands next to me and extends a hand, helping me to my feet. I don't mention the fact that he's put sock prints all over my clean tiles. I'll come back and finish it later. When I look around the room, I see that the kitchen is sparkling. When we moved in here, this room was a seventies-style brown and orange monstrosity. It was completely encrusted with grime. Fat was caked to every surface. I was glad. It meant I didn't have a problem persuading Tony to have it ripped out, and to let me choose a new one in white and chrome. It looks a bit odd in our funny little house – as if visitors from the future had arrived in our prehistoric dugout home, built their best kitchen, and rushed off again, back to 2020. At least it has a window. My kitchen always comforts me. Never, in my younger days, did I imagine myself capable of articulating a sentence like that.

I let him lead me into the bedroom, since Red has come home and taken up residence in front of the television.

'So?' I ask. I'm not giving an inch on this one. I know it's all about compromise, but I don't want to. He was in the wrong, and the fact that he has already mentioned my 'condition' means that he knows it.

He sits beside me on the bed. It is king-sized, with wrought iron at the head and foot. I had it delivered from Melbourne at massive personal expense, but it is glorious and it was worth it. It is my nest, my refuge. It is everything a marital bed should be. Once again, however, my strenuous efforts were unable to make our home into anything other than a dugout burrow in one of the least hospitable places on earth. However chic the bed, the bedroom is never going to have a window.

Tony takes my hand in his, and forces me to look at him.

'I'm sorry,' he says, with a little smile. 'Really. I'm sorry I wasn't very nice. It's just that it was the last thing I was expecting. Didn't even know it was a possibility. But I'm over the moon.' I scrutinise his face. He grins. 'Seriously, darl. Don't worry.' He pats my stomach, far higher than where our embryonic son or daughter must be.

I smile, despite myself, and move his hand from my lower ribs to between my hips. 'You are pleased, aren't you?'

'Truly I am.'

'But you weren't pleased when I told you. You didn't even look me in the eye.'

'I know. Hey, you know how men are. We're shite. Even whatsis-name in Bombay couldn't have been perfect *all* the time.'

'Oh, no, he would have been. But don't worry about him. As long as you really are happy. I don't want you pretending and then going complaining to Andy and Pete every night.'

'Of course I'm happy. It blew me away, darling. Tell you the truth, I didn't think my boys could do it. Didn't reckon they could swim that far. It's great news. I'm going to be a dad. It's the best thing that's ever happened.'

He sounds as if he means it. I force myself to smile. 'It is, isn't it?'

'Come here.' He hugs me. I breathe in his smell. When Tony folds me into him, we almost become one person. He makes me feel like a small delicate lady who needs to be looked after. He can pick me up under one arm, with ease, and at the end of an evening at the pub he often does. I know that I'm not someone who wants to sit back and be provided for but, from time to time, I like to indulge the feeling.

'Shall we tell Red?' I ask after a few minutes.

'No,' he says straightaway. 'I was thinking about that. If we tell him, we might as well tell the whole town. I guess you don't want to do that yet? Have a bit of leeway before my mum gets on your back. Hey, we were dismal in the Test. We're going to have to bowl them all out tomorrow if we want a hope in hell. Three hundred and five, all out.'

'We could swear him to secrecy. Make him realise that he mustn't tell anyone.'

'Lina, get real. He's ten years old. However shit I might be, Red's going to be over the bloody moon. It's going to make his day, his year. You, of all people, know that his favourite activity is chatting to the girls at school. We can't make him keep this a secret, because he wouldn't be able to, and you can't blame him for that. So say he tells Tabitha. She goes home and tells Jen. Jen tells the other mothers outside the school, or she mentions it in the pub. In no time someone's said to Mum, congratulations, Marg! You must be over the moon, and then we've got her on the bloody doorstep smashing my head in and demanding why she was the last to know.'

I think about it. He is absolutely right. 'So we keep it secret from everyone? Can I tell Beth?'

'Later. When's it normal to tell people?'

'Twelve weeks. The risk of miscarriage is a lot less from then on, and I think that soon after that you start looking pregnant.'

'How many weeks would you be now?'

'About four or five.'

'Already?'

'They measure it from the date of your last period.'

'Yeah? Why? And how do girls know this stuff?'

'We just do. Particularly if we've been at it for years. You know, the due date they give you is only approximate, based on you conceiving in the middle of an average cycle. Beth had some books when she and Andy were trying. And every sodding magazine seems to have had an article, in the week when I've found out I'm not pregnant, every single month for the past two years.'

He puts his arms round me. 'And what happens in the week when you find out you are?'

I smile up at him. 'I think that's when you buy some books of your own.' I think about it. 'Better get them on mail order, or everyone'll know.'

Suddenly I feel overwhelmed with love. Tony and I might have our ups and downs, but we are a team. Whoever this baby takes after, it's going to have a fantastic, if unusual start in life.

Since we're friends again, we stroll into town to celebrate. Red barely raises his tousled dark head to say goodbye.

'Off to the pub, yeah?' he says, waving a hand, his eyes not leaving the TV screen, where two lithe blondes are strolling down a beach wearing tiny bikinis. His cheeks are rosy, and his face is freckled. Like me, he has a pale complexion; something I have achieved for him with liberal daily applications of sunblock.

'Maybe. For a walk, anyway. What are you watching?'

'Looks good, mate,' comments Tony.

'*Home and Away*, for your information. So it *is* suitable. Have fun.'

We are, without a doubt, the only household in Craggy Rock that could afford satellite television yet chooses not to have it. I know I'm going to have to give in soon, because the pressure is increasing from both sides. Tony wants his sport, and Red wants everything. It is the nature of the 'everything' that makes me hold back.

I don't tell them, but I wouldn't mind some satellite TV myself. I'd like the BBC, and Channel Four's film channel. I think a British childhood leaves you convinced, for ever, that their television is the best in the world. I imagine spending the rest of the gestation period curled up on the clean sofa, watching repeats of *Bagpuss* and *The Magic Roundabout*. It might make for the perfect pregnancy.

I weigh up the merits of my comfort television versus the demerits of my son being able to watch porn whenever I'm out of the room. I realise that I'll never get my quality time, anyway, if those two have unlimited channels, and I decide to hold my ground a little longer.

'Bloody winter,' my husband mutters, linking his arm through mine. It is dark, and surprisingly cold. 'What month will the baby be born?'

We grin at each other in the light of the streetlamps, excited by the unfamiliarity of the conversation. I pretend to count on my fingers, even though I have already calculated not only eight months from now, but the more specific forty weeks from the beginning of my last period.

'March,' I tell him. 'I think it'll be due around March the seventh.'

'Autumn. That's good. So you get to be pregnant all through the summer. Wait till I tell the boys.'

We're strolling down our road. This time we've turned right. We pass the empty house, which is agreed, by a general consensus of Red, Eric, and all the other kids in my class, to be haunted. I know they climb in through the windows to scare themselves, but they don't know I know it. I checked that it wasn't abandoned on safety grounds, and then left them to it. An old white sheet went missing from the cupboard recently. There are, I reason, worse things they could be doing than playing at ghosts in an empty house.

I look up at Tony.

'Yeah?' he asks.

'Nothing.' We walk on. 'You really do want this baby, don't you? Did you think I was mad, earlier?'

'Not really. No more so than usual.'

'Things are going to get a lot more hormonal from here on in.'

'Are you going to be sick?'

I shrug. 'Probably. I'm sure I'll feel sick, anyway. You're going to have to be very nice to me, you know.'

'I'll do my best.' He stops, and turns me towards him. 'I've just thought of something. Are you going to stop drinking?'

'Alcohol? Yes, of course. Well, I'll be able to have a few units a week. Why?'

'Everyone'll guess. You know it.'

It is one of the curiosities of life in a small, heavy drinking community that pregnancies never go undetected. The moment a woman of childbearing age turns down anything alcoholic, the cry goes up. 'You're pregnant!' someone shouts. 'Aren't you?' At that point, the woman in question traditionally turns pink, and mutters something about not planning on telling everyone yet.

We are heading for the pub, and I will be rumbled in approximately four minutes.

'What can we do?' I ask. 'I don't really want to risk harming the baby just to stop our neighbours sussing us out.'

'We'll get you a drink anyway,' decides Tony, 'and you can pretend to drink it. I'll neck it back. We'll get you a glass of water as well. No one's going to notice that.'

'Water. Mmmm. Nine months of water. Lucky me.'

The darkness is broken up by the lights of the town centre, but the streets are deserted. We reach the pub, and as we stand on the threshold, Tony gives my hand a squeeze.

'I love you,' he says.

'I know,' I tell him. 'Me too.' I push the door open. We walk in, smiling, and join the crowd.

chapter two

On the day I turn nine weeks pregnant, I wake up in a filthy temper, and reach for Tony, who is snoring. Unhelpfully, yet predictably, he declines to wake up.

One of the things I hate about living here is the fact that, to see whether it's daylight yet, I have to lever myself out of bed, put on a dressing gown, and go into the living room or the kitchen, because they are the only rooms blessed with windows. I give Tony a sharp squeeze, but he doesn't stir. I can't face the idea of getting up when it's probably the middle of the night. I'll need the loo soon. As a preliminary, I reach for the alarm clock and press the button for the light.

It's five past five. That is the worst possible time. Any later, and I could reasonably get up. Anything past four, and I would manage to lull myself back to sleep. As it is, I'll just lie here feeling sick, and putting off the moment when I get up for a wee. This is the beginning of my day. It's a day I've been dreading, and it's starting early.

Nobody tells you what being pregnant is really like. The conception is still a secret between me, Tony, and Dr Angelos. The doc is a prominent member of the community who has been known to discuss his patients in the pub for dramatic effect. Tony had to take him aside and extract an oath of confidentiality, by reminding him of some obscure events involving a mineshaft and a donkey. I have no desire to know the details.

Every single day, I act as much like a normal teacher and mother as I can, even though I am sick once every morning, and once late in the afternoon. The rest of the time, I struggle to stay awake. I feel nauseous when someone walks past me if they're wearing perfume or aftershave. I can make myself gag by thinking about the revolving doner kebab in Mick's shop. The other day, Tony said the word 'offal' in some context, and I had to sit back and breathe deeply until the nausea passed.

I'll get up in a minute. I'll have to.

The children are the closest to guessing. They have noticed, although they're keeping it quiet, that I no longer run after them in the playground. The truth is, I can't do it. When I'm on playground duty, they get away with new levels of bullying and extortion, while I look the other way and pretend not to notice. I just sit on a step, sipping from a bottle of water, and occasionally I lean forward to shout, 'Jess! Where's your hat?'

I turn over in bed and try to find a comfortable position. Sleeping is terrible already, and I don't even have a bump yet. I suppose I'm glad it's Saturday, even if we do have a wedding to go to. Sometimes, at school, I have to make a dash for the toilets. Often I only get as far as the little children's ones, and find myself vomiting inelegantly into a knee-high dunny and hoping that none of the five-year-olds will catch me. The teachers are hopeless. I am willing an adult – any adult – to guess, so I will be forced to own up. If my colleagues caught me throwing up, they'd write it off as food poisoning. If they realised I was sick every morning, they'd never translate that into 'morning sickness'. I can turn up in the staff room with a small salad and two litres of water for lunch, and the only comment I get is, 'Lina! You don't need to diet, love.'

'I'm not dieting, I'm detoxifying,' I lie, transparently, and no one questions me.

Socialising has been even worse. Few activities can be quite as miserable as pretending to drink. Today is going to be the worst of all. I'd rather stay at home and vomit solidly for eight hours than sit in the church (no ethical scruples for them) and watch my former pupil Rachelle pledge herself, body and soul, to my best friend's recent ex-husband, Andy.

I am a closet misanthrope at the best of times. Today I will have to make myself as pretty as possible, offer insincere congratulations to two people who know I despise their union, and pretend to drink with every single inhabitant of this town. Not only that, but I am personally responsible for making Tony and Red look respectable before we go.

I switch on the bedside lamp, but my husband doesn't stir, so I climb over him. One arm is thrown back over his head, displaying a thicket of soft blond armpit hair. I resist the temptation to tickle him, or to drop something into his open mouth. His breath smells of stale beer. I pull on my cotton kimono, and head, with accelerating steps, for the bathroom. When I get there I wonder, briefly, whether the vomit or the urine is the more pressing need, before the vomit answers my question in no uncertain terms. Another joyful day awaits.

By the time Rachelle makes her grand entrance, I am awake only because the pews are so uncomfortable. I am wedged between Tony and Red. All three of us are scrubbed up. I'm wearing a fairly new linen dress that will crease so quickly that I'm not sure why I bothered ironing it. It's dusty pink, and I bought shoes to match, but I draw the line at wearing a hat. I've tucked my necklace inside the dress, to avoid spoiling the neckline. I look sideways at Red. He looks like a gorgeous little posh schoolboy. I yelled at him, after lunch, until he donned smart trousers, a tidy shirt and his school shoes. By then I was so cross that I slicked his hair down with gel. I've always loved the English public schoolboy aesthetic. Red has no idea how adorable he is. Without a doubt he'll be going home to change into skateboarding gear before the reception, and by then I will be beyond caring.

On my right, Tony looks equally uncomfortable in his suit and tie. He's even got a carnation in his buttonhole, as he did when we got married. I've tried to make him buy a new suit, but he refuses. The only suit he possesses was bought for a court appearance, years ago. It is navy blue, and shiny, and I am not in the least bit surprised that, both times he's worn it, he's been found guilty. On its third outing, he married me.

The church contrives to have a solemn, oppressive atmosphere despite its location. On a winter afternoon like this one, it's as cold and dank as any English church, and it even has the stations of the cross on the walls. It seems that all our neighbours are present. I wish I'd cried off. Finding an excuse – any excuse – was my first concern when the invitation arrived, three weeks ago.

'Oh, how horrible!' I exclaimed to Tony, walking into the kitchen with it in my hand. 'I'm not going.'

'What?' demanded Red, leaving the breakfast table and snatching it out of my hands. 'The wedding of Miss Rachelle Hunter and Mr Andrew Fisher? That's not yuck, Mummy. Why aren't you going? I thought you liked weddings. Is that *the* Rachelle?'

I had to think quickly. I have gone out of my way not to let Red know any details of Beth's marital catastrophe because I don't want him dwelling on the impermanence of marriage (a concern which, until now, might not have occurred to him). Besides, Red is the Oprah Winfrey of Craggy School, and spreads gossip without even noticing.

'Yes, it is. And I know I like weddings, but I meant, how horrible for you and Tony because I know you guys hate having to get smartened up. Also, Tony'll probably have to make a speech at the reception because Andy's his friend.'

Red was astonished. 'You mean Andy's name is Mr Andrew Fisher?'

'Certainly is.'

'*The* Andy? Wow. Will I have a posh name if I marry Tabitha?'

'You will. You'll be Mr Red Pritchett.'

'Ohhhhhh! That's boring.'

Tony, finally, looked up from his copy of *FHM*. 'Not half as boring as this wedding's going to be, mate.' He slid the magazine across the table. 'Here, look at this. You should ask your mum to get you a surfboard.'

As the organ pipes up with 'Here Comes the Bride', I crane around in the traditional manner, and catch Margot's eye. She's sitting between Tony and Pete, wearing the same outfit she wore to our wedding. If she knew I was incubating her grandchild, she'd have me sitting in a comfy chair with my feet up for the whole nine months. I have never known a woman as fiercely protective of her children as Margot is of her boys, and I'm sure our baby will also benefit from her lioness tendencies. Tony reverts to a six-year-old in her presence. The other day I caught her inspecting his nails and sending him to wash his hands before lunch.

Margot's wedding outfit is a peach skirt and jacket with a crimson blouse. Her hat is peach, with a crimson rose on the front. Her lipstick (an item which is normally anathema to her) is crimson, and her foundation appears to be peach. Her earrings are crimson, her clumpy shoes peach. Margot is so perfectly colour coordinated at weddings that I half expect her grey hair to be dyed peach for the occasion. I always wonder why she doesn't choose to coordinate herself in colours that actually complement each other. Nonetheless, I have become deeply fond of my mother-in-law. She's the closest thing to a mother I've got, and she'd do anything for our little family.

We smile, and Margot winks. I follow her gaze, and see Rachelle emerge, blinking, into the underground cavern. Her blonde hair is newly bleached for the occasion, right down to the roots, and it's piled stiffly on top of her head. She affixes a rictus of a smile to her face. Rachelle is seventeen years old, and she has no idea what she is letting herself in for. I feel a brief pang on her behalf.

I expected her dress to be bad, but she has surpassed my every fantasy. She is moving at the centre of a heap of net curtains. The bodice is covered in ruffles, and the full skirt has flounces galore. It sticks out so far that she reminds me of one of those dolls that sit on toilet rolls in the name of modesty. A nylon veil goes all the way down her back, and her face is grotesquely over made up. The picture is completed by two young bridesmaids, one of whom is crying. The other drops her bouquet and runs towards her mother.

I breathe a huge sigh of relief. I have promised Beth that I will call her when I get home and furnish her with every detail of the occasion, and I had imagined that I would exaggerate the horror of the proceedings. Now I see I can be perfectly honest.

Margot leans across Tony. 'Doesn't she look a picture?' she smiles.

The afternoon degenerates into a huge drinking session. Although Rachelle opted for the classier of the available marriage venues, they are holding the reception at the drive-in cinema. 'No Explosives' warns a huge sign on the fence. Workers have been known to call in for a movie in their work trucks, and dynamite has been known to spoil everyone's enjoyment.

Dirty Dancing is playing silently on the screen. I try to imagine whether this has long been one of the features of Rachelle's dream wedding. She has lived in Craggy all her life, and so I imagine it probably has. To be fair to the girl, she has used her imagination with the limited materials available, just as I used to tell her to do at school.

I clutch a glass of wine. The very idea of alcohol makes me sick. Faux drinking – remaining uptight while everyone else loses their inhibitions – is such a grim way of passing the time that it makes me want to have an abortion.

I have long stopped thinking of this town as strange. On the rare occasions when we go somewhere normal, like Adelaide, I see that world as odd, and mine as normal. The best I can manage to say for the people here is that they are mostly well-meaning. They are friendly, if you're white, and cheerful, and they adore a drink. Alcoholism rates are sky high.

I look at the crowd, and spot Duke talking with Bob and a group of the other hardcore miners and drinkers. Duke was one of the first people I met here. I estimate that he is in his sixties, although for all I know he could be thirty-eight and exceptionally battered by life. He drinks all day long, every single day, and when he's pissed he seeks out the Aborigines and sits with them, talking nonsense, and tugging at the legs of passers-by. He is, in fact, a lot less racist than most of Craggy's residents. I hope I haven't got used to the racism. I suppose I've learned to live with it, which amounts to the same thing. This is a completely segregated community with considerable ill will between the two sides. I take my cue from Tony, and live quietly in the white community, occasionally giving money or food to anyone who looks desperate. And just that pathetic act earns me the disapproval of my mother-in-law. Needless to say, today's gathering is exclusively white.

Duke staggered up to me in the street on our first morning here. I was reeling from the fact that life in the Outback was apparently just like Tony had told me it would be, except that he'd forgotten to mention the heat, the dust, and the fact that we would be living, indefinitely, with his mother.

'Hello, little lady!' slurred the strange man, taking my hand and caressing it, as I looked around, panicking. 'Where did you come from?'

'From Sydney,' I said primly, trying to extricate myself and hoping someone would save me.

'You're a lovely girl. Did you come to make your fortune? I did that. Rich as a king, I am. You wouldn't know it to look at me.' He tapped his nose. 'I keep it hidden, and *I'm not going to tell you where!*'

'Are you British?' I tried to use my Australian accent. It came out as '*Are*ya Briddish?'

'From Herererereford-shire, my love. You won't know what that is. Don't remember myself, come to think of it. Australia, the place to be. The best country. It's all in the opals.'

Tony appeared at this point, and with a cheery, 'All right, Duke?' steered me away. It turned out that about ten per cent of the residents fall into Duke's category. He is harmless, and over the years I've become quite fond of him. Duke will be working the crowd before long, grasping women's hands and hinting at his vast wealth. For all I know, he might even be telling the truth.

Rachelle is giggling with her girlfriends, most of whom were in her class at school. I taught some of them English. They only left last year. I wonder what her life will be like now. Marriage to Andy was a trial even for Beth, and she didn't have to contend with the age difference. Rachelle and Andy could be soul mates, but I doubt such a thing exists, really. It's just a question of two people wanting the same thing at the same time.

'What do you reckon?' asks someone at my shoulder. I look round, and see Tony's brother, Pete. When I met him, I refused to believe that Pete and my lovely Tony could be related. Tony talked about him so much and with such affection that I had imagined them to be identical twins. I thought the Pritchett boys would be two muscular teddy bears, both of them blondish and balding. In fact, Pete is dark and swarthy, as, apparently, was their father, Brian. He is as wirily small as Tony is big and burly. Resolutely single after two divorces, he despises anyone, including Tony, who settles down with a good woman. He never says so to my face, but I think he loathes me on principle as well as in reality. He's only ever civil to me, or to any other woman, when he's drunk, unless he's trying to get the woman in question into bed. Luckily, Pete draws the line at attempting to seduce his own sister-in-law. Either that, or he doesn't fancy me.

'What do I reckon about what?' I ask warily.

'The happy couple. How long do you give it?'

I look at Rachelle, exclaiming over Denise's ankle tattoo. Then I search the crowd for Andy, and spot him with Tony at the bar, laughing loudly.

'Two years, at the most,' I say. Pete whips a notebook out of his back pocket, and a pencil from behind his ear, and writes something down.

'Lina,' he says as he writes. 'Two years. Right, give us five bucks and you're in. Actually, Mick's already got two years. Can you be more specific? Yeah? Most of these are in months.'

I am mildly appalled, but I join in. I don't want to antagonise him.

'All right then. Say, twenty-two months. Are we counting until the separation, by the way, or divorce, or the initiation of proceedings?'

'The day one of them moves out and takes all their stuff. Minor bust-ups don't count.'

I hand him five dollars. 'You're a terrible man, Peter Pritchett. Does your mother know you're doing this?'

'Mum? You want to know what she thinks? Yeah? Five months, max.'

Although it's winter, it's a warm day. They've been luckier with the weather than we were, and before long I shake Pete off and sit down by the fence, in the shade of the 'No Explosives' sign, where I pour away half a glass of wine. I am dizzy, and I think I've got about forty-five minutes before I'm sick. The outdoor setting makes fake drinking easier, but nothing can make it enjoyable. I'll sit here and collect myself, and then I'll slip off home for a rest. My weekends are too precious to be spent like this.

The cinema is heaving with people. Even the residents of Clarrie's backpackers' hostel appear to have been invited en masse. I watch them, vaguely, from afar. They always intrigue me. Some look as old as me, just touching thirty. I wonder whether I could have ended up being them, and vice versa. I could have been them, all right. I *have* been them. I don't believe, however, that anyone else could have ended up as me. My circumstances have been very specific.

Three years ago, Craggy saw just a few of the most persistent travellers. This year, it has, apparently, been included in the Lonely Planet guide to Australia, and the numbers have increased beyond anyone's wildest expectations. Clarrie runs the hostel along the principle that there is nowhere else for her clients to stay, since they can't afford the motel, so they'll pay whether or not it's habitable. Now she's so oversubscribed with travellers who need to put a tick beside 'the desert' on their itinerary that she's talking about building an annexe before anyone introduces an element of free market competition. We also see a stream of overland trippers, who clunk into town in their bashed-up station wagons, and repair to one of the pubs for an evening's hard drinking. The backpackers, who get off buses and labour to Clarrie's under the weight of all their worldly goods, always stick together and only talk to their own kind, while the overlanders prefer to become part of the community for the night. I suppose the backpackers are making new friends every day, while the overlanders have been stuck in a hot car with each other for weeks on end. No wonder so many of them are delighted by an evening in Duke's company.

Tony catches my eye and waves. I make a gesture that I hope conveys, don't worry, I'm absolutely fine. He smiles and goes back to his conversation with the treacherous bridegroom. Tony has dumped his suit jacket, and rolled up his shirt sleeves. Now he just looks like an unusually fit insurance salesman in a very bad pair of trousers.

I swallow some bile and wonder whether I'd get away with a glass of water. I can't wait to go on maternity leave. I can't wait to tell people. I can't wait to grow a bump, and to realise that I really am going to have a baby; to accept that I'm not ill, and to realise that the thing making me sick and miserable is, contrary to my irrational fears, not a tumour or an intruder attacking my vital organs, but just a baby. Just a human being that I'm going to have to look after every day for the next eighteen years or so. Just someone who's going to draw their succour from my breasts and invade my sleep. Pregnancy has reduced – or raised – my body to a two-legged incubator. I am a host organ. Seven months from now I'm going to toddle into hospital, a comical, bovine figure, and go through agonies that a man, or a childless woman, or, indeed, any woman who is not going through it at that moment, could not imagine. Then I'm going to come out with my stomach folded over one arm, and a frowning purple baby tucked under the other. It is an enticing prospect.

'Hey, Mum. You dropout!'

Red sits next to me. He's been home and changed into his baggiest shorts and a huge dark green T-shirt with a logo that depicts a turtle standing on its hind legs, with a pint of beer in its 'hand'. I miss his aristocratic look. His eyes are dark and shiny, and his cheeks, as ever, are rosy. I take the cup from his hand, and drain it of orange juice. I feel a little better.

'Sorry,' I tell him. 'Dehydrated.'

In retaliation, he grabs my wine, and I allow him a gulp.

'Do you think Rachelle looks pretty?' he asks, staring through the crowd. He's always had a crush on his erstwhile babysitter. I look at the bride. She is, surprisingly, looking at me, and quickly averts her eyes. I wonder what kind of girl gets married when she's seventeen. All kinds of girls do, I suppose, but most of them haven't actively stolen their husbands from their previous and proper wives. I study Rachelle, in her cheap nylon dress, and try to work out whether she could be hiding the same secret as me. She is drinking straight from a bottle of Southern Comfort, which is being passed around her friends, and in the other hand she holds a cigarette which is dropping ash down the front of her dress – so probably not. However, she is young enough not to appreciate the implications. I can't imagine why else Andy would have rushed into a second marriage so soon after bailing spinelessly out of his first.

'She looks quite pretty,' I say to Red, vaguely.

'Beth would be sad if she was here,' he notes abruptly. 'Is that why you said it's horrible?'

'Yes, partly.' I pull him back into the shade, and we both think of my best friend.

'Andy is married to Beth. I didn't think you can be married to two people.'

'Not two people at once,' I agree, 'but sometimes, if people are married but they don't like being married any more, they can get unmarried. It's called divorce.' He looks blank. 'That's what Andy and Beth did,' I continue. 'That's why she moved away. And when you're divorced, each person can marry someone else if they want to. Some people have been married and divorced eight times, with different people. Only in America, though.' I can't believe Red has got to the age of ten without knowing about divorce. Maybe he overcame the odds and managed to lead a sheltered life. I always dreaded having this conversation with him, because I feared it would be a heartbreaking, 'Mummy and Tony don't love each other any more' discussion. The fact that it isn't cheers me up no end.

'So will Beth marry someone else?'

'Probably. One day.'

'Why did they get unmarried?'

'They just weren't friends. They had lots of arguments.'

He doesn't need to know the details. He doesn't need to know that half the people in town, including Tony but excluding me, knew that Andy had been screwing the teenage receptionist from the motel for months. He never needs to know about the day Beth and I called into the motel bar for a spontaneous drink after school, and saw Rachelle and Andy pressed up against each other, eating each other's faces. It won't last. I probably don't need to tell him that, either.

We are interrupted by a young man who squeezes into our modest patch of shade, smiling a little nervously. He's one of the backpackers. For a backpacker, he's exceptionally friendly. He looks about twenty, and has long greasy hair and an Ayers Rock T-shirt. He offers me one of the cans of lager he is clutching.

'Hiya!' he says cheerfully. 'Can I join you? Do you live here? I've been hoping to talk to a *local character* but they all seem a bit scary.'

'Scary!' Red looks at him curiously. 'Why?'

'Well, you two aren't, that's why I'm talking to you. Everyone else seems, how shall I put it, as mad as a hatstand.'

I revise my estimate of his age. He can only just have left school. I think, from his accent, that he's Welsh.

'They look worse than they are.' I force a smile. The last thing I want today is a new friend. 'Are you from Wales?'

'Yes, South Wales. How do you know? Are you British?'

'No, Australian, but I grew up in Britain.'

'So what the fuck, if you'll excuse my language, made you come to live here? Don't you get bored? Because it is, frankly, famously boring, isn't it? All the backpackers stay one night, and then they move on. You'd go out of your mind if you stayed longer than that. Everyone says so.'

'Then everyone is closed-minded. I know it's not to everybody's taste, but it's certainly not boring here. It's the opposite of boring. Look at it.' I gesture to the stony desert in front of us. 'It can send you mad, if you think about it too long. It goes on and on. There's nothing there. It's uninhabitable, and yet here we are, inhabiting it. Pulling the stones from the ground in the hope that one of them might turn out to be valuable. Their value, of course, being an entirely random manmade concept. You can breathe the air. The sun shines almost all the time. It's us against the elements, out here. It makes me think of how the world used to be. I half expect to see dinosaurs. You have no idea how many films they shoot round here, whenever they want another planet, or prehistoric earth. Red here has been an extra in a Mel Gibson film.'

Red nods. 'I have too. I was even in it when we had it here, at the cinema. For about three seconds.'

'No shit?'

Red beams, and I continue, 'Nature is so much more important than it is in London, or Cardiff, or New York or Paris or Sydney. I mean, look at our houses.'

'Do you live in one of those funny ones? Underground?'

'We have a front door and two windows, and then the house goes back into the hillside. The walls and the ceiling are the bare earth. There's a vent that goes right up and comes out in the hill. We lie in bed in the mornings, and if you can hear water pinging on the metal of the vent, you know it's raining. Which isn't often.'

'Do you live in a dugout?' Red asks him.

He laughs. 'No, mate. I live in Barry, and we don't have too many dugouts there.'

'Would you like to live here?'

'I'd go out of my mind.'

'Some of us would go out of our minds if we lived in Barry,' I point out. 'All that rain, the grim houses, the people everywhere.'

'You've never been to Barry.'

'True. But I can imagine it.'

'You'd be surprised.'

'Would I?'

'No.' He drains his lager and smiles at me. 'Can I take your picture?' he asks. 'Both of you together?' He's troll-eyed, but I like him. I like being admired. It doesn't happen much these days, and it will happen still less when I've lost my figure thanks to the baby. I am grateful for his harmless attention.

'Sure,' I tell him. Red sprawls on my lap. After we've squinted into the winter sun, I suggest we top up our drinks.

If I'd stayed in the shade and made Red and the Welsh boy bring me a glass of water instead, I might have been all right. Instead, I stand dizzily by the drinks table and chat inanely about the relative merits of wine and lager, until the other backpackers come along, en masse.

'Even in Barry,' I am saying, 'they must have Jacob's Creek.'

'I think Lambrusco's as classy as it gets,' says my new friend. 'Sorry. Look, these are my roommates. I don't even know your name.'

'Lina,' I say, sneaking a swig of water. Only here do they tut suspiciously if they catch you at a party with a can of lemonade. You're bound to be hiding something. Either you're pregnant, or you've decided to kick your alcoholism.

'Well, I'm Huw. It has been a delight to meet you, Lina. This is Vikram, Mark and Sophie.'

I look round, smiling. They are all about my age and I wonder what they make of their new, enthusiastic best friend. I make eye contact with one of them – Vikram – and we exchange an indulgent smile behind Huw's back. Then I look at Sophie, who is staring at me with intense interest. She has long brown hair and a pointy face, and her eyes are clear, blue and accusing.

I stare back. I hold her gaze, steadily.

She has an odd look in her eyes, and when I try to look away, it seems I can't. We stand and scrutinise each other for several minutes, while everyone else, inexplicably, doesn't seem to notice that anything is amiss. Then I pull myself together.

'Hello,' I say, as brightly as I can, and using an Australian accent. 'How are you all doing?' I look away from this woman, at the other three. 'Anyone need a drink?' I add, and as the boys answer, I turn to the table and busy myself pouring liquid into plastic cups.

Sophie appears at my side. I can feel her looking at me.

'Daisy,' she says quietly. She has a cut-glass English accent.

I look at her, shocked. 'No,' I tell her, suddenly remembering to smile. 'Not Daisy. My name's Lina. Are you confusing me with someone?'

She shakes her head. 'No. You look like Daisy and you have the same voice. Different accent, that's all. I'd recognise you anywhere. I *knew* you were still alive.'

I stare straight at her. 'I'm sorry,' I tell her, 'but I really don't know what you're talking about.'

She stares again, hostile now, and challenging. I see tears forming in her eyes, and I wonder what could make a grown woman, the same age as me, travel to the opposite side of the earth and bum around like a teenager. Anything, I suppose. I did it myself, and plenty of young Australians make the voyage in the opposite direction.

'You do,' she insists. Her voice is hard. 'You know it and I know it.'

I take a deep breath. 'Honestly,' I tell her, 'I'm sorry, but I don't know what you mean. My name really is Lina. I'm Australian. Lina, short for Noeline, but that's such a terrible name I don't let anyone use it.' I look around, and beckon Red over. 'Here, you can ask my little boy if you don't believe me.'

He comes over, cheerily. 'What?'

'Hello,' says Sophie. 'What's your name? How old are you?'

'The name's Red, and I'm ten.'

She looks at me. 'You vanished ten years ago.'

'I didn't,' I assure her. 'Red, this is . . . Sophie? Tell her what my name is.'

'Noeline.'

'Or?'

'Lina.' Luckily, he doesn't comment on my accent. He's used to my flipping into Australian from time to time.

'They do say everyone's got an exact double somewhere in the world.' I smile brightly. 'It sounds as if you know mine. What a strange coincidence.'

She's looking at me again, and looking at Red, and frowning. Eventually, she shakes her head, and smiles.

'Yes,' she says lightly. 'It's bizarre. You are the absolute spitting image of my best friend. I haven't seen her for years. Sorry to have accused you like that.'

'I hope you find her one day.'

'Oh, I think I will.'

We pause for a moment. I consider mentioning that sometimes people don't want to be found, particularly if their former friends are as odd as Sophie seems to be. I say nothing, and then she walks away.

'Do you know that lady?' demands Red, gazing after her.

'No, honey, I don't. What a strange woman.' I take him by the hand. 'Go and find Eric, or someone,' I tell him. 'I'm going home for a while. I'll see you later. Be good.'

He kisses me, and I transport myself and my embryo home along the dusty roads, checking, all the time, that I'm not being followed.

chapter three

2 September

My career plan allotted me two years in this job. I have seven months left. Unless I do something spectacular, and prove that I am not the run-of-the-mill hack (despite what everyone thinks), then I will start lagging behind. I will be stuck as a general reporter for ever. It's a graveyard here. I need to break out. The only way to do that is to show some initiative. People who don't show initiative end up getting sacked.

That's why I'm in early today. I balance my cappuccino on the edge of the desk, and pick up the pile of press releases and general crap, and chuck them into the bin. This clears enough space for my breakfast: a ham and egg roll followed by a croissant. There's a coffee machine in the office, but if you're the first to use it, that means you have to switch it on. In other words, you have to ferry some water over from the kitchen, measure coffee into the filter, assemble it all, and press the switch, and all for others' benefit. I barely even know where the kitchen is. I buy my own to last me until a secretary arrives to do the boring stuff. Sometimes I buy two, just in case.

I need my own story, that's the trouble. I can follow up someone else's story or hang around on doorsteps as well as the next man. Much better than the next man, given the general calibre of next men round here. That's not the point. I need to start setting the agenda. I need to leave all this behind. I need to surprise people. So I'm one of the top home news people. Big deal. Next step is a specialism, or an editing job. I'd rather be a specialist. Crime, I think. I need to be crime reporter before I'm twenty-eight. Otherwise the rest – the horrible precocious youngsters – will start overtaking me.

I love coming in early, particularly now that my girlfriend has gone away without me. It was a little crushing when she announced that one. Since I have nothing else to do except improve myself on the PlayStation, I've decided that these four months must be dedicated to work. In my uni days, I used to fantasise about being able to afford a grande latte from a chic takeaway chain, and some posh pastries in the morning, and about eating them on the move. I suppose, by that measure, I have achieved my youthful ambitions. It's not the best measure, though. Awards juries don't take it into account. No one save my brothers would be impressed.

When you say you're a reporter for one of Great Britain's finest tabloid newspapers, people seem to think you rush around shouting about stories and tips, and screaming at people on the phone. Not to mention running into the printing plant and yelling, 'Hold the front page!' Last time I was home, Mum confessed that she pictured me and my esteemed colleagues wearing some kind of Panama hats with cards bearing the word 'Press' tucked into the brim.

In fact, it's often more like a library. People talk quietly on their phones because they don't want their colleagues to know what they're up to. The ladies wear skirts, and most of the men wear suits. I had to buy a second suit last month because I realised that I'd worn the same one for eighteen months and never had it cleaned. In truth, it never occurred to me that suits needed cleaning. If it hadn't been for a passing comment from my girlfriend before she went on holiday, I would never have thought of it.

What happens if I'm not good enough?

I can't think where this thought has sprung from. I am good enough. I know I am. I've been a journalist for five years now, and I'm known throughout the old Fleet Street for being one of the best and sharpest in the business. That may, on reflection, be a slight exaggeration. I was mentioned in the *Press Gazette* once. I've never won a physical award, but lots of old farts in the business hate me, and that's enough to be going on with. I'm doing as well as (but not better than) the other notables from my journalism course. An actual award would be good. I'd like one very much. Then no one could tell me I'm not good enough. That's what I need to do next: I need to become the crime reporter, and get an award. In either order.

My previous resolution was to organise myself and keep meticulous notes. I have several colour coded notebooks now, and I use them for different things. It seems vital. I had a close shave with a libel scare a few weeks ago. I hadn't libelled this crumbly old lord, but he thought I had (everyone knows he's gay, and I think it was a reasonable assumption on my part that it had been printed before. I assured the lawyers that it had, for a quiet life, and they should have checked). He sued immediately. I was going to have to hand over my notebooks. I was petrified. I almost wet myself when the in-house lawyer appeared at my desk. The worst thing was that I couldn't whimper and phone my mum. I knew that everyone was listening, and that I had to put on a brave face. Sometimes I feel ten years old. I used to put on a brave face then, as well.

'Right you are, Jasper,' I said nonchalantly. 'What are the chances of it reaching court?'

'That is largely up to you,' he said. Jasper is small and insignificant looking, yet his approach across the newsroom can turn the fiercest of news Rottweillers to jelly. 'What were your sources? If you have impeccable records that will stand up in court, then we'll take it all the way. Can you gather together your tapes and notebooks and get them to me first thing tomorrow? Unless you have them to hand now.'

I shook my head pathetically. My sources were impeccable, insofar as gossip and common assumption are usually right. My notebooks were a mess, incorporating wish lists of porn videos Kev and I had made, and revealing that my grasp of shorthand had slipped somewhat. As for my tapes, there weren't any.

'Sure, Jasper, not a problem,' I said loudly, with a grin.

'And Larry,' he added, 'try not to look quite so scared.'

Peter, at the next desk, laughed loudly, and quickly went back to his pretend reading of the *FT*. As it happened, I had the last laugh, because, by a marvellous chance that almost made me believe in God, the gay lord died that afternoon. I could not possibly be as lucky next time.

Now I have a 'Personal' notebook, which is more like a diary, and I have my usual work books. They stay meticulously separate. The diary stays on my person at all times. The work stuff is as legible as I can make it. There is now no chance of my innermost musings ever being read out in the High Court.

I take out my diary, and start a new page in my best handwriting.

CAREER

Things that would make it better:

1. New role in the paper.
2. Award.
3. Friends with editor & other important pple.
4. Big, big scoop of story that wd raise me above others, eg find Lord Lucan alive & well, discover hard evidence of sex scandal (maybe incest or bestiality?) in royal family, politics etc, find financial scandal involving similar. Force resignation of someone high up somewhere. Pref scandal should be about someone very powerful & part of the establishment who I could bring down. The kind of story which gives me fame forever – when I'm old, I'll be subject to venerable admiring profiles. I will be a Bill Deedes-esque grand old man of British letters.

ACTION TO TAKE

1. Continue to do current job to best of abilities (goes without saying).
2. Let it be known that I have received advances from rival papers, even though I haven't (tread carefully with this one – don't play this card too soon or too often).
3. Go to pub on regular basis and become drinking buddies with important people though don't become an alcoholic.
4. Work overtime searching for scoop.
5. Today, call all contacts searching for no.1 story. Targets: anyone who can be accused of immorality and/or hypocrisy. Surely that is not overly much to ask???

Now that I know what I have to do, I'd better put this book away, and get down to it. I'll start making some calls. Surely, one day, someone will be able to help me.

By half past six, I am bored out of my brain. I need to get out onto the tennis court and thrash a few balls around until my life makes sense again. A good PlayStation session would also suffice. At least with S. away and Kev out tonight, I'll get a good run on the telly, and won't have to watch *Brookside* or share the PlayStation.

The big stories are eluding me, and I haven't even got any interesting normal ones. I've spent most of the day following up an agency story about protests over the price of fuel. How dull can you get? I haven't even got a car. Get a car. I fish out my notebook again, and decide to make a wish list: something I can refer to for motivation in the months to come.

WISH LIST
Good, unassailable job, with steady path to rise to editor.
My name mentioned when people speculate about who next editor will be.
Six figure salary.
Buy own flat in Notting Hill, Hoxton etc.
Come top in the tennis league this year.
Have more friends, of both useful and sociable varieties.
Go on holiday without feeling insecure about missing work (eg could have gone to Sydney if I'd felt able to leave, but didn't).
Family stop treating me like a deluded wanker (heard Luke use that very phrase last Xmas).
Get a car.
Domestic stability? Not easy when girlfriend is on extended holiday without me.

I should stay late to do some more brainstorming. I'm sure there's something hanging about, and all I need to do is clear my mind and put my finger on it. Sadly I have no idea what it could be. I don't have the same contacts as the people who've been in the business for ever, and those people don't have my energy, my hunger. I try to imagine how many stories never break because of this discrepancy. Maybe the best thing would be for me to steal someone's address book and nick all their contacts. I wouldn't be doing it for myself, I'd be doing it for the paper. For society. Looked at like that, it's actually my duty.

I can't do it tonight, though. It needs to be a carefully targeted operation. I mean, whose would I go for, for starters? Someone who is thorough, yet vague. I must remember to go through all the likely candidates this evening.

People are drifting away, and the couple of reporters on nights have just hung up their coats. I used to do nights. I quite enjoyed it, but it was no fun stopping work at two in the morning. There's nowhere to go for a quick drink to wind down, unless you want to hang out with pimps and lapdancers. I'm on the waiting list for Soho House, but that could take years. Going straight to bed after work would be like going home now and crawling under the duvet. S. was never very up for chatting, because she started work at nine. We barely saw each other until I was promoted to days.

I wonder whether I should be worried about the fact that I haven't really got any friends at work. I suppose I should make more of an effort, not just for networking, but also for a bit of a social life. If I had a good, work-centred social life, I think that would be a step on the way to success. It pains me to admit it, but the only friends I really have now are S., who's a million miles away, and Kev, and that's just because he's my flatmate. The other twentysomething reporters tend to be girls with dyed hair and bright lipstick, who are falsely chatty with everyone and go for long lunches with each other. One of them, Christie, is scurrying around now, inviting everyone to the pub. I am hoping for an invitation, to help me put a few resolutions into practice, but for some reason it does not seem to be forthcoming. I don't care. I probably wouldn't go anyway.

chapter four

Craggy Rock

This wasn't meant to happen. I was not meant to see Sophie.

The walls are closing in. I curl up on the sofa, with my legs tucked underneath me, and crane up at the bare earth of the curved ceiling, and the white plastered walls, all of them lumpy with desert soil. They are moving towards me. I huddle closer down into myself. I make myself as small as possible. If you live underground, there's always a chance that your house might collapse. The walls are approaching me now, and I'm glad. I curl up, on my side, and listen to my own gasping breaths, and wait to be crushed.

Nothing happens. When I open my eyes, the room is normal, and I sit up, glad that I'm alone in the house. For the past hour, I have been fighting an urge, which is almost overwhelming, to run away. I wonder whether you can have prenatal psychosis and, if so, whether it can happen this early in pregnancy.

Today's wedding, and reception, and accusation was the last straw. I don't want to live here any more. It's horrible. It crushes me and stifles me and I don't want my baby to have to live here either. I don't want her to have a life like Rachelle's, if it's a girl, or like, say, Pete's, if it's a boy. This is a sad, incestuous little town, and I want to go somewhere anonymous, like Beth did. For the past week, she's been living in Renmark, down south where they have modern luxuries such as plants, water, and windows. There are enough people there for her to be able to walk around without being dogged by gossip and speculation. She lives on a boat. I'd like to live on a boat.

Instead, I languish, pregnant and immobile, in this subterranean shithole. I never used to swear. I didn't use bad language of any kind. When I was young, I swore all the time. Then I had to shed all my defining characteristics, and so I stopped. Besides, I don't want to use the same adjectives for everything, whether it is good, bad, grotesque, beautiful or ugly. I try to save the bad words for special occasions. If I don't swear, then I know I won't accidentally tell one of the children to fuck off. Suddenly, though, I don't care. Fuck it. Bollocks to it. All the children can fuck off. Nothing about my petty, pathetic little life matters any more. An English girl saw me, and she recognised me. That is not allowed to happen. That will ruin everything.

I look around at the pathologically tidy room. Everything is in its place. The sofa and chairs are arranged at their usual angles, with the television discreetly in the corner so I can pretend we're the sort of household that reads books rather than gazes mindlessly at the box. Even the sofa, which is unwisely beige, is not stained. Despite the dust, I insist on keeping it immaculate. This is one of my Sisyphan compulsions. One of my ways of passing the time so I don't stop and contrast what my life could have been with what it is.

My baby already has organs, legs, arms and a face. Even that can't calm me. In fact, it enrages me. Here I am, a woman who should be independent and in the prime of her life, chained down to this dump, and with another chain on the way. I should be the one travelling around the world without a care in the world, walking up to strangers and making accusations. I should be able to pack up my bags and slip away, right now, to try again. I should be considering settling down sometime in my thirties. My twenties should have been free, but they weren't, and now they're nearly over.

I walk into the kitchen, and, without allowing myself time to stop and think, I take Tony's whisky (it used to be mine as well. In fact, I paid for it) from the cupboard and pour myself a large tumblerful. Then I carry it carefully back into the sitting room and sit on the chair with its back to the window, just in case. I start to drink.

Whisky has long been my secret emergency remedy. Before I discovered I was pregnant, I drank far more than Tony realised. I drank it to cope with this life. It warms me. It reaches right down inside me, and it promises me that everything is going to be all right. In broad terms, so far, it has told the truth. I have been all right, after a fashion. I haven't, I realise, been much more than all right. I used to imagine a fantastic, thrilling future for myself. I never imagined I could be anything other than a dancer. I was going to travel, and dance. I was going to lead an ethereal and glamorous life.

I am falling apart. I need the whisky more than I need to protect my baby. It's all upside down. Women aren't meant to be this selfish. That's why we, and not men, have to give birth. I am despicable, and I don't care. My tentative sips give way to deep gulps, and I sit back and wait for its consolations.

There is no good in my life, at all. Red, I admit, is a blessing, but he is a part of me and I don't count him as a facet of my life in Craggy. He would come with me wherever I went. Tony and I have a good marriage. Everyone says so. It's hard to judge because I don't know what marriage is like for everyone else. We get on well. We have plenty of sex. We laugh together and fit our lives around each other. We are happy and comfortable. Occasionally we fight, but then we make up. Maybe that is as good as it gets.

We are different people, now, from the drifters who met in Sydney. Tony was a magical stranger then, and I was a glamorous nomad. I never imagined our lives could become so humdrum, that for days I'd think about nothing deeper than how best to keep the dust out of the dinner.

Tony and I met at a time when I was desperate to stop living as a young backpacker. Although I was a world away from blasé Huw and his carefree friends, Red and I lived as they do. I was a frantic traveller, not a leisurely one. I moved on all the time. I looked over my shoulder. I was wary of new people. I walked away whenever I heard a British accent. I travelled not to see the world, but to escape from it. On top of that, I was set apart from my travelling contemporaries by the fact that, soon after I arrived in India, I was travelling with a baby.

Red and I stalked nervously through Asia for a year before we arrived in Sydney. He took his first steps on the wooden floor of a cheap hotel room in Bombay. The maids congregated to applaud him. He spoke his first word on the sand outside a beach shack in Kerala. That word, unoriginally, was 'Mum'. I thought that, at the very least, given his life so far, he could have come up with 'karma' or 'shanti'. He was ill in Bombay, but I had enough money to take him to a private hospital, and they rehydrated him and released him, healthy and smiling. After that his health was never dire, and neither was mine.

For a while, I thought we would settle there. I wanted to be in a huge city. The chaos on the streets comforted me. I loved the smells. I would step outside, and sniff the spices that wafted hotly from the door of the restaurant downstairs. I'd walk down the road, and suddenly I'd know from the smell that the local beggarwoman and her weightless baby were approaching. At the corner, it smelt of stale piss. Down the road I would sometimes catch the scent of the sea even though we were seven blocks inland.

I loved the fact that I could easily slip away down a dark alley where no one would be able to find me. I set myself the task of learning the city's geography, and plotting my escape routes. I found a flat, and started teaching English to people's children. We were accepted by our neighbours as a young British widow and her adorable baby. After a couple of months, they even started matchmaking. I thought about Sanjay's offer for a week – sweet, adoring Sanjay who was happy to take on a foreign widow and a stepson that no one would ever mistake for his own – but then I turned him down. I didn't have the documents a widow would have needed to marry, and besides, it didn't feel right.

A week later, I saw a poster for the Academy Ballet, visiting from London. Even in a city of thirteen million people, I knew I could bump into someone who might recognise me. Worse still, I wanted to go and watch. They were doing *Coppelia*. I once played the doll in one of their productions. All I had to do was to sit on the stage for the first act, but I adored every moment of it.

Going to see it in Bombay would have been suicidal, even from a cheap seat at the back, and I could not allow myself the temptation.

My visa was about to run out. I'd already renewed it once. We had been in Bombay for three months, and in India for a further nine before that. I wasn't far enough away. My identity wasn't polished. I needed to travel further, and so I bought a ticket to Kuala Lumpur, and left in the middle of the night. I put a bundle of rupees on the table with a short note, and I removed Red from everything he knew, except for me.

We arrived in Sydney on the day he turned eighteen months. It seemed logical for an Australian girl to come and live in Australia. By now I had honed my identity to what seemed to be perfection.

Nobody gave me a second glance, and the day after we arrived, I got a job in a cafe in Bronte, where they were so laid back they didn't mind a lively toddler coming in with me. In fact, they adored him. The attention he received from Cathy and her staff, following the worship he had accepted as his due in India, has, I'm sure, made him the sociable boy he is today. After a few weeks, we moved into a big, airy room in a shared house, and soon after that I enrolled Red in a kindergarten.

Almost every day, someone would ask what my story was. How, they wanted to know, had a 21-year-old woman ended up in Sydney, with an English accent and a little boy? Sydney is full of drifters, and one of the ways strangers bond is by swapping tales of how they got there. I was always happy to share. I never once gave anyone the impression that I was hiding anything.

'I am actually Australian,' I would say. 'But I grew up in England because my parents emigrated when I was small. We were settled there, and I loved it, but then both my parents were killed in a road accident –' I always paused here to receive commiserations – 'and I decided to move back here. I'm an only child, so there didn't seem to be anything to stay for.'

Cathy's eyes would mist over at my tragic story. Even though she knew it better than I did, she'd always listen in.

'And tell her about Red,' she'd call over, in case the stranger in question didn't notice the little boy sitting at the corner table, colouring in (or scribbling over) pictures of desert islands and palm trees. The walls were covered in his drawings. The cafe was his home.

'OK.' I'd shrug and smile. 'I went to Asia first, to try to work out what to do. I was lonely, and one day in Goa, in India, I visited an orphanage. I wanted to give something back because I'd seen so much poverty. I'm not sure why I went to that one at that time. It was one of those coincidences. 'There was a tiny baby, who'd only been there for a few days. I know it isn't really allowed, but as soon as I saw him I loved him. I asked whether I could adopt him.'

'But he's white.'

'I know. He'd been left by some drugged-out hippies a few weeks before. He was kind of their star attraction, but I think they were quite relieved that a white woman wanted to adopt him. I wore a ring on my wedding finger and pretended I had a husband in London. Then I paid some baksheesh—'

'That's Indian for a bribe,' Cathy would interject from wherever she was wiping a table or processing an order.

'And we dispensed with the formalities. They produced an adoption certificate from nowhere, I paid a little more, and then suddenly we were away, me and Red.'

'Why's he called Red?'

'Because that's the name the hippies gave him. Either that, or it's the best pronunciation the orphanage workers could manage. He's probably called something like Edward, something normal, but I liked the name Red, and I didn't see any reason to change it. It suited him.'

I always hoped I wasn't telling my story to an immigration official, but nobody has ever expressed disapproval. Everyone is captivated by the romance. Red, more than anyone, loves his own creation myth. I thought that, as he grew older, he'd wish he was normal, but so far, if anything, he is moving in the opposite direction.

I was perpetually aware that I was living on borrowed time, that we had to move away from the city, full as it was with tourists. I knew it was only a matter of time before my cover was blown. Still, we stayed in Sydney for a year, and then we moved inland to Katoomba in the Blue Mountains, and north to a town called Inverell in northern New South Wales. From there, we headed north to Queensland. Wherever we went, it never felt quite right. Inverell came closest, but I was lonely there. I didn't feel confident enough to settle. By the time I turned twenty-five, I was still bundling all our possessions, periodically, onto buses, and I was still looking over my shoulder. Red was five, and he needed to settle down. In desperation, I took him back to Sydney for a few weeks, with a view to working at the cafe until I could afford a cross-continental move to Perth.

One lunchtime, Tony strolled into the cafe, and gave me a big smile. I immediately appreciated his physique, although I was intimidated by him as well. He had more hair then, but only just. What I really liked, however, were his eyes. They were deep blue, and they were honest. I liked the smile lines around them. He looked like a happy man, and he looked gentle, and he looked as if he liked me, and that was what I needed. It's what I still need. I'd had my fair share of men coming on to me during my waitressing years – and I had seriously considered marriage years before – but I'd never come close to trusting anyone. Yet the moment I saw Tony's face, I relaxed a little.

We sat outside in the afternoon sun, and drank three beers. The air smelt of the sea. We chatted about Sydney and I asked how he ended up there. He was from a tiny town in the Outback. Suddenly we were looking at each other, and the looks were full of possibilities.

'Actually,' I began.

'There's another thing,' he said, at the same time.

'What?' we asked each other.

'You go first,' he insisted.

'OK. I've got a little boy,' I said, and waited for his interest to wane.

'That's great,' he said, apparently genuine. 'How old is he?'

'Five. In fact, I have to fetch him from the childminder in half an hour.'

'I'd like to meet him.'

'Good. Come with me. So, that's my confession. What's yours?'

He looked me in the eyes, then looked away. 'Nothing so heart-warming. I came out of prison two weeks ago.'

I didn't know what to say.

'See,' he continued, 'you don't want me to meet your little boy now, do you?'

'What did you do?'

'Oh, I'm innocent. I was framed. Not really. I was in what folks seem to call a brawl. We were all drunk. I punched a guy, and got unlucky. Hurt him quite badly. I'm not proud of it.'

'How long were you in prison?'

'Two months. I tell you, you want to keep out of there if you can.'

'I'll bear it in mind.'

We smiled at each other. I really didn't mind that he'd been to prison, because he didn't seem threatening at all. In a way I found it slightly thrilling. Everything hinged on how he was with my little boy, and he passed that test. From that day to this, we've rarely been apart. It's just become normal. I suppose that happens to everyone.

I can already imagine how I'm going to feel, later. I haven't touched an alcoholic drink for four weeks, and I hadn't planned to have more than the most symbolic of measures until March. Part of my brain is very well aware that I shouldn't be doing this, but nothing else would console me. All I want is a few precious minutes' oblivion.

I look around, checking Sophie hasn't crept into the house to watch me. It is as tidy as it was before this happened. Everything is still in its place, but my own neatness, which sustains me day and night, is shattered. I pour myself a refill. It's making me feel sick, but I gulp it back all the same. I haven't lost control for ten years. The only way I've got this far is by exerting rigourous self-discipline. I had forgotten the liberating, heart-stopping knowledge that everything I have is at stake. It is unspeakably precious, and yet I am jeopardising it all. I laugh, a mad cackle. I'm tired, and my head is beginning to ache.

I wish Beth was here. When I think of stupid little Rachelle and pathetic Andy, led by his cock and by the mysterious 'things she can do' to him, I feel a wave of cold fury. It's their fault – their fault, and cancer's fault – that I have no real friend. They deprived me of Beth, and then they got married. By and large, I find that the only way to get by in a small community is to be tolerant, and so there are very few people I outwardly despise. For years, I have made myself as inoffensive as possible, and whatever I think of people, I keep it to myself. I am making an exception, however, for Rachelle and Andy. His infidelity has already forced Beth out of town. Now her humiliation is complete, and I am friendless.

Briefly, I consider phoning her. I know she is waiting by the phone for my report of the wedding. I'll do it later. It wouldn't help, just now.

Rachelle, I think nastily, will have a rude awakening sooner than she realises. She will discover that marriage goes beyond getting drunk in a flouncy dress, and going to cosmopolitan Alice Springs on her honeymoon. Rachelle is sixteen years younger than her new husband. She will, I imagine, be astonished once he stops being on his best behaviour and starts farting in the marital bed and staying out all night leering at Scandinavian backpackers. For his part, he will, no doubt, be amazed when she stops simpering at him and shows her true teenage colours. You don't expect your pupils – and I think of all of them, even the sixteen-year-olds, as children – to start stealing your friends' husbands. I'm just glad she didn't set her sights on Tony.

My glass is still half full. I seem to have stopped drinking. It's not doing what it should be doing, and I am compelled to confess to myself that I'm not enjoying it, after all. After the initial crackling warmth, the escape I was hoping for is apparently not on offer today. It's this bloody pregnancy. Nothing that's bad for me tastes good any more. I know this is a positive phenomenon, in almost every way. The smell of coffee makes me physically sick. Alcohol, it seems, turns my stomach. Any fatty food, even buttered toast, makes me retch.

I pull my knees up and rest my face on them. I don't know what to do. I have no idea what I'm going to do. I must not panic. I've always been all right in the past, because I've never allowed myself to panic. But I don't know what to do.

I have a couple of hours before Tony or Red comes back, unless there's a crisis that propels Red home early. He already thinks I've got cancer, so I wouldn't be surprised to see him back, checking up on me. Sometimes I come within a hair's breadth of telling him about the baby; he has interpreted my constant nausea and exhaustion as portents of a far more sinister growth. This is directly due to what happened to Nina. Red refuses to talk about it, but I know that he thinks and worries about it all the time. The things that go on inside a ten-year-old's mind constantly amaze me. I teach ten of them at the school. I loved it, until I became obsessed with my own nausea, and with daydreaming about the baby. The kids are too young to be really horrible, and they seem to like me because I don't yell at them very often. I appreciate the fact that Red is, quite clearly, head and shoulders above all of them. He has reserves of imagination and natural intelligence that the other children seem to lack. It must be partly because of his cosmopolitan start in life. Sometimes I have to pick on him to avoid being suspected of favouritism.

Giddy with whisky and confusion, I stand up and wander through to the kitchen. I cleaned it this morning, and there's nothing left to scour away. I wipe the surfaces anyway, before tipping my whisky down the sink and washing the glass, drying it, and putting it in its place.

Foetuses can survive a tidal wave of whisky. Plenty of women have no idea they're pregnant, and carry on drinking heavily for months after this. I'm sure my parents' generation drank throughout their 'confinements' and, arguably, it didn't do me or my contemporaries any harm. So, either I stop now and try to pick up the pieces, or I carry on drinking.

I sit at the table and apply myself to wondering how to leave Craggy. I know I have to do it. Abruptly, I jump up from the table, and vomit copiously into the sink. I feel horrible. I hate it when the sickness comes upon me with no warning like that. I'm lucky I was in the kitchen. Otherwise, I'd have had to explain why the sofa was newly stained with sick (not in itself a difficult one), and why, more trickily, that sick was giving off a powerful odour of whisky. I run the hot tap, and pour disinfectant all around, and scrub it clean. Then I fill the sink with hot water and bleach. I'll leave it to soak. My head is spinning and my knees are buckling under me.

I need to get out of here. I picture a girl with straight, brown hair and a pointed face. I hear her English voice say: 'Daisy'. She knows where I live. I want to see her, and yet I need to run as far from her as I possibly can.

I know I can't run away, so I need to formulate some other plan. I remember the misery of the years before we met Tony, and I don't want to go back there. Not with a ten-year-old, and a new baby as well. I can't do that to them, or to Tony, or to myself.

I'm going to have to take them all with me.

I persuaded Tony to take me back to Craggy with him because it sounded like the perfect place for me to live without ever bumping into anyone who might recognise me. For seven years I had been seeking the end of the earth, and now I had found it. As soon as we got here, I didn't know if I'd be able to handle it. It was full of rejects and runaways. All kinds of people wash up here, and by the time they get here, there's nowhere else for them to go, and so they stay. Their children reach seventeen, and hurry to one of the big cities as fast as they can, without looking back.

It's time for me to make a move. I don't want to be a runaway reject any longer.

By the time Red tears through the front door with Eric and Tabitha, I have pulled myself together. The sink is clean and odour free. The whisky is topped up with water and put into the cupboard. I have taken a single paracetamol – generally agreed to be the most suitable painkiller for a pregnant lady who insists on the best for her unborn child – had a cool shower, and changed out of my vomit-and-spirits splashed dress into some loose cotton trousers and a blue T-shirt. There is a load of washing in the machine. I have overcome my nausea and my drunkenness enough to decide that Red and I are going to have pizza tonight, although I haven't actually started preparing it. I know I won't see Tony until long past eating time, and that's fine. I don't want to see him, yet.

I can't run away from my marriage. We are going to move house. Ideally, Tony needs to think it's his idea. This will be a well-planned move. There can be no more drifting.

In the early hours of the morning, when he stumbles back from the tail end of the festivities, I hold my breath and cuddle up to him. Ripe alcoholic fumes waft over me from all his pores.

'Darling?' I say, pretending to be much more sleepy than I really am.

'Mmmm?'

'Had a good night?'

He perks up a bit. 'Hey, it was magic,' he says without stirring. 'Drank the bar dry. Had to start paying for our drinks. Rachelle wanted Andy to go home with her, wedding night and all that, so he went off for a bit of a root, and then he came back to spill the beans. Don't know what you taught her at school but it sounds like she's quite a girl.'

'How exceptionally romantic. Did you have anything to eat?'

'Yeah, doner and fries before Mick shut up shop. I tell you, it was a great night. Duke almost told us where his money was.'

I smile, despite myself. 'That'll be the day. Surely if Duke was going to give his secret away when he was drunk, the whole of Australia would know it by now. Don't forget, Duke is never sober. You are, occasionally, that's all.'

He nuzzles my neck. 'You have a point. You are my clever lady. I do love you. You know that, don't you? I love you, and I'm going to love that little baby.' He is maudlin and sentimental. This is my moment.

'Tone, can I ask you something?'

'Sure. What?'

'Can we move away from this place?'

'Where to?'

'Near Beth?'

'Don't see why not.'

'Thanks.'

'Night.'

After a couple of minutes, he pulls me towards him and sniffs me in a puzzled manner.

'You haven't been drinking, have you?' he demands.

'Nope,' I lie.

'Must be me then.'

'Must be.'

A moment later, he's snoring.

chapter five

The morning proves to be a struggle. I address myself sternly. You mustn't give in, I tell myself. You must make a plan, and stick to it. It's worked in the past. I'm always lecturing the kids about the value of positive thinking, and the absolute necessity of organisation. 'Cover every eventuality,' I tell them, perched on my desk at the front of the class, 'and you'll be able to do anything. You will amaze yourselves.' I look at their innocent, ten-year-old faces, sitting behind their Formica desks, and I hope they will amount to more than I have.

'Miss?' asked Eric the other day, for in many ways this town is old-fashioned, and I am universally hailed in this manner, sometimes by Red, in my own home. Were Rachelle to speak to me, she would call me Miss. 'Does that mean I can be a famous singer in a band?' The other kids laughed at him. Children are breathtakingly cruel. No one has made the slightest allowance for the fact that Eric is recently motherless.

'Yes it does, Eric,' I told him, and his face lit up. 'Like I said, if you cover every eventuality, you'll be well on the way. Anyone, what are the eventualities that Eric, as a potential singer, needs to cover?'

'Learn to sing?' called Tabitha, and everyone laughed.

'That's right. First of all, make sure your voice is strong enough, and if necessary get singing lessons. If you genuinely have the ability, you need to go to the right place, say Sydney, and introduce yourself to the right people. Don't do that before you've left school. It's essential that you have a strong education behind you. Finish year twelve. It took me a long time to understand that. Then, make sure you're presenting yourself well. Presentation is everything.' That is another of my mantras. I am arguably the best dressed woman in Craggy, largely because I have a very small and select band of competitors for the title.

The pop singer discussion was abruptly halted because I went weak at the knees and had to sit down and set them some work to do quietly, but I meant what I said. Now, I am putting it into practice.

The family breakfast is often my worst time of day. Today it's more of an effort than usual. Either I'm going to be sick, or something bad is going to happen, I tell myself. It's a little bargain that I make. If I'm sick, nothing will go wrong. If I sail through the morning with no illness, then that is the portent of doom. I pass Tony his coffee, inhaling its fumes, to encourage my churning stomach. It works.

'Won't be a second,' I gasp, and run for the bathroom. My pregnancy sickness is a strange thing. It is all-consuming while it lasts, and yet as soon as it is out of my mouth, I am able to observe it with detachment. I feel better straightaway. My vomit, this morning, is a mixture of homemade pizza and whisky. I can smell it. The stench is foul. I'm glad some of it's coming up. That suggests to me that it hasn't all headed ruthlessly, destructively, for the baby. The loo is full of tomato, sweetcorn, and honey-coloured liquid. I flush it away, and put bleach down after it to take away the smell and the germs. Then I brush my teeth twice, rinse with mouthwash, floss, and return to the table smiling. I have increased my teeth cleaning regime to eight times a day now, and that doesn't include post-sickness brushing, which is an exception. Not even Tony knows about the new rituals.

Red and Tony are eating their cereal in companionable silence. I reach for the bread. Dry toast and Vegemite is the best I can manage.

'Morning, Red,' I groan, as cheerfully as I can.

'Morning,' he replies drowsily.

'Morning,' Tony says to both of us, and we all lapse into a silence which is, variously, sleepy, pregnant, or hungover. In my case, it is all three.

Even the kitchen table irritates me. I am constantly fighting a battle against its size. It's the kind of battle I like. I have just as much determination as the table, and I suspect it is only just beginning to realise this fact.

It's its middle that causes the problem. During the installation of my dream kitchen, I spent money we barely had on a huge, pine farmhouse table. No one understood why. Tables in Craggy tend to be functional. They are covered with wipe-clean Formica, like the desks at school. Families do not eat freshly baked scones while cats slink around their feet. Even we don't do that. Families, including ours, often eat from their laps while watching the television. However, something inside me yearned for a solid pine table as the symbolic centrepiece of domestic life, and so I had one trucked in from Adelaide. The trouble is that when Red and Tony finish with anything, whether it's a cereal bowl, a circular from the school, or a dried-up felt tip pen, they send it, with a skid, into the middle of the table, a space which none of us can readily reach. I have to kneel on a chair to retrieve things, and this is not a good position when you're nauseous. Already, in my brief sicky absence, the table's centre has filled up with all the morning's post, an empty Weetbix box, and the sugar bowl.

'This table reminds me of a story someone once told me about Sierra Leone,' I chide them as I put some toast in front of Tony and lean forward to gather up the junk and open the letters. 'This guy was at a meeting with some high-up politicians, and he said they had a massive heavy conference table, and in the middle it was coated with dust and there were paper clips and all kinds of shit, all of it just out of arm's reach from any of the chairs. A great symbol of crumbling Third World dictatorship, or something. That's what it's like in this house.'

'What's dictatorship?' asks Red.

'Where's Sierra Leone?' asks Tony.

I know this is one of those educational opportunities, and give it a half-hearted go.

'Red?' I say. 'Do you know where Sierra Leone is?'

He is playing with his cereal. 'No, Ma'am.' Red is a fan of the Waltons, which is sometimes on before school.

'Go and look it up, then.'

He looks at Tony and rolls his eyes.

'Go on,' I tell him. 'Don't look to Tony for support. Go and look at the map.'

I pinned a world map to his bedroom wall last year, in a bid to broaden his horizons beyond this rocky, forgotten part of South Australia. When he asked me to point out England, I almost didn't want to. He was amazed at how small, and distant, it was. He used to want to go there, caught up by the reverent way people talk about the royal family, and the fact that I grew up there, but since then he's entirely lost interest. England, he immediately decided, was overrated. He was astonished when I told him that the little island comprised not just England, but Wales and Scotland too.

'Got to go to school,' he tells me jauntily. 'You have too. No time. Give me a clue.'

'OK. It's in Africa. Now, go and find it. Maybe we'll talk about dictatorships in class.'

Tony winks at him. 'You're all right, mate. Africa. That's all I wanted to know.'

They both laugh.

I thought Red would hate it when he and I started at the school at the same time, three years ago. In fact, he loves school, largely for the social life, and appears not to have noticed it's strange to have your mother as a teacher. It's even stranger to have your mother as an entirely unqualified teacher, equipped for the classroom only by the remnants of an English accent, which seems to be an accepted alternative for teaching experience in this particular outpost of humanity.

He pitches his bowl into the middle of the table, ignores my protest, and picks up his satchel.

''Bye, Tony,' he says. 'Come on, Mum, we'll be late.'

'You go on ahead,' I tell him. 'Call for Eric. I'll see you there. I just want to talk to Tony.'

Red narrows his eyes at me. 'Are you ill again?'

'No I'm not. Off you go.'

Once we are alone, I put my arms round Tony's ample waist.

'Do you remember coming in last night?'

'I think so. There's a bloody band of Aborigines playing didgeridoo in my head this morning.'

'Do you remember us talking?'

He frowns at me, his eyes blank, and I laugh and kiss him.

'I said can we move house,' I remind him.

'You did too!'

'And you said sure.'

'I did not!'

'Oh, you *so* did. I said, can we move house, and you said, where to, and I said South Australia, and you said sure.'

'Perhaps you're right, darling. We already live in South Australia.'

'Oh, you think you're so clever. I didn't mean moving across town, or moving into a bigger house for the baby. I meant moving south, maybe to where Beth lives. In fact that's what I said.'

'I kind of remember that.'

'And?'

'To be honest, I'd been wondering when you'd ask. As long as you don't want to go back to England.' He holds up a hand to forestall my protest. 'And I know you don't. So as long as we're still in Australia, that's OK by me.'

'You know your mother won't like it.'

He shrugs. 'She's a grown-up. She'll live. She might even come with us.'

I have nothing whatsoever against Margot. She has accepted Red entirely as her own grandchild, and she's going to be delighted beyond all imagining when she finds out about this baby. That doesn't stop me feeling desperate at the idea of her joining our family unit. I'm not sure what to say.

Tony prods my arm. 'Not really. I am thirty-three, and that's old enough for a bloke to cut the apron strings. Don't need to take Mummy with me. She'll be visiting, wherever we are.'

'True.' I smile at him.

'Are you thinking of a little riverside cottage where the kids can roam barefoot on the grass, and we can have lots more babies and the whole family can sit around the fucking outsize table stoned out of our heads during the long summer evenings?'

'Something like that.'

Tony already sitting smiles the smile that won my heart in the first place. He looks more animated than I've seen him in ages. We do get on well. We really do. This is our life. This is my life. It's my happy, normal life.

Red came home the other day spouting a trite little epigram one of his beloved older girls had taught him. 'Yesterday is history, tomorrow is a mystery, today is a gift – that's why they call it the present,' he recited solemnly. I laughed at his greeting-card sentimentality but, for some reason, the words keep popping into my head.

'We could sell this place, easy enough. But where, exactly, do we go to, darling? That's the question, if you ask me. That's the main thing.

We need to go down south ourselves and find a little place for chez Pritchett. Do I imagine you might be thinking of the very town where Beth lives? What's it called?'

'Renmark. Yes. I mean, it's not really off the beaten track, not like this place. It has schools and pools and shops and stuff. It's right on the banks of the Murray. I like the idea of being somewhere with plants and water, and somewhere the backpackers don't go. I mean, God, I wouldn't want to live on a boat with a new baby, but the fact that it's possible seems incredibly romantic and exciting.'

'And what am I supposed to do to put the crusts on the Renmark table?'

'I don't know. We'll find you something. You could be a fisherman. Go out on the river every day. Or a househusband. I could go back to work. You could stay at home with the baby.'

'Great. From a miner to a fisherman. I've never seen the sea in my life.'

'Haven't you? Where did we meet again? Because I thought it was Sydney, but it can't have been. It must've been Alice.'

'Yeah, it was Alice.'

'Liar.' I throw a jammy crust at him. Tony loves playing up to his tough boy from the sticks image, but he's much more cosmopolitan than he lets on. He spent five years in Sydney, including those months in prison. He would never have considered moving back to Craggy if I hadn't begged him to.

He stands up and paces around the room. 'So, here's the plan. We give Red to Mum for the weekend, and we drive to Renmark. Then we stay with Beth, and find our next home. When we've found it we can come back to break the news.' He grins. 'Both bits of news, I think. Something happy to lighten Mum's gloom.'

I am astonished. 'Are you sure?'

'Whatever makes you smile, my love.'

This makes me smile. I give him a big kiss. A weight lifts. It's a cliché, but I feel it, and it does lift. It lifts from my stomach. I hope the baby's OK.

'Have you spoken to Beth about this?'

'Would I talk to Beth before you?'

'Yes.'

I consider. 'I suppose I might, but I haven't.'

He takes my hand and sits me down. 'We'll move. We'll do it before you're too far gone. It'll be fine. In fact it's a good idea. Now, you have to go to work and so do I. I'll try to find the big one today. The rock that'll secure our future. So look after yourself and my baby, and we'll talk more tonight.'

I don't know where he gets it from, sometimes. I have found myself a gem of a man, a veritable life-changing opal, and I have to hang on to this life. I go to school feeling uneasy.

chapter six

28 October

To be honest, I am scared rigid. I mean, she was away for four months and one week, and we'd only been together six months before she went. And now she's back. I've been wondering whether she might just ignore me. I've had visions of bumping into her on the street with a bronzed surfing dude, or whatever they call themselves, on her arm. In my imagination she humiliates me in front of him.

'Sophie!' I say, excited, in my daydream.

'Hello?' she says, frowning. 'Oh, hang on, did I used to know you?'

The dude strokes her bum, and then they both laugh a private, lovers' laugh.

I know I'm paranoid. None of my relationships has ever gone particularly well, and when we were together before she left, I was constantly expecting the worst. Sophie's so sweet. It would be totally out of character for her to humiliate me. But even sweet people can manage phrases like: 'It's not you, it's me'; 'I really like you, Larry, but I don't think it's going to work out'; and 'Can we still be friends – and I know everyone says that but I really mean it?' We've kept in touch, by email, but you never really know what's going on from an email.

I'll find out tonight. She called me at work at ten this morning, and seemed to be waiting for me to suggest something, so I said, as casually as I could, 'It would be good to catch up with you sometime, Soph. Are you free for, say, dinner tonight?' Then I quickly added, 'Or tomorrow night, whenever?'

She appeared to leap at the chance. She only got back yesterday evening, so she did warn me she might be a little bit jet-lagged. She managed to sleep through the night and on the plane as well. That must be because she's so tiny. I've never been on a long flight like that, but I'm sure I wouldn't be able to sleep. I'm six foot two, and Sophie's five foot three. She can curl up in her seat and be happy as Larry, so to speak.

In fact, I'd forgotten exactly how tiny she is. When I open the door to her, I can hardly see her, she is so small. I wonder what her first impression of me is. I've put on a clean blue shirt. Alix, my last girlfriend, bought it for me, but Sophie's never going to know that. It's the nicest one I've got, and I ironed it specially. She's smiling behind her hair. Her breath is around her in a cloud, and she's stamping her feet and looking cold.

'Hello, Larry,' she says, and I am overcome with shyness. I hope we are not going to be awkward with each other for long. She really is stunning. I knew it before, of course, but now she's tanned and her hair's streaked with blonde. She looks all toned and relaxed, and I realise that my doubts about the whole relationship – which centre around the fact that she is now thirty and thus, according to Kev, might 'accidentally' get pregnant – are probably unfounded.

She's lovely. So, immediately, I start worrying about what she's been up to. What is she thinking? Is her reaction to seeing me as wholehearted as mine is to seeing her? I don't think I'll ever know.

I lunge at her for a kiss, hoping that this is what she wants. I aim for the corner of her mouth, because I really don't know what the form is on these occasions, but she laughs and holds my head and twists it round so I inadvertently give her a full-on snog.

When I see the flat through her eyes, I wish she'd given me a bit more notice. I offered to meet her at a bar, but she said it would be easier for her just to come over. If only she'd come on a Monday, that's when the cleaner comes in, but as it's Friday the place has already been reduced to rubble. The communal hallway contains a solitary piece of furniture, a brown table that is so ugly it's probably fashionable again. If it wasn't so sturdy, it would be bending under the weight of letters to long vanished tenants.

The brown stair carpet is threadbare, and she trips on a piece that's become detached. I catch her. She weighs nothing.

'Sorry about that,' I say.

'Don't worry. I should have remembered it from before.'

I notice, for the first time, that our front door is *dirty* and scuffed. The landlord will never clean it, because he doesn't live here and he can't be arsed, and we'll never get around to doing it ourselves because we don't intend to be here for ever.

The interior is worse. I did have a tidy up before she arrived, but it was too cursory to do any good. I shouldn't have loitered at work trying to steal stories off Dot. I should have actually done the washing up, rather than leaving it in the sink. Leaving it in the sink is a stupid idea. You have to take it out before you can do anything and by then it's all congealed. Things that started off reasonably clean become dirty. It was just a last-minute measure to make the unwashed heap look smaller. I haven't been to the offy, haven't got any food in, haven't changed my sheets. I am not conveying success and style. Not making myself look like a reasonably impressive catch. I remember all the nights I spent at her studio in Battersea. It was tidy there. I wasn't allowed to put my shoes on the sofa. Those were the days.

'Sorry,' I tell her, doing what I hope is a rueful smile. 'It's not looking its best in here.'

'It's fine. Where's Kev?'

'Out. I mean, away. He's gone to Ireland on a stag weekend.'

'Whose?'

'Simon's.'

'Is it his wedding already? Why aren't you at his stag?'

I feel like a bit of an idiot. 'Well, you know.'

'I don't know.'

'You were coming home, weren't you?'

'You mean you stayed away from a stag do just for me?'

'Was that silly?'

'No, it was sweet. Really it was.'

Sweet. Great. His house is a squat, and he's sweet. Quite the Lothario.

'Actually, I'm not completely staying away. I'm flying out tomorrow, to meet up with them for the second night.'

She looks a little bit relieved. I fling the fridge open to change the subject.

'Drink?' I ask, before I've looked properly. 'And when he got there the cupboard was bare,' I add, quite wittily. Then I start babbling.

'Lager, lager, lager? A glass of white? There's some here, but it's Kev's, but that doesn't matter. I'll replace it. But it's been open for a while. Sorry, I meant to get some in, but I just haven't had a moment. I'll tell you all about that later. Or we've got vodka, a bit of gin, Scotch, no, sorry, we finished that. Rum. Sake. Should have got some champagne in, shouldn't I? I can run to the offy. Tell you what, I'll do that now. Get some Pringles while I'm there.'

She giggles, though whether it's because she's so pleased to be back, or what, I don't quite know.

'Sit down,' she says mock sternly. 'Shut up and bring me a lager.'

She manages to sit on the sofa without a flicker of distaste. She kicks off her shoes and tucks her little feet underneath her.

'So,' I mutter. 'How was it?'

She grins. 'It was great.'

Now, what does that mean?

In my head, while she was away, I toned down her charms to stop me missing her so much. I tried to mould her into a normal girl. I spoke about her with a long-suffering tolerance like the other lads speak about their girlfriends. Now I remember that she's different.

However, I don't know about the etiquette of these kinds of reunions. She knows I didn't want her to go. I was amazed when she announced, out of the blue, that she was giving up her job and going on a solo trip to Australia. 'It's their winter!' I told her, desperate to make her stay without her realising just how attached I was becoming. 'What about your flat?' I added.

Nothing I said made any difference, and she promised, at the time, that when she came back we'd pick up where we left off. This evening, I am too nervous to ask.

'You must be wondering what's been going on with my job in your absence,' I suggest instead.

'Sure. You tell me,' she agrees, and I think we're both relieved.

It's all easier at the restaurant. I take her to a Thai place which Kevin recommended on the grounds that when he took Tania there he got a shag on the first date. Tania is a Hungarian au pair whom he met on the tube. We were all impressed.

'I thought Thai food might be appropriate for someone who had a stopover in Bangkok,' I say knowledgeably to Sophie, on the way.

'It would be.' She smiles. 'I stopped over in Hong Kong, but that's fine. I love Thai food.'

The walls are a deep maroon, and the seats have red velvet cushions. The tables are wicker and ornate, the lighting dim. A candle splutters on our table. Sophie takes my hand, and squeezes it.

'It's absolutely gorgeous,' she tells me.

'Thought you'd like it,' I agree graciously, making a silent toast to sexy Tania.

This time, when I ask about her trip, I really want to know.

'It was absolutely amazing.' She leans back in her chair. 'It really was. That sense of freedom, of having everything you own on the bus with you. Some weird stuff happened . . . but it was all interesting. And in Australia there are beaches, there's desert, there's everything. Sydney was wicked. You'd love Sydney, Larry, you really would.'

'I've heard good things about it. Sorry I didn't make it out there. I really wish I had. The time just seemed to fly by.'

While we eat, and drink wine, and chat about the Sydney opera house, the Great Barrier Reef, and my dull Sophieless summer in London, I keep noticing a flicker crossing her face. It is the flicker of things I did not witness, things I would not understand, things she will not even bother to try to explain to me. The flicker of adventures that she judges to be so entirely out of my experience that she simply won't waste her breath trying. She probably thinks I don't even see the flicker. But I do, and I have one question about it. Is it the flicker of holiday snogs, of abandoned sex on remote beaches, of salty skin and sweaty nights? Or is it just a flicker of excitement at having left Europe, alone, for the first time, and survived?

I can't bring myself to ask. Instead, we chat inconsequentially. We move on to dessert wine, and share a very un-Thai crème brûlée, which Sophie first declines, then reluctantly agrees to share, and which she ends up hogging. Then she looks me straight in the eyes, and starts to speak.

'One thing that happened out there, Lawrence, I can't get it out of my head.'

Oh great. Here we go, then. I knew this was too good to be true. Here we go, with the holiday romance.

'What is it?' Not that I want to know. Particularly if she hasn't been able to get it out of her head.

'You remember Daisy?'

'*Daisy?* Of course I remember Daisy.'

'Well, I – can I tell you something weird that happened to me in the Outback? You have to promise, absolutely promise, not to tell anyone. Particularly not anyone at your work, OK?'

'Sure, hon.' I chuckle to myself at the very idea that I'd talk to anyone at work about anything at all, let alone something that happened to my girlfriend when she was on holiday. I can't imagine where Daisy comes into it. Nobody remembers Daisy, apart from me and Sophie. I mainly remember her because she brought us together in the first place, and because I got a good story out of it. Now I sound like an uncaring bastard. I also remember her because she was Sophie's best friend. I know Sophie still thinks about her and that means I do too. I never even met her; she was long gone before I came along.

Daisy brought us together. Sophie and I met, less than a year ago, a couple of weeks after Kevin and I moved into this shitty flat. We had a badly planned and slightly shambolic housewarming. Sophie came, with one of Kev's many female friends.

I noticed her as soon as she walked through the door, and although I've done my fair share of putting it about, I don't think a woman had had that effect on me before, and I know that no one has since. I would never tell her this, but I can remember exactly what she was wearing that night: a very short black skirt, which was shiny in a classy way, and a red top with a big, scooped out neck. Her hair was loose down her back. The moment I saw her, I pushed my way through the crowds to take her coat. I couldn't think of a good line, so I just smiled and said hello, and by the time I came back from laying her coat carefully on my bed (and allowing myself, briefly, to imagine doing the same to her later in the evening), she had gone. Later, though, I ended up in the kitchen, leaning on the fridge and talking to her, through a cloud of hashy smoke, about my vocation, and when it first came calling. The music was thumping, so I had to shout. I liked the sound of what I was saying. I hadn't thought of journalism as a vocation before, but I was talking to a beautiful woman, and I was pissed.

'It's the people that make the job what it is,' I told her confidently. 'My role is to seek out the human interest in the world – ordinary people in extraordinary situations – and to act as a filter through which the public at large can view the remarkable world in which they live. The journalist is doing his job best when he's invisible.'

'So you don't approve of those columnists with big pictures of themselves next to all the self-righteous crap they write?' she asked, surprisingly vehemently.

'No, I don't,' I told her, although I know that if anyone offered me one I'd instantly compromise my principles. 'You sound very passionate.'

'I am.' She smiled. 'My best friend was one of those ordinary people you were just talking about, although I doubt anyone would have called Daisy ordinary. She was all over the papers ten years ago, and then she disappeared because of it. She killed herself. Probably.'

I touched her arm. 'I'm sorry to hear that. What was it all about?'

'Oh, you won't even remember it. She was, according to your colleagues, a "wild child". She was a trained dancer, and she got into drugs. Do you remember the name Giles de Montfort?'

'He died, yeah?'

'Do you remember anything else about it?'

'He was one of those Hugh Grant type boys, wasn't he? And he had a brother. They both overdosed, the same night, along with some of their friends. There was a girl, who sold them . . . was that her?'

'That was her.'

'I do remember her committing suicide. Is there some doubt about whether she actually did it, then?'

'In my mind, absolutely.'

I came to realise how damaged Sophie had been by her friend's tragedy. She and the wayward Daisy had been best friends, from the age of three. From time to time her friend's name comes up, or we meet someone else called Daisy (usually a cat), or someone mentions suicide or the Severn Bridge, and she gets upset. Last May, she cried because it was Daisy's birthday, although it took me ages to get the reason out of her and I spent about two hours trying to think what I'd done to upset her. Kev came home when she was sitting on my bed, hugging a pillow and sobbing quietly. Immediately, I sought the benefits of his superior experience where women are concerned.

'Your fault,' he said straightaway.

'But I haven't done anything,' I told him.

He shook his head. 'Doesn't matter, man. Still your fault. Such is the way of the female brain. She's probably had a haircut and you didn't notice.'

I suppose none of Kev's many and varied conquests have had a dead best friend, or at least not one that's impinged on the relationship.

I must confess that, although Sophie's sadness touched me like nothing a girl said had ever touched me before, part of me couldn't stop looking at her story with a journalistic eye. I'm not proud of that but still, it's the truth. First of all I made sure Soph and I were going to see each other again anyway, and to my delight she seemed receptive to that. Once our relationship was established I began to suggest that I could interview her, in the friendliest way possible, for our women's features pages. She did it, because it was me who asked, and we produced a fantastic double page spread on 'My agony after best friend's suicide: I always wonder if Daisy's still alive, says Sophie'. She was so sad, and so pretty. The photos were sensational. She spoke about their lives in Devon, their ballet classes, their unshakable friendship. She relived her sadness when Daisy went away to boarding school to be a dancer. She told the readers how she watched her friend going off the rails and the way she tried to help her but failed to get through. By the end she was the only person Daisy would talk to normally. And then, just as she and everyone else who knew her was preparing to see Daisy incarcerated, she was gone. For ever. It was a great little story, and it got me noticed by the features editor. The de Montforts wouldn't comment, but you can't have everything.

So I am naturally intrigued as to what bearing Daisy might have had on Sophie's holiday experiences.

'You're going to think this is so stupid,' she warns me, cupping her chin in her hands and looking cute. 'You're going to think I'm mad.'

I stroke her arm. 'No I'm not.'

'You are, but what the hell. I saw her. I really did. It was her. She's living in Australia.'

'You saw who? Daisy?'

'Yes, I did.'

I try not to smile. 'Up close, or in the distance?'

'I *knew* you wouldn't believe me. I spoke to her, OK? It was her. I know it was her.'

I feel a certain professional frisson. It is unlikely, but sometimes these things happen. 'Did she remember you?'

'Yes. Well, no. I'm sure she did, but she wouldn't admit it. She pretended to be someone else and she did an Australian accent.'

'So you saw someone who looked like her but who said she wasn't. Could it have been a double?'

'No.'

'Why are you so sure?' On the one hand, this would be fantastic if it were true, but on the other, it can't be. People are always thinking they see missing people, but invariably it's just someone who looks like the person. People project what they want to see. I'm not surprised Sophie projected Daisy onto some poor bewildered Australian woman then marched up and accused her of being a long dead disgraced socialite.

'I know her, don't I? I am one hundred per cent positive. This bloke, Huw, he said she'd sounded English before.' She pauses. 'Oh, forget it. I wish I hadn't said anything. Just forget I mentioned it.'

I worry that she's angry with me for not even considering that she might have been right; but she isn't. She changes the subject lightly, and we don't mention Daisy again.

All in all, an interesting and reasonably successful evening.

chapter seven

Even in the most trying and the least comfortable of circumstances, five months pregnant is a good way to be. If I can put up with this, I think I must officially be both 'glowing' and 'blooming'.

Red and I are on our way to Renmark. The air conditioning has broken on the bus, and, because it's supposed to be air conditioned, the windows don't open. Even the skylights in the roof are permanently closed. If there were a few chickens and goats under the seats, and about a hundred more people on the bus, this would be like travelling in the Third World, apart from the fact that in the Third World people wouldn't be complaining. Here, in the self-styled World's Best Country, there is a loud and permanent mutter concerning refunds.

I am sweating. In his sleep, Red is also sweating. He's leaning on my arm, and making it sticky and uncomfortable. I don't want to move, in case he wakes up.

With my free hand, I stroke my bump. My happy thoughts are vital for this baby's wellbeing. It's good that I have to think about other people. For the past ten years, my top priority has been Red. For the past three, I've had to look after Red and Tony. Now there's going to be me, Red, Tony and the baby. Together, we will make a classic family. A nuclear family. I've never liked that expression, with its uncomfortable apocalyptic resonances. We are a stable family: that's much better. The overtones there concern Mary, Joseph and the infant Jesus. That baby had unlikely parentage, too.

The bus rattles along. I look out of the window. We are passing through a tiny settlement, which seems to consist of two houses on each side of the road, a nasty looking cafe and nothing else. There isn't even a bus stop. Life in this place, wherever it is, must be even worse than in Craggy. The scenery is becoming greener, the trees less scrubby and more plentiful. The soil is transforming itself into proper earth, rather than grey dust. We have come a long way south. Australia is a remarkable country. It unnerved me when I arrived. It was too much like England. I didn't like the fact that everyone spoke my native language. I kept expecting to see someone I knew.

After a while, though, when all the people I met were resolutely strangers, I grew comfortable with the weather and the relaxed way of life. Before long, I decided I might well end up spending the rest of my life here. I smile, and direct a wave of love towards the unborn baby. I can almost convince myself that I'm happy and secure, that I have no past. I must, at least, be convincing the baby. She's too small to understand about lies.

I wish I knew whether everyone else's home lives were as argumentative, and yet as humdrum, as ours has become. I can't ask my own mother, obviously, and I also can't mention the subject, however delicately, to Margot. She would take it as a clear signal of my intent to leave her son and 'march off back to London Town', as she occasionally insists I will do one day. To Margot, all of England, and Scotland too, are contained within the borders of London Town. From the Outback perspective, they may as well be. All we hear of Great Britain, in Craggy, is the ongoing soap opera of the royal family. Everyone but me is sincerely fascinated. At first my neighbours expected me to have particular insights, or at least some inside information. They soon learned.

Everybody on this bus must be coated in a slick of perspiration. Everyone is miserable and cross. People have been complaining loudly all day, and their combined bodily odours and emissions hang above us all, an almost tangible polluting cloud.

I gaze out of the window and fight the urge that has besieged me for the months since Rachelle's wedding: the urge to think about my life in England. I'm not allowed to give it a moment's thought. That's my rule. It is out of bounds, forbidden territory. In spite of Sophie, it will remain so for ever. Instead, I force myself to visualise our new house. Tomorrow, Red will see it for the first time, and next week we will own it.

Renmark was exactly the way I'd expected it to be. Australia is like that, in a way that Europe isn't. You go to Sydney, expecting to see the harbour, the opera house, lots of trendy bars and gay men, and that is exactly what you get. Any visitor to Craggy has an idea of what they expect from a small town in the Outback, and Craggy Rock obliges with its dust, heat, stones and cold lager. Renmark, for its part, really is the relaxed settlement on the river that I'd hoped it would be. Tony and I had driven up to Beth's houseboat at sunset. The tall trees were glowing golden, and the river was wide and staid. Beth was sitting in a wicker chair on the bank, with a glass of white wine in her hand and a magazine on her lap. Her hair shone angelically, and she looked peaceful.

As soon as she saw us, she jumped up, and ran to meet us. I was so pleased to see her that I almost cried.

'Guys!' she said, embracing me and then kissing Tony, who handed her a six-pack of VB. 'You didn't bring Red!'

'I said we wouldn't. This is an adults only expedition.'

'Come in. Have a look at the boat and I'll get you a wine.'

'Could I have a soft drink to start with?' I asked. 'I'm really thirsty from the journey.'

'Sure.'

The boat was glorious. It was her perfect home. It was painted blue on the outside, and inside there was a small sitting room, a bedroom which was filled with a double bed ('it seemed too tragic to buy a single at my age,' she pointed out, 'even though it would have meant space for my clothes.') The wardrobe was in the tiny bathroom, and the kitchen was in a corner of the sitting room. Somehow, the overall effect was cheerful and snug. It made me think of Mrs Tiggywinkle's house.

Once Tony ascertained that she had an electricity supply, and hot and cold running water, he pronounced himself impressed. The best part of the house, by far, was the deck; and it was there that we sat and watched the sun set over the wide Murray River.

'I often see otters here,' she said. Then she looked at me. 'That's your second lemonade. Are you pregnant?'

We had planned to make a grand announcement. Instead, we just laughed and blushed.

The following day, we saw five houses. One of them was opposite the houseboat. It had four bedrooms, a sizeable back garden, and a shady, cool interior. As soon as we walked in, it felt like home. I've heard about that happening but had never experienced it before. The air there was cool, and it lacked the harsh dryness of the desert. I felt myself coming alive to new possibilities.

Ever since the week after we met, I've had a gnawing fear that, one day, Tony and I will wake up with nothing to say to each other – that we'll struggle through talking about the children until they leave home, at which point we will become one of those couples who sit in cafes in silence, not even able to look directly at one another. In fact, I've never truly believed we'll make it that far. We fight too often for that. I've always suspected that, one day, I will be abruptly overcome by horror at the lack of possibilities in my life, and that I'll bolt.

In Renmark, I realised we might be better off than I imagined. We conversed and laughed all the time. There were no sad silences. We barely argued. I can't imagine being without Tony. I know I have no choice. If I run away from the English girl with her accusations, I have to take the family with me. That is exactly what I'm doing. They haven't a clue.

Red stretches and yawns an enormous yawn.

'Are we nearly there?' he demands, his voice fuzzy with sleep. The road is now lined with real, serious buildings which have other buildings beyond them. I see an advertisement for Adelaide's Premier Bed Warehouse. There really are a lot of trees here, and I begin to imagine I can smell the sea air, although I know it's just the salt from people's sweat.

'We're nearly in Adelaide,' I tell him. 'Then we have another few hours to Renmark.'

'Bugger.'

'Don't say that.'

'But I mean bugger. What can I say instead?'

'Try bother.'

'Bother and bugger. I'm bored. And too hot.'

I will never get used to the heat. As soon as spring arrives, I'm the only person who's depressed. I'm delighted that the baby's due in March. Even though it means I have to be pregnant through a long hot summer, I can't wait for the winter with the newborn. We won't have to keep it out of the sun, to cover it with cream all day long, every day. It won't have to spend almost all its time indoors. The timing couldn't have been better. I manage to deal with the heat at home because the underground walls keep us cool. I can deal with it in Renmark because of the river, and because our new house will be shady, and protect us. I will deal with it on Beth's boat because she has ceiling fans. The only place I can't handle it at all is on this bus.

'It's cooling down now,' I tell him, with more certainty than I feel. 'Look, it's almost four thirty. It's hardly the midday sun.'

'I know but there's no air coming in, so it's just built up through the day.'

'You're too clever for your own good,' I tell him crossly, but he is already distracted.

'HELLO, BABY,' he shouts into my bulging stomach, cupping his hands to intensify the sound that reaches the foetus. The woman sitting in front of him turns round, startled, then smiles indulgently. 'IT'S OK, BABY, WE'RE NEARLY THERE. WE'RE IN ADELAIDE NOW.' I feel the baby reacting to his loud invasion of her space, and kicking him away. He can probably feel it himself.

The coach terminal is concrete and functional. Despite its slight grubbiness, all three of us are delighted to be here. Red and I take deep breaths. The baby settles down. Our connecting bus leaves in forty minutes, so we haven't got time to go into town. We're going to have to sit in the drab building, even though we've been sitting all day. There isn't a single spare seat. The plastic chairs are the sort I remember from school in England, and most of them are cracked. They don't have legs; instead, they are stuck to a block of concrete that runs down the room. About a third of them are occupied by sprawling backpackers, some of whom, I note disapprovingly, are taking up more than one seat. They snooze with their legs stretched over the chair next to them, or they pile their bags up on seats rather than the floor. They are oblivious to, or careless of, the crowds of grumpy, seatless passengers glaring at them.

I try to imagine myself as one of them, travelling from one random place to another without any responsibility. The days when I could have done that, I tell myself sternly, are long gone. I've done it enough for a lifetime. It was not a carefree life, for me. I look down at Red, and am glad we managed to settle. The backpackers are grimy. Their bags are bulging, with enamel mugs and hiking boots tied to the outside. I would hate to live like that.

I make accidental eye contact with a young man of about my own age. His eyes are surrounded by smile lines, and his face is weatherbeaten. His hair is implausibly yellow. Despite myself, I am smiling. I like the look of him. I like his messiness, because it's so different to my own neatness. I like his cotton collarless shirt and his checked trousers. He seems to be drifting around without any responsibilities, and yet he looks focused on something.

Even with my son by my side, I am immediately drawn to him. This hasn't happened for years.

He stands up, and walks towards me.

'Hi,' he smiles. He's American.

'Hi,' I tell him, and I try not to blush. I am, after all, a married woman.

'You need a seat?' he asks, pointing to the one he has just vacated.

I cannot help feeling crushed. I see myself through his eyes: a woman in a crumpled dress, hot and bothered from a long day's travelling, burdened with two bags and a boy. He didn't see me, Lina. He saw the stressed woman with the child hanging off her arm and nowhere to sit. He was just being gentlemanly. I didn't even think I was that noticeably pregnant, yet.

Sometimes I forget that, as a mother and a wife I am invisible as a sexual being. I love Tony, and I am happy with our lives, but I'm still in my twenties, just, and I'd like to be noticed, harmlessly, from time to time. My whole identity used to be built on being attractive. Now I am a teacher, a mother, a wife. I have no *je ne sais quoi,* any more. People look at me, and they think they know it all.

'Thanks,' I tell him, and we take the seat.

I can't wait to hang out with Beth this week. I miss her and Nina terribly. Having no friends makes me feel like I did in my first, bewildering weeks in Craggy Rock. Everyone in the town was focused on Tony's return, particularly as he had brought an English girl, and a little boy, with him. I could scarcely leave Margot's house without a friendly neighbour rushing up to introduce herself, to give me some tips about living in the Outback, and to form an assessment which, Margot told me, would always be presented to her, with regard to how long I'd stick it out. Looking back on if, Pete must have had a book going on the duration of my stay in Craggy. He was probably taking bets on whether or not I'd leave Tony as well as the town. I wonder whether anyone's going to get a payout, now that we're off.

I'd never lived in so stifling a community, and I wasn't used to finding that everyone knew my business without my telling them. I couldn't imagine how I was going to stick it out, and I lay awake every night plotting my escape, while Tony slept peacefully beside me, an alien being who had returned to his own planet. No wonder he'd fled.

Beth didn't help. She hated me on sight, and I didn't blame her. The first time we met, I had been shopping. I'd performed my nervous manoeuvre of backing slowly away from Mavis as she lectured me on the good honest hard work that makes the townsfolk what they are.

'I daresay, love, you find us a bit lacking in the fancy city manners,' she told me, and as I took a step backwards, I simpered that no, that wasn't the case at all. 'But stick with us. You'll find us good friends.' I smiled as sincerely as I could, and made it through the door. 'You take care of that boy of yours!' she called after me. I wondered whether this was just an expression, or whether she actually believed I might be neglecting Red. I had no idea; I couldn't connect with anyone at all. I felt autistic in Craggy Rock. Then I ran straight into Andy.

He put his hands on my shoulders and steadied me. He is even bigger than Tony. His fingers are about as thick as my arms.

'Lina! Watch it!' he admonished. Then he looked at me. 'How you doing? Come for a beer.'

I was too dazed to refuse, so I followed him into the bar and drank three lagers, while he rambled on about nothing in particular, and knocked back five. An hour later, Beth strode in to fetch him. She shot vitriolic looks at me, even when she knew who I was and even as she purported to be welcoming me to Craggy life.

'Hello,' she said coldly. 'I would say welcome to Craggy Rock, but you seem to have found your feet already.'

It took her several weeks to work out that she had the wrong woman, but once she did, and when I met Nina, the place began to seem bearable. For years, we were a unit. Nina, Lina and Beth. We tried to persuade Beth to change her name to Tina or Gina. Then, within the space of three months, Nina was abruptly and belatedly diagnosed, and died, and Beth divorced her cheating man, and left.

*   *   *

69

'Mummy, is this Renmark?'

I shake myself awake, and look around. Red has his nose to the window. I don't know how long I've been asleep, and I feel terribly confused. I look around the bus. I expected to wake up in a lying down position, and it takes several minutes to get used to the fact that I am sitting on a seat, crammed into a small space with a hundred other people. It's not right. Not civilised.

It's dark outside, and we appear to have stopped at a garage. I peer through the window, trying to make out whether it could be our destination. We are definitely in a town. A group of people is waiting for the passengers to disembark. Head and shoulders above most of them is a blonde, freckled woman. Red spots her at the same time as I do.

'It's Beth!' he yells. At her request, we tried to get him to call her Auntie Beth for a while, but he wasn't interested in being patronised. He knew that no one else called her Auntie Beth, and he also knew that she wasn't his aunt, so nothing we said could induce him to be cute for our benefit.

In a second, we are off the bus, and Beth is carrying our bags to her car. Red looks around at the gas station and the wide road in front of it.

'So, here we are,' he says grandly. 'Good evening, Renmark. My new home.'

Red is wide-eyed as soon as he sees the boat. He transforms himself into an angel child, eats all the food Beth has prepared for him, drinks a glass of milk, and asks to go to bed. He loves the idea of sleeping on the river, and we tuck him up in Beth's bed so we won't disturb him. I wanted to carry him into the sofa bed with me in the middle of the night, but Beth insists that, on account of my condition, Red and I must have her bed. I argue for a while, before giving in gracefully.

When I come back from tucking him up, Beth has poured a glass of Banrock Station Sauvignon Blanc for herself, and a mango juice for me. 'It's fresh,' she smiles. 'You can get everything here. Trust me, it's a world away from Craggy bloody Rock.'

'Red certainly feels at home.'

'We can take him to the pool tomorrow if you like.'

'Do you have any idea why either of us stayed there so long?'

'None. Cheers. To Craggy Rock, and the great joy of leaving it.'

'And to Nina.'

We clink glasses, and Beth goes to the kitchen to fetch the dinner. I feel completely relaxed. This is where we are going to live. It's somewhere new. Somewhere with flowers and trees and fresh fruit juice. We are only a few hours from the sea. It's like being in a different country, and yet we're still in the same state. I occasionally curse Australia for the fact that, like a convict, I have no option but to remain here, exiled from my old life. I'm on the other side of the world, walking upside down. If I dug a deep enough hole on an English beach, I'd end up where I am today.

'I've booked you in to see the house in the morning,' Beth says as she hands me a plate of grilled fish, new potatoes and salad.

'Thanks. Wow, this looks amazing. I hope Red likes the house. He'd have preferred a boat, clearly. He doesn't seem to mind the idea of leaving Craggy, not one bit.'

'Red can join the club. I'll introduce you to some neighbours as well. I think you'll find them different from the good, honest, hard-working folk of the Outback.'

'The *self-proclaimed* good, honest, hard-working folk.'

'That's the ones. It's very relaxed around here.'

'I'll look forward to seeing how Tony settles in.'

'He seemed happy enough when you were down here. I suppose he has lived in civilisation before.'

'He can fit in anywhere, as long as it's in Australia. Prison, Sydney, you name it. He only moved back to Craggy because I wanted to.'

'You crazy woman. You don't want to go back to England, then?'

I stretch my feet out in front of me and flex my calf muscles. 'No, I don't.' I'm lying – I'd love to – but it's a lie I've repeated so often I barely even notice it any more. This time I do notice it, because my carefully cultivated nonchalance is still upset by Sophie's appearance. Nonetheless, I am still able to lie without flinching. That is my most valuable skill. 'I know that Red should be able to go there and see his adopted heritage one day if he wants,' I continue, 'and so should the baby, and that's up to them, but there's nothing there for me any more. No parents, no family to speak of, nothing but sad memories.'

'Does Red ever ask about your parents?'

'He has done, but I just tell him the truth. There's no point lying or trying to make it sound more palatable than it is. There are only so many ways you can dress up the fact that they died in a car accident when I was younger. Children are tough. He has no concept of my parents. He's far more cut up about Nina.'

'Poor love.' I'm not sure whether she means Nina, Red or me. All three, probably. 'He's very stable, isn't he?' Beth continues. 'Do you know anything about his birth family?'

'Not a sausage.'

Beth fiddles with her drink. 'You know, I sometimes wish you did want to go to Europe. I'd tag along.'

'Excuse me, madam, but you don't need me to take you to Europe. You're a big girl. Do lots of shagging and see some cathedrals. Be one of those scruffy bastards who clog up bus terminals. You'll have a ball. I'm afraid I've come round to the Pritchett point of view – that is, I've decided that I don't need to leave Australia. I've done my travelling. Maybe we'll go to New Zealand one day.'

'Oooh, you two are so adventurous. So you don't want a grand girly trip with the kids.'

''Fraid not.'

'Shit. That means I'll have to find someone else to go with. Or go on my own. Could I go on my own? I don't think I could.'

'Of course you could.'

'Do you think so?'

'I know so.'

'OK. So you can help me plan it. Where would you go if you were me?'

This is an excellent challenge. We spend the rest of the evening poring over an atlas, and writing Beth's itinerary. I make sure she knows that she should spend time in France, Italy, Spain, and perhaps even North Africa. Britain, I impress upon her, is seven times smaller than Queensland, with more than three times Australia's population.

The house is just right for us. Every time I see it, I like it more.

'Hey, this is cool,' Red announces, walking into the biggest room, earmarked as the sitting room. 'This can be my place. No one else allowed in, except the baby.'

'Sorry, honey, but this is the sitting room, for all of us, and that is not up for negotiation. You and the baby can still have a playroom. There are four bedrooms, you see, and we're only going to need three.' We'll get a sofa bed to go in the sitting room too, for when we have visitors.

The garden is huge and full of possibilities, and the kitchen is three times the size of our current effort. On top of that, it is already done tastefully enough. All in all, it's going to be a fresh start. It's going to be perfect. I'm glad we've still got a little bit of money hidden away, because this is in a different league from our dugout home.

I'm happy. Our offer has been accepted, Andy and his child bride want to buy our little house in the hillside, and we will all be moving to this fertile town where all the fields appear to be planted with vines.

'Hey, Mum,' says Red. 'This is good.'

We spend a week squeezed onto the houseboat, planning Beth's big trip and meeting our new neighbours. And like an alcoholic tentatively trying to go back to drinking in moderation, I begin to allow myself to remember the way things used to be, twelve thousand miles from here.

chapter eight

Daisy 1982

'To Daisy,' read the card. 'Our little ballerina. We are so proud of you. Have a wonderful time, and remember to call us every week. We'll miss you. Much love from Mum xxx and Dad x.'

She looked up. 'I'm not a ballerina,' she told them. 'No one's a ballerina when they're twelve.' She pushed away the butter, and spread her toast with plain Marmite.

'But you're *our* ballerina,' her mother objected.

'I'm not. I'm your daughter. You can call me your dancer if you really have to be so naff. Margot Fonteyn was a ballerina. Alessandra Ferri is a ballerina. I haven't even gone to ballet school yet.' She took a swig of black coffee. She was trying to force herself to like it because she knew it was going to be her preferred drink from now until the end of her working life. She was going to draw her energy from black coffee and Diet Coke. It was exciting.

Ed looked up. 'For Christ's sake,' he muttered. 'It's a bloody card. Brat. Note, Mother, the ingratitude of your youngest offspring.'

Daisy propped the card up next to her plate. 'Thanks,' she said sulkily to her mother. 'Thanks a lot. Can we go soon?'

'You're welcome, darling,' trilled her mother, ignoring the question. None of the children knew it, but she was well on her way to an antidepressant dependency. If Daisy had known at the time that her mother was a drug addict she would have treated her with more respect. Instead, she jiggled in her seat, trying to retain a degree of nonchalance. She wasn't nervous. She was leaving home, to become a dancer. Not a lapdancer, or a pole dancer, despite what the papers said about her afterwards. She wasn't any of the types of dancer that is synonymous with prostitution. She was a ballet dancer; the most pure profession known to little girls all over the western world. From as early as she could remember, this was what she had wanted. She might have been a prima ballerina if things had been different. Before it all went wrong, she was being pushed that way. She could have been a soloist. She might have been lots of things. It was all ahead of her.

Her father got up from the table. 'Are you packed?' he demanded.

'Yes.' He knew she'd been ready for days.

'Let's get this show on the road.'

'Do you have to go so soon?'

'Mum, you know I do! I've got to *be there* this afternoon!'

'But it says to arrive between midday and six. I don't see why you have to get there at twelve.'

Rosie and Ed looked at each other. Daisy despised them.

'Let her go, Mum,' said Rosie, speaking for both of them. 'Then we'll get some peace and quiet.'

'Yes, let me go, then I won't have to see their hideous faces.'

'Release her from the parental bonds. Allow the fraternal twins to use her redundant bedroom as a study.'

'You cannot! Mum, tell them it's still my room.'

Their mother stood up, wearily. 'It's still her room. You all know that. Don't tease her, Edmund.'

He rolled his eyes, and, when she thought their parents weren't looking, Daisy gave him the finger. Her father saw her. She caught his eye, and looked away.

She took deep breaths to overcome her nerves, and she told herself, again, to remember that she was doing exactly what she'd always wanted. She had been dancing for nine years, since the age of three. She could barely remember a time when she didn't go to ballet. She grew up loving it. She was never particularly clever at school, and she only had one good friend. She was bratty at home because she had to be, and she was shy and withdrawn away from it. Ballet was her salvation. It was the thing that kept her going. By the time she was ten, she was the star of the local dance school, which, admittedly, wasn't difficult.

The school consisted of one studio with a wooden floor that was polished three times a year. It had high windows, a barre along three walls, and an out of tune piano in the corner. The walls were covered in peeling yellow paint. The teacher styled herself 'Miss Mary' and terrified her pupils. She had uncompromisingly short hair, and eyes like lasers. She shouted obscenities, she raged and, from time to time, she ejected a tearful girl from the class, on the grounds that she wasn't pointing her toes enough, or for some similar minor infringement of the balletic code. Mary had set out to reach the pinnacle of the dancing world. She had trained at the Academy and thought she was going to make it, until, when she was sixteen, she was told bluntly that she was too stocky. Thus she ended up, frustrated, in charge of the girls of Kingsbridge.

The class that changed Daisy's life had taken place seven months before, when she was eleven. She and Sophie were the youngest in grade five, and they had just been put in for the exam. The whole class were in the centre, in rows of four, doing arabesques. Most of the girls were wobbling and giggling and falling over as they tried to hold themselves on one leg for longer than they'd ever done it before. Sophie was wobbling slightly, and Daisy was concentrating with all her might, and managing to stay like a statue. Miss Mary, who invariably dressed for teaching in a pair of black towelling flares and an orange towelling top, stopped in front of her, and stared. She took Daisy's front hand in hers and adjusted her balance by a minuscule degree.

'Everyone except Daisy, that's enough. Gather round.'

Daisy redoubled her concentration. She knew that no one but Sophie liked her, because she was so young, and because her thighs looked good in pink tights. She had no breasts, where the other girls bulged, and while the rest of them tugged at their leotards in a vain attempt to cover themselves, Daisy and Sophie were unselfconscious. The fourteen-year-olds glared at them for an hour every Saturday.

'This is how first arabesque should look. It's a shame it takes a little girl to teach you clodhopping great oafs.' She showed them the way Daisy's hips were straight, level with the floor. She pointed out the line from the tip of Daisy's middle finger to the end of her big toe. She made her go up on tiptoe to see if she could hold the pose. She could. Daisy felt waves of resentment coming from the class, and she tried not to care. Finally, Miss Mary let her go.

'Come and have a word after the lesson,' she said as she walked away.

'Spastic,' said Fiona Day. Her friends concurred.

After class, Daisy stood in front of her teacher, expecting that a touring production needed some children for, perhaps, *The Nutcracker*. That was normally why Daisy and Sophie were kept behind.

'Have a seat,' she said, with a gesture. This was unprecedented. As Miss Mary perched on the edge of her desk, Daisy sat on the rickety chair that was reserved for mothers needing to chat about their darlings' progress. She put her feet up on the crossbar of the chair, and made sure she pointed her toes. While Miss Mary was putting away all the money – three pounds a girl – Daisy looked at herself in the mirror. One of the reasons she loved ballet was because it changed her image and made her beautiful. In her normal clothes, most of which were Rosie's cast-offs, she looked like a runty misfit with a scrawny body. In everyday life, she wanted her sister's soft curves. When she was wearing her black leotard, tights and a crossover cardigan, with ballet shoes which she had recently upgraded to satin ones tied with ribbons, she liked herself just the way she was. She looked like someone completely different. Someone with an art. She liked the way her face suddenly looked interesting, with her hair swept back into a bun.

'Stop admiring yourself,' said Miss Mary abruptly. 'Have you thought about auditioning for the Academy?'

'No.' Daisy was amazed.

'Would you like to think about it?'

'Do you think I'd have a chance?'

'I wouldn't suggest it if I didn't, would I?'

And so Daisy ran out to the car, still in her ballet clothes, and brought her mother in for discussions. Three months later, her mother had taken her on the train to London for the audition, and now she was leaving. Ballet had, unexpectedly, proved to be a passport out of home. It was her saviour, her guardian angel.

She heard footsteps on the gravel path, and ran out to meet Sophie. Both girls were small-boned, but Daisy was reasonably tall. Sophie was like a little fairy. Although she was twelve, she looked nine. Her hair was long and silky, and she had blue eyes and a pointed chin. They hugged, and stepped back and held each other's hands.

'I can't believe you're going today!' Sophie complained.

'We can write all the time, and I'll be home for holidays,' Daisy told her. 'I'm glad you're coming in the car to take me there at least.'

'I couldn't believe I was allowed! I get to go inside the *Royal Academy of Ballet*!' She said it in the poshest voice she could muster. 'So I'll have an idea of where you are when you write your letters. I wish I could have gone with you.'

'You could have. You'd have got in.'

'I wouldn't. I don't want to be a dancer.'

Daisy said goodbye to the twins as nonchalantly as she could. She knew she wouldn't miss them. She hated them both. They spent all their time together, shutting her out from their whispered conversations. They'd make up little private jokes just to spite her. She'd always wanted to be their friend, and they had always been mean to her. They would talk loudly about their golden age in the years BD (before Daisy). They'd tell her how much better their life had been before she came along. Ed would use stupid long words. They would shut her out, and laugh at whatever she said or did.

She particularly resented Rosie. Ed was a nerd. He wore thick glasses, and he studied far too hard. She would never have been mates with him anyway. Rosie, on the other hand, was pretty, and she wore nice clothes. She was Daisy's big sister, and she had no interest in the role whatsoever. Daisy wanted to sit on the edge of her bed while Rosie brushed her hair and put on lipstick. She wanted her to talk about boys. Rosie looked, Daisy thought, like a prettier version of herself. Her hair was long and thick, and she conditioned it every day. They both had bushy brown eyebrows, but Rosie plucked hers twice a week. They had the same freckles, but on Rosie they looked cute, and on Daisy they were just bratty. Rosie had a beautiful figure that was both slim and curvaceous, while Daisy couldn't imagine ever needing a bra.

'See you then,' she said over her shoulder. All the bags were in the boot. The two girls were going to sit in the back, like stately passengers in a limousine, despite the fact that it was Dad's old Maxi.

''Bye,' said Rosie.

'So long,' said Ed. He raised a dismissive hand, and they went inside before the car pulled away.

Daisy was so happy that she wanted to laugh and sing. The only person she was sad to be leaving was Sophie, and they weren't parting quite yet. She appreciated what a big thing this was for Sophie to do, because she was terrified of Daisy's dad, and yet she was subjecting herself to an entire return journey to Devon alone in the car with him. She would have to sit in the front then. Daisy prayed he wouldn't do anything embarrassing on the way home.

Sophie had always been her best friend. They met at ballet when they were three, and were each other's only friends when they started school the following year. Daisy didn't want to leave her behind, because even though they were different, Sophie felt like a part of her. Sophie was a normal girl. She had a group of good friends, and she was popular at school. She was fast on her feet, so she was chosen early on for the netball teams. She was able to chat to anyone about anything, and even when they were eleven, people would go to Sophie with their problems. Daisy, on the other hand, kept herself aloof, because she didn't know how else to be. People put up with Daisy because they liked Sophie and the two came as a package.

Daisy had nobody else. She would have to make a new friend when she got to the Academy. Sophie, though, would be fine. She was happy. Perhaps that was the difference between them.

'We'll still be best friends, won't we?' Sophie asked.

'Of course we will,' Daisy told her firmly. 'We'll always be best friends, for ever. Just because I've *escaped from home*, it doesn't mean anything's going to be different.' She said escaped from home loudly, as a dig at her father. He ignored her. 'I'll still be back for holidays, worse luck,' she added.

'Shall I see if Mummy will let me come and visit you?' asked Sophie.

'Of course! Maybe this year she might not let you, but you know it's going to be amazing. I've got it all worked out. I'll be there till I'm about eighteen, and that means you can come and see me and we can go out in London and no one's going to stop us. We can do whatever we like!'

There was a snort of laughter from the driver's seat. Sophie and Daisy smiled at each other. He knew nothing.

chapter nine

11 November

Time to put my plan into action. The only way I'm going to get ahead is by cheating a little. It probably doesn't even count as cheating. There is probably an unspoken rule somewhere that states that, in all matters journalistic, the end justifies the means, and that the only thing you can do wrong is to get caught. In fact I'm sure I've heard that said somewhere – quite possibly on my journalism course.

PERSONAL CODE OF ETHICS
1. Don't libel anyone or do anything else that's going to cost the paper embarrassment/money.
2. Try to get own stories before resorting to nicking other people's.
3. But advancing myself at the expense of others' careers/happiness is OK as long as I don't get found out. In fact, this is simply an extension of the newspaper's very existence – we use other people's lives to advance ourselves, i.e. raise circulation. Therefore I am practically honour bound to do the same thing in my private working life.
4. There must be another ethic? Must think of one.

It hasn't taken me long to work out that the most useful information in the office belongs to Dorothy, the current incumbent of my putative next job. Dotty Dorothy has been crime correspondent for approximately the past one hundred and twelve years, and she knows everyone, on both sides of the law. She does, I admit, get good stories, but she's getting on a bit now, and she must be up for retirement. In the event of my taking over from her, she would give me some contacts. So I'm not really stealing them, I'm simply anticipating the event.

Today is Dotty's day off. Earlier in the week, I ascertained that we don't have security cameras in the newsroom. When no cleaners are anywhere in the vicinity, I pick up my coffee, and pour a slug through the vents on the top of the terminal. Then I switch it on. It happily invites me to log on. I pour in some more coffee, and add some to the keyboard for good measure. It insists that I must enter my user name and password. Since when have computers been so bloody hardy? I consider unplugging it, but I know that, somewhere along the line, I'd just end up looking silly. In the end, I pull a cord and hide my keyboard under Pete's desk next door. I squeeze it right to the back, behind the bin. I'll go in early tomorrow and retrieve it.

'Arse!' I exclaim, with a rich Somerset 'r', for the benefit of anyone who is within earshot. 'Someone's nicked my keyboard.' Then I pick up all my things, huffing and puffing at the inconvenience, and move them to Dotty's desk. That's the normal thing to do if your terminal doesn't work. You find out who's off, and you shift to their desk instead.

Then I go back and programme my phone so all the calls go through to Dot's extension, and I settle in for the day.

Her top drawer contains hundreds of pens that almost certainly don't work, and a few pencil sharpeners, pots of dried-out Tippex, and curled up Post-it notes. Some have numbers on them, but without names they are no good to me. Her second drawer houses a million pieces of paper – exactly what I am looking for – and the big bottom one is packed with unread books with notes from their publishers attached.

When I look around, I notice that Christie has arrived. She is looking at me. This is not good. I shut the drawer hurriedly, and log on to the system.

'Morning, Christie, how are you?' I call casually across the room.

'Fine, thanks. What are you doing here so early?'

'What are you?'

'Catching up on correspondence. You?'

'Same.'

She is looking at me rather too closely. I try not to blush. Christie is one of the quieter hacks, but for all that she could be dangerous. I don't really know her. She came from a local rag, somewhere up north. She probably spends more on cosmetics in a week than Sophie does in a year, and yet she's not nearly as attractive. Quite pretty, but overly painted. Her eyes, cheeks, mouth, everything's been coloured in. You wonder what the real person underneath looks like. I think nature intended her to be mousy, but she's streaked her hair with terrible white highlights, no doubt at an extortionate cost. She's much chunkier than Soph, and she always wears bright red lipstick. Her clothes, today, are tight and kind of beige and black.

'My keyboard's gone walkabout,' I volunteer, 'and Dot's off today.'

'Why don't you just nick her keyboard then?'

'Nicer to work at a tidy desk,' I say lamely. 'Change of scenery. And Pete's been getting on my nerves.'

She nods. She doesn't trust me, I can tell, any more than I trust her.

'What's wrong with Pete?'

'Oh, nothing. Just too loud on the phone.'

She smiles. No one could argue with that. So we work at our desks, separated by a reasonable chunk of newsroom. Damn her. Damn her stupid painted nails and her high-heeled shoes, kicked off under her desk. Damn her grande Macchiato, exactly the same as mine but no doubt with 'skinny' milk. Catching up on correspondence, my arse. She is no more doing that than I am. She is putting in the hours, that's what she's doing. Spying on me.

I edge the second drawer open, keeping an eye on her all the time, and, without looking down, I remove a wedge of papers and slip them inside my own file. I take a pen, to make me look businesslike, and start going through them.

By the time the room fills up for the day, I have discovered that it is the lot of the crime reporter to receive hundreds of mad letters from people who are either in prison or living their crazy paranoid lives in the outside world, convinced that 'They' are out to get them. There are drawings, there are poems, there are rambling letters typed with such vigour that all the dots go through the page. Some of them are actually written in green ink. The cliché of the 'green ink letter' come to life. I begin to reassess my ambition. Being a political correspondent, I think, could be just as good for me.

Buried among the green ink letters, however, is some curious information. I wonder how she distinguishes the good stuff from the crap. Unfortunately, by the time I have sifted through, there are too many people around, and I am sick of closing my file hurriedly to trot out the 'no keyboard' excuse. I slip the correspondence into my bag, for lunchtime photocopying. Christie watches me, all day long. I wonder whether she's older or younger than me. She's probably about the same. I can't have her overtaking me, and she seems serious.

At six thirty she strides over, intimidating in her tight black trousers, black jacket and beige top. Her bag is slung over her shoulder, and I immediately tell myself that, whatever she says, I will deny it.

'Coming to the pub?' she asks casually.

'No! I mean, me?' She's never asked me to the pub before. Nor have any of her friends. In fact, I am hardly ever asked. I'm not very good at social skills in the office, and try to work on the basis of the individual cultivation of people, rather than being one of the gang. I'm not a one-of-the-gang kind of lad.

'No, I meant the Pope. Of course you, you twat.'

'Oh. OK. Just give me a minute. I'll catch you up.'

'Your stories are filed. So what's keeping you?'

'Nothing really.'

'You've caught up on your correspondence, I know that much.'

'As have you.'

'Indeed.'

I have been outmanoeuvred. She wants to keep an eye on me rather than enjoy my company. The moment we enter the pub, she steers me to a table populated by chattering, over-fashionable colleagues, and waits while I reluctantly scour the room to find two wobbly stools. The pub is hidden behind the office, and is visited solely by journalists from the *Herald* and the *Sunday Herald*. No normal person would want to drink in a place like this. It's a dark, slightly sinister room, with an aroma of stale beer and tatty furnishings, and a regular array of middle-aged drunk men propping up the bar. The King's Head is the last remaining eyesore in an area that positively gleams with trendy bars with chrome furniture and cranberry juice. When Sophie comes to meet me after work, I wouldn't dream of taking her to the office pub. In fact, I haven't been here for weeks.

It is, though, congenial, in its way. It is strange to walk into a drinking establishment where, as in *Cheers*, everybody knows my name. I know that they know it for banal reasons – these people are not my friends, and they only know who I am because just about every single one of them is a colleague – but it's quite heart-warming all the same. It's not often, in London, that you get a sense of faux community.

The barman sees us walk in, and immediately pours Christie a vodka and tonic. That proves that I really don't put in the hours here like I probably ought to. He has to ask me what I want, and I decide on a Guinness. I quite fancy a vodka myself, but fear I'd look girly.

'Lawrence Golchin!' says Abigail, as I sit down. 'Hey there, stranger.'

'Don't often see you in here, mate,' adds Tim, whom I barely know at all. He sits four desks away from me.

I smile at them. 'It's a pleasure to be here,' I say, then worry that I sound wanky. When I look at Tim, I decide I should perhaps update my work wardrobe, and make it funkier. His charcoal suit is cut differently from my navy one, and his shirt is burgundy, but he looks good.

'So, what's with the mysterious overtime?' asks Abby conspiratorially.

'What mysterious overtime?' I reply with a smile. 'Nothing. You should ask Christie here the same question.'

A girl called Patsy laughs. 'Methinks he doth protest too much,' she says archly.

'So, who's going to be watching the England game on Saturday?' I say innocently, and to my delight I get a laugh. After that, I begin to enjoy myself. Add to to-do list: Drink in the King's Head at least once a week.

I am about to go to the bar again when my mobile rings. I have set it to play the William Tell overture, which I think is quite amusing. I notice Abigail and Christie exchanging glances.

'Hello?'

'Hi, hon, where are you?'

I am so glad to hear her voice. 'Sophie! Hi, hi. I'm in the pub. Where are you?'

'I just thought you might like to meet up somewhere, but if you're with work people, it doesn't matter.'

'No, it's OK. Where shall we meet?'

'But don't feel you have to. Are you doing that important networking? If you're with the editor or anything, just say so, and I'll see you tomorrow. Or you can come over later. It's just a spur of the moment thing, you know.'

'Soph, don't be silly. I'm not with the editor, just a bunch of people.' I see a few of them looking at me. 'I'm with esteemed colleagues,' I tell her, 'and now I'm coming to see you. I'll come to yours and we can take it from there.'

I press the red button and smile around. I catch a few raised eyebrows. I pick up my things, mutter that the missus wants me, and bid them all goodnight. As I walk out, I hear Christie's voice.

'Did you hear that? *I'm not with the editor.* Why would he be with the editor?'

I let the door slam shut behind me. Let her wonder.

chapter ten

2 December

The London Underground in the rush hour never seems quite so bad if you've got a seat. I enjoy sitting here, with people jamming their briefcases into my knees. I know they would happily poke my eyes out or disembowel me with a blunt umbrella if it meant they got my seat. I never normally travel this early in the evening, so it's a bit of a novelty. Sometimes I try to catch my fellow passengers' eyes and smile smugly. The man right in front of me has a thin face and a dogged expression. I wonder whether he's thinking about the fact that he's standing on a hot train on a cold day with thousands of other people all just like him. Maybe his mind is a million miles away. He's probably thinking about sex.

He won't look at me, so I can't taunt him. Instead, I stare hard at an ad for car insurance (cheaper for women, apparently). Paddington is the next stop. I'm taking Sophie home for the weekend, and it seems like a worse idea by the minute. My family don't even like me. I suppose Mum does, but Dad doesn't really care either way, and Luke thinks I'm laughable. He thinks I talk bollocks, which is rich, coming from the bullshitter extraordinaire. Because of Luke, Matt laughs at me too. Matt follows Luke's lead like a puppy.

I hope the weekend's going to be all right. Months ago I made the mistake of admitting to Mum that I had a girlfriend. Her nagging has finally become too much to bear, and my brothers are sending emails which suggest, in the crudest terms, that Sophie is either a figment of my imagination or a blow-up doll.

It's been a washout of a day so far. I took one of Dot's contacts out for lunch but found myself entirely unable to distinguish what was definitely bollocks and what might not be. He was a well-dressed man with an expensive haircut and a charming line of patter. One minute he told me he'd done twelve years for fraud, and half an hour later it had mutated into three separate stretches for armed robbery. Early in the conversation, he claimed to be a misunderstood homosexual, and that he'd left the true love of his life in prison, while later on he was getting married next year, and was the father of four infants by three different women. The stories he wanted me to cover included a vice ring operating within Buckingham Palace and encompassing several minor royals (if only!), and the fact that a major British charity was a front for child pornography. For all I know they might both be true, but I wouldn't exactly like to rush into print. It was a waste of a good lunch, and I had to put down 'Labour Party worker' on my expenses slip and hope no one asks which champagne socialist, exactly, ordered lobster at Quaglino's (I would never have got away with that in John Smith's day) and what story I had to show for it.

The train shudders to a halt. I get up and five people fight, silently and without any facial expressions, for my seat. The thin-faced man gets it, and smiles smugly as he lowers himself. One of the women who was beaten huffs and puffs, turns sideways to display her figure, and finally addresses him directly with the words, 'In case you hadn't noticed, I'm pregnant.' He doesn't even look up. He's got his paper out now and everyone ignores her. It's a tough world. The fittest survive in London, and that is why I need to take active steps to propel my career along. I wonder whether that's why it's called a career, because, done properly, it consists of a headlong dash. I need to career towards Dorothy's desk. I need to career in the direction of the editor's chair. I need to career onto the front page with a wonderful story. Such as the discovery of someone long presumed dead, someone disgraced and tainted by mass death, living in the Australian bush, and, by chance, coming face to face with her oldest friend.

For some reason, Sophie's far-fetched tale of spotting her friend keeps coming back to me. Imagine if it was true, and I ruled it out without making even the most perfunctory of checks.

I elbow along with the crowds. The walls and the floor seem to be covered in ancient dirt, and we all ignore a homeless woman and child sitting in one corner with a placard saying 'hungry please help'.

I'll talk to Sophie about Daisy again, maybe on the train. I have my tube ticket in my hand for a speedy exit, but the woman in front of me appears only just to have realised that she'll need her ticket to get out, and stops, blocking my chosen exit, while she looks through her handbag. She's only small, and she's probably a European on holiday. I squeeze past her with a very mild 'Excuse ME!' and she steps back in confusion, losing her place.

The inside of the mainline station always surprises me. They've done it up, so it's all shiny and clean, and you can do better shopping there than you can in Wandsworth.

I spot Sophie before she sees me. She's standing by the Paddington Bear stall, looking at some overpriced teddies. She's all wrapped up in her big winter coat, with a bobble hat on, brownish lipstick and no other make-up. Her slightly pointed nose and chin make her look like a pixie. Poor little damaged Sophie. Sometimes I feel that I want to make it my life's work to take care of her. I wonder how she'd feel about that. I can't tell her, because sometimes I don't. Sometimes I forget about her altogether.

I walk round in a big arc so I can come up behind her, and then I put my arms round her waist. She inhales sharply and spins round. In the second before she realises it's me, I see the panic on her face, and I could kick myself.

'Sorry, darling,' I tell her.

She laughs. 'You great idiot. You terrified me.'

On the train, I try to prepare her for meeting my family. I've never talked about them much, but I desperately want her to think they're all right. More than that, I want them to see her and to realise that I'm not a loser. That I can get the girl.

I try to get us into weekend first, but the conductor tells me sharply that on a Friday, first class is exclusively at the disposal of people who are paying first class fares. We get a table instead, and end up sharing with an elderly couple who sit silently, listening to our conversation, all the way to Bath. I drink lager. Sophie drinks gin and tonic. We share a packet of smoky bacon crisps.

'They're just normal,' I tell her. 'Don't worry about them.'

She smiles and licks her fingers. 'I'm not worried. Not really. It'll be nice to see where you come from.'

'Soph?'

'Yes?'

'You know when you thought you saw your friend Daisy?' I look sideways at the elderly couple, but they don't seem interested. Sophie looks surprised.

'Yes.' She sounds cautious.

'Well, I've been thinking about that. How certain are you that it was her?'

'Completely. But it's OK that you don't believe me. If someone else thought they saw her I wouldn't necessarily believe them, although I'd want to. You must remember, I know her. I know what she looks like. I knew her for more years than she's been gone. It was her, but that's OK. I'm happier just knowing that she's out there, and that she's fine. In fact, if I get on to a masters, I might go out again before it starts, and talk to her this time.'

'So if it was her, how would she have ended up there?'

'She was determined. She could have done it. People vanish all the time, don't they? We only hear about the ones who get found. Who knows how many people pull it off? I bet it happens a fuck of a lot more than we would imagine.'

I consider this. 'True. But before you saw the Australian woman . . .' I decide to be more diplomatic. 'Before you saw Daisy, did you ever believe that she could really, truly have done that? I mean, faking her own death, writing suicide notes. It's quite a fantastical cliché. Not something one's friends would do.'

'Nothing Daisy did was what one's friends would do.' She crunches an ice cube, and smiles sadly. A lock of hair has fallen across her face. She's never got over what happened to her best friend. She keeps the goodbye letter beside her bed. I think it's affected her even more than her mother dying. I've tried to talk about Daisy a number of times but, since that first interview, which I think she regretted, she's never wanted to talk about her at all.

'Sorry I didn't take you seriously before,' I tell her. I know the old couple are listening but can't imagine they're a dangerous audience. 'It seemed too incredible. But let's talk about the woman you saw. What did she look like?'

'Medium height, thin, dark, like Daisy but older.'

'Dark?' Daisy was as blonde as it's possible to be.

'Yes, her natural colour. She was always a dark girl. Chestnut colour.'

'Like you.'

'Just a little bit darker. We used to compare.'

'Actually, I do remember it. Didn't someone print pictures of her as a child?'

'Everyone did. Her sister gave them to the press for some reason. I was in a few.'

'So, the woman in Australia?'

'Yes, well, she looked thirty, which is what she would be. She was drinking wine out of a plastic cup – it was at someone's wedding party, and a load of us from the hostel went along. There was this very young bloke staying there, straight out of school, and he'd been talking to her. He seemed to fancy her. In fact he was half in love with her.'

'She hasn't lost her touch, then.'

'She was much mellower. At first. And he introduced us all to her. Her name was Lina.'

'Lina? Funny name.'

'Whatever. She had a boy with her. He's ten – I asked him.'

Sophie looks me directly in the eye, then looks at the old couple. 'I'll show you something later,' she says quietly.

As we pull into Bath and start to get our things together, the old couple get up, with much huffing and puffing, to let us out. Sophie squeezes past the woman, whose grey hair is worn, not in the customary tight curls, but in a perfectly executed chignon.

'I hope you find your friend, dear,' she smiles.

Sophie grins back. 'You never know, we might.'

Home never changes. I wonder how old you have to be before you stop thinking of your parents' house as 'home' and your own as some kind of temporary, term-time digs. The house is big and sturdy and as ugly as ever. It smells the same as it always has. It is a smell of cooking, and the washing machine, and various other comfy things. I hope Mum doesn't ask whether I've brought any dirty laundry home. I hope she's put me and Sophie in the double bed in the spare room. I'd be mortified if Sophie got the spare room and I ended up in my old single bed with the 'manly' grey and black striped duvet cover.

As soon as they meet Sophie, Luke and Matt trail around after her, taking her coat, sitting her down in the big leather chair, which swamps her so she looks like a little doll, and bringing her a second gin and tonic before she's even had time to meet my father. He has to be summoned from his study, where he pretends to be working. His pretence is shattered every time anyone tries to make a phone call: it's the white noise and the mysterious random melodies of the internet that give him away. Last Christmas, I decided to check out what he'd been looking at. The array of gay porn sites that made up his recently visited list made me resolve never to question him again. I didn't tell my brothers, although they've probably discovered it for themselves. I haven't told Sophie. I've told no one. I can no longer look my father in the eye.

'Hello, Larry,' he says heartily in his artificially deep voice, the one he keeps for when we've got company. 'And this must be Sophie. Welcome to our humble home!'

'Nice to meet you, Mr Golchin.' She smiles, and betrays her nervousness by taking a huge gulp from her glass, and coughing. 'Sorry,' she adds, pushing me away as I go to thump her on the back.

'What's all this Mr Golchin business?' he demands. 'Call me Alan.'

'And I'm Maggie,' adds Mum. I always found it embarrassing, in the eighties, that my mother had the same name as the despised Prime Minister. She once went mad when Luke, Matt and I started a campaign to get her out of the bathroom one Sunday morning, with a chant outside the locked door of, 'Maggie, Maggie, Maggie. Out! Out! Out!' The woman had no business having a long bath in scented bubbles and reading a colour supplement. Not when we needed a lift into town.

'How was your journey?' Mum – Maggie – asks Sophie. A good, polite question to start things off. It's when these questions have dried up that we'll find out whether they really get on.

'It was fine,' she responds, smiling. 'It's lovely to get out of London. I always like seeing fields and trees out of the window. It's like you never notice you miss it, and suddenly you feel like you're coming home.'

'Are you from the country, then?' mutters Matt, all teenage and awkward. My youngest brother has changed his look since I last saw him. He used to model himself on Ali G, apparently unaware that Ali G was taking the piss out of people like Matt. Now he affects a skateboard 'chic', for want of a better word. He wears baggy trousers and huge sweatshirts that would be more at home on Puff Daddy. I'm proud of my own style, these days. I've followed Tim's lead and smartened up my act. No one has commented.

'Sorry?' says Sophie, with an apologetic frown.

'I can interpret that,' I tell her. 'My little brother wants to know if you're from the country.'

She turns to Matt. 'Yes, I am. I grew up not far from here, actually, in South Devon.'

'Cool.'

All through dinner, which has been prepared extra-late in honour of our eight thirty arrival, I note my brothers looking at Sophie, and looking at me, and wondering what she sees in me, and whether they have, perhaps, underestimated me. Good. She manages to chat to my parents charmingly, and if I didn't know know otherwise, I'd think my father fancied her. Mum is, quite clearly, planning what she'll wear to the wedding. In her head she's coming up with suggestions for grandchildren's names. All in all, the evening is a success. But it's still only Friday, and we're here till Sunday.

The parents go to bed, as ever, as soon as dinner is cleared away. Mum says awkwardly, as she stacks the dishwasher, 'Larry, I made up the spare room for you and Sophie.'

'Thanks, Mum,' I say gratefully, and give her a goodnight kiss.

I can only hope that she and Dad don't go to bed so early to shag. God knows what would be running through his head if they were.

Sophie and I accept Luke's invitation to his room. Both my brothers are shameless dopeheads, as are all their friends. I feel that getting stoned might be a reasonably pleasant evening activity. Luke did his A levels last summer, but he's still dossing around the parents' place, not working, not studying, not paying any rent. I can't believe they haven't chucked him out yet. Also I can't believe any relative of mine could be so utterly and depressingly devoid of ambition.

His bedroom is meant to be the place where he has free rein to express his personality. He managed to paint one wall purple, before he ran out of energy and left the others magnolia. His posters show such diverse paragons as Sarah Michelle Gellar, Louise Nurding and, just for rebellion's sake, Marilyn Manson. I note that he has tidied up, by sweeping all the dirty clothes away somewhere. Either that, or Mum's been in recently.

We sit on the bed and on the beanbags that your parents buy you when they're trying to convince you that a couple of beanbags in your room will, somehow, make you into a fully fledged adult.

Luke has put the Verve on the stereo, and lit a stick of incense. This is Luke doing 'seductive'.

'Here,' he drawls, passing the joint across me to my girlfriend. I intercept it and take a toke before passing it on.

'Where are your manners?' he asks languidly.

'Oh, don't be nasty,' says Sophie. 'I'd feel I was the one with no manners if I let you pass it straight across poor Larry.'

Ignoring me utterly, Luke slides down from the bed, and sits next to her. He looks into her eyes. Luke fancies himself as a ladykiller, and I am amazed to see him cracking on to my girlfriend right before my eyes. 'What are you doing with him, Sophie?' he demands. 'You're too good for him, can't you see that?'

'Oh, right,' she giggles. 'So I'm meant to go out with you instead, is that what you're saying?'

'You see? You're perceptive as well.'

'Well, thanks for the offer, but I happen to think Larry is a lovely bloke. And I think you're too young for me, and anyway, talking to me like this in front of your brother would mean you're not the kind of person I'd want to go out with anyway.'

He laughs. 'Yeah, but it's Larry. My dorky big bro.'

'He's not dorky. He's an interesting man.'

Matt mumbles to himself in the corner. 'An. Interesting. Man. Wow.'

'Yes, he is. Come on, Larry, stand up for yourself.'

I am mortified at being told off by my girlfriend in front of Luke and Matt. They snigger a bit, and I stumble to my feet.

'I'll find your coat,' I tell her. 'Let's go outside.'

The moon is full, and we sit on the bench with our feet up on the table. Sophie leans against me and I stroke her hair. I feel slightly awkward as I do so. I am self-conscious, particularly now she has seen how I am viewed by my own family. I feel guilty for having a family at all, when Sophie's only got her dad. Out here in the moonlight, under the yew tree, everything looks silver, and we seem ridiculous. Like people in a black and white movie. I feel Sophie is about to burst into song.

She doesn't.

'What were you going to show me?' I ask, hoping it doesn't sound like a bad line – like 'show us your tits'.

'It was something to do with Daisy,' she begins. She looks at me, and I can see her mistrust. She tips ash from the end of the joint onto the grass.

'What is it?' I make my voice as gentle as possible. Sophie takes her purse out of her coat pocket. Tucked into the back is a photo. She takes it out and hands it to me.

A woman and a little boy are squinting out at me. Behind them is a tall wire fence with a sign on it reading, rather bafflingly, 'No Explosives'. Beyond that are some scrubby trees. A lunar landscape stretches off into the distance. The boy is dressed in exactly the same style as Matt, but he's years younger. The woman is wearing a pinkish dress that's a bit creased. Her dark hair is tied up with a clip with a flower on it. They are both sitting on the ground, both smiling. They look happy.

I have seen enough pictures of Daisy Fraser to recognise her when I see her. For some reason, though, I play it cautiously.

'The resemblance is certainly very strong.' I hold it up to the light of the moon. 'Soph, I can see exactly where you're coming from now.'

'It's not a *very strong resemblance*. It's her.'

'Did you have this all along?'

'No. There was this young guy there, I mentioned him before. When I asked him afterwards what she'd said to him, he went on about this conversation they'd had about Wales, and how she'd said she'd grown up in England, and then he said he'd taken her photo. I made him absolutely promise to send me a copy. I even gave him money to get one done. I took his parents' phone number and told him I was going to ring them if he didn't send one. He thought I was loopy. It arrived a couple of weeks ago.'

'Why didn't you show me before?'

She shrugs. 'Why do you think?'

'But this is kind of proof.'

'I don't want you only to believe me when I happen to have concrete proof of something. I wanted you to believe me because you trusted my judgement.'

'So why now?'

'Because you brought the subject up on the train.'

I don't speak for a while, and nor does Sophie.

'There's another reason why I know it's her,' she says eventually.

'Mmm?'

'I'm probably only telling you this because your dad got me pissed and your brother got me stoned.'

'That's a good reason.'

'I think she was planning to escape.'

The information penetrates my brain slowly. 'She was planning to escape,' I repeat.

'She was sorting it out. She told me. Or rather, she hinted at it. She didn't tell me in so many words, but she as good as told me.'

'What did she say?'

'Oh, she said enough.'

I can see she's clamming up, but I need to know more.

'When did she tell you?'

'You know. Just before she went. When she was at rock bottom, waiting for the trial to start.' She looks at me. 'Journalists are wankers, you know that? Present company excepted.'

'I'm sure you're right.'

'So she was at home with her parents, and she was just so miserable. I was doing my A levels and I used to go and see her every day. She knew her trial was starting soon, and she knew she was lucky to have got bail at all, and that most people would have loved to have seen her get a life sentence. She was terrified – petrified – about what would happen to her in prison, and she knew she'd be found guilty. She was so young and fragile, and she couldn't cope with it.'

'And when did she say she was going to run away?'

'The last time I saw her. She was with her family, but she wasn't talking to them and they weren't talking to her either. I felt so sorry for her mum. She was dosed up on tranquillisers, a zombie, just to get through the days, I think. She hadn't been able to deal with any of it – first of all that her darling daughter was such a wild child and was hanging around druggy circles and shagging posh people when she was meant to be becoming a ballerina. Really, Larry, the blokes she hung out with were vile. And then that Daisy had survived that evening but she could easily have been dead. Then all the tabloids crucified her, and she was headed for prison. Mrs Fraser was completely bewildered. None of the family knew what to make of Daisy. She was a horrible embarrassment, the black sheep. So anyway, Rosie let me in, and I went into Daisy's bedroom, and she was just sitting there with a passport and some other pieces of paper. When I came in, she put them away quickly, and asked me not to tell anyone, ever, that she'd been looking at them.'

'Did you see the name in the passport? Or even the nationality?'

'No. I asked her if she was going away travelling, and she said, kind of. So I said I promised I wouldn't tell, and she said, "I can't tell you anything. I can't tell anyone, but if I could, I'd tell you. Just, don't be surprised. And know that I'll always be thinking of you." I asked if she was going to come back, and she said she doubted it. So we got absolutely plastered, the most drunk I've ever been in my life. Luckily I didn't have an exam the next day. It took me until the afternoon to get over the hangover, and when I did, I called her, and she'd gone. The day after that it was all over the papers, about her car being found.'

'Did you think that everything she'd said could be interpreted as meaning she was going to commit suicide?'

'No. I've never believed that. How do you explain the passport?'

'She was trying to make it easier for you?'

'I surprised her. She didn't know I was coming.'

'But you came every day. You've never mentioned this to anyone else before?'

'Never. I shouldn't have mentioned it now, either.'

'It's OK. I'm on your side, remember? So let's say that she did go to Australia. It's a reasonable place to end up. Did you go looking for her?'

'Not at all. It really was a holiday. It was all to do with turning thirty and never having left Europe. I never, ever imagined seeing her there.'

'So how are you feeling at the moment, Soph?' This seems to me like an excellent thing to say. The sort of thing girls like to hear. My head is spinning. I am frantically trying to make my concern for my girlfriend take precedence over the insistent voice in my head that is proclaiming one fact: this could be the one. It could be the story that makes the difference.

'I've been a bit shaky since I saw her, but I'm feeling quite stable,' she says, leaning on my shoulder. 'It's nice to know that she's all right. But I can't help wanting to go back and talk to her properly. Just the two of us. I want to persuade her that it's OK for us to talk, that I'm not going to blow her cover.'

'Do you want me to come?'

'Only if you absolutely swear you're not going to write about it. Only if you come as my friend, my partner.'

'Of course! I promise. I wouldn't mess you around, Soph. You should know that by now.'

Even through my fuzzy head I can see that Sophie and I might have a divergence of interests at the point where we tracked her down. Sophie would be anxious not to blow her cover, and I would be madly keen to do the opposite. I want to summon the entire media army to some remote town in the Outback, and present them with a story on a plate. Daisy Fraser: you won't remember her, but she's back from the dead. I think Sophie's being a little naive by telling me all of this. It means part of her must want it in the paper. I am, after all, a reporter. She won't even remember my promise in the morning.

Sophie throws the end of the fag into a flowerbed. I want to pick it up, but if Mum finds it she'll only blame Luke.

'Got any chocolate?' she asks. 'Or crisps?'

'Sure,' I tell her, squeezing her shoulders. 'Let's raid the kitchen.'

chapter eleven

We are moving this afternoon, and I am six months pregnant. Thus, I have the perfect excuse to do nothing. I stand outside for a while, and watch the men loading boxes into the van, which has been borrowed from Alcoholic Bob for the occasion. Pete's coming to Renmark to help us at the other end, and he's taking the van back. It is usually used for, among other things, the transportation of explosives to and from the quarries. I personally clambered into the back today, to check that no stray dynamite was going to blow Tony and Pete up en route. It was, as Bob had promised, clean. Now, Tony, Pete, Merv and anyone else they can bully into helping is heaping our household goods into it. I can't bear to watch them manhandle my precious items without a regard for the care with which I selected each one.

The heat is debilitating. I feel my brain throbbing, and I wonder how everyone else manages to stay so blasé. If it was up to me, we'd spend the whole summer indoors with the curtains drawn, sipping iced water and waiting for autumn. In fact, that's what I'll do as soon as we reach Renmark.

The school term ended two days ago. When the pupils go back, I will not. They will return to the cleaned and polished school, and they will find a new teacher. They will forget all about me, unless the new teacher is some kind of monster, in which case they might occasionally remember me with residual fondness.

That, at least, will probably happen. I helped interview for the new teacher. Normally the interview process is redundant because the school is trying to persuade the teacher to take it on, rather than vice versa. This time we had two candidates. I remember when I was offered the job. The early days in Craggy were starting to drag, and

I was putting off the day when I traipsed around the shops asking everyone if they had any vacancies. My main fear was that they might say yes. I could not imagine spending all day, every day, in the company of, say, Mavis in the store. One afternoon, as I was strolling around killing time until I had to pick Red up, I happened to walk past the school. I stopped to read the noticeboard outside, which detailed end of term fairs and appeals for funds. As I stood there, a woman rushed out and stood next to me, smiling pleasantly. She was about my age, with curly chestnut hair in a ponytail, and she was wearing jeans and a white shirt, with red flip-flops (or 'thongs' as they inexplicably call them here). I recognised her from our road, although we hadn't met yet.

'Hi!' she said, looking at me intently.

'Hello,' I replied. 'Are you a teacher?'

'Yes, and I'm the deputy head as well. We haven't met yet but I know you're Lina. My name's Nina.'

'Pleased to meet you.' God knows, it was refreshing to meet a woman of my own age, but I had no idea why this earnest teacher had run out to talk to me.

'I was just in the staff room,' she said, indicating it with her hand, 'and I saw you through the window. The thing is, we're short of a teacher. I wondered if you might be interested in applying. I know your little boy's here. Mine's in the same class, Eric. Thought you must be kicking your heels a bit and it might suit you.'

I was amazed. 'But I'm not a teacher. I have no training at all.'

'You wouldn't be the first. You look right. You sound good. You'd be fine. We're only looking for a class teacher for year five. It's nothing too tricky. Oh, and you'd have to teach a bit of English too, but since you *are* English, how hard could that be?'

It seemed like a more interesting prospect than working in the garage. I started work the following week.

I sigh, and go inside. Nina was intense and intelligent, and I miss her. If she was alive, I'd be round at their place, staying well out of the way of all the removals. Instead, I find a few chairs in the kitchen, put the kettle on, and sit down. I take a few deep breaths, and sing a little song for my baby. I've been singing it '*O mio bambino caro*', which I think is by Puccini. I can't hit the high note, and I hardly know any of the words, but I figure that if anyone's going to forgive me for that, it'll have to be someone who hasn't even been born yet. I rock the bump in my hands, and hum to her, or him.

I tried to inject an element of formality into the two interviews for the new teacher, both of which were conducted by me and Simon – Mr Andrews – in the bar. Simon, who is so shy that he can hardly bring himself to speak to me, roars at the children in a manner that would put a sergeant major to shame. Simon is now the deputy head. They tried to make me do it after Nina was too ill to work, but I had no interest in any extra responsibility, and besides, I felt like a fraud as it was.

Simon's interviewing technique, without me there, would have consisted of three questions: 'Would you like to tell me about yourself?' 'There must be questions you'd like to ask me?' and 'Another drink?' I smiled at the candidates, and asked them what their weaknesses were. Everyone knows you're meant to say 'I'm a workaholic and a perfectionist', and indeed one candidate, Jane, who was straight out of teacher training college in Brisbane, said exactly that. I smiled conspiratorially at her, and she smiled back, relieved. The other, Thomas, was baffled. He was a red-faced man from Alice who was leaving his last job for unspecified reasons. 'My weaknesses, love?' he echoed. 'My weaknesses?' I waited, praying that he was going to say something like, 'I steal from my employers and download child and animal porn onto the school computers.' In the event, the best he could come up with was, 'Well, there was that business . . .' I was agog, but he checked himself. 'S'pose a bloke likes a drink at lunchtime, if that's a weakness.'

Simon gave Thomas the job, on the grounds that he knew what to expect from Outback life. Simon hates being outnumbered by women.

I'm bored. We're having an early Christmas lunch at Margot's in about an hour. Only after that ordeal will I be able to get behind the wheel of our car, with Red beside me, and leave this life. Every minute drags, in this heat. Being indoors provides some considerable relief, but I still know what it's like outside, and I still know that I'm going to have to go out into it sooner or later. I have spent the past week waddling between home and school, and wrapping, packing and labelling all our possessions in every spare moment. Every lesson at school has been devoted to my pupils' creativity as they glued cotton wool and glitter onto paper to make festive Christmas cards. We made snowflakes and stuck them in the classroom windows, where the midsummer sun beat down upon them so intensely that I thought they would melt. The boys put tea towels on their heads and pretended to be shepherds, and Tabitha dressed in blue and self-consciously rocked a pink plastic doll that signified the baby Jesus.

We did, in short, all the Christmas activities that I remembered from school in England. We have done the same things for the past three Christmases. Left to myself, I would have happily made seasonal and geographical adjustments – a stable in the desert, for example, rather than in snowy northern Europe, or a Father Christmas clad in a red vest and fur-trimmed shorts. In my first year, however, I tried to make some sensible alterations (I think I had surfers trekking to the middle of the desert to see the infant king in his dugout) and there was uproar amongst the spectators. 'It's just not right,' Margot said, on behalf of all the onlookers. 'It makes a mockery of the Christmas story.'

I put the kettle on. I am making tea for everyone, yet again, largely to create an excuse to clean the kitchen one more time. I sense someone standing in the doorway, and turn round.

'Hi, Andy,' I say, without animation, as I warm the pot and drop in three tea bags. 'Do you want a tea?'

'Please. That'd be great.'

As I am waddling to a cardboard box to fetch another cup, Andy walks into me. He jumps back.

'Sorry! I was going to get it for you. You shouldn't be doing that, in your condition.'

'I can still pick up a cup, thanks. I'm just passing on the heavy boxes and furniture side of things. But go ahead, do the tea if you like. It'll be your kitchen in two hours, after all.'

Andy hangs his head. I sit down and watch him fiddling with the milk, and pouring the tea. He does a good job. Rather sweetly, he used to make tea for me and Beth on a regular basis. In fact, I used to envy her. Tony would get me an alcoholic drink any time I fancied one, but it has never once occurred to him to make tea.

'There are some biscuits here,' I tell him. I line up the mugs on a tray, and put the plastic bottle of long life milk, and a bag of sugar, next to them. Andy snatches them from me. I put my tea and the biscuits down on the table.

'I'll take them to the lads,' he says, ingratiatingly. 'Then, erm, if you've got time for it, it would be kind of good to have a chat. If you've got a moment.'

I shrug my shoulders. 'As you can see, I have moments in abundance.'

Andy, apparently, wants to pour out his heart. I find this odd, as he is sober.

'You know about being married,' he says urgently.

'Not as much as you do.' I smile. 'I've only done it once.'

'So you know more. You've done it right.'

I nod, and eat a biscuit. 'How's it going with Rachelle, then? Looking forward to moving in?'

He smiles, then puts his head on his hands and rocks back and forth, groaning.

'Come on!' I say cheerfully. 'You've only been married three months.'

'Three and a half.'

'That bad?'

He reaches for my hand. His hand is unfeasibly large and pink. 'Lina, why didn't you stop me? She's seventeen bloody years old! And I'm thirty-three! I have nothing to say to her. We sit in the pub and she tells me about this new nail varnish she wants to order from a catalogue, or about how she wants to model our marriage on Catherine Zeta whoever and Michael bloody Douglas. She tells me about Denise's new boyfriend, and Raelene's new shoes. I don't think I can take it.'

Apparently, he really does expect sympathy.

'Remember when Beth and I saw you with Rachelle in the bar?' I say sharply. I know it's callous, but I don't care. I'll never forget that afternoon. We had been shopping, insofar as shopping is possible in this town. It was fairly hot, and we innocently stopped at the motel bar for a restorative beer. It was my idea. I felt guilty for weeks about that. As our eyes got used to the light, we saw the shapes of two people joined at the lips. She was sitting on his lap, kicking her skinny legs in the air. His huge hand was on her thigh. Her matchstick arms were round his neck.

Beth nudged me. 'Way-hey,' she said. 'Bit early in the day for . . .' Her voice tailed off as she saw who it was.

Rachelle spotted us over his shoulder when she came up for air, and burst into shrieking giggles. I touched Beth's arm and tried to turn her round. I don't know why; it seemed that leaving was the only thing to do.

'I used to babysit you, you bitch,' said Beth, and we walked out.

What would have happened, I wonder, if it had been Tony, and not Andy? It is just as plausible. Would I, perhaps, have been a tiny bit relieved? It would have been an excuse to escape.

'Yeah, sure I remember,' he says quietly, and takes another biscuit. 'Worst thing that ever happened to me.'

'It didn't exactly *happen to you*. You did it. Andy, are you wondering whether or not Beth would have you back?'

He looks up and squeezes my hand. I extricate myself. He's never appealed to me physically, and I have to contain the part of myself that is delighted at his unhappiness. He inflicted so much of it on my best friend, and now he's suffering himself. It is, I tell myself, karma.

He looks at me like a huge pink puppy. 'What do you reckon?'

'Is Rachelle pregnant?'

He is shocked. 'Did Tony say something?'

'No, he bloody well did not!' Tony is far too loyal to Andy. I have only just forgiven him for neglecting to tell me when Andy was cheating on Beth. Now I'll have to hold this against him as well.

'Well, the truth is, no, I don't think she is.'

'So why would Tony have said anything?'

'She was. That was why we got married so damn quick.'

'I have to say, I'd more or less worked that one out for myself.' It would have been nice to have had it confirmed by my husband, though. I remember asking him what he thought, and he shrugged.

'She had a miscarriage. We were both a little bit relieved.'

One of the worst things about being pregnant is the way it messes with your emotions. There's nothing wrong with a seventeen-year-old girl losing an embryo she doesn't want. It was probably a blessing for everyone, most of all the potential baby. Yet I find myself blinking, and sniffing, and trying desperately not to let Andy see my sadness. I think of my own baby, who gives a reassuring kick. Then I think of Rachelle's tiny cluster of cells, giving up the ghost.

'Have you been using contraception since then?' Three years as a teacher has conditioned me, a little, as a counsellor. It was never one of my natural skills because I was never interested enough in other people. Now I can do it with my eyes shut, even with someone I dislike.

He looks ashamed. 'No. So she might be. She's two days late.'

'Andy, that is just *pathetic*. You know as well as I do that she's probably pregnant again. Are her periods normally regular?'

He goes red. 'We don't talk about that.'

'So you wait until you've probably created another life, and then you come to me to ask whether you can go back to Beth. If Rachelle's pregnant, you definitely can't. Beth wouldn't have you back anyway, she's very happy as she is, but can you imagine what she'd say if you went crawling down to Renmark, saying um, darling sorry I cheated on you with a teenager, sorry you had to walk in on me with her, sorry you had to move miles away from your home to get away from me and from her and from her family and friends laughing at you. Sorry I forced you to start out all over again in life, but hey, Rachelle's pregnant and I'm not happy with her, can I move in with you please? And when I get divorced, can we marry again?' I stop for breath, but I could easily carry on. I am outraged.

'I guess she wouldn't be impressed.'

'I'll ask her for you if you like. It's a flattering offer.'

'I was, kind of, thinking I could come in the car with you guys today, and ask her myself.'

'Andy, you have bought this house. You're moving in this afternoon. This is your kitchen now. These are your biscuits.'

'No they're not. They're still yours.'

'OK, but everything else is yours. You can't do that. You have to face up to what you've done. Find out whether Rachelle's pregnant, and if she's not, and if you don't like being with her, you can leave her, and get another divorce. It's not the end of the world, and she'd get over it.'

'She'd get over it in bloody no time. What if she is?'

'Then I can't help you. She could have an abortion, if that was what she wanted – but that's her choice, not yours.' I hate talking about abortion. I want to cover my foetus's tiny ears. I believe in it wholeheartedly, but my emotions are too haywire to countenance the thought. 'You should tell her how you're feeling so she can make an informed decision. Otherwise, you could leave her, pregnant, which wouldn't be exactly noble, or you could buckle down and lie on that bed you've made. I'll tell you one thing, kids are fantastic. But then you'd know that. You're married to one.'

He opens his mouth, about to speak, when Pete shouts from the living room.

'Oi! Andy, you still here?'

He jumps to his feet, clearly relieved. 'In the kitchen, mate, helping Lina.' He winks. A second later, Rachelle is in the room.

'Christ!' she exclaims, in her squeaky, child's voice. She wouldn't, of course, be looking pregnant at just over four weeks, and for a moment I envy her skinny frame. The envy doesn't last. 'I've been looking all over for you. We are *supposed* to be moving house today, yeah? As in packing up our things in boxes and bringing them over here. What are you doing helping here and leaving me all on my own?'

'You're not on your own. You've got your entire bloody extended family over there. I needed some peace and quiet.'

'Yeah, well.' She looks at me with narrowed eyes. I beam back. I feel sorry for her. I know what it's like to be in over your head at such a young age. She hasn't got a clue what she's let herself in for.

'Hi, Rachelle,' I say. 'We'll be out of here in an hour or so. Then it's all yours. Andy was asking what time it would be OK for you guys to start moving in. So he is trying to help.'

She tosses her bleached hair at me. 'Thank you, Miss. That's all very well for him to say, but his place is by my side.'

As they leave, Andy gives me a pathetic, pleading glance. I'm not sure what he expects me to do. Am I, perhaps, supposed to run after them, grab him by the arm, throw little Rachelle to the floor, and proclaim, 'No, you cannot take him. Andy belongs with Beth!'

I don't say a word.

Margot has cooked a heavy Christmas lunch, with no concessions whatsoever to the fact that we're in one of the hottest places on earth, at the hottest time of the year. The walk across town to her house leaves me panting and leaning on Tony's shoulder. I am hungry, but I'm craving salad and fresh fruit juice. I couldn't get them in Craggy if I tried (and Margot hasn't), but I will feast on them in Renmark.

'Yum!' shouts Red as we approach the house. 'I can smell chicken!'

'You can't, mate,' says Tony. 'Don't say that to Mum. It's turkey, yeah? Because it's Christmas.'

'Why,' asks Eric, who is joining us for lunch, 'do we have turkey at Christmas? And never any other time of the year?'

'Americans do,' I tell them, reverting to teacher mode. 'They have Thanksgiving at the end of November, and all the family gets together and they have huge amounts of food. The main dish is turkey.'

'Do they have turkey at Christmas as well?' asks Red.

'What's Thanksgiving for?' says Eric, at the same time.

Tony raps on the door, and Margot answers it within the space of a second. She must have been waiting in the hallway.

'They have turkey at Christmas too, or sometimes goose,' I tell Red, while Margot embraces Tony. 'At least the ones who celebrate Christmas do. There are lots of different religions in America.' Then I turn to Eric. 'They were originally thanking the local Indians for helping them survive in America.'

Margot, by now, is standing in front of me, waiting, her hands on her hips, for her hug.

'Come on, darl,' she says, 'the lesson's over,' and she clasps me into her stocky frame. 'How's my grandchild? Come in and sit yourself down. It's not a time to be outside, in your condition.' I am bustled inside, and pushed into the sitting room and into what is universally known as Brian's Chair. Brian died in 1978, and his chair is a huge leather thing stuffed with horsehair. It smells a little bit old, and it has the best view of the TV. Under normal circumstances it is reserved for Tony or Pete, but since I've admitted to pregnancy, it's been mine. Despite the aroma, I like it. I like the fact that I can curl up into it, as if it were a nest.

Tony follows his mother into the kitchen where she has a beautiful retro seventies flavour going on. I hear his voice, and Margot's, and Pete's, and I smell apple crumble mixed in with the turkey and vegetable smells. I like my enforced exile.

Red appears and puts a glass of orange squash beside me. The ice tinkles as he puts it down.

'Margot said we have to ask you if we can watch telly.' He smiles, charmingly.

'Of course you can. Only if you come and sit here with me, though.'

'I knew it! Eric! She said yes!'

Red burrows into the chair next to me, and as Eric appears, with the boys' drinks, I feel a sudden pang. If there was room, I'd ask him into the chair with us, but there's not.

'It's all right, actually, Red,' I tell him. 'You can sit on the sofa with Eric.'

He shrugs. 'Fair enough.'

I enjoy perfect peace while Red and Eric sit silently staring at an old episode of *ER*. The baby shifts itself around, and I rub it reassuringly, at the same time as vaguely admiring George Clooney and wondering whether, if life had worked out differently, he could have been the father of my child. Meanwhile, raucous sounds come from the kitchen, and I know it won't be long before Christmas dinner is served.

When we told Red we were having a baby, he didn't believe us. He had become so convinced that I, too, was dying of a brain tumour, that he accused me of lying to him to make him feel better.

'You're not having a baby,' he shouted at me. He was in his Spiderman pyjamas, all ready for bed, and he was getting more and more agitated. I despaired of getting him to sleep at all. Tony and I had been fighting, quietly, about when we should tell him. I was assured by Dr Angelos that, after ten weeks of uncomplicated pregnancy, nothing was likely to go wrong. Tony wanted to wait until we'd had a twelve-week ultrasound to give us a serious all-clear. We fought for a week, and then it seemed that we might as well wait. Tony, in short, had won.

Neither of us had predicted Red's reaction. We expected smiles, relief, and stroking of my stomach. We thought he'd want to choose a name. We never imagined that his lip would tremble, and his eyes would become hostile.

'It's not a baby,' he shouted again. 'I know what it is. It's a tumour. You're not going to have a baby. You're not. You're going to die. Stop lying to me!'

Tony left the room, and returned with the scan pictures. I hoped they were clear enough to satisfy Red. They looked a little like a satellite map of rain over Tasmania.

I struggled for things to say. He wouldn't let me hug him.

'I promise you, sweetheart,' I said, there's nothing wrong with me. There's just a baby growing in my tummy. We've talked about that before, haven't we? That one day there might be a baby. You've always said it was what you wanted.'

'Oh yes,' he said bitterly. 'Of course I'd want it *if it was true*.' He pulled away from me. I was deeply disconcerted by the adult way he was talking. I wondered if it came from too much *ER*.

'Red,' I said firmly. 'This is ridiculous. I am pregnant. I know that we were all upset about what happened to Nina, but it's a very rare thing, and it's not happening to me. If it was, I would tell you. Eric's been very, very unlucky to lose his mother so young. I'm not going anywhere, and you are a very lucky boy because you're going to get a brother or a sister.'

'If that was true,' he said guardedly, 'could Eric help us with the baby as well?'

'Yes, of course. You know we're not going to be living in Craggy, though?'

'But he can come and stay in the holidays.'

'Of course he can.'

Tony sat in front of him. 'Here you are, mate,' he said, and put the small, cloudy pictures in his hand. 'You're the first to see these. See, this is the head. This bit down here is the spine. You can see that, and it goes all the way down, and these are the legs, curled up.'

'If it's in Mum's tummy, how come we've got a picture of it?'

'The hospital took them. They have a special machine.'

Red accepted that. 'And no one knows except for me?' He touched the photograph.

'You are the very first, mate,' Tony assured him. 'So how about, in the morning, we all go over to my mum's, and you can break the news to her?'

Now that the bump's existence is indisputable, to the point of occasionally kicking him, Red has forgotten his previous concerns. His main worry, now, is what Eric will do when he's gone. They have become so inseparable, in recent months, that I had to beg Margot to let Eric come for Christmas lunch. I share Red's concerns. Eric's father is a lovely man but he does not have the first idea about coping with two bereaved sons. He can barely look after himself any more.

* * *

Lunch is as heavy and as filling as I had anticipated and we struggle through mounds of turkey slices, heaps of roast potatoes, and a seemingly endless supply of brussels sprouts and carrots. The whole thing is drowned in thick gravy. There is champagne, as this is a special occasion. I have half a glass, and try to regulate what Tony drinks, since immediately afterwards he will be driving all our possessions across the state. We're staying in Adelaide tonight. We won't get there until midnight, and that's assuming we leave according to the schedule, at half past two.

'Oh, Margot,' I say casually, trying, and failing, to refuse a second helping of potatoes. 'I've been having a bit of strife with some tax authorities in England. They're chasing me for tax on the money my parents left me.'

'It's taken them a while!' she exclaims. Pete is watching me intently.

'Lina thinks they might come and look for her,' adds Tony. Poor Tony. It wouldn't occur to him to doubt me.

'So if anyone turns up from England, asking after me,' I continue, 'please don't tell them anything. Don't tell them where we live now, and in fact it would be best if you pretended you didn't even know me. It's just that I didn't pay the tax at the time, and now we haven't got the money any more.'

Margot taps her nose. 'Consider it done,' she says. 'Those mongrels, who do they think they are? Coming here after all these years when a girl's about to have a baby. We'll see them off, don't you worry.'

'And tell everyone else, too?'

'We'll spread the word.'

I look at Pete, and he nods curtly. 'Leave it to me.'

I feel enormous as I push the seat back and clamber behind the steering wheel. The scales have been packed away for days, but last time I looked I weighed sixty-four kilos. I have never weighed anything like that before, and I know that the worst of the weight gain is yet to come. I wonder, for a split second, what Jonathan, the ballet master at the academy, or even Miss Mary, would make of me now. I'd confidently assumed that, because of my early physical training, I would be one of those women who grow a neat, clip-on bump and lose all the weight immediately after the birth. I am fast realising that

I am depressingly normal. I'm putting it on everywhere. I'm eating all the time.

The back of the car is filled with odds and ends. It's packed so tightly that I have to use the wing mirrors to see what's behind me. A box of kitchen appliances has been unwisely strapped to the roof rack. I don't have the energy to rearrange things, so I'm just going to hope that it stays in place until we get to our new home. Our old, underground home, meanwhile, is empty and clean. Andy and Rachelle will take possession of it at any moment. It will be the scene for their newlywed bliss. At least they won't be able to fault its cleanliness.

Tony leans in through the window and gives me a kiss.

'See you in Adelaide, darling.' He smiles, his eyes betraying the excitement he has been hiding from Margot. He gives Red a salute. 'As for you, mate, make sure she doesn't drive too fast, and if she gets tired, she has to pull over, yeah?'

He returns the salute. 'Right, boss.'

And so we drive off, me and Red in front, and the van following us. Most of our friends and neighbours have come out to see us off. Eric waves his best friend away stoically. Simon pretends to be sad to see me go. Mavis and Nora say fond farewells and immediately return to their discussions of Andy and Rachelle's marriage. I see the couple, as we round the corner onto the tarmacked road, walking hand in hand towards their new home. They are doing a reasonable job of looking happy.

As for me, I am ecstatic. I have never been happier. I've got away. I have done it again. Here I go, driving a car into my new life.

chapter twelve

19 December

Fuck. Fuck it fuck it fuck it. I am a twat, an arsehole, a wanker. I deserve to be publicly humiliated in the pages of *Private Eye*. I do not deserve the life I have.

Still, it looks like I might get away with it. I take the office stairs two at a time and remind myself to be casual. There is a strong chance that the gossip has travelled already, and I must deny everything and ride it out until they think of something else to talk about.

It all began yesterday, with the department Christmas lunch. Before that, I was doing fine. Life has been good recently, and I've even stopped going to the office so early. I kept catching sight of myself in mirrors and thinking it was someone else. Someone with pudgy skin, and with black bags under his piggy, bloodshot eyes. Sophie has been nagging – sorry, asking – me to stop spending up to fifteen hours a day at my desk when my official shift is half that. I must admit that, physically, I have been suffering, and the story I'm working on now doesn't involve the office at all. I've got a file of photocopies of old stories about Daisy Fraser. She did have a hard time of it. Now I wake up at eight and come into the office at quarter to ten, and it's still usually empty so no one is any the wiser.

I've bought Sophie's Christmas present, namely two return tickets to Melbourne. I hardly flinched at taking the time off. After all, it's not just a holiday, and I must admit that the guaranteed sunshine is looking more appealing all the time. We leave on January the ninth. I've already told Sophie about it so she could arrange her time off, and buy some more clothes or whatever it is girls do.

I can't even think about her without despising myself.

Yesterday, I got all my stories filed in the morning, because there was nothing going on. I was planning to get drunk at the newsroom bash at lunchtime with Tim, Christie and Abby, my new office buddies, and I didn't particularly fancy running through the pre-Christmas ritual of staggering back to my desk at five, making a few nonsensical phone calls, and filing a dyslexic piece that would immediately be spiked. The day before, I'd managed to concoct a straightforward story from Dot's stuff, and it was printed, so I was perfectly entitled to go easy on myself.

The office didn't feel like work today anyway, because all the serious news is drying up (though you do have to keep a sharp eye out for announcements the government's trying to slip through when no one's looking). The room is choked with freebies from desperate PRs. I added a piece of public relations tinsel to the nearest dismal pot plant, and considered that I had done my bit.

I stride into the room and look neither right nor left. Nobody shouts or jeers when they see me, but I wouldn't expect them to. Gossip is more insidious than that. I can hear a few fingers tapping on keyboards, and there is approximately a fifty per cent chance that they're sending emails to each other about me.

I have kept to my resolution and been to the pub more than once a week in the past couple of months, so now I consider almost all my colleagues to be friends. It's strange that, for eighteen months, that social life was available to me and I never even noticed it. I've also purchased myself a third suit recently – this one's a smart one from Armani, and it cost more money than I care to consider. Coupled with some Ted Baker shirts, I think I look more the upcoming Young Turk these days. I look like Tim. The lunch was fun. Large quantities of food and alcohol were consumed, and many people were slandered.

The trouble began during the collective meander back to work. The Diary column had already promised to open a bottle of the champagne they keep under their desk to exchange for stories, so there wasn't much danger of anything actually being done. I was considering slipping away and going back to shag Sophie, when Christie caught up with me.

'Hiya!' she called in a sing-song girly voice.

'Hello,' I said, smiling as soberly as I could.

'How are you?'

'Fine,' I assured her, and walked straight into a lamp post. She grabbed my sleeve.

'Not that fine.'

'Fine enough, cheers.'

'You doing any work when we get back?'

'Nope. I filed this morning.'

'Cool! Then we can carry on drinking.'

I looked at her. She was drunk, and I was too. I tried to remember what I was meant to be doing. Probably just hanging out with Sophie, as usual. We've been getting a bit domestic lately. Which is good. Obviously.

Maybe it was the alcohol acting as a soft focus filter, but Christie seemed to look less ghoulish. Her hair was less harshly coloured than usual. I thought it was a bit longer, too.

'Is your hair different?' I asked her.

'What a funny question for a bloke,' she replied, and explained at length about how she felt she needed a change with her highlights. She wanted, apparently, to be taken more seriously, to model herself on TV stars she admires. 'I needed a more classic look,' she said. I was wondering why I used to be so scared of her. She was a little flushed. She is nowhere near Sophie's league, because Sophie doesn't need to wear make-up at all, and Christie still seems to be fairly caked in the stuff – but kind of intriguing, nonetheless. I've discovered in the past few weeks that I like Christie, as a friend. Yesterday, I even wondered whether I could take her home to meet Soph, before deciding that it probably wouldn't work.

We were outside a bar. It wasn't the office pub. It was a different one, a trendy one. Christie took me by the hand. She didn't give me much choice. 'Come on, then.' She attempted to pull me through the thick glass doors. A barman was looking out at us, and smiling. I thought he was smiling.

'I'll just make a call,' I told her. 'You go on in. I'll be there in a sec.'

She planted her feet firmly on the step. 'No way. You'll just get told to come home and you'll run away. I'm staying here.'

So, with Christie watching me, and both of us swaying slightly, I phoned Sophie.

'Hi, hon,' I said.

'Christ, are you OK? You sound weird. Are you ill?'

'Maybe a little bit drunk.'

'Well, it was your Christmas lunch, wasn't it? Are you still drinking?'

'Yeah. I'm with some of the boys, you know, the important ones. Is it OK if we give tonight a miss? To be honest I wouldn't be much fun for you this evening if you're sober and the last thing I want to do is make you get up to let me in at two o'clock.'

She laughed. 'Of course it's fine, Larry. I'm not some nagging wife, you know. This is a grown-up relationship. You stay at yours, and I'll speak to you tomorrow. In fact, you can call me when you feel up to it.'

'Thanks, darling. You're a star, you know. Love you.'

'Yes, I'm sure. You tell me that when you're sober sometime, OK?'

'Babe! Of course I will.'

As I put the phone away and followed Christie into the bar, I wondered whether that counted as lying. I suppose implying that Christie was several important company executives wasn't great behaviour. And I didn't really imply it so much as say it straight out. I rationalised it, eventually, on the grounds that Sophie wouldn't have been happy if she'd known I was there with just one girl, so I was just sparing her some needless anguish.

Christie came back from the bar with a jug of pale green liquid and two glasses with salt round the rims.

'Are we on margaritas?'

'We certainly are. Cheers!'

The evening must have flown by, because in no time our chatter was interrupted by the barman.

'We're closing now, folks. Off you go.'

'How did that happen? Are you closing early?'

'It's quarter past eleven. Time you guys were out of here.'

I looked at Christie. We were holding hands across the table. We'd probably been doing that for hours. I couldn't think what came next.

'Where shall we go?' I asked her.

'We could either carry on drinking, or, could we go back to yours?'

'Um, we could. It's a bit of a tip. In fact it's rank.'

'I won't mind.'

I must face up to what happened next. It felt so inevitable that it didn't even seem wrong. In the cab, I kissed her. I snogged her. She was an amazing kisser, and, through my remorse, I already wonder whether I'm going to want to do that again. Of course I won't, because I've got Sophie. Sophie is an amazing snog, too. I've just never been that drunk with Sophie.

I slid my hand under Christie's top, and felt her smooth skin. At the time, I liked the fact that she was bigger than I was used to. There was more to grab hold of. I undid her bra with one expert movement, and cupped her breasts in my hands. She seemed incoherent but happy. I wanted to see her tits. More than anything in the world, I wanted to see her naked. I think I started trying to take her top off, over her head, and I remember her stopping me.

'Not now, Larry,' she said sternly. 'Not in the cab.'

I ushered her up the stairs as quickly as I could, and took her to my bedroom. We sat side by side on the bed, and I lifted her top off. She raised her arms in the air to help me, and I was thrilled by the glory of her bosom. She has huge tits. They are spectacular. I'm going to want to see them again, I know I am. I held them, two overflowing handfuls.

'You are beautiful,' I muttered, and I slid a hand inside her knickers.

I sit down and gulp back a swig of coffee, then wince at its bitterness. I know I should be drinking water and orange juice, and, indeed, I will move on to them shortly. For now, I need a jolt to keep me going. I sneak a look around, and catch Christie's eye. We both look away, quickly.

I'm dreading Pete getting in. He loves to torment me. I'm going to have to sit here with him all day long, and try to ignore all the innuendoes and the mocking laughter. Maybe he won't turn up.

If it wasn't completely against my personal code of conduct, I would have taken the day off as well. Unfortunately, however, I don't do sickies. I felt genuinely ill when I woke up this morning. I felt like shit, physically, emotionally, and in any other way that's possible.

I've never cheated on anyone before. No one I've cared about, anyway. It took me a while even to remember what had happened. At first, all I could think about was my hangover. My head ached and I could barely move. So, naturally, I did what I always do in that situation, and reached for Sophie. She was there all right, curled up next to me. I grabbed her round the waist, but she felt different. She was more substantial than usual. I nuzzled into her neck, but she smelt different. I managed to force my eyes open, and then I saw that Sophie wasn't there at all. And, finally, it hit me in a rush of shame and remorse and self-hatred.

I peered blearily around the room. The hangover suddenly seemed much less important. I saw a condom wrapper on the bedside table. It was not, I told myself, conclusive proof of anything. Many different things can happen to a condom after it is unwrapped. However, there it was, used, on the floor. Its contents had oozed onto the brown carpet. That meant one of us must have stepped on it. That, in itself, is nothing new – before I met Soph, if someone had left an ovum on my bedroom floor, they could have grown a baby – but the sight of my own sperm has never horrified me before.

Then, and now, I couldn't find any weaselly argument to justify my behaviour. I love Sophie. I am going out with Sophie. I'm taking her to bloody Australia in two weeks, to find her friend and achieve my professional breakthrough. I don't love Christie. I probably don't even like her very much. Yet I shagged her. I am the worst person in the world.

Occasionally, this morning, isolated images are creeping back to me. I have a vague and terrible memory of Pete coming into the bar at one point during the evening, and laughing at us.

I email Christie, trying to adopt the correct tone for our circumstances. 'all right there?' I write. 'how are you feeling? do I look as rough as I feel? have a slight memory of pete in the bar last night. say it aint so.' I hesitate, wondering whether to add a kiss. In the end, I do. Just a small, lower case x.

She writes back immediately. 'yep, he was there. glad it's you not me over there. am feeling shite, obviously.'

No kiss. That's fine. Christie seems to remember the evening much better than I do. If I was the girl, I could accuse her of taking advantage of me. I think she asked me about what I'm working on. I remember consciously stopping myself from telling her about Daisy.

When I looked at her sleeping face, it was all smeared with make-up. She's not even pretty. A cursory glance in the mirror confirmed that I wasn't, either. The most important thing seemed to be getting up without waking her.

I sat in the kitchen, in a pair of boxers, and I loathed myself. Stupid wanking fucking twat. For the first time in my entire life, I'm in a good relationship with a sexy, wonderful woman. So then of course I have to jeopardise it all by shagging some tart from the office. I knocked at

Kev's door, but he wasn't there. He stays at Tania's more often than not, as she has a self-contained flat in the basement of the family's house. Au pairs, it seems, get far better perks than journalists. Moments like this are when Kev comes into his own. I decided that the first priority was to get rid of Christie, and the second was to ensure that Sophie never, ever finds out.

I was unsure of the etiquette of one-night stands with colleagues, but it seemed only fair to make Christie a cup of tea. Then I started thinking that I'd better be more than civil to her, because otherwise she could turn into a bunny boiling nutter and wreck my life and my chances of finding Daisy. I mustn't be so nice to her that this accidentally happens again (although shamefully I already remember some events with a certain guilty pleasure). It's a fine line to tread. So I made her tea and toast and a Beecham's Resolve.

I was sitting at the table, rehydrating myself, looking idly through the post that had piled up for me since I was last at the flat, and trying not to think of Sophie, when Christie wandered in.

My first thought was that I couldn't imagine what I thought I was doing. My second was that she really does have fantastic tits.

She was wearing one of my T-shirts, and her knickers. Her thighs are very different from Sophie's. I smiled weakly, and pushed her tea and her Resolve towards her. She smiled as pathetically as I did, and sat down.

'Thanks,' she said.

'Um,' I started.

'Yes. Hard to know what to say.'

'Not premeditated.'

'And no doubt fun at the time, if only we could remember.' She looked up. 'Can you remember?'

'No. The condom on the floor jogged my memory a little.'

'How sordid we are. Doesn't matter, hey?'

'No, there's nothing we can do about it now.'

'What's the time?'

'Twenty past nine.

'Shit, can I use your phone?'

I gestured to it. 'All yours.'

She took a big swig of Resolve, and carefully dialled 141 before the number.

'Hi, hon.' She sounded strangely chirpy. It was an impressive act. 'Yeah, OK, not too bad. I just wanted to check in, really. I stayed with Abby last night, you know, from work. Sorry, I meant to call you but by the time I noticed the time it was too late. You weren't worried, were you? I did leave a message on your mobile . . . Yeah, it was a good night.' She winked at me, the harlot. 'A bit fragile. I seem to have got off lightly compared to Abby though. Yeah, straight to work. I'll see you after. Love you. 'Bye.' She hung up.

'I didn't know you had a boyfriend,' I said. I don't care. I'm hardly going to be gutted by this revelation.

'We are a pair of shameless slappers, aren't we?'

'Don't remind me.'

'Aren't you going to call the wonderful Sophie? Elfin. That's what you called her last night.'

'Later. If I call her now it might make her suspicious.'

'Well, no one's ever going to call me elfin, as you've noticed. Can I use your shower? In fact, can I use your toothbrush?'

'Sure.' I pointed her, listlessly, in the right direction. Fuck, fuck and fuck again.

I should send Sophie flowers, but for one thing I couldn't make the call from my desk because everyone would laugh at me, and Christie would hear about it in no time. Besides, everyone knows that sending a woman flowers makes her suspicious. I rack my brains for the one thing that would make Sophie happier than anything else. Whatever it is, it's the least I can do. I don't feel I can ask any of the women at the office for ideas, for obvious reasons. Every time I walk up behind anyone, they get flustered and click on to the PA headlines. This is a sure sign that they really are exchanging emails about me. I just hope it's all speculation, that Christie is keeping quiet.

At lunchtime, I turn down the offer of a mass Christmassy exodus to the pub (please!) and go to Hatton Gardens, handily located within a few minutes' walk of work. I spend loads of money – what with this and the Australia tickets I'm almost cleaned out – but not enough to assuage my conscience. Then I take the liberty of anticipating the outcome, and call the airline, on my mobile, to request an upgrade as we're going abroad to celebrate our engagement. I accept the press officer's congratulations with grace. I arrange to meet Sophie after work.

Unfortunately, she wants to come to the office, to pick me up. 'I've never seen where you work,' she complains, 'and you spend so much time there, I feel like I'm missing out on part of your life.'

'You don't want to come here!' I bellow, too loudly. 'I mean,' I add quietly, 'it's not very exciting. I mean, I've never seen where you work either.'

'That's because I don't work.'

'You do. Sometimes.'

'Oh yes, of course, temping. I'm really going to go into an office for a couple of days at a time and bring my boyfriend in. To introduce you to people I don't even know myself! It's not the same and you know it.'

'Suppose. It's just that I like to leave work behind at the end of the day. OK, though, we'll meet round here if you like. Why don't I see you in the Red Bar.'

I give her directions and wonder what the fuck I am up to. The Red Bar is the scene of last night's disgrace. I consider my compulsion to return. Maybe I did it to atone for my sins, to offer recompense to someone who doesn't even know she's been wronged. I'm keeping it from her because I know it was just a drunken mistake that could happen to anyone. She wouldn't see it like that. I suppose I'm protecting her. On the other hand, perhaps I'm just a wanker.

With her usual antennae working full time, Christie appears at my desk the moment I put the phone down.

'You all right?' she asks, smiling. I look around, paranoid.

'Of course. Why wouldn't I be?'

'Oh, I don't know. You had your head in your hands, that's all. It's all right, Lawrence. It's not the worst thing that's ever going to happen to you.'

I say nothing, and she wanders off.

When Sophie walks through the door, I savour her. I love times when I'm looking at her and she doesn't know I'm there. She's my pixie, my doll, my darling. She's slight and light.

I made sure I got to the bar first, so I could give the barman a fiver and warn him not to mention the fact that I was in there last night with a different girl. He thought it was hilarious and tapped his nose a few times. He's a bit of a tosser, actually.

Someone else's office is having a Christmas party, and they're wearing pink paper hats and pulling crackers and generally acting in a way that is not appropriate for so fashionable a bar as this one. The mildly amusing thing is, they are clearly a highly trendy company – probably web designers or similar – and everyone is impeccably dressed. They've just lost their cool through alcohol.

Sophie stands on the threshold, tiny in her coat, her face flushed with the cold, and she looks confused. She seems to believe she's come to the wrong place, stumbled into a private party. She is about to turn and go, when she sees me waving.

She flings herself down on the seat. 'I didn't see you.' I am waiting with an expectant pout, so she leans across and kisses me.

'You're looking lovely,' I tell her, sincerely.

'No I'm not, I'm just looking normal. I only put my lippy on on the tube.'

I can't wait to give her her present. I'm too scared not to, so I do it before I even get her a drink.

'Sophie,' I say, taking both her hands in mine. 'I've got something to ask you.'

'What?'

'Um. I don't really know how to put this. You know how much I love you?'

'Mmm. Kind of. Are you still drunk?'

'No! I really do love you, and I've been thinking, I can't imagine ever being without you. So . . . will you marry me?' I did it! I can't stop myself grinning. I reach into my pocket and push the box across the table to her. 'I got you this, to prove I mean it.'

Sophie is gobsmacked. I suppose it's every girl's dream come true. I am waiting for her to say, 'Oh, Larry, of course I will!' so that I can reply, 'Thank you. You've just made me the happiest man on earth,' in a Trevor Howard kind of a way.

But she doesn't. Instead, she almost cries, and asks me to give her a bit of time. 'You are so unbelievably sweet. I wasn't expecting this at all,' she says with a small smile. 'But I don't want us to rush into this. And I'm not completely sure your heart's in it.'

I am, I confess, a little crushed. We agree to talk about it properly over Christmas, and she says she'll give me a definite answer, if I still mean it, in the New Year. So I'd better be on my best behaviour.

chapter thirteen

As the clock begins to strike, the clientele erupts into cheers. Beth raises her glass, and Tony, Red and I do likewise.

'Cheers!' we all shout, above the uproar.

'To a happy New Year,' adds Beth, 'and a happy new baby.' She looks at me expectantly.

'To everybody needing good neighbours,' I improvise, 'and to Beth's meeting the man of her dreams this year. And to the internet,' I add, unable to stop myself.

We both look at Tony, and I will him to stop sulking. He can, at least, pretend. He doesn't actually have to like me. He just has to be civil to Beth.

'To Red,' he shouts eventually, above a rousing rendition of 'Auld Lang Syne', 'and a good start at school, mate. And to everyone we left behind in Craggy. And everyone Lina left behind in London.'

I suppose I asked for that one. I try to catch his eye, but he won't look at me. Red holds up his glass. 'Well, I say, to Renmark, and to the baby, and to Beth's boat, and to no divorcing.'

We clink again, and we all drink.

The new year has begun, and Tony and I have never been less close. I hope this isn't a portent. This should be a joyful time, a new start. Today marks the twelve-day anniversary of our arrival in our new home. Red loves it. I would, ordinarily, love it. Tony doesn't mind it at all. Yet today we can barely speak to one another.

Beth organised our New Year celebration in a restaurant on the river bank, about a mile from home. When she came to pick us up, I was lying on my side on the bed, feeling the baby's reproachful kicks. I knew my eyes were red and puffy, and I couldn't be bothered to get changed. My New Year's outfit was laid out on my chair, but I didn't want to wear it. I was supposed to be showing off my curvaceous figure in a tight red dress. Instead, I was still in my gardening clothes. I was wearing Tony's worst pair of tracksuit shorts, which fit me nicely round the middle, and a big, shapeless T-shirt. Both were splattered with mud. I had been intending to get up and have a shower, but it hadn't happened. The only thing I'd managed to do was to scrub my fingernails, to protect me and the baby from toxoplasmosis.

I curled up tightly, and listened to their conversation as Tony let her in. I was intrigued to see whether he would turn his usual manners back on and be normal to Beth, or whether, at last, I had finally made him crack.

'Hi, guys!' she trilled, too brightly. 'You ready, then? We've got an hour till the table's booked, so we could have a drink here if you two aren't set to go yet.'

'Beth,' I heard him say quietly. 'Come in. Red with you?'

'He was. He's still at the boat. We're supposed to phone him when he needs to come over here.'

Tony did one of his snorts. 'Didn't fancy a return to the house of hell just yet? Can't say I blame him. Can I go to your boat myself?'

There was a short silence, and then Beth said, 'So, where's Lina?'

'Search me. In the bedroom, I think. I know my place, Beth and that seems to be in front of the TV with the cricket on. Either that or at the computer. Go and have a word if you like. I'm sure she'll let you know what it's all about. I'm ready to go whenever you are. Tell you what,' he said, as an apparent afterthought (which shows that I really had messed with his mind), 'I'll pour you a drink. White, red or beer?'

'White, if you've got some open. Thanks, Tony.'

I briefly wondered whether to stay as I was, self-indulgently curled up against the world, mirroring my own foetus, or whether to make a show of trying to be brave. I knew I was going to have to face Tony sooner or later, so I decided to make a token gesture, and swung my feet round and sat on the bed. Our new bedroom is going to be beautiful. I want it to be so stunning that it could be featured in an interior design magazine. In fact, I want it to *be* featured in such a mag. That, I think, is going to be my next project. I've put white linen on the bed, and vases of white flowers all over the windowsills.

There is one vase fewer now than at the beginning of today, but I've cleared up the wreckage, and the effect is still the same.

There was a knock at the door, and Beth came in without waiting for a reply.

'What's going on?' she demanded, sitting next to me and looking at my dirty clothes and my ugly puffy face.

'Oh, I was planting some roses. You know, the dream home, a white picket fence and roses around the front door. A place where everyone's happy? And then I put in my jasmine bush, so it all smells sweet on the summer nights. I want this place to be just perfect.'

'I didn't mean that – as you know. I meant, why did I have Red showing up on the boat crying his little eyes out, and telling me that you and Tony weren't going to live together any more? Why did he refuse to come over here with me now? Why is Tony acting so strangely? I thought nothing you did got a reaction out of Tony.'

I sighed. 'We just had a fight, that's all. He was vile. I'm seven months fucking pregnant – I'm allowed to be emotional, aren't I?'

'What was it about? What was he saying about computers? Actually, please don't go into it if it'll upset you. Mainly, we need to get you guys back on speaking terms pretty bloody quick, otherwise Red and I will end up seeing in the New Year on our own, and quite frankly that might be more fun.'

'Maybe the three of us could see it in, and we could leave Tony here with his cyberfriends.'

'No we couldn't. So, how did it start, and how can we patch it up?'

Now that midnight's past, all I want to do is to go home. We've limped through the evening, pretending to be jolly whenever anyone Beth knows pops over to the table. We've discussed such diverse matters as whether Australia should ditch the British monarchy (we all agree that it should, although I think Beth secretly likes them) and how funny it was that Andy wanted Beth back. I've commented on the three babies who are in the restaurant. Tony and Red talked about soccer for a while, and, as I always do, I insisted it should be called football. Every conversation petered out. Every moment has been a strain. I wait for an opportune moment to take Red home.

Red and I spent this morning at the local pool, where I lay in the shade and read a book and fended off friendly questions about my bump, while Red teamed up with some other children and learned to dive off the side of the pool. I taught him to swim in Sydney and although he hasn't had any practice in the past three years, he has remembered his skills admirably. Soon he was diving from the low board, delighted with himself.

We came home smiling. We both love the water, and we love the easy-going nature of Renmark. No one has marched up to us, so far, and accused us of being new in town. No one has confronted us with the fact that Renmark people are hard-working and don't suffer fools gladly (one of Craggy's great self-delusions). I have never felt, as I walk away from a cluster of people, that they are gossiping and speculating about me. Here I feel free.

'Hey!' I called, in greeting, as we came into the shady house. Red ran to dump his trunks in the bathroom and get himself a glass of squash with five ice cubes.

Tony didn't reply. I looked for him in the garden, and then in the sitting room. He wasn't nursing his cannabis plant; nor was he watching satellite television. When I tried the door to the small room that I grandly call 'my study', I was surprised to find that it opened. Tony was sitting in front of the computer, gazing intently at a picture of a woman with her legs splayed. His shorts were unzipped, and his penis was in his right hand, which was making rapid movements. Just as I opened my mouth, though with no idea what I was going to say, his semen spurted everywhere.

I couldn't speak. I turned, and shut the door loudly.

'It didn't mean anything,' he said when he caught up with me in the garden.

'I don't think for one second that it did mean anything,' I said coldly. I was trying to play him with his own tactics. I wasn't going to lose my temper and pummel him. I was quietly getting on with planting my jasmine.

'So, why are you so mad?'

'Why am I mad? I hope you mean mad, as in angry, and not mad as in insane?'

'Don't come the fucking English teacher with me, Lina. You know I mean angry.'

'Perhaps because you ignored us when we came in. Maybe because it's purely by chance that it was me and not Red who walked in on you. And that's only the beginning.'

He looked embarrassed. I supposed that was good. 'Didn't hear you come in. Sorry. Won't happen again.'

'Oh, I'm sure it will. I'm sure it's been happening for years. Just try not to get caught again, that's all I ask. But Tony, how could you? It's so cheap and tacky. I mean, internet porn, for Christ's sake! What were you doing? Do you think that woman was enjoying herself when she posed for those pictures? She was doing it because she needed the money and she was desperate. She's probably got kids and the only way she can feed and clothe them is by posing for wankers like you, so you can pretend to yourselves that she fancies you. It's tragic.'

I was beginning to lose my cool. I desperately tried to rein in my temper.

'And another thing,' I added.

'Oh yes, here we go.'

'Just because I'm pregnant, it doesn't mean I'm training as a nun. We haven't had sex for weeks, even though we could perfectly easily do it if you wanted to. I want to. You don't. You push me away if I try. You've made it perfectly plain that, now that I'm bigger than a size ten, you don't want anything to do with me. I like my body now, and I like the fact that it's housing a child. I still think it's sexy. But you don't. Do you have any idea how that makes me feel?' I looked up. I was still kneeling by the flower bed, and I suddenly thought to check that Red was nowhere nearby. He wasn't.

Tony knelt beside me. I hoped that, now, we might be able to make up. We could send Red round to Beth's boat and perhaps, finally, we could have sex. The sun was beating down on my head, and suddenly I was exhausted.

'The thing is,' Tony said, with an edge in his voice that I hadn't heard before, 'sometimes it seems to me that you're barely there at all. It's like I'm some inconvenient extra that you don't want or need. Like you'd be happier if it was just you and Red and the baby. Like you've got my sperm, you've got yourself fertilised, and you've got your big house, and that's all you wanted. Like I could drive back to Craggy, or Sydney, this arvo and it would take till tomorrow before you even noticed I was gone.'

'Tony, that is the biggest pile of crap I've ever heard and you know it. It's just bollocks. I love you. I love our family. I can't wait to hold the baby, and to watch you holding the baby, and to get our physical life back as well. You're just trying to turn things back to me because you were in the wrong, wanking off in the house where Red could have seen you, and you know it.'

'Yeah, that wasn't the most intelligent thing a bloke's ever done, but it's hardly as if I'm the only bloke in Australia looking up chicks on the internet. Every bloke jerks off, babe. Most do it every day. Red'll be doing it soon.'

'Shut up! Shut the fuck up!'

That was when I started losing it. I brandished my trowel at him, and he caught my wrist and held my arm in the air where, however much I struggled, I failed to free myself. I used my other hand to punch his stomach, but he didn't flinch. He caught that hand as well, and held it away from his body.

I looked at his face. He was angrier than I had ever seen him. His eyes were furious, and any sense that he was in the wrong seemed to have deserted him. His cheeks were puce, and he looked as though he hated me.

'What is it with you, you cold bitch?'

'You can't speak to me like that,' I shouted, squirming. 'I'm your wife, and I'm having our baby in eight weeks. I'm not some tart off the internet.'

'At least tarts from the internet are honest. You won't speak to me about anything. You've shut me out ever since you met me. It's been more than three years now, and I've been waiting and waiting for you to talk to me properly. It was always, *oh, I don't talk about my life in England, it upsets me too much, I won't tell you about it, you have to understand*. And I've been so fucking understanding, Lina, because I thought you'd tell me when you were ready. And now I've just realised that you're not going to, are you? Sometimes I read your emails just to see if there are any clues in there.'

I tried to kick him, but failed. 'You read my emails? You fucker! I'm going to start reading yours. Anyway, if you read them you'll know that I've got nothing to hide and I don't talk about England to anyone. OK, my parents died. You know that. It was a great shock to me, and I vowed I would never go back. I haven't been back, I've cut all ties, and that's the life I want for myself.'

'That's fine, but you don't talk about anything a-fucking-tall. I don't know what sort of school you went to, what studying you did, I don't know where you lived in England, or whether you've got any family or friends still there. You must miss things about it, but you never, ever mention them. Because, like I said, you're shutting me out.'

I'd never seen Tony like this before. I tried to work out how to defuse the situation.

'I just went to the local school.' I was desperately trying to remember what I might have told him before. 'Well, the local private school. We lived in London. None of it's that interesting.'

'It's a bit unusual, don't you think, for me to have to force this out of my own wife?' His grip on my wrists was tight. I wanted him to let go.

'Tony, for Christ's sake. You're being a prick. If you can believe it, this has nothing to do with you. It's not personal. My way of dealing with what happened to Mum and Dad has been to block out everything to do with them. Maybe it's not healthy, but it is what I do. It's as simple as that. You're playing with fire, here. If you're going to make me sit here and recall it, while you hold me so I can't move, then I warn you that you're going to be opening Pandora's box. There are things I never want to think about again. Coming to Australia was supposed to be so I could start a new life. You can't force me back to the old one. It's not that I don't love you because really you know I do. It's all to do with what happened before I met you.'

'But it's spooky. It's like you didn't have a childhood at all.'

'I know. But it's not a case of me shutting you out. It's me shutting myself out.'

He let me go. 'I don't like it, Lina. This is nothing like a marriage ought to be. It's not what I expected from my life. I don't want my baby to have a fucked-up mother.'

I straightened my shoulders. If only I could be just a tiny bit dignified. I felt like a buffalo.

'Well, I don't want it to catch its father having a fucking wank!' I shouted as he started to walk towards the house. 'If you hate our marriage so much, why don't you get in the bloody car and leave, like you said? We'd be fine without you. Go and find some bored internet whore and see if she satisfies you.'

Tony didn't look round. Then I saw Red standing in the doorway, staring at me, aghast.

'What are your New Year's resolutions?' asks Beth as Tony orders another bottle of champagne. I am still sipping from my half glass.

I look at Beth, and frown. I've been desperately steering the conversation away from any matters that might inflame Tony.

'Oh, I don't know,' I say lightly. 'Live in Renmark. Have a baby.'

Red joins in. 'Mine is to learn to do really good dives off the top diving board. I might become an Olympic diver, actually. I could represent Australia. Would I be allowed to represent Australia, Mum, even though you found me in India?'

'Yes, of course you would, darling, because you're an Australian citizen.'

'Cool. So that's what I'll do.'

Tony stirs himself. He has been sitting in the corner, with a thunderous face, ignoring anything I say to him, all evening.

'Not a bad resolution, mate. You could try out for Australia's cricket team while you were at it if you wanted.'

Red thinks about it, and yawns. 'Nah. Cricket's boring. Tony, what are your resolutions?'

'God knows.' He stands up, and pushes past the back of Beth's chair to get to the toilets. I catch Beth's eye and roll my eyes.

'I'm exhausted,' I tell her, 'and I know that this young man is too. I think it's time I took him home to bed.'

'I'm not even tired at all,' says Red.

'Fine. So you take me home to bed then. Look after your poor old mum.'

Red and I walk back along the river path. I look at the full moon reflected in the water, and I wonder what will become of me. I should have known that I wouldn't be able to relate to anyone properly, that I could never have a lasting marriage. I wonder whether this fight with Tony is going to blow over, or whether it's one of those issues that will never go away. I have no idea. When I outlined Tony's concerns to Beth (considerately leaving out the full drama of the cyberporn incident), she brushed it off.

'We all know you're touchy about your past,' she said, coaxing me into my clingy dress and spraying my wrists with perfume. 'Tony knows it's nothing to do with him, really. For Christ's sake, you're heavily pregnant. You should be allowed to get away with anything at the moment. Here, brush your hair. I'll have a word with him, if you like.'

I looked at her, gratefully, and took the hairbrush. 'Would you?'

I have left them to talk about us. I hope Beth makes some headway.

'Mum?' asks Red in a small voice as we walk slowly together.

'Mmm?'

'Are you and Tony going to get divorced, like Andy and Beth?'

'No, honey, we're not.'

He looks up at me. 'Promise?'

'Promise.' I sincerely hope that I won't have to renege on this one. 'All grown-ups have arguments,' I tell him. 'They don't happen often, but when they do, they just end up clearing the air. We're all happy to be in Renmark.' I pause as we pass a group of three drunken young men, who nod elaborately at us and wish us a happy New Year. 'Happy New Year to you, too,' I tell them, smiling. 'So, I'm very, very sorry that you had to hear the fight today, because that's the sort of thing that children shouldn't have to listen to, but I promise you that we still love each other, and that, from when you wake up in the morning, we're going to be happier than we've ever been. We've moved house now, after all, and our new house is wonderful, isn't it?'

He nods enthusiastically. 'It certainly is.'

'And what's the next major event?'

Red grins. 'The baby's going to be born.'

'And will that be fantastic, or what?'

'I think it will. Mum?'

'Yes?'

'You know you said about the internet? Were you talking about the pictures Tony looks at, of the ladies with no clothes on?'

I stop, and look at him. 'How do you know about them?'

'It's not exactly difficult. It's on the web history. Why do the ladies take their clothes off like that? I think they look disgusting.'

I take his hand. 'Good,' I tell him. We walk companionably home.

chapter fourteen

12 January

Most of the other passengers are, perversely, smiling as they get off the bus. Even Sophie looks happy. I can't imagine why. We have exchanged air-conditioned relative comfort for the furnace of the grim Australian Outback.

'Look at it,' she says, turning to me with a grin. 'Isn't it amazing?'

I have been watching the road, wondering when the buildings would start, when I'd see traces of civilisation. The answer, clearly, is a resounding 'never'. There is nothing here at all. The bus roars off in a cloud of dust. A couple of buildings line the road. There are a few strangely shaped hills dotted around the place. Essentially, we have been dumped in the middle of the desert. The tarmac springs beneath my feet. My temples are starting to throb.

'You're sure this is the place?' I ask Sophie.

'Of course it is!' She laughs. 'Craggy Rock! We're there.'

'What a fucker.'

'I know. Don't you just love it?'

This place is far, far worse than I ever imagined it could be. It looks like some kind of apocalyptic nightmare. I'm on the wrong side of the world, in a town so horrendous that it's awesome. Only someone as fucked-up as Daisy Fraser could possibly think of making a place like this her home. It's like being on the moon, but hotter, probably. It will be the perfect setting for my story. The camera will love it.

I, on the other hand, am thinking of dark, cold, grumpy old England with longing. If I really was here just to track down an old friend of Sophie's, I'd be complaining twenty-four seven. I'd persuade Soph to go to the Great Barrier Reef with me, and find her friend by phone.

It's the middle of winter, and yet the temperature is at least forty-five degrees centigrade in the shade. My system is screwed by the sudden change. We left Heathrow in a storm, three hours late because of ice on the runway. At the time I complained that we never get the right sort of winters; the ones with deep blue skies and crisp sunshine. Now I would kill to be back in the Dickensian gloom.

In many ways, I wish Daisy had taken it upon herself to build a new life in Manhattan. As it is, I've still got my winter cold, and there's nothing designed to make me cross quite as efficiently as a stinking great cold in summer.

As I follow Sophie to the motel, leaving the handful of backpackers to the burly woman who is ordering them to follow her, I realise that my summer cold doesn't matter. 'It's the story, stupid,' I mutter under my breath. Despite everything, I am excited to be here at last. It's good, really, that she didn't choose a more congenial setting. I start composing intros in my head. 'The harsh conditions in Craggy Rock,' I tell myself, 'denote its status as, literally, the end of the earth. It is here that Daisy Fraser has found refuge. The sun beats down on the dusty soil . . .'

Sophie strides ahead of me, looking every inch the keen back-packer. Her hair is tied up on top of her head. She is wearing a short pink skirt and a white cotton blouse. I look at the nape of her neck, and the contours of her legs. They retain the traces of a tan from her previous travelling, and they are small and perfectly formed. I was never aware of her exercising in London, but she must do something to keep them trim. Her muscles are beautifully defined. Perhaps it's all the shagging we do.

For a moment I think, she's too good for me. That's what everyone will say. I promised Sophie that I wouldn't do a story on Daisy, and I knew perfectly well, as I said it, that I was lying. I made the promise because it was the only way I was going to get Sophie to bring me here. I proposed to her because I was feeling guilty about shagging Christie, and not because I have any intention of marrying her. From what she's implied, she's shortly going to say yes. Not only am I going to betray her trust, but I'm going to force her to betray the trust of her best friend. Plus I've had sex with Christie again since then. What a bastard.

But it will be worth it. It will be worth the ruthless sacrifice of Sophie, and it will be worth putting up with this evil weather. I know I look stupid here. I'm out of my element. Kev offered me his backpack, but it was filthy, and bore the traces of far too many camping expeditions. Even if it had been new and shiny, I couldn't have brought it. I travel with a suitcase. That's just what I do. It has a handle, and so it should be easy to wheel it behind me, apart from the fact that the 'road' upon which we are now walking is made of stones and dust. I'm wearing my smartest summer clothes: light beige trousers, and a white linen shirt. I should feel good, but everyone else is in shorts and flip-flops. Nobody else has a laptop computer. They make me feel uptight, like a colonial gentleman in India. I know my nose is red. This alone must betray me as a newly arrived Englishman.

Despite the weight of her rucksack, which is almost bigger than she is, Sophie is practically skipping. She is as excited as I am, and much less shocked. When we sat outside the bus terminal in Adelaide this morning, Sophie was like a cat, turning her face to the sun and almost purring with pleasure.

'Larry, isn't it glorious?' she demanded. 'Doesn't it make you happy, just feeling it on your face?'

'I suppose it does,' was the best I could manage. I've never really been a sunshine sort of person. I'm northern European, through and through.

'It's so easy to forget, when you're at home,' she wittered on. 'You just forget what sunshine is like. This is how life should be. Maybe we could come and live out here. You could get a job on a paper.'

Australian journalism is hardly the cutting edge. I could walk into a newsroom in Sydney and tell them I work on Fleet Street, and everyone would know exactly what I meant. They'd punch each other's lights out in their competition to be my best friend. Whereas if I went home in five years and told them I'd been, say, news editor of the *Melbourne Age*, they'd just tell me to switch on the coffee machine on my way out. I admire Rupert Murdoch, and he had the sense to get out of here (indeed, to renounce his citizenship) in order to make his name. I'm hardly going to do the opposite.

I smiled. 'Maybe.'

No, my mission is to bring even just one other journalist to Craggy

Rock. That will show the bastards. For the first time in my life, I am going to set the agenda.

Even later on, when we'd been sitting, cramped, on the bus for five hours, Sophie came back to the subject. She was flicking through some free paper she'd picked up at the bus station.

'Sod temping,' she announced. 'There's a job here working somewhere called the Riverlands, which sounds nice, doesn't it? Assistant manager of a vineyard. I'm sure I could do that. How about it? Let's stay here and make wine for a living. My God, I would love to drop out of that whole London thing for ever!'

'You wouldn't really, though. You'd miss it.'

'Oh, I *so* would not. Not at all. Do you really think I would? Do you think I'd miss tramping into someone's bloody office with all its little cliques and in-jokes, and being referred to not as Sophie, but as "The Temp", and having to make the coffee and go out to buy the chocolate, and do the filing that no one's touched for three years? I loathe temping. It's really not me at all. I also wouldn't miss being inside for all the daylight hours, and not having any money, and living in Battersea and taking a mainline train *and* a tube to get anywhere. There's no comparison whatsoever with the way things work here.'

'Don't you think you're being a little bit idealistic? We're on holiday. You don't get any real sense of a place on holiday.'

She looked at me and pulled a face. In a way, I admire her for being so adaptable. I'd hate to live in Australia. Apart from anything else, it's so bloody far away.

It was, though, nice to leave Britain in this particular instance. Sophie took three weeks off her temping, rather than two, and spent the week before we left in Devon with her father. So muggins came down on Friday night to pick her up and whisk her off to Heathrow for a Saturday lunchtime check-in. Which meant I spent the night at her father's house. Worse: in her father's bed. I had managed to avoid it over Christmas, largely by avoiding Christmas altogether and volunteering to work. It got me a few jeers, but Christie was working as well, and we got drunk together in the afternoon. Best to draw a veil, actually, over what happened after we'd reported on the Queen's speech and a train crash in Russia (few casualties, no fatalities). Suffice to say that working on Christmas Day was less dull than everyone had predicted, and suffice then to add that Christie's assets are as magnificent as ever.

When I got to Sophie's father's house, they were watching television together. They didn't even switch it off when I arrived. Indeed, her father, meeting his putative future son-in-law for the first time, wasn't even going to get up to say hello. Sophie forced him.

He looked old and tired, but he was a bastard. I knew he was a retired professor. He had the abstracted air of someone who's constantly calculating the value of pi to three hundred decimal places; someone for whom conversation is a distraction that might well make him lose his place. His hair was wispy and grey, and his glasses were on top of his head, like Professor Brainstawm's.

'The famous Lawrence,' he said, shaking my hand with a grip that was firm, or even harsh. 'I've heard your name a lot this last week. You take care of Sophie for me.'

'And Sophie will take care of me, too,' I pointed out.

'And me as well. I think we're probably luckier than we realise with this one.'

I wasn't sure what to say to that. I hesitated to agree with him, and thus to lump myself into his category of hopeless males, but I didn't want to draw a distinction too rudely. I hated the whole evening. Sophie cooked dinner and we opened the wine that I'd brought. Then we watched crappy television. This was the life of my in-laws. My in-law, in the singular. This was what I might be marrying into.

It got worse when I tried to get him talking about the Frasers, during *The Bill*.

'You must have known Sophie's friend Daisy and her family,' I said casually. 'Were her parents friends of yours?'

He looked at me, with an expression I couldn't work out. Normally I'm good at interpreting faces, but this time all I could divine was that it wasn't particularly friendly.

'I used to ferry Sophie there and back five times a day.'

'Dad, you did not. I used to walk.'

'Not when you were five, you didn't.'

I tried to steer the conversation. 'And Mr and Mrs Fraser, how were they after she disappeared?'

'Oh, they weren't great friends of ours. But how do you think they were? How would I be if it had been Sophie?'

'They don't live in the area any more, do they?'

'No, and before you ask, I don't know where they are, or how depressed they are on a scale of one to ten, and to tell you the truth I don't think we need any more journalists around here asking questions about them. Particularly not guests in my house.'

There was a long silence. I wasn't going to say anything, because if I did it would have come out angry, and a war between me and my putative father-in-law would not have been a good tactical manoeuvre. He clearly had nothing more to say, and didn't want to back down. It was left to Sophie to get the conversation going again.

'Dad, Larry is my boyfriend,' she said. 'He's interested in Daisy because she was my friend. Not in his professional capacity. He cares about her because he cares about me. Not all journalists are the same, you know.' Then she turned to me. 'Larry, you have to understand that we had a horrendous time with the press after she vanished. It was bad when she was arrested, but I didn't really notice because I was so concerned about what she'd been through and what she was going through. But when she went, we were completely besieged. They stayed for weeks. They knew I was her friend, and they thought I must have some idea what had happened to her.'

Her dad was looking at her. 'Darling, you still say "she went". We all know that she didn't "go" as such. She died. They found her car, and they found her suicide note. All her suicide notes. You've got one.'

She was pink in the face. 'They didn't find her body.'

'That's because they never find bodies when people jump off the Severn Bridge. Her body was washed out to sea. You know that. I know that. So does Larry. Even the Frasers came to accept it. I know it was easy to believe that she'd disappeared. Irresponsible speculation stirred up by the press.'

'There were lots of sightings of her,' I pointed out.

'Thank you. More irresponsible speculation on the part of Her Majesty's press. If I recall correctly, there were conclusive sightings of her in China, Argentina, India and Moscow, all within the same week. Any white girl with brown hair suddenly became little Daisy. Sophie, if they'd seen you in Anchorage, say, you'd have been her. People see what they want to see, particularly if they're going to get a fee for it from the lazy hacks.'

Sophie looked at me. 'Dad, you know we're going to Australia?'

'You might have mentioned it once or twice.'

'Well.' She hesitated. I silently begged her not to tell him. She was thinking about it, I could tell. I didn't want to be there when he discovered that I was going with her on one of these wild goose chase outings. He'd know immediately that I'd lied. I didn't like Sophie's dad. He unnerved me.

Luckily, she thought better of it at the last minute.

'I loved it there, Daddy, I really did. I was thinking about going to live there, one day, but I'd only do that if you came too. How about it?'

He laughed, relaxed, and sipped his wine. 'I'd certainly give the matter some thought, my sweet girl. I'd contemplate it.'

He made us sleep in his double bed, while he repaired to the austere single in Sophie's old room. I couldn't shag her in his bed. He knew I wouldn't be able to. He'd done it to freak me out. I realised I was going to have to keep an eye on him. He was nothing like the cuddly and tragic figure he pretended to be.

There are a few people around on the streets. A burly man, taller than me and three times as broad, is mooching along the road with his hands in the pockets of his shorts. Next to him, a rough-looking girl with bleached hair is tripping along, whining.

'There was no way you had to phone her, yeah?' she's saying as they pass. 'She divorced you. There should be nothing between you. Your place is with me.' He looks miserable.

Sophie waits for me to catch up. 'I think I went to their wedding!' she laughs.

The motel, rather weirdly, has a front but no sides and it definitely doesn't have a back. It is a dugout. Sophie told me about them, but I didn't take much notice. But the people here, it seems, really do live in holes in the ground. Apparently it keeps them cool. They are fucked up; I'd go for air conditioning every time.

The woman at the reception desk welcomes us. She is large, with raw pink cheeks. She doesn't ask our business. I suppose there's no reason on earth why she'd care what brought a pair of Brits with contrasting luggage into such a backwater. By definition, everyone who checks in here has drifted to the backwater. She'll care, though, when she finds out that they've had an escaped criminal living in their midst for God knows how long.

'Room fifty-four,' she announces, handing us a key on a huge wooden keyring. I would have thought it was a piece of driftwood but for the fact that we are hundreds of miles from the sea. 'It's desert oak,' she adds, seeing me handling it.

'Are they common?'

'Yep, you'll see them all over. We run tours into the desert every Tuesday and Thursday afternoon. Will I put youse two down for one?'

Sophie takes over, smoothly. 'We'd love that. I'll tell you what, give us this evening to plan our stay, and then we'll let you know which day would be best.'

'How long are you planning on staying then, love? Normally they're in and out in the blink of an eye.'

'I've been here before, actually. I was here back in the summer – in the winter, I mean. I liked it, so we thought we'd stop for a few days this time.'

'On your way to the Alice, is it?'

'Yes,' says Sophie, at the same moment that I say, 'No.' I am telling the truth, but Sophie's version is, of course, the more plausible.

The woman guffaws. 'Well, which is it?'

I look at Sophie, and leave it to her. 'Yes, of course we are, but not straightaway. After this we'll go to Coober Pedy, and make our way to Alice slowly. My boyfriend hasn't been here before, and his geography isn't very good.'

I smile guiltily. 'It's true. I've never been this far from home.'

'You look like you haven't. Youse two enjoy yourselves. Any time you need anything, just give us a yell. There's always one of us here, whether it's me, Dave, or Rachelle. I'd get Rachelle to show you to your room now, only she's not about. She's turned into a shocker since she got married. Out the front door, round to your right into the courtyard, and you can't miss it. Room fifty-four. And I'm Nora.'

'Thank you, Nora,' says Sophie, sweetly.

'You're welcome, love.'

'And there is one thing you might be able to help me with. Last time I was here, I met someone I was hoping to see again. I know she lives here. Maybe you could help me find her?'

137

'Sure I can, darl. I know everyone. What was her name?'

'Lina. She had a little boy as well, called Red.'

I study Nora's face, and my excitement mounts. First it registers recognition. She is about to tell us about the so-called Lina and her little boy, Red. Then she holds herself back, and finally her face becomes a mask.

'Sorry, love, I don't know anyone by those names. Are you sure she lives here? Plenty of people pass through.'

'I'm positive. She lives here. She's about the same age as me. Taller, with dark hair.' She fumbles in her bag, and produces the cherished photograph. Daisy smiles awkwardly, one arm around the little boy. It is a smile we have analysed countless times. 'Here she is. Are you sure you don't know her?'

'Never seen her before in me life. Sorry I couldn't help.'

'Never mind. Thanks anyway.'

'That's OK.'

I'm sure that, as soon as we leave, she picks up the phone.

In our bare, dark bedroom, we dissect the meaning of Nora's obvious lie.

'Maybe she was telling the truth,' says Sophie, upset. 'Perhaps Daisy doesn't live here, after all. She could just have been visiting.'

'Of course she wasn't. Remember all the things that Welsh boy said? He said she lived in a dugout and that she liked it here because of all the nature, although frankly she must still be on drugs if that's what she goes around saying. So if she was passing through, which might be a reason why Nora didn't recognise her—'

'She didn't recognise me,' Sophie interrupts.

'Exactly. Well then, that would be a different matter. But the woman in the photo wasn't passing through. We know that.'

She agrees, a little reluctantly.

'So,' I continue, 'Nora wouldn't have lied just for the hell of it, would she?'

'No. Daisy must have told her to.'

'Precisely. So the upshot is, that woman must have been Daisy.'

'Yeah, I know. I knew that before.'

'But it's exciting to have proof, don't you think? Not only is she

Daisy, but she's one step ahead of us. It's a challenge. We have to find her.'

'But I don't want a horrible challenge! I just wanted to see her, and now she's hiding from me.'

'From you, or from someone else.'

'Yes, maybe from you too. You, as in the press. She must have known that if I knew I might talk about it. She's done it again, Larry. I know she has. She saw me, and so she's vanished again.'

'That doesn't mean we give up. First of all, for all we know, that Nora woman might have moved here since you were last here. We need to ask some more people. Even if they are all covering up for her, someone could let it slip. In fact I'd be surprised if they didn't. We'll identify some likely culprits in the bar tonight, and we'll buy them beers till they tell us. If we have no joy with that, we'll think of something else. Having that photo, Soph, is a major blessing. You did well to get that. It's going to be our best friend.'

She sat up and hugged me. 'She was talking about Rachelle getting married. I'm sure that skinny girl was Rachelle, the one we saw in the street. That was the wedding where I met her. So let's find her again. I couldn't do this without you, Larry.'

'I would never ask you to.'

We grin at each other. We are equal to this challenge.

chapter fifteen

I thought Renmark would be cooler than Craggy, but it's just shadier, with more water. Our back garden is enclosed, and our front garden, open to the quiet street and, beyond that, the river, is shaded by two huge gum trees. The front garden, we have discovered, is a sociable place. All we have to do is to take a table and chairs, or a rug, onto the short grass, enjoy the cool breeze from the water, and wait to meet our new neighbours. It doesn't take long.

'Hi there!'

I look around. A man is standing in the next door garden and peering at us.

'Hi!' we call back.

'You've just moved in? I'm Henry. I live two streets away. Just visiting.'

As he speaks, Henry climbs delicately over the small fence that separates our garden from the neighbours'. He has a bottle of Foster's in his hand.

'Henry, mate, I'm Tony,' says Tony, smiling and standing up.

'And I'm Lina,' I add, forcing myself to my feet and extending my hand. Henry is in his late twenties, and has blue eyes and black hair. He is good-looking, I decide, and he is clearly friendly as well. Maybe I'll introduce him to Beth. In fact, she probably knows him already.

As soon as he sees my huge stomach, he does a double take.

'Wow, pleased to meet you, Lina, *both* of you! That's great.' He turns to the garden from which he's just come, and shouts, 'Jess! You have to see this!'

Jess turns out to be his wife, and her baby is due a week before ours. I feel better the moment I see her. She is blonde, pretty, and massive.

In fact, she is so magnificently pregnant that she almost makes me feel small.

I fetch each of us an iced grapefruit juice, and Jess and I sit on a blanket and talk about pregnancy, in the shade. I realise that, in the past seven months, I haven't met another pregnant woman, apart from Rachelle and people I've seen at the surgery. Now I'm going to have a neighbour with a baby the same age as ours.

'How are you finding the kicks?' she asks me.

'I like them. Except when I'm asleep.'

'Oh, do you get that too? My little bumpkin does that to me. It drives me mad sometimes, but hey, you can't stay angry with Baby for long!'

I overlook the twee use of 'Baby', on the grounds that I'm happy to have someone to talk to. Tony and Henry, sitting at the table, seem to be getting along. Suddenly I realise what we are doing. We're making friends. Tony and I have been friends as well, recently. We both managed to apologise, with varying degrees of bad grace, for New Year's Eve. Tony agreed to make allowances for my pregnancy emotions (and I succeeded in biting back any objections to allowances being necessary) and I promised I'd tell him all about my English childhood after the baby is born. Perhaps I will. I'd rather tell him the truth than invent some more lies, but I know it would be dangerous. I've only just stopped looking over my shoulder as it is. Sophie could always find me if she really wanted to, now.

The upshot of our January the first discussion was that neither of us wanted to split up, least of all shortly before the birth, and nor did we want to upset Red any further.

'Better make the best of it then.' Tony smiled weakly, and I wasn't sure whether he was joking or whether this really was the strongest endorsement of our marriage that he could manage.

'I'll put up with you if you put up with me,' I suggested.

'I'd get you a beer, if it was wise.'

'Sod it,' I told him, 'I'll have one anyway.'

As he set off for the fridge, I called after him. I couldn't stop myself. 'Tony?' He looked round. 'You do love me, don't you?'

He laughed. 'You know I do, darling. Of course I do. We're all right, you know? We're going to be all right.'

'I love you, too. Thank you.'

Jess and I are discussing the likelihood of perineum tearing when we are interrupted by Red.

'Mum?' he yells from the front door. He's been playing on his PlayStation.

'Oh!' says Jess, her eyes wide. 'So you've been through all this before, then?'

'No,' I tell her, 'he's adopted. It's all new to me, too. What, darling?'

'Phone. It's Margot. She wants to speak to you, not Tony.'

I excuse myself. As I approach the phone, I am happy. We have friends. We have a wonderful house. I am having a baby.

'Margot!'

'Hi, darl, how are you?'

'Fine, thanks. We're all brilliant, in fact. We've just met some neighbours whose baby's due on March the first. You'll meet them when you come. When are we going to be seeing you down here?'

'Thought I'd come over in a couple of weeks, love. That way I can stay around for when the baby's born, and I'll be there to look after young Red if it pops along early.'

My heart sinks. If she comes in a couple of weeks, Margot will have a solid month before the baby's due. There'll be no getting rid of her afterwards. I resign myself to a good six months with my mother-in-law residing in the nursery. I suppose this is the price you pay for moving away from the bosom of your husband's family. The bosoms can always follow.

'Great!' I say, as enthusiastically as I can. 'You know you're welcome any time. Red's been asking when we were going to be seeing you.'

'Has he?' He hasn't, in fact, but I'm feeling charitable.

'Of course. Now, tell me everything that's been going on in Craggy.'

'Oh, nothing changes here, love. Andy and Rachelle are expecting as well – did you know that? We're not meant to know, as such, but Rachelle was sick every bloody morning last week when she was on the early shift at the motel – every bloody morning! Once or twice you can write off as a hangover. Nora ended up saying to her, look, love, you're newlywed, you're sick in the mornings, is there anything you need to tell me? And so it all came out.'

'If she told Nora, the whole town must know by now.'

'Oh, they do, love, they do. Oh, now you've made me remember what I was phoning for in the first place. You remember those tax inspectors you were saying about? Well, they're here. You were right. No need to worry, though. Everyone knows not to say anything about you. We've pulled the wool over their eyes, good and proper.'

I sit down and rub my bump. 'Good God. I never thought they'd actually turn up. Not so soon, anyway. I thought it was just a threat.'

'I wasn't going to call because I didn't want to worry you, not in your condition, but Pete said that it was best for you to know. Just in case they do manage to track you down.'

I think about it. 'You know, they probably will. How many of them are there?'

'Two, darl. A boy and a girl.'

'What do they look like? I might have had dealings with them before, you see.'

'I haven't met them close up myself, but Nora knows them – they're staying at the motel. I suppose you wouldn't get the tax inspectors dossing at Clarrie's! She said the girl was very small, and the boy was tall and bright pink in the face. You know the way these people are, Lee. Very English.'

'What are they like?'

'Oh, Nora said the girl's sweet as. She likes her a lot. But she's got no time for the boy. Very rude, she told me.'

'Do you know their names?'

'Sure I do. Now, where is it? I wrote them down. Jotted them on the back of the water bill and threw it in me handbag. Here we go. Lawrence Golchin and Sophie Johnston. That's who they are.'

I keep my voice steady. 'That's who I thought they'd be. Thanks for that, Margot. I appreciate the warning. Now I'll have to decide what to do about them.'

'You forget about them, love. It's only money. You'll be right. Have you seen the new doctor? How's my baby doing?'

Back at the front of the house, I try to breathe deeply. I force my nails into the palms of my hands, and exhale from the abdomen, as instructed by various pregnancy handbooks. I concentrate on walking to the group in the garden, and I think about looking normal. My heart is racing. My baby is kicking.

'Hi,' says Jess happily as I sit down with her again. I'd rather chat about pregnancy and babies than go anywhere near Tony right now.

'Hi,' I say, as normally as I can. 'That was my mother-in-law.'

'The dreaded in-laws! Does she live locally?'

'No. We used to live near her – we moved from the Outback, from a place called Craggy Rock, just before Christmas.'

Jess giggles. 'Craggy Rock! What a funny name. It sounds like Renmark might be more baby friendly. Have you thought about nurseries?'

When, eventually, Jess and Henry leave, I stay on the rug, pleading tiredness, and lie on my side. My relationship with Tony is fragile as it is. Sophie and Lawrence, whoever he may be, are looking for me, with a view to unmasking me, in Craggy Rock. Sophie has already travelled halfway around the world, again, to find me. This time she's brought a reinforcement. I know she won't go away. If she turns up in Renmark, my marriage will probably be over and I'll be a single mother before my child is even born. This baby will no more have a father than Red does. If they stay in Craggy, then the moment either of them says anything about me to anyone, Margot's sensors will be alerted and I'll have an irate mother-in-law informing Tony that I'm not who he thinks I am. My only choice is to get to Sophie before she gets to anyone else.

I lie on my side on the blanket and pretend to sleep. I could tell Tony and Red that I need to go and sort out my finances in Craggy. Tony won't believe it's that simple, but he'll think I need to get away from him for a few days. It won't occur to him that there's anything else going on. Red will miss me, but he'll be all right. Then I can find out who Lawrence is (her lover, I assume) and how much danger I'm facing. Perhaps, once I know, I will be able to take appropriate steps. Whatever they might be.

I brush a fly away, and heave myself up into a sitting position. It's time to go and lay the groundwork.

chapter sixteen

12 January

The bar is like something out of *Crocodile Dundee*. It's horrible. I thought pubs here would be like Australian themed bars at home, but it's not at all. I suppose some of its paraphernalia is (I think there are some Australian rules football posters, or some sporting pictures, anyway, on the walls), but the clientele is different. At Walkabout in London, you get Australians who have moved to London. You see the people who have had the good sense to get out. The Walkabout customers might not be sophisticated, and they might leave a trail of vomit all the way to the tube, but if any of them had the misfortune to be born in Craggy Rock, at least you know they remedied it as soon as they could walk. Whereas the people in this place are adults who have made an informed choice to be here.

Most of them are white men wearing denim. Their faces are lined and weatherbeaten. They look as though they've been sculpted from leather. Everyone is drinking solidly. This, I suppose, is the way the Outback should be.

We find ourselves a small table, and sit on wooden stools. Sophie picks up the overflowing ashtray and six used glasses, and puts them on the floor. I look around. It is five o'clock in the afternoon, and yet the room is crowded and smoky. Much of the clientele has clearly been here for hours. This is, no doubt, a Sunday tradition.

There is a sprinkling of women, and they are a mixed bunch. I thought they'd be either terrifying old witches who would snap me in half with the flick of a wrist, or overcompetent young blondes who have babies without even noticing, while they're rounding up a pack of wild horses. I dwell, occasionally, on whether a sophisticated British lad such as myself could tame a wild Outback woman and take her to London. I realise I am basing my images of the resulting hilarious mayhem on the film. Outback Woman has no idea how to cross the road. She greets everyone she passes in the street with a cheery 'G'day'. I take her to a smart dinner and she embarrasses me yet reveals some fundamental truths to all present. My female Dundee is not in this bar, where the women look weatherbeaten but disappointingly normal. What, I ask myself, would I be wanting with a crazy Australian woman when I'm practically engaged to Sophie?

'Right, Soph,' I say, as I put the drinks down. It was hard to get them, because when I asked for a pint, the guy pretended not to know what I was talking about. We've ended up with big glasses. I think it's more than a pint (trust the Australians to come up with a measure that's bigger than anyone else's) and that's fine by me. We need to look as if we blend in.

'Right, Larry,' she answers, and I wonder whether she's taking the piss. I've been wondering that quite a bit, lately.

'We'll get some of this down us, and then I'll start doing some asking around, all right?'

'Who will?'

'Us.'

'But we discussed this. It's my thing, isn't it? My friend. So I'm going to do the asking, aren't I? Remember?'

'Yes.' She's annoying sometimes. 'But I wish you'd let me do it. It's what I do. It's my job.'

'You're not here to work, are you?' She actually sounds quite angry.

As she appears to be waiting for an answer, I feel obliged to say, 'No,' while looking as sincere as I can. Then I rally. 'No, I know I'm not,' I tell her. 'All I meant is that these kinds of investigations are nothing new to me, so maybe, as I'm more experienced, I should be the one to get the ball rolling.'

'Daisy's my friend, and I'm going to do it.'

I realise, once again, that although I've always assumed Sophie to be sweet and unassertive, when she cares about something she can be tougher than my mythical Outback Woman. She gets up, nudging the table and spilling my beer, and walks away from me without another word.

At a nearby table, a group of denim-clad men are drinking and laughing. She stops beside them, and I see her smile and begin to speak.

'Sophie!' I say crossly as I jump up and take my place, protectively, by her elbow. She ignores me. One of the blokes glances through me, and then turns back to Soph.

'So what's her name, this friend of yours?' he asks.

'If she's around, Pete'll know her,' says another. 'Pete's never been known to let a lady pass him by.' He leers, in what I imagine he takes to be a comical manner.

'Her name is Lina,' Sophie tells Pete, clearly. 'She's the same age as me, but taller, and she has a little boy, who's called Red. Do you know her?'

At the far end of the table there is a bit of whispering. Pete glares at them, then turns back to us. I say 'us'. In fact, he turns back to Sophie. None of them has acknowledged my presence, not even to register disapproval. I try to convince myself that this, at least, is a positive sign.

'No, sorry, my sweet, I don't. And I would know her if she was here, you can be sure of that.'

'He would,' confirms the other.

'How about I get you a drink?' adds Pete, pointedly, to Sophie.

I take her by the elbow. 'No, we're fine, thanks,' I answer, because she's looking as if she'd like to say yes. 'We've got some drinks over there,' I add, gesturing towards our table.

'Hey, mate, I wasn't talking to you. You can go over there and drink your little drink. I was inviting Sophie to join me and the boys. Me and the boys like Sophie, and we'd enjoy her company. We might like to get to know her better. So, go on, mate. Do one.'

Instead of telling him where to go, Sophie takes me aside. 'How about if I stay and have a chat? They're drunk. They'll let something slip. I'm sure they will.'

'Oh, fucking right they will. They'll let their cocks slip. Into your mouth.'

'Larry! You're being a wanker. As if. I just want to talk to them. Not because I've suddenly transformed into the kind of slapper who fancies blokes like that. Do you really think that I'd get off with *Pete* right in front of you, just because I was flattered by his attentions?

Is that what you think I'm like? Is that what you think all women are like?'

'No.'

'Are you sure?'

'Oh, fuck it. Sorry, Sophie. Of course I'm sure. But you'd be giving them entirely the wrong impression and you could end up in a lot of trouble. Don't lead men like that along, Soph. They're dangerous.'

She looks at me, and suddenly she doesn't seem to like me at all. 'Larry, I am thirty years old. I've travelled on my own, which is more than I can say for you. I know how to spot the danger signs. Give me an hour, and they'll be too drunk to stand up, let alone to attempt to force themselves on me.'

'I really don't want you to do this.'

'I'm not doing it because I want to. They're repulsive. I'm doing it because we're here to find Daisy. If you were with one of the girls from your office – Christie, say – and you were on a story, you'd let her do this, wouldn't you? You'd ask her to do it. You know and I know that these people know Daisy, and that they're covering up for something. They don't want to talk to you. They want to talk to me. She's my friend, and I'm going to find her, whatever it takes. Christ, I wish I'd been a bit more forceful last time I was here.'

'Why did you mention Christie? You haven't even met her, have you?'

'Because she's the only female colleague you ever talk about, apart from Dotty the crime correspondent, and I can't see you and Dotty out on a job together, not when you've been nicking her stories.'

'Fair enough.'

'It's OK, Larry. I don't mind you working with women, you know. Sometimes I think you want to wrap me up in cotton wool. You want to create a happy little Sophie world where nothing can ever upset me. Well, I don't need that. I can be just as strong as you, or Christie. You miss that. You shouldn't.'

'I'm not going far away.'

'Good. Don't come over unless I call you. You'll get into worse trouble than I would.' She stalks off, pink in the cheeks, and squeezes onto the end of Pete's bench. He looks down at her – Pete is small and skinny but everyone's bigger than Sophie – and smiles a nasty, lecherous smile. Then he looks at me, and gives me a sarcastic thumbs up. I reciprocate, unsure whether I'm being ironic or pathetic. I don't really care.

Twenty minutes later, having drunk both our beers, I am wondering how, exactly, it came to this. Why am I sitting, humiliated, on my own, while my girlfriend chats merrily with a group of rowdy men? I decide to join a table of three backpackers. They are all female, all blonde, and none of them can be over twenty-one.

I pull up my stool. 'Hello', I say awkwardly, glancing over at Sophie who has not yet noticed my retaliation. 'I'm sorry to disturb you, but would you mind if I sat with you for a moment? I've been on my own for ages and I'd appreciate a little bit of company.'

The girls look at each other and burst out laughing.

'Fine,' says one, in lightly accented English. 'You may join us, sure!'

'You are from England,' says another.

'I am,' I admit, with a little bow. 'And you?'

'Oh, we are Swedish.'

'And you're all travelling together?'

'Of course.'

'How long for?'

'In all, one year. So far, two months.'

'Two months and one week.'

'And three days.'

The three of them grin at me. I'm not sure what to say next.

'Can I get anyone a drink?' I hazard. This was clearly the right thing to say. I'd forgotten that backpackers invariably have no money. Booze is the only language these people understand. Apart from English, and, no doubt, Swedish, and probably twelve other languages as well.

While I'm at the bar, I catch Sophie's eye, and wink. She smiles, and waves. Either she's doing a good job of pretending, or she really is enjoying herself. Well, I can do that too.

The bedroom is swaying slightly. I look at her challengingly.

'So?' We are both drunk. She looks a little wary.

'So I think I might have found out a little. I mean, they were definitely pretending.'

'You mean the famous Sophie charms didn't melt their little hearts and lead them to confess all?'

'How about you? Did you gather any clues from those three nubile young things who were *so* obviously residents of this town? They really were the clear choice, of all the people in the bar, for you to talk to, weren't they? Or did you forget why we're here?'

'Sophie, may I point out that you are in no position to be jealous?'

'You may, but unfortunately for you I'm not jealous. I just think you're pathetic. You knew why I was talking to Pete and Merv, and it wasn't to upset you and it wasn't because I liked them. Christ! You should have understood that much – you keep boasting that you know how investigations work. So then you storm off to chat to three blonde girls and you keep sneaking little triumphant glances over at me. I never thought this before, but sometimes I really notice the difference in our ages.'

'Yeah, well, sometimes so do I.'

I regret that as soon as I've said it, but I'm also quite pleased with the slick way it came out. She doesn't reply. She just gets into bed and turns away from me.

'Sorry,' I say grudgingly, five minutes later. Her response is to reach out and turn out the light on her side of the bed.

'I didn't mean that, I really didn't,' I add, after ten minutes. I'm sure she's not asleep. We've never had an argument before, but I'm certain Sophie wouldn't be able to switch off from it to such an extent that she'd fall asleep. 'And I'm sorry for talking to those girls. I would have been wandering around the bar asking everyone about Lina, but . . .'

'I'm listening'. Her voice is muffled by the pillow. 'I'd like to hear this.'

'But I thought it was your thing. You wanted to do that, you said so. I felt completely redundant. I was bored, but I couldn't leave the bar in case you got in too deep and needed me. So I went to talk to the only other people there who were obviously outsiders.' I like this version of events. It sounds plausible to me. In truth, it didn't even occur to me to do anything else.

'Whatever. Go to sleep. We'll talk in the morning.'

In the morning, it transpires, we are both too hungover to say anything, beyond a resentful 'Hello', and 'How are you feeling?' and 'Not so hot, actually, how about you?' The argument appears to be over, for now at least, but I don't think it's resolved.

'Let's go to the school,' decides Sophie over a breakfast of lukewarm coffee and soggy Danish pastries in the nearest cafe. 'She had that little boy. I guess she isn't around here any more, so he's probably left the school, but you never know. He might be there.'

'We can talk to some kids. They'll tell us if they know her. Kids won't remember to cover up. In fact, we can switch to asking them about him. Show them the photo. That's a great idea.'

'Seems a bit mean to trick innocent children.'

'So we can go to the school, and you can look for the boy in the photo. While you're doing that, if I'm chatting to a kid, well, that won't do anyone any harm, will it?'

'If I didn't notice that you were doing it I suppose I wouldn't mind.'

'I don't think you'd have the option of minding.'

'So, do your worst, journalistic scum.'

'Do your best, child-stalker.'

One thing is worrying me. 'Do you think they have a school in a place like this?'

I'm not sure you can really call it a school, but they have a building, a proper one, which isn't dug into the hillside. It even has air-conditioning units on the outside. We turn up at lunchtime.

The place is deserted.

'Maybe they keep them all inside in the middle of the day,' says Sophie. 'They can hardly, really, send them out in this weather.'

'You think there might be a mass siesta going on in there? But it doesn't look like there's any sign of life at all.'

'Maybe we should go in. Larry, you're the expert, you come up with a cover story.'

'Tricky. Everyone's bound to talk, and so anyone we meet will already know that we're looking for "Lina".' I make quotation marks in the air with my fingers, to emphasise that I am not taken in by Daisy's disguise. 'Maybe we could pretend we've got a child and we're thinking of moving here, but who in fuck's name would believe a thing like that?'

Sophie looks at me. 'That we've got a child?'

'No! That people like us would come and live here.'

'Daisy's like us. She's like me, anyway, and she did.'

We cross the playground, which is made of some kind of turf that springs underfoot. I step back, because I know Sophie wants to take the lead, and she tries the handle of the main door. It is locked. We both rattle it a few times, but to no avail.

I start walking round the back, to see if there's another entrance. As I go, I pass a noticeboard, and stop to read it. Then I look more closely.

'Soph!' I shout. 'You've got to see this!'

In amongst the photos from the nativity play, and the list of term dates (which reveal why there's no one here on a Monday lunchtime in January), there is an end of term circular from the deputy head teacher, Simon Andrews. As soon as I looked at it, one name jumped out.

'Look,' I say, tracing the words with my finger. 'This Christmas we say a sad farewell to Mrs Lina Pritchett who has taught year five for three years, and who has proved a most popular English teacher and member of staff. We wish her and her family the best of luck in her new home.' I look down at Sophie. She is beaming.

'They don't say where her new home is,' she points out.

'That's a shame. But she exists. Your mate's been a teacher for the past three years.'

'Daisy, an English teacher? She hated academic work. If she was a dancing teacher, I could have understood it. How *weird*.'

'G'day.'

We look down. A small girl is standing beside us. She's wearing shorts and a T-shirt. Her hair is dark blonde, and her face is sweet. For a moment I wish she was Daisy's child. She'd look great in the paper. She looks about the same size as Daisy's boy.

'Hello,' says Sophie, smiling at her. 'What's your name?'

'Tabitha. What's yours?'

'Sophie. This is Lawrence.'

I bend down a little, to her level. 'Hi, Tabitha. Do you go to school here?'

The girl laughs. 'Of course I do, but not in the holidays. What are you doing?'

'We're looking for a friend of yours,' Sophie tells her, 'but he doesn't live here any more, I don't think. Do you know a boy called Red Pritchett?'

She laughs. 'Red's my second best friend! But he's moved. We write each other emails, though.'

'Do you know where he's moved to?' Sophie continues, showing no signs of the excitement I'm feeling.

'It's R . . . R . . . I can't remember. It begins with R. You have to get two buses to go there. I'm going to go and visit, maybe in the Easter holidays. They live by the river. Do you know Red?'

'No, not really,' says Sophie, smiling, 'but I do know his mum, Lina.'

'Mrs Pritchett, you mean. She was our teacher. Now we're going to have some *man*. But we're not allowed to talk about Mrs Pritchett.' She looks up at Sophie. 'You've got the same voice as her.'

'That's because we both come from England. Tabitha, do you think you could find out Red's new address for me, please? Or tell me his email? Because I want to write a letter to Mrs Pritchett, since she's my friend.'

Tabitha puts her head on one side. 'Suppose. Shall I meet you here later?'

'How about at four o'clock?'

'OK.' She turns and runs off.

At four o'clock, we are back outside the school, waiting for her, but Tabitha never turns up. Neither of us is the least bit surprised.

chapter seventeen

My heart is pounding as we pull into town.

'Ladies and gentlemen,' says the coach captain. 'We are now entering the bizarre world that calls itself Craggy Rock. Watch out for the mineshafts, and enjoy your stay if this is your point of disembarkation.'

I have been dreading this. I've been trying to concentrate on making the journey last for ever. I've hoped the bus would crash. I have fantasised that it might become a fireball of such intense heat that my fellow innocent passengers are incinerated beyond all possibility of being identified. Somehow, we escape the flames, my baby and I, and we spend months living in the desert, during which time I give birth with the help of some wise Aborigines. At some point in the future, we emerge in Perth, paddle a canoe to Indonesia, and start a new life.

The absence of so much as a skid from today's journey is not the only thing that makes this fantasy scenario impractical. It doesn't work like that. New lives take months of meticulous planning. They only work when you can cut all ties and never allow yourself to look back. I can't do that. This time I have to face what's coming.

Margot had some more information when I called her back to announce my visit.

'My Pete was chatting to the young girl in the pub,' she confided. 'Said she was a nice girl but all she wanted was to talk about you, and he wasn't letting on that he knew you. But he said the fella was a different matter. Didn't take to him. He looks young, you know. Younger than her. Pete said he didn't know what she was doing with him.'

Alarm bells have been ringing loudly ever since. It's like tinnitus. Sophie, Sophie. I could deal with you on your own. I hold my bump for reassurance. If I really believed that, I'd have dealt with her at the beginning of September, at the wedding. If only I had. I know she was at least a little bit sympathetic to me, because she left me alone. We might have been able to sort it out.

An elderly man struggles to his feet across the aisle, and tries to manoeuvre his bags down from above his head. I get up and reach to help him. He turns and beams gappily at me.

'Thank you, my dear!' he says, and immediately notices my bump. 'But I should be doing this for you.'

'Oh, I'm fine, thanks,' I lie. 'I can manage.'

I spot Margot outside the window. She is beaming. A visit from me, after all, necessarily incorporates a visit from her unborn grandchild. Margot knows that anything connected with money can only be a minor-to-medium irritation, and she believes that my visit is largely social. Tony and Red are of the same opinion.

'Come back soon, yeah, Mum?' said Red, as Tony loaded my bag onto the bus at the Renmark garage this morning.

'Of course I will.' I smiled and kissed him. 'When I come back, it won't be long before we've got the baby. I'll talk to you soon. Good luck with your diving.'

He clung to me for several minutes, and I know he was hating the thought of doing anything without me. It's bad enough that I'm not going to teach at his school any more. Red is used to seeing me all day, every day. He has seen me every day of his life. I try to convince myself that I'm going to Craggy, now, for his benefit. I have to keep him out of the spotlight. I remind myself that I have been lying to all of them for ever. There is no logical reason to start feeling guilty about it now.

As I climb awkwardly down the steps, after the old man, my heart sinks at the familiarity of it all. I hope that the day will come when I can say I've forgotten what Craggy Rock is like. That its relentless sun and the way it makes the back of your neck ache, its singular architecture, the haze of eccentricity that hangs over it where normal towns have clouds, has all slipped my mind. Unfortunately, however, we only left a few weeks ago, and Craggy still seems more like home than Renmark does. Renmark is indisputably gorgeous, and no one would ever use that word to describe Craggy. Even Margot speaks about it defensively, particularly to a girl from London Town such as myself.

Nora passes by as I awkwardly descend the steps.

'Hi, Lina!' she says. 'Back so soon? Some people were looking for you, but don't worry, I didn't let on.' She winks, and lumbers on her way.

Margot hugs me. 'You're looking great, darl!' she exclaims. Then, as ever, she bends her wiry body and put her mouth approximately where my belly button is.

'G'day, little bubba!' she bellows. I feel the baby stirring crossly. Tony, Red and Pete also practise this method of communicating with the foetus. It must terrify the poor little shrimp. I wouldn't do it, even if I could. Normally, when people do this, I point out how shocking such a sudden loud noise, amplified by the amniotic fluid, must be for the baby, but I am too tense today. A startled baby is the very least of my worries.

I aim as relaxed a smile as I can muster in Margot's direction. I have already scanned the road several times for Sophie and pink Lawrence. I want to get into Margot's house and have a lovely cup of tea before the confrontation takes place. I am jittery. I cannot believe I have come, on purpose, to the place where I know I will be found.

Margot takes my bag. 'So, we'll go to the pub, will we?'

'I'm not drinking, remember.'

'But you don't mind coming with your old mum, do you? Have a lemonade, or a glass of wine.'

Wine, in Margot's book, is a soft drink. 'It's grape juice,' she once explained with a shrug.

'Do you mind if we go back to yours first?' I say, pathetically. 'I'm really tired after the journey, and I could do with a shower.'

'Oh, sorry, love, I'd forgotten what it was like. Mind you, I was always in the pub when I was having my boys. There was no one around in those days, you see, telling us not to drink. Drank like a fish, I did. Smoked like a chimney.'

'These days we have to smoke like a fish and drink like a chimney.'

'We'll have a cuppa. You're allowed tea, aren't you? I forget. It seemed like you were just on the water at Christmas. They take the fun out of everything.'

'You know, if I was doing it properly, I probably wouldn't even have tea, but I do. You can't give up everything. I figure the baby doesn't mind the odd cup.'

'Course she doesn't.'

As we walk up the dusty track, I try to keep an eye out for the intruders, and, at the same time, to appear relaxed. I am relieved to see Margot's shack. It is a shack in the most palatial sense of the word. In fact, it is one of the most upmarket homes in Craggy. The fact that no part of it is built underground lends it perverse cachet, as everyone knows that this means it has air conditioning.

At the door, I sigh with relief. So far, so good. I know, however, what Craggy is like, and I know that word of my return will already have spread throughout the town. Nora has doubtless already sought out Sophie, and said, oh, you know that girl you were looking for, well, I was mistaken, I do know her, and she's back in town.

Margot forces me to sit in Brian's huge old armchair, and brings me a cup of strong tea, into which she has emptied the sugar bowl. I tuck my feet underneath me, glad to see that they're all right (my feet are strangers to me most of the time), and I drink the tea slowly. As I do so, lost in my thoughts, Margot knocks back a can of lager, and talks.

'In actual fact, I was thinking of coming back with you, when you're done with the tax inspectors. Only Pete says, Mum, you can't just go to Renmark now, you should give them time to settle in, but I said, I can't wait, I'm just dying to see this posh house of theirs and young Red's been asking about me – I don't want him forgetting all about me, but Pete said, don't be silly, woman, he's not going to forget you, not in a week and not in a year.'

'You know we'd love you to come whenever you like,' I say absently.

'I know, darl. But the upshot is, I think I'll come in a couple of weeks. You'll need a bit of help around the place. Then I'll be around when the baby comes. Is Tony going to the hospital with you?'

'Yes, of course. I think he's looking forward to it.'

'Brian wouldn't have come within a mile, and to be honest I was glad. The blokes weren't allowed in those days – a good thing in my book. You'll find out it's not very dignified. In my day you had to lie flat on your back with your legs in those stirrups. Jesus Christ, I can still remember the pain. Why I went back for another I'll never know.'

I smile at her. 'I'm glad you did.'

'Otherwise you'd have had to marry Pete!'

There is a knock at the door. I look at Margot, horrified. She puts her tinny down and strides off to answer it.

'Are you expecting anyone?' I ask her departing back.

'No, could be anyone,' she says cheerily. I try to curl into the chair, and I listen to what is said.

'G'day!' I hear her exclaim. Margot is indiscriminately hospitable, unless it's someone with whom she happens to be feuding. 'Come on in. Guess who's here? Only Lina, come back to visit us!'

I look up. Margot comes back into the room, smiling. Behind her is Pete.

'G'day, sis!' he exclaims, kissing me on the cheek.

I beam. 'Hello, Pete.' The baby and I have blood and adrenaline pumping around our bodies. It must think we're being pursued by a pack of lions.

Early in the morning, I wake up in one of the spare rooms. This used to be Red's bedroom when he occasionally stayed at Margot's, and I can smell him on the Superman sheets. The bed is single, and I've wedged a pillow under my bump. There's not much room to manoeuvre. As soon as I open my eyes, I stretch out and realise that I have to get up.

Margot went to the pub without me last night, so I'm sure she's still sleeping off her hangover. For a hardened woman who has spent her entire life in the Outback, she doesn't get up very early. When I first came here, I assumed everyone would be up at the crack of dawn, just out of habit, but as there are no animals to feed or crops to water, the only people who need to put in an early appearance are the miners.

I love the early mornings. I put on my clean Capri pants and iron a linen shirt. I have spent the evening and the night in air-conditioned comfort and I feel relatively good. Being in Craggy Rock is irritating but normal. Nothing, I tell myself, can go that wrong, because Sophie doesn't want to bring me any harm. I wonder whether I can call Tony and Red, but decide that six o'clock is far too early.

I am quite safe walking around at this time of day. The air is crisp, which is a blessing. Nobody is about, even though this is the most wonderful time. Craggy is silent, and I look at its slumbering weirdness. It is so familiar. I thought I had left it behind in favour of water and greenery, and yet here I am, still pregnant, and still here. Perhaps I'll never really escape. I suppose we'll be visiting periodically, when all this is over, since we have no family anywhere else.

The Outback is dotted with towns like Craggy. Tough people live from the land all over inland Australia. All over the world, people exist far from urban centres. People fend for themselves. Their main priority is survival. I think back to villages I visited in India. They were completely different from this, and yet they were the same. Everyone's daily goal was to feed themselves and their families, and to take whatever the land had for them. It was so different from my previous urban life. I was dazed and exhilarated.

I half walk and half slide down the path to the road. Nobody is around, so I walk beside the street for a little way, and then struggle up one of the bizarre manmade hills that pepper the town. It is dusty, and the exertion is quite extreme for me, accustomed as I am to taking no more exercise than what is necessarily involved in taking Red to school and keeping the house clean and tidy. I smile at the idea that I'm walking on someone's roof. I never got used to that.

At the top of the hill, I survey the town. The industrial mining equipment is still and ominous at the edge of the settlement. This place would not exist were it not for the opals in the desert. I see the water lorries on the road from Adelaide, approaching the town. As human habitation, this is fantastically unlikely.

I breathe deeply.

'Excuse me,' says a woman's voice behind me. I gasp, and turn round. I had thought I was entirely alone.

She is standing a few metres away. I watch her face as she recognises me.

'You're pregnant,' she says.

'Yes,' I agree. 'I am.'

For a long minute, neither of us says anything.

'When's it due?' she says eventually.

'Beginning of March.'

'Congratulations.'

'Thanks.'

She walks towards me. I know there is no point in my pretending not to know her this time. I look at her. She makes me feel enormous. I wonder whether she still dances. I don't ask.

'Why did you come back?' I say, as we stand side by side, looking out over the town.

'To see you.'

'It's not that simple.'

'I know. I'm sorry. I could see the first time how much you didn't want to talk to me, but I had to see you. I can't believe you're alive. Do your friends here know who you really are?'

'Of course they don't. I hardly remember it myself now, most days.'

'You think I'm going to tell everyone, don't you?'

'I've known all along that anything like this would be disaster. The moment the two worlds come together, it's over. You know what the consequences could be for me. It doesn't bear thinking about, not with the baby.'

'I'm not going to let that happen. I came to see you, not to arrest you.'

'But you've already told someone. Who's Lawrence?'

She laughs, and hesitates. 'News travels fast, doesn't it? He's all right. He's on our side. He's my boyfriend. In fact, my fiancé. Sort of.'

I sigh. 'Did you have to tell him?' I ask her.

I watch Sophie's face as it changes. She becomes defensive.

'Daisy,' she says, and I shudder at her use of a name I haven't heard for a decade. 'You made me think you were dead, for ten whole years. I'd just about *got over* you. Do you have any idea what that's like? We were best friends, and then you killed yourself, except there was no body, and now I know why. I've been half grieving, half thinking you'd escaped and were living happily somewhere as someone else. Here you are, with a family, and a baby on the way, and you begrudge me telling the person closest to me about the thing that has occupied my thoughts for every moment of every day since that stupid wedding.'

'I do know what it's like,' I tell her quietly, 'because it's been the same for me, although I did know what was going on. But I knew that I couldn't contact you, or anyone, ever again. Sophie, in lots of ways I'm absolutely amazed and delighted to see you. It's something that I never believed would happen. If you'd asked me a few more times at the wedding, I'd have told you everything then. But you must know that you've got me over a barrel here. I'm kind of at your mercy. What are you going to do?'

Her eyes fill with tears, and she reaches out and touches my arm. 'I want to feel that you're real. I want to talk to you. I really really want you to tell me how you did it. I won't blow your cover. No one will ever know.'

I'm close to tears as well.

'I've missed you,' Sophie adds, 'so much.'

For me, this is the last straw.

'I've missed you, too,' I confess. 'All the time.' I start sniffing.

'I almost followed you home when I saw you before. I watched you leave the party, but I thought, Daisy doesn't want to see me, and that's up to her. I was too shocked to do anything else. I couldn't work it out. I knew it was you. And I could see that no one else knew. I didn't want to ruin it all.'

I smile. 'Thanks.'

'As soon as I got back to England I knew I had to come back. Did you move away because of me?'

'Honestly? Yes. Nobody knew. We'd been here long enough, anyway, but seeing you and realising that everything could be shot to pieces gave me that special motivation. I was petrified. I don't want to go to prison.'

'They've done a fantastic job of covering for you.'

'It's a close-knit place, and my in-laws are here. It's really not so difficult to arrange that level of protection. They think you're the tax authorities from England. That's why they're so determined to send you packing.'

'That's funny. It makes sense. We found your name on the school noticeboard in the end, and a little girl helped us out. She said she was Red's second best friend.'

'Tabitha,' I tell her.

'Exactly.'

'Where does Red come into the story, Daisy?'

'I adopted him in Asia. Partly as a disguise.'

We sit down on a nearby bench. 'You know we're on someone's roof,' I point out. 'That's their air vent, over there.'

'They can't hear us, can they? Didn't you go mental here? I suppose

161

it was the right place for you.'

'It was perfect.'

'Where are you now?'

I hesitate.

'You don't have to tell me. I know it begins with R, it's by the river, and that you catch two buses to get there.'

'Tabitha's contribution? Maybe I'll fill in the blanks later.'

We look at each other. I am deeply wary. 'You look great,' I say.

'You look good too. You look very healthy. I can't believe you're about to have a baby. So if you've got in-laws, you must be married.'

'I've been married for years.'

'To . . . ?'

'Tony. He was at that wedding but I don't think you met him.'

'And the marriage is a good thing?'

I try to work out what she's getting at. Then I realise.

'Sophie, it's a great thing. It's one of the best things that's ever happened to me. We have our moments, for sure, and most of them spring from the fact that I won't talk about my old life. I've spun everyone a little story about dead parents. Don't think that I married Tony just out of convenience, because I didn't. I was on my own with Red for years before I met Tony. He might not know everything about me, but we have a strong relationship, largely. I don't think any marriage is perfect, but I've been stable, over the past three years, for the first time in my life.'

'Do you think he'd be OK if he found out about your past?'

'That's something I don't intend to test. But, no, I don't.'

It's getting warmer, and slowly the town below us is coming to life. I see Merv putting the sign outside the garage as he opens for business. A few people are walking to work, and the street plays host to the occasional car. I am anxious to turn the conversation away from my own life.

'Now, tell me about you,' I insist. 'What's going on? What were you doing here last winter?'

'I was travelling, the same as everyone else.'

'How long for?'

'Just four months. I'd had itchy feet for a while, and I decided that if I didn't save up and go away on my fantasy holiday, I'd never forgive myself. It's easy to forget about it out here, but England can be the most depressing fucking place you can imagine. Have you been back?'

'Of course not.'

'Lucky you. So I came away over the English summer. I have to say, the Australian winter was, by all accounts, warmer.'

'Where does Lawrence come into it all?'

'I'd been seeing him for a while before I went away, but I couldn't stay at home just for a man. I was starting to resent him. He's a funny boy – I think you'll like him. I hope so. He says he wants to marry me but I don't believe him. So I decided to go anyway. I made it very clear he wasn't invited, but he's so engrossed in his career – his job – that I don't think it would ever have crossed his mind to ask if he could come. When I got back, I found I had missed him, and we've been a bit more serious since.'

Despite myself, I laugh. 'You have definitely not changed. I bet he thinks he calls the shots in your relationship. I bet he doesn't realise what a tough cookie you are. You were always like that. The girl who's secretly in charge.'

'You know, not many people know that about me. My dad does.'

'Your dad! How is he? How's your mum?'

'My mum?' She looks taken aback, and rubs her eye. 'Fuck. Don't forget we've lost ten years. Mum died four years ago. She had breast cancer. Dad hasn't come close to getting over it. He's still got that sarcastic wit, but he isn't the same. I know he thinks about her all the time. He was horrible to Lawrence just before we came away. Really made him squirm, but underneath it all, he's just sad. When it was just him and Mum and me, with the outside world shut out, he was completely content. Now, even when I'm there, he knows it's not the same. Even I can't make him happy.'

I take her hand. 'Sophie, I'm so sorry. That's awful news. It must have been terrible for you.'

'It was. It is. But it was no worse than losing my best friend. Sorry to be harsh, but it's true. I know you did it to save yourself, but you must have known what you were doing to everyone you left behind. I read your letter almost every day. I've got it here, with me. At least Mum led a full life. At least she'd had a child and all that. You'd cut yourself down in your prime. That's what everyone thought. Because of your own recklessness.'

'But it turns out I've got children too, and a husband.'

'It's like a bizarre dream. I keep expecting to wake up. I used to dream about finding you, alive and well. But I thought if you'd pulled it off, you'd have let me know, somehow.'

'Sophie, I was dying to let you know. I practically told you before I went. But I couldn't look back. I had the choice between running away, or really jumping off the bridge. If I ran away, I knew I had to do it properly. I couldn't afford for anyone to know what I'd done. Neither running nor jumping was the right choice for you, or for my family. Nor was prison. Don't you see, there wasn't a good option.' I see her about to speak. 'Don't talk to me about the family, by the way. I'm not ready for that.'

'OK. I haven't seen them, or heard anything about them, for years, anyway.'

It's starting to bustle down there. I see a group of three blonde backpackers starting to walk up the hill.

'We're going to have to go. I can't ask you round to the house because as you know I don't live here any more. I'm staying with Margot, my mother-in-law. Can we meet up again later, to talk some more? In a very low-key way?'

'Of course we can. Where and when?'

'Margot and Pete, that's Tony's brother, are going out tonight. Andy and Rachelle are having a housewarming – they were the ones who got married. They've moved into our old house. I can cry off on the grounds of pregnancy, and anyway they know I don't want to go because Andy used to be married to my –' I nearly say 'best', but hold myself back at the last minute – 'my friend Beth. Why don't you come round to the house? If anyone comes home we'll have to switch to a conversation about tax. Come about eight.'

'Pete? Is that Pete who's kind of short and dark and skinny? I spent an evening with him. How weird. He wasn't letting on at all. So, where do I go?'

I tell her. We stand up. As we are about to go, I hold her sleeve.

'Sophie, just you, yes? I'm not ready to talk in front of anyone else. In fact, I never will be.'

'Yes, of course just me. Maybe I'll send Larry round to the housewarming.'

'Warn him that he's a tax inspector. And I can't stress enough how important it is that he doesn't say a word to anyone about me.' I remember her saying he's obsessed with his job. 'What does he do, in real life, anyway? Not tax, presumably?'

'Sophie looks at her feet, suddenly embarrassed. 'He's a journalist,' she admits.

Fuck, fuck and fuck again. I storm around Margot's house, kicking the furniture. I ring Tony, and tell him that the tax people are upsetting me by reminding me of my dead parents.

'Do you want Pete to get the lads to see them off?' he asks immediately. I sense that he's happy that I've mentioned my parents spontaneously.

'Not at the moment. Maybe later.'

'Just say the word. Craggy law can always be applied for you.'

'I know. And I appreciate that.'

Sophie isn't stupid. I don't understand her. I was beginning to think that, together, we might be able to save the situation, that she might be able to go home without ruining my life. It had even occurred to me that, if anyone could keep this secret, it would be Sophie. She might even be able to become a part of our lives: mine and Tony's and Red's and the baby's. They would be delighted to have a friend from England. We might get away with it.

Then she mentions that she has brought a member of the press to my doorstep. She cannot be so naive as to believe that he won't write about me. I know what they are like. Even if he was a genuine and lovely person, and I know that the chances of that are slim, the secret has moved one step away from me. Sophie couldn't keep it to herself. Lawrence has less incentive than she did. It's an interesting piece of gossip. He won't keep it quiet, whatever he says. He'll tell a friend, or a colleague, or his mum, and then it will be one step further still. It will get out. It would, even if he wasn't a journalist. I have been here before. My life is about to fall apart, to shatter. There is nothing I can do to stop it. This morning it was different; it was salvageable. Now it is not.

Margot contorts herself into the room. She's bending under the weight of a cot. It is fully assembled, and it smells of paint.

'Look what Pete got for you!' she says. 'It's second-hand but he gave it a lick of paint.'

'Do I have to take it on the bus?'

'Oh, no worries about that. We'll put it on for you, and Tony can take it off the other end.'

'But I have to change in Adelaide.'

'So one of the blokes can carry it for you.'

'Is it collapsible?'

'Ah, now there's the thing. It was, but now he's painted over the places where it collapses. So the answer is, not any more. You'll be right, though. A lovely cot for the baby, that's what matters.'

'Yes, it is. Thanks, Margot. I'll go over to see Pete in a bit and thank him too.'

'No worries. No worries at all, darling.'

A stupid, non-folding cot is the least of my worries.

chapter eighteen

14 January

I reach for Sophie, like I always do, but she isn't there. As soon as I begin to regain consciousness, I make that movement automatically. I wonder if it means I love her. I think it probably does, but I don't think I love her enough. Today, I do not wonder for long because she has gone.

She does this from time to time, even in London. She gets up early and sneaks away, on her own, for what she insists is 'a walk'. The first time she did it, I assumed I'd been dumped. It was February in London, so she was hardly going to be dancing for dawn joy under the cherry blossom. I had a shower and started getting my things together, savouring the particular humiliation of being dumped at Sophie's flat without even a note, and wondering whether I should leave some vengeful havoc in my wake. Then a key turned in the lock, and she came back, rosy-cheeked and frisky.

'You're up!' she chirruped, putting the kettle on. 'I hoped I might be able to crawl back into bed with you.'

'Where have you been?' I demanded. 'I thought you'd left me.'

'For a walk. I bought the paper and some milk. I'll make you a coffee. You sit down. It's gorgeous out there. All crisp and wintry.'

Sophie, I came to realise, is not like other girls. I do not like the thought of her traipsing around Craggy Rock alone at (I press the button for the light on the clock) ten past six in the morning. Not with all those disturbing men around.

I switch on my bedside light. This room is almost completely dark without electricity. It smells of sweat and sex and dirty clothes. Nora allocated us the end room, so we live further into the hillside than any of the other guests. When the sun is directly overhead, a faint beam forces its way through the air vent, many metres above our heads. Otherwise, it is pitch black.

WORSE PLACES TO BE THAN CRAGGY ROCK
    On a submarine.
    Living in a subway tunnel like the Mole People in New York.
    Stuck, for several days, on a crowded Connex train going nowhere in the rush hour.
    Buried alive, listening to my own funeral.
    Stranded on a desert island with the Parliamentary Conservative Party.

I try not to feel uneasy about Sophie's absence. I know we're on borrowed time. The day is almost upon us when I will have to choose between her and my story. She doesn't know that yet, not unless she's read my notebooks. I wonder if I'm being spineless. I needed her to bring me to the woman who will change my life. I suppose it might have been a more honourable course of action to have stolen the photo, dumped Sophie, and come out here on my own. But Sophie wanted to come so much. To date, I have taken the path of least resistance. The resistance, I feel, cannot be avoided for much longer. It is just around the corner.

I have a weak shower and hope Sophie comes back before I am obliged to wander around looking for her. Today I will dress as a lad on holiday, not a man at work. I decide on shorts, and a PlayStation T-shirt. No one can argue with the power of PlayStation. The T-shirt was actually a freebie. Christie appeared at my desk one November afternoon and threw it down. 'You're the only person I know sad enough to wear this,' she said with a cheeky grin, and walked off. That was before our dalliance. You could say it was during our courtship.

My legs are white, and hairy, but I am pleased that the hairs are blond. If I had black wiry hairs on my legs I'd look really vile. The unformed whiteness of my legs would shine through. I squeeze my stomach. In London I didn't mind that I was developing a sturdy belly. Everyone has one. No one has time to exercise. In fact, by the standards of most of my male acquaintances, I am svelte. The men here, however, mostly work in the opal quarries. They have six-packs and defined muscles. They are fit and tanned. They make me feel ugly and unattractive.

I'm going to feel bad about myself if I choose the story over Sophie. I should think of some activities to boost my self-esteem.

I will start dieting. It's that or exercise, and no one in his right mind would go jogging in this heat. I wrote a piece, last summer, about how the guy who invented jogging had died while indulging in that very pursuit (not exactly original subject matter, I know). It was a feature in which I outlined my manifesto (invented as I went along) for a happy life. Drink coffee in the morning to make everything seem possible. Work hard to earn good money. Drink alcohol in the evening to relax and socialise. Don't worry about exercise. It was crap, but my byline looked good on it, and I decided I was probably right. I had one angry letter, from the British Heart Foundation, betraying a certain disappointment that one as irresponsible as myself was allowed space in a national newspaper. Otherwise, my manifesto was roundly ignored, even by my mother.

Today I, too, will ignore my manifesto commitments, and start slimming.

Purposefully, I walk down the road to the supermarket, holding my stomach in. Normally, we have Danish and coffee, but today I'm going to surprise Sophie by buying fruit for breakfast. And juice. Four Aborigines are sitting outside the shop. One of them shouts something at me, but I ignore him. Race relations are not the strong point of this town. The racial lines appear to be drawn as strongly as they ever were in apartheid South Africa.

It's a drab little shop. There is no piped music, and there is a marked absence of the kind of convenience foods that make my local Tesco Metro a reasonably pleasant consumer experience. Most of the produce is presented in the cardboard boxes in which it was delivered. There are rows and rows of non-perishables. I am unimpressed by the display of two-minute noodles. The pasta looks halfway decent. Everything else must be past its sell-by date. I pick up a jar of pasta sauce whose label has turned brown and is starting to flake off. 'End Feb 1996' advises the label. I consider pointing this out to the nearest shop assistant, but turn away when I see her ferocious face and gladiatorial muscles. She looks more like a Roman gladiator than a contestant from the old TV show. She's not polished enough to join Jade, Hunter, and their gang. Instinctively, I realise that she would not appreciate my pointing out the inadequacies of the stock, so I meekly return it to its pride of place at the top of a precarious pyramid.

When I get to the fresh produce, I realise my diet is up against some fearful odds. The fruit section comprises three melons, a couple of moulding apples, and a wrinkled mango. All the other boxes are empty. It's going to be a Danish after all.

'Hi there, love, how are you going?' bellows someone behind me.

'Fine, thanks,' I say, turning round to see Nora. 'I was hoping to buy some fruit,' I add.

'Fruit, were you? You'll be lucky. The fresh stuff arrives tomorrow morning, that's why. You'd want to come early. Sunday at seven thirty. That's when you see this place heaving with heaps of people.'

That would explain it. 'So this lot has been here for a week?' I gesture to the pathetic display.

'Oh, you don't want to go near that rubbish. Hey, I was looking for you and Sophie, darl. You'll never guess who I saw? That girl in your friend's photo, she came off the bus yesterday. She'll be around town, if you're still looking.'

'Really? That's wonderful news. Thank you very much indeed. Sophie will be delighted.'

Nora winks. 'You're welcome.'

In the cafe, I roll my Danish up into little pieces and eat it slowly, in an attempt to stop myself wanting a second one. I wonder whether Sophie already knows that Daisy's back. It might explain her disappearance. On the other hand, she probably just woke up early and went out. I'm sure the phone didn't ring in the night. I wonder whether I'm the bearer of exciting tidings, or just the person she's left behind in her excitement.

Through the smeared window, I catch sight of her on the other side of the street. I bang on the glass to attract her attention. The three other people in the cafe look at me curiously. She doesn't see me. She's wearing a little dress, and looking exquisite, but she also looks sad. I can't see her with any degree of definition, owing to the dirt that stands between us, but I think she's been crying.

I stand in the doorway. I don't want to get beaten up because the cafe owner thinks I'm trying to leave without paying.

'Sophie!' I call, waving exaggeratedly. At last, she looks over. She crosses the road and allows me to hug her. 'You've been crying,' I tell her.

'I haven't.'

'Yes you have, I can see it. Did you know that Daisy's come back?'

'No.'

I put my arm round her shoulder, and guide her to my table in the cafe.

'Coffee?'

She nods. I go up to the counter, then sit down opposite her. Her eyes are puffy, and she's not looking me in the eye. I wait for her to speak. The coffee arrives. I look around, searching for the right thing to say, the right question to ask. This cafe could do with a lick of paint. There are wide gaps between the windows and the thin plaster walls. It doesn't matter, of course. The windows amplify the heat, whereas the gaps let some air in.

'Actually, I do know she's here,' Sophie admits eventually, and takes a sip of coffee. She winces. I think she's burnt her tongue.

'Did you see her?'

'Yes.'

'Did you talk? Is that what's upset you?'

'No, I stubbed my toe. Of course that's what's bloody upset me.'

I could be imagining it, but I think she's a little hostile towards me.

'Did you bump into her? Or did you get up early to go and find her?'

'Look, don't you get all resentful with me. She wouldn't have spoken to me if you'd been there. I am entitled to see my best friend on my own, you know.'

'I didn't say you weren't. Christ!'

'Well, I got up early because I couldn't sleep. You were out for the count and I knew it would be beautiful outside. I went for a walk, and I walked up this hill, and at the top I saw a woman. I didn't think it was her, not even for a second. You see, this woman was heavily pregnant. She looked nothing like Daisy from the back. So

I said excuse me, because I just wanted to know what time it was. She turned round, and then I saw that it was her.'

'Did she pretend not to know you this time?'

'No. She talked to me straightaway. She wouldn't say where she lives now, but she came back because she heard that we were here looking for her and she didn't want us turning up at her new home.'

'Sophie, that is absolutely wonderful. Well done! We lured her back.'

'Yeah. Well done all right.'

'What? This is what you came for. I don't understand what the problem is.'

'I suppose you don't. Lawrence, you're the problem.'

'Moi?'

'Oui, toi.'

'Why?'

'Well, Daisy and I were getting on fine. It was incredibly strange, but we were kind of managing to talk to each other, and I promised her I wasn't going to ruin her life, because she's married and everything, and her baby's due in a couple of months.'

'And the problem is?' I am uneasy now.

'She was quite worried that I'd brought someone with me, because she doesn't want anyone to know who she used to be. I promised her you weren't going to tell anyone, and that was OK until she asked me what you did. I'd been talking about how you're so into your career, and later on she asked what your career was, and as soon as I said the word journalism, she just collapsed. I was worried about the baby.'

'Don't you trust me?'

'I did trust you, because you made me a promise. Now I'm not so sure. Daisy said I was being incredibly naive and that no journalist, and particularly not one who's obsessed with his career, is going to walk away from a situation like that. And I thought about it, and I thought, she's right.'

'So you really don't trust me.'

'It's not a question of trust. It's a question of knowing what your priorities are. I should never have expected you to be able to keep this secret. And yet I wouldn't even have come here again, or not so soon, if it wasn't for you. Tell me honestly, Larry, *please*, did you get our tickets out here because you wanted to get the story?'

'No, I did it because I knew it would make you happy. We've been through this before.'

'You see, now I can suddenly see that she's right. You're lying.'

'No I'm not.'

'Look me in the eye and tell me that you will come home with me next week and never ever breathe a word to anyone about the fact that someone we all thought was dead is in fact alive and well with a happy family life, and living in Australia.'

I take a deep breath, look her straight in the eye, and give it my best shot.

'I won't say anything, Sophie. I really won't. Not if Daisy doesn't want me to.' Suddenly, I realise that I don't need to lie any more. I should be taping Sophie, talking about her. If 'Lina' has admitted to Sophie that she used to be Daisy, then all I need is Sophie's story, and I've got it in the bag. Even though I'm not taping her, I know my story's true, and it is on my doorstep. Perhaps I should try to talk Sophie round. With her on my side, we could persuade Daisy that doing an interview with me would be the best course of action available to her. She might hate me for a while, but it would work out in the end.

'Actually,' I say.

'Here we go.' I've never heard Sophie sound bitter before.

'All I'm saying, Soph, is that actually, now that you and I know that this is Daisy, the story's bound to get out sooner or later. She might even want it to. It seems to me that the best course of action all round might be for me to do a sympathetic interview with her. Then she would have a chance to put her side of the story before anyone else gets in there first.'

Sophie looks at me with a poisonous expression I've never seen before.

'Larry, you know perfectly well that if you write about her in the paper, she'll end up in prison. You *know* that. If the only reason you're here is for your story, just fucking well say so. It's me, remember? Sophie, your supposed girlfriend. I know you steal your colleagues' stories, and I'm sure you've used that "better for you to do a sympathetic interview" line many times before and equally I'm sure you sometimes get people into a position where they have to go along with it, but Larry, this is me. I know you. I'm supposed to be your fucking fiancée. You're not supposed to screw *me* over for a story. The bottom line is,' she says, glaring at me, 'that if you publicise the fact that Daisy's here, she'll go to prison. And it'll be in the paper for a week, and then everyone'll forget about it. And you will have ruined her life. What about her little boy, and her unborn baby?'

'What about the people she killed?'

'That was eleven years ago. She was as much a victim as they were. She didn't do it on purpose.'

'Surely that judgement should be left to the criminal justice system. And she jumped bail. She's a fugitive. There's nothing wrong with bringing a fugitive to justice. In fact, it would arguably be wrong to do anything else.'

We are talking quietly, because we both know it would be disastrous if we were overheard. I need my exclusive. We hiss at each other. As I suspected, Sophie seems to have forgotten that she's supposed to love me. Part of me wants to cave in, to promise her that I'll keep the secret. Even though she hates me, Sophie is still the best girlfriend I've ever had, by a long chalk. We've had happy times together. She's been good for me. Everyone has said that. If my main ambition in life was to get married and have a couple of kids and a stable family life, I'd put Sophie above the story and sacrifice my big break for the sake of her and her friend.

I know I don't have a choice. I've known all along what I'm going to do. I have dreamed about it, day and night. I bought the tickets and put up with the heat and the discomfort and the humiliation, for one reason. In many ways, I would love to be the kind of man who's selfless enough to give up a chance like this for love, but I know I'm not.

'Don't pretend to be so bloody righteous,' she says quietly, and with venom. 'You wouldn't know morality if it bit you on the bum. This isn't about the administration of justice, and nobody's going to believe you if you say it is. This is about Larry Golchin and his career.'

'What did you expect me to do? This will make me. It will transform my life. You can't have seriously expected me to sit back and ignore it.'

'Call me stupid, Larry, but actually I did. I thought you were a good person, underneath it all, and I believed you cared about me and about our future together.' She is blinking furiously.

'I do care about you.'

'Like fuck you do.' She pushes aside her empty coffee mug, stands up, and walks out without looking at me.

I watch her departure. Sophie is walking out of my life. I wait for her to come back. She'll have to. She'll need to ask me what I'm going to do next, so she can warn her friend. After a few minutes, I order myself another coffee. Then I ask for a second Danish to go with it. I hope I've got enough cash on me to cover my bill and Sophie's too.

I decide to prioritise. Now that I'm on my own, I have to get everything right.

THINGS TO DO
1. Find out where Daisy is staying (Nora will know).
2. Confront her, take some pix, and get a reaction. If necessary can write story without conclusively saying it is her.
3. Ask some locals for reaction to fugitive in their midst.
4. Call Patricia in London and offer story.
5. Alert Scotland Yard/Australian equivalent.
6. Sit back and watch career and story take off.

I have to leave my credit card with the cafe guy, even though they don't take them. I'll get it back when I return with the two dollars that I lack.

'I can't get the money out without the card,' I tell him.

'Should have thought of that before,' he retorts, and I realise I'm going to have to get it from Sophie. How ignominious, to betray my girlfriend, to watch her leave me, and then to go crawling back for two dollars and twelve cents.

Nora is overjoyed to see me.

'Your things are here, darl,' she grins, ushering me to her side of the reception desk. I see my suitcase, my shoulder bag, and a few odd items on top of them.

'Did Sophie put them there?' I wonder what she told Nora.

'She did, love. I gather there's been something of a domestic. Don't worry. It'll blow over. Now, do you want to wait and talk to her, or will I give you a room of your own for now?'

I indicate the direction of our old room. 'Is she in there?'

'She went out, love.'

'You'd better give me a new one, for now.' I try to look rueful. 'It was my fault,' I add.

'So she said. You've got a sweet one there, if you don't mind me saying so. Try to hang on to her.'

'I will, Nora, don't worry.'

I take the key. I need a room more than ever, now. This one will be my strategy centre. My plotting room. It will be the centre of my operation.

chapter nineteen

'I tell you, I've never known a boy make so many friends, so quickly. He's in his element, Lina. We shouldn't have worried about moving him, not for a second. He misses you. Keeps asking me when you'll be back.'

'So you'll want to know what to tell him.'

'Forget what to tell *him*. I want to know for my own purposes. I miss my wife and my little babe.'

'And we miss you too. Your babe has had his or her knobbly feet stuck in my ribs ever since we left, but we're both absolutely fine. Look, Tony, is it OK for you to talk? I mean, no one's listening, are they?'

'Home alone, darling. He's gone to Beth's with his new mate Daniel. She lets them play cricket on deck. And fish the balls out of the river with her net. The woman has the patience of a saint.'

'Good. I hate to even talk about this, my love – I'd far rather be chatting about Red and the cricket balls – but it's something quite important. Things are about to get complicated.'

'How do you mean? Is it those tax people?'

'Sort of. You see, it turns out that they're not really tax people at all, but they are from England and they are connected with my childhood there. At least, one of them is. She used to be my best friend.'

'Hey – childhood. Well done. That's good, isn't it?'

'Not really. It's good to see her, in many ways, but it's more complicated than that.'

'You mean all that stuff with your parents?'

'I've never told you the full story.' I stop myself. I have to be honest now. 'I've never told you the *true* story. I'm so sorry, Tony. I just couldn't. It was too difficult.'

'What are you saying?'

'About my life before I met you. Before I met Red and before I came to Australia.'

'We've been through this before, haven't we? If your friend's here, then bring her down to meet us. That's what I've always wanted. Lina, I know you've never wanted to talk about it, and you still don't have to if it upsets you. You're about to have a baby. My job is to look after you. Beth made me see that. Not to nosy around in your past. We've got our own past now. Three years' worth.'

'Do you mean that?'

'Don't I sound like I mean it?'

'But do you really mean it? I mean, are you saying that I could tell you anything at all about my life in England and it wouldn't change how you felt about me?'

'It couldn't. The only thing that's ever bothered me has been not knowing. I kind of know you didn't go up to Craggy just to sort out some money. You went to have a break from me, and that means I haven't been looking after you like I should.'

His belated concern for me is breaking my heart.

'That's not true. I wish I didn't have to do this on the phone.'

'So come home. Bring your mate.'

'No time. Listen, this is really hard, but I'm going to have to do it. What if I told you my name wasn't originally Lina, or Noeline, and that I'd broken the law in a wide – enormous – variety of ways? What if I'd run away on bail, and I was likely to go to prison?'

'How do you mean?'

'Just go along with me for now.'

'I'd be surprised. And I'd want to know what you'd done. You know I've been no angel myself. As long as you hadn't killed anyone, that would be OK, I guess. But you don't mean going to prison now, do you?'

I ignore that salient point. 'What if I'd killed people by accident?'

Tony pauses. 'Babe, you're freaking me out.'

'What if you might have already read my name in the paper?'

'I know your name.'

'My original name. My birth name. My other name. I don't think of it as my real name, but I suppose you could call it that. What if I was someone who had been vaguely well known a while ago?'

'I doubt your fame could have reached Craggy Rock.'

'Actually, I think you're right. I was only briefly notorious in Britain. Otherwise I'd never have made it all the way out here. Have you ever heard of a girl called Daisy Fraser?'

'No.'

'She was a British girl who got into loads of trouble. She was one of those wild children who go out drinking and taking drugs underage.'

'Like Drew Barrymore?'

'Not that extreme, but yes. And like Drew Barrymore, she's been rehabilitated. She went to boarding school to learn to be a dancer. She used to go out a lot in London, even though she wasn't allowed to. One day she bought some drugs on behalf of all her friends, and they turned out to be contaminated, and, because they injected them, four people died. She didn't do it on purpose.'

'So what happened to her?'

'She was arrested for supplying and on suspicion of manslaughter. There was a huge amount of publicity about it because she was so young and she went to a famous ballet school. So she was out on bail, and she committed suicide. She wrote suicide notes to everyone she knew, and to a newspaper, and to her school, and drove her car to the Severn Bridge. It separates England from Wales. Then she jumped off it. Her body was never found.'

'What you're telling me is, she didn't actually die?'

My voice will scarcely come out. 'Yes. No. I mean, I am telling you that. She ran away. She bought a new identity. She did a deal with her drug dealer that she'd keep the dealer's name out of it, and she'd get a new passport.'

'What was the name in the passport?'

'What do you think it was?'

'Noeline Jennings?'

I nod. I know he can't hear me, so I manage to say, 'Yes.' Then I add, 'No one knows that in the whole world.'

Tony doesn't say anything. I'm not sure if he's still there.

'I'm just going to fetch a drink,' he says in the end. 'In fact, I'll call you later.'

'Tell Beth, if you like.'
He hangs up.

I know I am about to lose him. And I know that, although I have custody now, purely thanks to the fact that the baby is still in my womb, Tony will be the one who brings up our child. I will be locked up. Years ago, I checked out Australia's extradition treaty with the UK. Needless to say, they have one. Australia, after all, started off as the extradition centre. If only I could convince a court that I'd punished myself by transporting myself to a former penal colony. No one would buy that. Everyone knows the former penal colony offers a better quality of life.

Even if I didn't end up in prison, there's no way that a judge would offer custody to a dead drug dealer rather than a genuine, hard-working, honest Australian. Tony may have a criminal record, but he's no fugitive. And he's never killed anyone. Even Red might be better off with Tony. I pace around the house, thankful that everyone's at the party. If Red stays with Tony, and the baby goes to him too, and if I'm alone, in a cell – and I really think it will come to that – then nothing will be left of my life. Nothing. I turned my back on everyone when I left England. I built myself a new, dishonest life. I always knew that I had to lie to everyone, and that everything I gained, I gained only on the understanding that I could lose it all at any time. And I knew all along that, if that happened, I might as well find a bridge and jump off it this time.

I can't do that while I'm pregnant. I will have to have the baby first. I stroke it. The poor little chicken is feeling what I'm feeling now, and must be wondering where its safe, calm world has gone. Suddenly, it is swamped by misery, guilt and despair. It's probably already psychologically scarred. I owe it the best I can give it, and at the moment, all I can offer is my survival until its birth.

I switch the television on. It is an old episode of *Coronation Street*. I switch over in disgust, and eventually slump in front of the adverts. I can cope as well with Aussie kids being Weetbix kids as I can with anything else.

I haven't thought about why I ran away. Not for years. I'm not strong enough. If I'm not strong enough to think about it, then how will I cope with seeing it analysed in the world's newspapers? I know that the sensible answer is to ignore the papers, but I couldn't do that last time, and this time it is beside the point. It's not what the journalists say about me that's going to matter. It's the fact that Craggy Rock will be invaded – Renmark, too, when they discover it – and all my friends, family and acquaintances will be interviewed about me, and (oh fuck, this is the worst of all) my original family, my parents, and Eddy and Rosie, will be dragged away from whatever lives they now have, to join in the slagging off. And they will have every right to do that. And I will be arrested. I hope they let me wait till the baby's born. I try to imagine myself as an ashen-faced woman in prison uniform, giving birth while chained to a hospital bed.

Somebody bangs on the door. I do not have the energy to get up. Margot's air-conditioned shack is my temporary haven, and this is likely to be one, or a combination, of three people. Sophie. Sophie's scummy boyfriend, Larry. Tony, come to confront me. I strike Tony from the list. He hasn't had time to get here. But he has had time to call Pete to come and tackle me on his behalf. Perhaps it's someone entirely different, in which case I will have to pull myself together.

I lever myself up, and shuffle to the door. This morning I felt crisp and capable in my Capri pants and my shirt. Now I am crumpled, huge and ungainly.

It is, under the circumstances, the best person it could be. She is alone.

'Come in,' I say weakly. Sophie looks almost as miserable as I feel. I lead her back into the lounge, and switch off the television, which is now showing a mindless game show.

'I'll pour you a drink,' I say. 'Unless you're pregnant too?'

'Not that I know of.'

'Or a recovering alcoholic?'

'Not recovering. I'm just getting started.'

Margot has a fine stock of whisky. I give her a bottle every birthday and every Christmas, to ensure there is always some in the house if I want it. Over the years, I've varied it between different brands of Scotch and Irish. Once I even bought a bottle of 'Mount Everest' whisky from Clarrie after a traveller left it at the Backpackers'. It claimed to be 'the world's fifth selling whisky', a claim I would love to see supported by fact.

'Here.' I hand Sophie a glass of Teacher's. Margot likes that one, because I am a teacher. She calls it 'Lina's special drink' and saves it for when Tony and I are there. Between the three of us, we can drink a bottle in an evening.

'You look like things aren't going so well,' I add. 'That seems to me to spell disaster.'

'Daisy, I don't know what to say. Lawrence promised me he was coming with me to help me find you, and that he wasn't going to write about it. If I'd thought for an instant that he was lying . . .' She stops and looks at me. 'It was staring me in the face, of course. My dad saw straight through him. If I'd told Dad why we were coming here, he'd have stopped me. I was so excited about seeing you that I didn't allow myself even to consider what Larry might do. I've ruined everything, haven't I?'

'That depends, rather. Tell me what's happened with him today.'

As she tells me about meeting him in the cafe, and his admission that, naturally, he was not planning to pass up on this story, I watch her drinking, and wish I could blot out the mounting horrors by any kind of artificial means. I'd even go back to speed if it didn't cross the placenta. I assume it does.

'I moved his stuff out of the room before he came back,' she finishes. 'I'm keeping our room. Nora's put him in a different one. I don't know what we can do.'

'You don't want to see this in the papers, then?'

She stares at me. 'Why would I?'

'Oh, I wouldn't blame you. You said this morning, what I did to you and to Mum and the twins was horrendous. You said it was just as bad as when your mother died. I hadn't been able to think about that before.'

'Forget that. That's the least of our worries now. Water under the bridge.' She looks up at me and smiles. 'So to speak. You did what you had to do. What about the future?'

'I could be extradited and tried. In fact, I'm sure that's what'll happen unless I quickly escape to somewhere without an extradition treaty, and I'm too pregnant to fly to Brazil. Or to anywhere else.'

'Do you really think they'd bother? They were never going to charge you with murder, and it did happen a long time ago.'

'There are a lot of bereaved families out there who I imagine won't rest until they see me put away. They're not exactly obscure people.'

'Daisy, I think we should run away. We could go tonight. That was what I was thinking. It won't take Lawrence five minutes to discover that you're in this house. He's probably got the address off Nora already, and a little map drawn to go with it. Once he turns up on the doorstep, you will essentially be public property. I warn you, when he's on the case he can be a cunt. If we go right now, we could get away, somewhere.'

'I've been thinking the same. Any ideas where?'

'Into the desert. The perfect place. Have you got a car?'

'Not here, but we could take Margot's. Say we do. There's a chance that Lawrence and the police and everyone else would get the registration number. So we disappear into the desert for a week or two, but we can't stay there for ever. We'll always be looking over our shoulders for the police, like Thelma and pregnant Louise, and look how they ended up. Say we swap the car for a rental car, then the car rental people will have our details and the bank will be able to trace us, and in no time everyone would have the new registration. I can't leave Australia, because they'll be looking out for me at the airports. I can't go anywhere without Red, so we'd have to go and pick him up, and then either we'd see Tony or he'd go out of his mind with worry about what had happened to Red. I can't work out how we could do it properly.'

'You did last time.'

'It took weeks and weeks of meticulous planning. I've been thinking about this, because you're right, it is the obvious thing to do, but I can't make it work this time. I'd like to charter a plane to take us somewhere like Papua New Guinea. Is there anything at all we can do to call him off?'

She shakes her head.

'I told Tony.'

I should be crying by now, but I'm not. I'm not feeling anything. I know that I'm going to have to call on reserves of strength to get me through this. I have to think about the baby. I can't fall apart. Suddenly, this house seems like a trap. I'm sitting in it, waiting for the next knock at the door. When it comes, it will be Lawrence the pink journalist.

'I led him to you. It's the worst thing I could possibly have done.'

'I wish I'd spoken to you at the wedding. I was too shocked. If I'd managed it, this might not be happening.'

'It would still have happened, as long as Larry was in my life.'

'How long were you together?'

'Less than a year. I was away for four months of that. What's going to happen with you and Tony, do you think?'

'I don't hold out much hope. He didn't really take it all in. I only spoke to him about an hour before you arrived. It's our third wedding anniversary next week.' I can't bear it. I stand up. 'Let's go.'

'Where to?'

'The desert. If your friend comes looking for us here, then at least he won't find us. He would never in a million years locate us where we're going now. In fact, let's go away all night, and then see what we want to do after that. Fuck being sensible. We have to get out of here.'

'Are you sure? Isn't it dangerous? In your condition?'

'No, it's more dangerous to stay behind, especially in my condition.' I rush into Red's bedroom and pack some of my things back into my bag. I add my toothbrush, toothpaste and moisturiser, and put on a sweater. I write a note on the kitchen worktop. 'Margot,' I write, 'I've borrowed the car for a while. Nothing to worry about – I just wanted to show Sophie, the girl from England, some of the local sights. Have also taken the torch. See you later, hope you've had a good evening, love Lina x.' It's as jaunty, and as ambiguous, as I can make it.

I'm exhilarated as we drive away, but I drive as cautiously as I can. You never know when a kangaroo's going to appear from the darkness and land on your bonnet. I don't want the seatbelt to slice into my womb. We're running away. We have no plan. We don't know where we'll sleep tonight. In the car, probably. We'll have to go to Renmark soon, and after that, we'll be able to do whatever we like, as long as we're not found. I'll find somewhere to have the baby. I'm going to miss an antenatal appointment tomorrow. As it's in Renmark, I'd have missed it even if we'd stayed in Craggy. I'd sense it if there was anything wrong with the baby. It's all right. I know it is.

Sophie and I grin at each other. Margot's car is hardly glamorous – it's small and full of junk, and I had to throw lolly wrappers and old magazines into the back just to make room for Sophie in the passenger seat – but suddenly I feel a new respect for it. It is our ticket out of here.

Our smiles fade quickly. This is an unusual situation. I ruined her life by pretending to die, and she's done the same to me by bringing her boyfriend here. Now we are both attempting an escape, for the sake of an unborn baby. Somehow, underneath it all, I feel as though we've never been apart.

I veer off the tarmac road down a rocky track. We bump along in silence for a while. I begin to wonder about the details of the plan.

'Have you seen the stars?' I ask her, after a few minutes. She bends forward and looks up through the windscreen.

'They are fantastic,' she concedes.

'Wait till we see them from the top of the rock.'

'What rock?'

'You'll see. I always think of it as Craggy Rock, but I think that's just a generic term given to the place by some English settlers who thought it sounded appropriate.'

I drive for ten minutes. The main amusement Craggy has to offer me has always been the climbing of hills. I've never found this strange before.

Finally, I stop the car, in the middle of nowhere.

'We're here,' I say as cheerfully as I can. I'm wondering, now, whether this is freedom or folly. It is hardly a bed for a night, but it's the only place I could think of. We'll go somewhere else from here. We'll drive all night. I switch on the torch, and lead Sophie up the path, wishing that I had my usual energy. In the winter, Red and I used to race up this hill, and when we got to the top, we'd lie down and pant and laugh and look at the sky. Tonight, I take slow steps and pause to breathe every couple of seconds. I hate being incapacitated.

'Here,' says Sophie, taking the torch from me. 'We're just going up, yeah?'

'We are. You'll know when you get there.'

'You don't mind if I go ahead, do you?'

'That's fine. I'll be with you as soon as I can. Be careful where you step. I can see by the moonlight – I'm used to it. You're not.'

My head is hurting. I've been having strong Braxton Hicks contractions all day, and even though there's nothing in them that makes me feel anything's actually happening, I am still constantly alert for any sign that this trauma is driving the baby out of its cosy home in the womb. What happens if I go into labour miles from anywhere?

If that happened now, the baby would be premature, and it would need medical attention. Without it, it might die. I feel guilty about this child's wellbeing before it's even been born, and I cannot imagine what family situation it will be born into. Will it have two parents and a brother? Will it have a doting grandmother? Will it live in Renmark? All the certainties of its little life are gone.

Eventually, I struggle to the very top of the hill. Sophie is lying on her back, in exactly the way Red and I used to. She's looking at the stars.

'Sometimes Tony and I used to come up here with a bottle of wine,' I say.

She props herself up on her elbows, and smiles.

'We could have brought one now,' I add, 'except I never remember to think about anyone else's drinking requirements now that I don't have any of my own.'

'Doesn't matter.'

'We are in an odd situation.'

'We certainly are. Tell me what happened when you ran away. I mean, how the fuck did you manage it? My dad always says you couldn't possibly have done it, because everyone was looking out for you and it simply wasn't possible.' She does an impression of her father. '"Your mother and I were very fond of Daisy, and without a doubt she had a degree of intelligence, but no one, least of all a girl with her problems, could have contrived an escape like that one." He thought I was being sad, or mad, fantasising that you were still alive.'

'Did you believe it all along?'

'Not really. I always told myself that I was just hanging on to false hope because I hadn't seen your body. That was what my head said, the same as everyone told me. In my heart, though, I think I always knew the truth. I never let go of the absolute conviction that we'd meet again one day. I used to dream about you, and I'd wake up happy. I thought if I saw you again then the rest of my life would be one long smile. I thought I could never be miserable if you came back to life. I suppose everyone thinks that way when someone dies, don't they?'

'I'm sure they do. I had a friend here, Nina. She died recently. I have those thoughts about her, even though she had a brain tumour, and I saw her body.'

For a moment, I think of the trip we made to Adelaide, to be with Nina when it was clear she was about to die. In many ways, she was dead already. She was alive, and awake, but she was barely there at all. Her two sons clung to their father, scared of her. Her eyes were hollow, and she squeezed my hand weakly. We all went back to our motel for the night, and by morning, she had died. My lively friend was gone. Sophie's lively friend went in the same way, and now I'm back.

'I do wish I'd let you know in some way that I was all right,' I tell Sophie. 'I could have done it, couldn't I, without giving everything away? You know when you came in and saw the passport? I was quite relieved then, even though it wasn't what I'd intended at all. I thought you'd know. Once I got away, I found I could only deal with things by blocking them out completely. I forced myself not to think about anyone or anything I'd left behind, because if I became preoccupied with, say, seeing you again, I thought I'd never be able to live out the rest of my days without leaving Australia, and I knew I had to do that. Are you angry with me?'

'I was, I was furious. Not any more. I don't think I can be. I don't have the right to anger, not after I put you in this mess.'

'This is the lull before the storm, you know.' She nods. 'Even if we run away, it won't last. Is there anything whatsoever that we could do to stop him?'

'I wish there was.'

'The only solution I can think of is very much an Outback one, and I don't think that would get us very far.'

'You mean violence?'

'There are guys in this town who would do anything if Tony asked them to. Christ, Tony would do it himself.'

'We can't actually *kill* Larry.'

'I suppose not. I was thinking more of having him dumped in the desert and leaving him there to fend for himself.'

'How long would he last?'

'He wouldn't. Last month they found the body of a Dutch boy not far from here. He'd wandered away from a tour, got himself completely lost, and in the four hours he was missing, his body had dehydrated so much he was desiccated, like a mummy. He was only nineteen.'

'So the dumping in the desert option is kind of the same as the killing option.'

'Well, yes. Tempting as it is, I think I'm just going to have to face what's coming. Sooner or later.'

'First of all, tell me what happened.'

'Can I tell you later? How long are you staying in Australia?'

In the silvery moonlight, I can see from Sophie's expression that she hasn't thought about it.

'Our tickets home are for next Friday,' she says slowly. 'I haven't got a job at home. I've just been temping since I got back from Australia – see how you unsettled me? – so I haven't got much to hurry back for. I'll change the ticket and stay out here as long as I need to.'

'You could live here.'

'Maybe. So, OK, you can tell me later. That's fine.'

'I haven't thought about England for years. It feels like it all happened to a different person. I suppose that kind of separation is the only way to stay sane.'

'It must have been. I hope you haven't got it all stored up, undealt with, in your psyche.'

'I don't think the major trauma's going to come and get me in the night. That was so horrendous at the time that I imagine I must have worked through it, or whatever you're meant to do. I don't think about the guys at all any more. You know, the ones who died. I can't bear to.'

'It was a long time ago, Daze. You're allowed to get over it.'

I lean back and look at the stars. They are bright, each one defined. I like the smudges where they seem to merge together despite being millions of miles apart. When I look at the Outback sky, I can see why people used to believe they were protected by a giant dome with holes pricked into it, and the light of heaven shining through. I take a deep breath of warm night air. I can smell the faint scent of a plant we must have trodden underfoot. I killed people. It was me. Everyone's going to know.

'There's the Southern Cross,' I say, pointing it out. 'You'll never ever see that one in England. If we stay out here long enough, you'll see it move across the sky. I've always loved the Southern Cross.'

'It reminds you that you're not at home?'

'It reminds me that I am.'

I remember the day it all started; the terrifying arrival at the new school, the tearful goodbye to Sophie, the shocking unfamiliarity of everything and everyone around me. My instinct was to retreat into my shell, and yet that was the one thing I'd promised myself I wouldn't do. This was my opportunity – the first – for self-reinvention. It turned out to be something I was good at. I gritted my teeth, and told myself to conquer my shyness and be popular, whatever that took.

You won't be the best in the class any more, twelve-year-old Daisy said to herself, clenching her fists. You won't be the youngest, either. You won't know what's going on, or where to go, or what to take with you.

Outdoors and in, the big stone house was teeming with athletic girls, their parents, and the occasional, robust looking boy. Parental vehicles, almost all of them grander than the Maxi, were parked everywhere, and boxes and cases were piled up next to them. Daisy wished it was the end of term, and that the boxes were going in, rather than out. All the girls were greeting each other enthusiastically. They paid her no attention at all. She was invisible. She barely existed.

'Jacqui!' yelled a ginger-haired girl right next to Daisy's left ear. Jacqui, who was standing primly on the grass beside her mother, was blonde and held herself like a proper dancer. She bounded over and the two girls embraced and hopped around each other.

'Happy to be back?' demanded the redhead, raising her eyebrows to signal her irony.

'Oh, we had a wonderful holiday,' Jacqui gushed, pointing a leg behind her. 'We went to St Lucia. I danced on the beach every morning and then a man made me enter a talent show, and guess what? I got the silver medal!'

'I went to summer school in Paris. It was brilliant! We put on a new ballet. Michel choreographed it specially. *Figaro* reviewed it!'

Daisy looked at Sophie. Her mouth was open.

'No real ballerinas have red hair,' Sophie managed to whisper.

It transpired that they probably did. That little girl, Mary Futter (or Maria Fortinova as she rechristened herself) was briefly a member of the Academy corps de ballet, and an important mainstay of both the black hair dye and the 'diet pill' industries, until her untimely death, in an amphetamines incident, at the age of nineteen.

The dormitories were clean and warm. It was the temperature that Daisy noticed first; her family home was so draughty that she was used to huddling in bed wearing pyjamas, a sweatshirt, and two pairs of socks. Here, girls were strutting around in leotards and tights. Some of them didn't even wear their ballet cardigans. She didn't think she'd need a jumper here from one term to the next. She breathed in the institutional smell. It was the smell of her new life.

As I lie on the rock now, I can smell it as though I were back there. It was a smell of polished floors, and mass catering, and excitement. In some parts of the building you could smell the ballet paraphernalia: the sweat, the chalk to stop pointe shoes slipping, the discarded tights.

Together, the two girls located Daisy's dormitory, and sat on her bed. It was surprisingly comfortable. There were only four beds in the room, and one of the occupants wasn't there yet. Daisy was petrified, but was quashing her fear as much as she could. For now, she ignored her roommates, and concentrated on the bed linen. There were nice big duvets – hers had a plain blue cover – and the furniture was pine.

'Are you going to be all right?' whispered Sophie. 'It's a bit posh.'

'I'll show them,' Daisy grinned, pushing her fingernails into her palms.

One of the other girls was watching them curiously. She was tall and willowy, with blonde hair. In fact, she looked like a girl from an advert.

'Have this,' Sophie said to Daisy, and took her hand. She wrapped Daisy's fingers round a small packet. Before she could open it, Dad came back into the room with her last bag.

'Your luggage, madame,' he said in a joking, pompous voice that made Daisy cringe. She looked at the blonde girl, but she didn't seem to notice his presence at all. He turned to Sophie. 'And as for you, ma'am, your carriage awaits. Fraser's cabs at your disposal.'

'Are you going, then?' Daisy asked.

'We have to if we're going to beat the traffic,' he confirmed.

She and Sophie exchanged glances and stood up. Daisy took both her hands.

'I'll write,' Daisy told her.

'So will I. Every day.'

Dad stepped in, and gave Daisy a horrible hug. She cringed away from him.

'Look after yourself,' he told her. 'See you at half term.'

Daisy didn't go down to wave them off. She was on her own.

The room was silent for five minutes.

'Hi,' said the blonde girl languidly. She offered her hand. Daisy had never shaken anybody's hand before. She remembered that this was her opportunity to be someone new, and before she had time to think about it, she drew the tiny, pale hand to her lips, and kissed it. The blonde girl laughed.

'Pleased to meet you,' she said. 'My name's Leila.'

'I'm Daisy.' They grinned at each other.

She couldn't believe she'd pulled it off.

'Remember the necklace you gave me at the Academy?' I ask Sophie. I know I shouldn't lie on my back for too long, because the weight of the baby can cut off the blood supply to all sorts of important locations. Who would have imagined that tiny little dancer growing into the lumbering heffalump that I am today?

'Mmm?'

'It's the only thing I brought with me. That and the clothes I was standing up in. I've still got it.'

'You haven't?'

I reach inside my shirt and take it out. There's a small, silver fairy on the chain around my neck. I've never taken it off. Sophie sits up and looks at it.

'Bloody hell,' she says after a while.

'Funny, isn't it? So I was thinking of you all the time. I had to tell Tony my mother gave it to me when I was little.'

'You've really worn it all the time? I didn't even know you kept it. I assumed you'd probably lost it when we were about thirteen. Did you have it on at that wedding?'

'Always.'

We look at each other and burst out laughing.

'You know,' she says after a while, 'I was so jealous of you, that day at the Academy.'

'You never said.'

'Of course I didn't. But we'd been dancing since we were so tiny, and this was ballet school. It wasn't even just ballet school – it was the Academy, the best. We'd talked about it practically all our lives. There you were, training to be a dancer, and there I was, going back to school, where they told my mum I couldn't be in the circus because I was too short. Do you remember, I made her ask at parents' evening once? And they said I had to learn to type instead. And on top of that, at ballet I was the only twelve-year-old in that class and I had no one to talk to. I used to screw it all up on purpose, just so I'd get kept down. Miss Mary knew exactly what I was doing, but she never said.'

'Why didn't you audition, with me?'

'It was you she kept behind after class, not me. I didn't feel I had the option.'

'You must have hated me.'

'I didn't hate you. It wasn't your fault. I did miss you.'

'Did you learn to type?'

'We all end up knowing how to type these days, don't we, by default. We had a few lessons in school. We'd sit in front of those clunky old BBC computers with tape recorders attached. I don't suppose you had to do that at ballet school.'

'They tried their hardest to pretend to give us a rounded education, but no dancer is going to voluntarily spend hours typing when they could be grand jete-ing across the room.'

'We had to type out "The quick brown fox jumped over the lazy dog", and "He said she said they said Fred's dead". The computer would sound this big clanging alarm if you made a mistake. But in spite of my teachers' expectations, I didn't end up as a secretary. I went to uni and studied English. I specialised in Chaucer, and I loved it. I loved the literature.'

'Where did you go?'

'UCL. I lost myself in London for a while. I saw you in crowds over and over again.'

'You know I was an English teacher?' Sophie nods, smiling. 'I mean, how unlikely is that? I wish I'd finished my education. I've thought about doing a degree time and time again, but there are limited opportunities round here. I'd have had to do it by correspondence, and that didn't appeal so much. Writing essays at the kitchen table seemed like an unnecessary extra complication. I haven't even got any A levels.'

'You can still do it.'

'Maybe.'

'Is there a uni where you live now?'

I think about Renmark. I'm fairly sure Flinders University has a campus nearby. 'Near enough. If this doesn't blow up too much, I could enrol there.'

I shut my eyes, and see the imprint of an iris on the inside of my eyelid. It's yellow and black and throbbing. I feel a little bit dizzy. I am intoxicated and scared by the fact that I am now allowed to remember my early years. I've shut them out for so long, and now they are back.

I'm so tired. I roll over onto my side and pull up my legs. I should have brought a pillow out, to tuck under the bump. It makes sleep so much easier. I remember Mrs Thickett, the Australian woman who tried to keep me and Leila on the straight and narrow. I respect her, now. I wonder whether she's still alive.

It was Mrs Thickett who noticed, long before the dance teachers, that Leila and I were wilfully swerving off the rails. When we were fourteen, our transgressions involved nothing more serious than running up and down the fire escapes simply because we weren't allowed to; and walking innocently to the edges of the grounds and stepping outside into the street – the Real World – for a few minutes at a time. Our fantasies about running away into London and doing any number of forbidden things were unformed, and did not, as yet, involve boys in anything more than the vaguest of ways. Pathetic though this rebellion was, Mrs Thickett kept catching us. We would be late for registration because we'd been deep in conversation, or we'd drop bits of lunch onto the dining room floor, and she would be the one to spot us. One day, she kept us behind after classes.

'Mrs Thickett,' said Leila, graciously batting her lashes and smiling winningly. 'We really can't stay. We have a national dance class at four thirty and as you know we're expected to eat something first to keep our strength up.'

'Leila, you cannot expect to get around me by looking pretty. That kind of behaviour does not, as a rule, work on women. Nor most of the men round here, come to that. It won't take long. I've been noticing that you seem to be deriving a lot of pleasure from breaking rules. I know that my classes are not the reason you joined the Academy, but they still deserve to be respected. Respect is something you should learn at any school.'

'But we're here to dance,' I told her rudely. 'We respect everything to do with the ballet.'

'I'm sure you do. But you're not here purely for ballet. You're here to get a rounded education.' We looked at each other and stifled giggles. 'You are also the least mature girls in this class. The other girls all realise that they will need their education. What if you can't be dancers when you're older?' She silenced our nascent complaints with a frown. 'I know you're good at it. So is everybody else in the school. What if you injure yourselves? You know it happens. You could fall and break your backs. You could end up the wrong shape, or your feet could give up on you. Believe me, girls, I've seen it happen time and time again. And even if you survive as dancers, what happens when you're thirty-five?'

'We come back here and teach. Or we move into other areas of dance.'

'Daisy, there are a lot fewer teachers here than there are students. You can't all do that. All I'm saying is, you need every skill you can lay your hands on in this day and age. You need some maths. You need some languages. You might be taken on by the Berlin ballet, and you'd be in an excellent position if you spoke German. I've had letters from past pupils who have discovered just that, and who have been grateful for what I taught them. You'll have a better time all round if you can appreciate some literature to read on the journeys between dancing engagements. If you paid any attention to human biology –' we were still juvenile enough to snigger at the words – 'Shut up! Then you'd know that, physically, you can't dance every day while chucking half your food away. It's just common sense, and that is something you two lack.'

'Sorry,' we told her meekly, looking at the ground and sensing that the lecture was coming to an end.

'Off you go, then. And think about what I've said.'

We laughed about it for the rest of the day.

I wish I'd listened. I thought of her when I arrived in Australia. I half expected to see her in Sydney, with her glasses balanced on her head, sweltering in her woollen suit. Even though I put her and everything else about that school (upon which I heaped so much disgrace) from my mind, I think I based my teaching methods almost entirely upon hers. I wonder what she'd say if she knew. I suppose she'd be pleased.

Somebody is shaking me.

'Daisy!' says a voice, sharply.

'Not Daisy,' I say, batting it away. 'Lina.'

'Sorry. Lina, then. We should go somewhere. It's three o'clock.'

'No it's not.' I rub my eyes, and sit up. I look at my watch. It is ten past three. I look around. I'm still on top of the rock, and I'm cold. My joints are aching. The baby starts to kick. The desert is all around us, lit up by the moon and the stars. Its bumpy, uninhabitable landscape is reassuring. I look at Sophie, who appears dazed. She is shivering. I am, too. We need to go home.

'Fuck,' I say. 'It's freezing.'

'I can't believe we slept like this.'

'I've never slept up here in the night before. We must be mad.'

'So what do we do? Drive somewhere?'

I consider it. I know that the idea of a completely unplanned escape is a stupid one. I can't stay awake, driving, all night long, and even if I could, it wouldn't solve anything.

'Soph, I think we need to go back to the house. We can't just rush off randomly. It's not fair on the baby. We won't get away with it. I can't force you and Red and the baby to live like fugitives with me and it'll only make things worse in the long run. I was eighteen before. Now I'm nearly thirty. I've got responsibilities.'

'So what are you saying?'

'I've got to face it. It's not your fault, Soph, it's mine. It would have caught up with me sooner or later. You do what you like. If you want to go back to England, go.'

'I'm not doing that. You'll need me here. As if I'm going to bugger off and leave you with just Margot for company.'

Lawrence has been here. He has been inside the house. He has stolen the book that I was reading. He went through my drawers. He thought he'd left everything the way that he found it, but I know how I fold my clothes, and all of them have been moved.

I should have packed up all my things and taken them with me. I thought about locking the door before we went out, but if I'd done that, Margot wouldn't have been able to get back in. I don't even know where to find the key, if there is one.

I consider going into the other guest room to tell Sophie, but there's no point. He won't have been through her things. She hasn't got anything here. I put on my pyjamas, and refold all my clothes. They go back into the drawers, the way they're meant to be. It's quarter to four. I don't think I'll sleep tonight. Instead, I go into the kitchen and fill the kettle. Margot is home – her handbag is on the counter, and she's poured herself a glass of water before bed, and left it by the sink. My note isn't there. I look in the bin. I have left notes for Margot countless times, and they stay on the side for weeks. Lawrence must have taken that, too.

I sit on one of the prized bar stools. This would be a good time for a drink. A hot whisky might temporarily hit the spot. Instead, I make some coffee. I gave Margot the cafetiere when I realised that nobody in Craggy makes proper coffee, and it languishes in one of her units, in a state of constant anticipation of my next visit. Now I get it out, the poor redundant thing, and set about filling it. I close the curtains. No one has ever needed to shut these curtains before, because the possibility of being watched is simply not an issue here. In the bedroom, of course I close the curtains (there was no need in our old house thanks to the absolute lack of windows) but in the kitchen the drapes are purely decorative. He could be outside, watching me, right now.

I am dead inside. And yet I contain a living baby. Inside my body, two hearts beat. I worry intensely for its health and happiness. For the rest of the night, I sip coffee, force myself to eat the occasional piece of toast, and I try not to relive the events that led to my flight.

At one point, I stand up and attempt an arabesque. I want to recapture my dancing days, the innocent days, but I can't balance with my new centre of gravity, and I sit down again. That, then, is a skill I have lost. As the light appears around the curtains, I know that I am Daisy again. The past ten years have been a dream, an interlude. I should be talking to the baby, and thinking happy thoughts in its direction, but all I want to do is pretend it's not there. God knows, we'd all be better off if it wasn't.

This life is over. I'm back at the Severn Bridge. I have to pick up where I left off. I'd rather be dead.

chapter twenty

15 January

At half past eight in the morning, I knock on the door. My palms are sweaty, and adrenaline is pumping through me. It is vital to get her to stand up the story as soon as possible. In a way I was tempted to wait for the fingerprints and the handwriting to be analysed, but I knew she'd just run away. I need a current photo of her, and I need a comment. Beyond that, I don't care what she does. If she pegs it this time, we'll all chase her.

Sophie kept the snapshot when she threw me out. I should have thought of that, and made a copy before we left England. It would have been a wonderful prop: 'the picture that revealed the truth'. I miss the photo more than I miss the girlfriend. In a way, I wish I was pining for her. It would be more acceptable. She's pretty, and she never did a single thing to hurt me. I should be feeling terrible. I proposed to her, for God's sake, even if I did just do it out of guilt. I made her lead me to this story. Now she's gone and I'm glad. Having Sophie around would just distract me from the matter in hand. The truth is, I am on a huge high. I am loving every minute of my time here. The town is a shithole, I've been dumped, I don't get served in the bar any more, and I stole private property last night. None of that matters. It is happening for me.

I know she's here. There is a car outside, where there wasn't one last night. No one answers the door. I stand firm where the doorstep would be if there was one. The house is disgusting. I try to imagine someone erecting a shack like this in London. You wouldn't even find it under Waterloo Bridge any more, now that they've tidied it up. It is made of plasterboard, like those mobile classrooms you used to get at school. The roof is corrugated iron, which must be hot. Ugly air-conditioning units hum underneath the windows. That proves someone's in. She can hide, if she likes. I've got all day. I've got all week. If it came to it, I could have all year.

Last night, I was only planning to bang on the door and see what happened. I thought that, if I got into any trouble, I would use Sophie as my excuse. I would pretend I was looking for her. Nora drew a little map directing me to the door, and when no one answered, and all the lights were off, I tried the handle. I did it because that's what someone would do in a film. It swung open. In my book, if you know you're being pursued by a journalist, you don't go out and leave your door open. It was practically an invitation.

Moments like that are why this is the best job in the world. You can spend years rewriting PA copy and being passed over for promotion, and when you find yourself creeping around someone else's house on the other side of the world, searching for evidence, it all becomes worthwhile. I switched on as few lights as possible, and wished I'd brought a torch. If there is a next time, then I will.

I found the kitchen. It was foul – a monument to bad taste. I never notice things like kitchens, generally, but this one was worse than mine and Kev's, and that's a phenomenon I don't think I've seen before. It was all brown and cream, and the tragic thing was, it was tidy. Someone actually cares. They like it.

On a fawn Formica sideboard, there was a note. I swivelled it round. Now I know it off by heart. 'Margot,' it said, in scrawly pencil. 'I've borrowed the car for a while. Nothing to worry about – I just wanted to show Sophie, the girl from England, some of the local sights. Have also taken the torch. See you later, hope you've had a good evening, love Lina x.'

I folded it neatly, and put it in my pocket. I was buzzing.

It didn't take me long to find her bedroom. She's sleeping in the kid's room, even though there's a spare room with a double bed in it. There were maternity clothes in the drawers, and all sorts of lotions and potions in the bathroom. I hadn't expected her to be so tidy. It was a bit freaky. None of her stuff was very interesting, but I put her book (some paperback called *Monkey Puzzle*) in a plastic bag and took it away with me in case we need fingerprints.

I calculate that she's in no position to sue me. In fact, I'd love to see her try.

Now the sun is just beginning to beat down upon me. I'm glad I have some idea of what it's like behind that rattly door. I can imagine Daisy Fraser pacing about, scared of me. From time to time, a car passes, and covers me in dust. I've dressed for work today, in my cream trousers, newly laundered, and black T-shirt. The trousers are suffering already, but I feel reasonably efficient. I know I'm pink in the face, but can't help that. On the plus side, the excitement has largely stopped me from eating, so I hope to see a stomach reduction before too long. Perhaps I should have brought my hat out with me. It was vanity that stopped me. Ace reporters don't wear sun hats. I look ridiculous enough as it is.

On my third rap, a woman comes to the door. This must be the famous Margot. I have seen her in the street. She is at least fifty, probably sixty. She's small and skinny, and her hair is tousled. A dressing gown and a pair of fluffy purple slippers complete her Craggy Rock chic.

Margot peers at me. 'Yes?' she demands.

'Good morning.' I almost call her madam, but something tells me she wouldn't appreciate it. 'I'm sorry to disturb you. I was hoping you might be able to help me. I'm looking for Lina. Is she here? Or Sophie?'

She looks at me. 'No, she's not here. Nor Sophie, whoever that is. And you're not wanted either. So bugger off.' She slams the door.

I smile. So far, so much as expected. I can wait. I buy myself a takeaway coffee, and sit on the ground, just outside Margot's little fence, sacrificing the bum of my cream trousers as I do so.

In twenty minutes, the old woman is back. She informs me fero-ciously that if I don't fuck off away from her house she's going to call the police.

'I'm not actually on your land,' I say politely, 'so the police can't actually do anything.'

'The police round here bloody well can, sonny,' she retorts, and I believe her. I move a little further away, and sit on a rock. I am loving this; every moment of it. She is defensive. I'm winning.

I sit for more than an hour before Sophie puts in an appearance, thus proving Margot to be a liar. I see her face at the window shortly before she comes out, and give her a friendly wave. She still looks pretty, but I don't regret my actions. In fact, seeing her leaves me entirely unmoved.

'Lawrence,' she says coldly, standing in front of me. 'You broke in last night.'

I consider denying it, but can't see the point.

'I didn't break in,' I object mildly. 'It was open.'

'It wasn't *open*. It was unlocked. That meant you had to try the door to find out.'

'People who leave their doors open get burgled. Anyway, I didn't exactly steal the family silver. If there was any, which I doubt.'

'You stole enough. It's still stealing. No one locks their doors round here.'

I shrug. It feels strange that Sophie is towering over me, and so I stand up and, in doing so, kick over my coffee. It splashes my trouser legs, further ruining the efficient Englishman abroad effect.

'Can I see Daisy, Soph? I won't take up much of her time.'

'I can't believe I wasted almost a year of my life with you. No, she isn't here, so why don't you just go home? It's the least you can do. You're not going to see her, because she's gone. A long way away.'

'Tell her I can still do the story without her. We've had tests done on the fingerprints on her book, and on her handwriting, and so we know categorically that she is Daisy Fraser. I'm not going anywhere, and I'm sure she isn't either. Pass that message on. And tell her it's not going to be as bad as she imagines. It happened a long time ago, and people are going to be interested and sympathetic. No one's going to condemn her.'

'Oh, except perhaps for the police and the criminal justice system.'

'This woman is a fugitive from justice.' I stop as I see Sophie's face. That is a bad line to follow. 'I can stop it being too awful for her.'

'You lying twat. By the way, have you got anything to say about the way you used me? The way you abused my better nature? Are you in the least bit sorry?'

I don't know how to answer that. 'Yes,' I say, in the end. 'I am sorry. But I don't think you'll take that in the spirit in which it is intended.'

'Fucking right.' She stalks off, and slams the door.

I begin to feel the heat. I wish I could go for another Danish, but I don't want to give Daisy an opportunity to leave. If I deserted my post for ten minutes now, I'd never be completely certain she was still indoors. I need something, even if it's just a snatched shot of her in the distance, to illustrate my story. So I sit on my rock, and I look at the house, and I wait. I should have brought something to do. I've only got my notebook. If I had a paper or a book to read, or even some kind of Gameboy or something, the time might not drag quite so much. I'm still excited, but my face and arms are burning, and I've got a headache.

PEOPLE WHO WOULD BE EVEN MORE EXCITING IF THEY WERE INSIDE THIS HOUSE
Lord Lucan
Elvis Presley
Princess Diana
Bill Clinton, receiving a blow job from Margot

I decide to make a more sensible list, of points I must remember to cover if and when she agrees to an interview. Before I write a word, however, I feel a hand on my shoulder. I gasp. Someone has crept up behind me, and I didn't hear them at all. This can only mean trouble.

'Larry, it is you, you old slapper,' says a voice as I turn round, expecting the local bobby.

I am baffled. It looks just like her, and it talks just like her, but it can't possibly be her.

'Christie?'

'You look like you're working,' she says cheerfully. 'Don't I get a kiss?'

I can't begin to imagine what's going on. 'What the fuck are you doing here?' Quickly, I look at the house, hoping that Sophie isn't watching. Not that she'd know who Christie was.

'I read your notebook. So sue me. Am I too late? Is anything happening?'

'You read my notebook? When? I keep it with me all the time.' I try to think what she would have read. Everything about this story, that's for sure.

'Not quite all the time, Larry. You might find that when you're hungover and feeling guilty, you leave it in your bag in your bedroom without a second thought when you go and make the tea.'

'You read it then? That is *so* out of order! And then you followed us here? You're a bloody nutter.'

'I've been up for a good story for as long as you have. I remembered who that girl was from your feature. I looked it up again. I knew that if it was true it would be such a fantastic story, and hey! I didn't want to be left out. I needed a holiday anyway.' She sounds brassy, but she looks nervous.

'But I came here with Sophie!' I tell her, confused. 'What were you planning to say to her?'

Christie looks around, laughing. 'I don't see Sophie. And according to the friendly woman at the motel, you're in separate rooms now, and Sophie didn't even come back last night, whereas you did, after a bit of creeping around. So I don't see Sophie as a terrible problem. Don't worry, though, I got my own room. What happened? You got what you wanted and then you dumped her?'

I open my mouth to rebut the accusation, then think better of it. 'Something like that,' I admit. Christie has seen the worst of me already. She's not going to care. 'But this is *my story*,' I tell her. 'It's not yours, OK?'

'Ooooh, it's my train set and I'm not going to share!' she mocks. 'So it's happening, then? Is this where she lives? Are you about to get the scoop? If so, you go right ahead. I'll just do some colour or something. I don't want a joint byline or anything like that. I just thought you might like some help. It sounded like fun.'

I shake my head. 'You're weird,' I tell her. I still think she's a mirage, but it's surprisingly good to have company.

An hour and a half later, I am refreshed by the Coke and ice creams that I made Christie buy me. We are gossiping about our colleagues. Abby and Tim have, apparently, become embroiled in a relationship that they are vainly trying to keep secret. This annoys me, for some reason.

'Office affairs are nothing but trouble,' says Christie, grinning wickedly.

'That's right,' I tell her solemnly. 'No good can ever come of them.'

The front door opens slowly. I hear the squeak, and get to my feet. Christie stands a little way behind me.

There she is. It's her, beyond a shadow of a doubt. I am sorry for doubting Sophie for one second. This is Daisy Fraser. Daisy at home. Daisy pregnant.

I walk towards her. As I do so, I hear Christie behind me, taking a series of photos, as instructed.

Daisy is wearing a short pink dress made of T-shirt material, and no shoes. Her nail varnish matches her dress. I wonder whether this is intentional. Barefoot pregnant women in short skirts, I now realise, are remarkably sexy. It must be something to do with all those curves. Fleetingly, I remember a photo of my mother, pregnant with one of us in the seventies, wearing a minidress.

Up close, Daisy looks tired. I wait for her to speak, but she doesn't.

'Hello, Lina,' I say, extending my hand and hoping that she won't shake it. It's too sweaty. 'I'm Lawrence. I work for the *Herald*, in London. It's a national newspaper, as you already know. I'm delighted that you've decided to talk to me, and I can promise you that I'll look after you.'

She doesn't answer. I reach into my pocket, and turn the tape recorder on, as subtly as I can.

'For the record,' I continue, when she fails to respond, 'I know that your real name is Daisy Fraser, and that you were in considerable trouble with the law ten years ago.' I look to her for a response. None comes. 'Independent analysis of your fingerprints and handwriting confirms it,' I add, even though she must know that I couldn't possibly have got that confirmation overnight. I'm sure it *will* confirm it, and that's what matters.

'You can't base a story on tests performed on stolen goods,' she says finally. She looks knackered, and more pregnant than I'd expected. Nonetheless, she looks better dark than she did blonde. 'Margot is calling the police right now, to get you away from her house. The authorities can be draconian when they want to.'

'We can run the story anyway, and we will.' I feel more confident with Christie behind me, literally and metaphorically. It's nice to be plural. It makes up for the fact that my employers don't even know I'm here. 'Can I ask you, for the record, whether you were formerly known as Daisy Fraser?'

'Do you have a tape recorder? Because if you do you have to tell me about it.'

I take it out of my pocket. 'There you are.'

'I have no comment to make whatsoever on your story, beyond the fact that this type of so-called journalism is intrusive and destructive. I don't know what you want with me, but I'd thank you to leave me and my family and friends alone.'

'So are you denying it?'

'OK. Yes, I am denying it. I am also promising legal action.'

'Lina, we both know you're on shaky ground.'

'And you're on shakier ground than you realise. This town can be dangerous. There are people here who don't like . . .' She is looking at my tape recorder, and her voice tapers away. 'Off the record,' she continues, 'there are people here who don't like outsiders stirring things up. I have a lot of friends.'

'They certainly covered for you well.' I smile, hoping for a little banter. She glares.

'Please leave us alone. This has nothing to do with the owner of this house, and I'd appreciate it if you stayed away from her property.'

'Sure. No problem.' I smile, and turn round and wink at Christie. Together, we walk down the track, towards the motel. Christie looks back, but I don't need to. This is it. We have our photos. I have my story.

chapter twenty-one

I didn't handle that well. In fact, it was entirely inept. I actually threatened him, with his tape recorder running. I need to smarten up if this is going in the direction I fear.

As soon as I close the door, I decide to start telling people the truth. Margot likes me at the moment, but she is a fierce woman, and her main concern is to protect her boys. I try to calculate how far she might support me over this. She's always had sneaking suspicions of my motives, apparently believing I was, otherwise, too good to be true, and now she has been vindicated.

Pete is a veteran of two divorces. He cheated on his first wife, over and over again until she left him. Margot, much to Pete's disgust, maintains friendly relations with the first Mrs Pritchett to this day. The second wife, however, was practically run out of town when it became known that she'd been the one playing away. She had to move to Alice Springs. Even though fidelity (except the cyber kind) is not an issue with me and Tony, I think I'll be kicked firmly into the same category as the second Mrs Pete. I have wronged a Pritchett boy.

I can smell coffee. I deduce that Margot is making it in the cafetiere, for my benefit. I walk, as slowly as I can, towards the kitchen. I don't want to face this. The cot's in the hall, looking all innocent. I stroke the baby as I walk past. 'I've looked after you this far,' I remind it. 'Can you maybe try looking after me for the next few weeks?' I know this is a lot to ask from one whose eyes can barely open, who has no sense of the mass media, drugs, or lies. I can only hope it was some kind of a guru in its previous life. My antenatal appointment with the midwife in Renmark is in two hours, and I haven't even told them I'm not coming. This baby is going to have to get some care from some quarter, soon.

Sophie is perched on a bar stool, wearing one of Margot's washed-out nighties, with a bowl of Frosties and a steaming mug in front of her.

'Hey, darl, you come and sit down and tell me what that was all about.' Margot smiles, holding out a bar stool.

'Actually, I'll grab a chair. My back's aching.'

'Sure. We made the coffee that you like. It won't hurt the babe just this once.' She positions herself in front of me, and leans down to address the person in question directly. '*Will it, bubba?*' she bellows. She makes a show of pressing her ear to my stomach. 'The baby says no it won't,' she tells me. 'Sophie said you'd appreciate a coffee because you look so tired, and I said, you know what, Sophie, I think you're right.'

I lower myself into the chair, and take the mug Sophie offers me, with a weak smile.

'Thanks, Soph,' I say.

'How was that?' she asks under her breath.

'Bad. I'm going to tell Margot now.'

'I'll leave you to it.' She straightens up, tips most of her cereal into the bin, rinses her bowl in the sink, and turns to Margot. 'I'll go for a shower now, thanks, Margot, if that's all right.'

'Sure, help yourself, pet. There's towels in the cupboard outside Lina's room. Take one of the pink ones. They're the guest towels. For best.'

'Thank you. I will.'

'You know, we used to say that pommies don't like showering. It's because you live in a cold climate, you don't need to. We used to say they don't use deodorant as well. But I can see you're the exception. Lina here, she's the other exception.'

'We do our best.'

'That bloke of yours though, Soph, he'd be the one to prove the rule! Never seen a young man sweating so much.' She cackles with laughter.

'Who's that girl out there with him?' I ask, not really interested but putting off my moment alone with Margot. 'She looked just as bad.'

Sophie frowns. 'Australian or English?'

'She didn't say anything. She looked out of place.'

She shrugs. 'A martian? Like I care.'

With Sophie gone, I know the moment has arrived.

'Charming girl,' says Margot, with a grin. 'She's a love. I'm wondering whether Pete might like her. Two pommy girls in the family. That would be quite the thing. I'd be the smartest woman in Craggy.'

'You're already the smartest woman in Craggy.'

'You know, I'd never have had her down for a tax inspector.'

'That's because she isn't one. She does temping work in offices, but she's thinking of coming to live in Australia.'

'You wouldn't blame her for that.'

Margot is infuriating me. She isn't asking any of the right questions. She must wonder why Sophie's here, and why I was talking to Sophie's boyfriend on the doorstep, and what this crisis is about, but she is wilfully not asking.

'Margot,' I say. I am so tired. I just want to curl up around the baby, and block it all out by sleeping for one hundred years. 'I need you to know what's going on. It's not what you think, not at all.'

And so I tell her.

Her eyes dart from me, to my bump, and to the door. The door, I think, is representing Sophie.

'And that is the truth, is it?' she says at last when I've finished filling her in on the basics. It goes against all my instincts to admit it. 'Not just something those journo scum are saying, but the actual truth?'

'Yes. I'm sorry.'

'Does Tony know?'

'Yes.'

She is silent. I stand up and go to pour myself yet more coffee. I shouldn't be drinking it. My mouth tastes foul, and my heart is pounding, though I'm not sure how much of that is attributable to caffeine. My hands are shaky, and I feel off balance. If it's affecting me like this – and this will be, I think, my sixth cup since the early hours of this morning – then I shudder to think what it's doing to my poor, darling baby. Even if the heart and the shakes are attributable to fear, well, that, too, crosses the placenta.

'I'll do that for you.' Margot takes the cup, and pushes me back towards my chair. 'Now, will you explain some more? Tell me exactly what happened, and who this Sophie girl is, and why you never told us before. We all make mistakes, darl. It's being lied to that I don't like. But if it's us against those scum out there, then we'll have to be with you.'

I smile, and put my head on the table for a second. 'You have no idea what it means to me to hear you say that.'

'Tell me all about it, and then you can go for a little sleep.'

By the middle of the afternoon, Margot has rallied to my cause. She has announced, rather ominously, that we will sort out 'your actual rights and wrongs' at a later date. I have heard her on the phone to Tony, telling him sternly that he has to support me because of the baby, and that for now, all that matters is getting rid of the journalists.

The news spreads. Neighbours call by, to gawp at me. Lawrence is staying away. Tempting as it is to interpret this as a loss of interest on his part, I know that's not the case. Sophie is charming the local people who, now that they know she is a friend and not a tax inspector, are reassessing her. Pete discovers a new degree of family feeling. It compels him to spend all his time at his mother's house, trailing after Sophie, attending to her needs.

I hide in my bedroom whenever Margot allows me. Here, at least, everything is ordered. There is a comforting aura of Red. I have my things around me, apart from my book. I can control what happens in this room. I keep the curtains closed, and I lie on the bed, on my left side, as recommended by the baby books. I have brought the cordless phone in with me, and I spend my time chatting as brightly as I can to my little boy. He knows – of course he does – that something is wrong. My heart is heavy.

'When are you coming back, Mummy?' he demands. 'I need you back. I miss the baby.'

'The baby misses you, too, darling. And I miss you. There's just a lot of stuff going on here that I need to sort out. I'll be back as soon as I can.'

'Why don't me and Tony come and see you there? Margot did say I could come and stay whenever I wanted to.'

'I don't know, darling. It's all a bit busy here now. There's lots of boring grown-ups' stuff going on that you wouldn't like.' I hate patronising him, but I know that the only way to stop him wanting to jump on the next bus to Craggy is to impress the potential boredom upon him.

'Tony's a bit cross. He's grumpy with me.'

'Don't worry, he'll be OK soon. It's not your fault. Margot wants to talk to him again in a minute. She'll make him be nice.'

'I'm going to Beth's boat when she comes home from work. Maybe Beth would take me to Craggy.'

'You ask her then.' I can say that safely, secure in the knowledge that it would take, at the very least, the tragically premature deaths of both Andy and Rachelle to bring Beth back here. 'Tell me what you've been doing.'

'Oh, you know. Playing. Mainly with Daniel. He lives on our road. We go to Beth's and we play cricket. He's got a girlfriend! When school starts he says I can have one too. Maybe.' He tails off, suddenly shy.

I am overcome with a longing to see him. I miss everything about him. I miss him in his turtle T-shirt, and his shorts. I miss his dirty hands and knees when he comes in from playing. I miss the way he loves his unusual name. We've been companions through everything, until now. When this is in the papers – tomorrow, probably – all his friends will see it. Daniel will ask him about it. People will point him out when he starts at school, and he won't have me there to comfort him and promise him that everything's going to be all right. I will never be able to make that promise again.

Most of all, I miss his innocence. That, I realise, is something that, by the next time I see him, will be gone.

I'd better call Beth.

'You *what?*'

She doesn't believe me. So Tony didn't tell her yesterday, after all.

'I'm sorry, but it's really true. I was in trouble, I ran away, I kept it secret and now I've been found out.'

'When I first met you, I *thought* there was something strange about you. I *knew* you were hiding something. You'd never say what your real story was, and when I got to know you better, you were just Lina and I forgot all about it.'

'Do you mind that I never told you?'

'No, in lots of ways I don't. It feels strange. I wish I could remember seeing you in the papers. What was your name, then?'

I hate saying it. 'Daisy. Daisy Fraser.'

'That's a pretty name. I don't remember it. Normally you hear when someone disappears, don't you?'

'Not always. It happens all the time. It was just seen as a suicide. It might have merited a small paragraph in Australian papers because of the aristocratic connections, but I doubt even that. I covered my tracks pretty carefully. It seems all wrong that everyone knows now. If there was any way I could leave Craggy, I would.'

'So, do. More journalists will arrive, won't they? It sounds pretty irresistible for them. Even if it is going to be in the papers, spoil their fun. Run off. Everyone'll cover for you.'

'We tried that last night. It couldn't work. There's nowhere to go, and I'm having a baby.'

'How's Margot?'

'She's rallying around. She's a star. I mean, she's not exactly letting me off the hook, but she knows that the problem is the journalist. Nobody's going to help him with his inquiries, that's for sure. Apparently he's been trying to talk to people about me, but no one's playing. He can't even get served any more. Mick's just decided that he's banned, and if the pizzeria does the same, and the supermarket, we could starve him out of town.'

'Get in the car with this Sophie girl and come to Renmark. So what if they find you here eventually. Come and see your boys. You should get a medical check. You know, Red's here now, with his new mate. They keep me company every day.'

'Thanks so much for putting up with them.'

'Not a problem. I like them. Guess what? I met a man. Early days, but interesting. Anyway, that's something I'll tell you about later. Does Red know everything?'

'Not yet. He's a little bit confused, but I don't really know what to say to prepare him for tomorrow, if that's when it's going to be in the papers. I'm praying he won't get dragged into it.'

'This is going to be a big deal, isn't it?'

'Yes. You know, I could well end up in prison.'

'Not if you don't go back to England, surely?'

'We have an extradition treaty with England.'

'They wouldn't bother, would they? I mean, you've exiled yourself to Australia. You've done their work for them.'

'If only it were still that simple.'

'Like I keep saying, you really should run away while you've still got the chance.'

'I am obsessed with the idea. I think of little else. But I can't think how it would work. I can't sort out the details.'

'Keep it simple. You and me and Red, and Tony if he wants, and Sophie, we can all just get in a car and go. Do it now. Pack your bag, take a car, and bugger off down here.'

'Then where?'

'Western Australia? It's huge out there. We could drive around WA for months without seeing another person.'

'We kind of need to see another person. In March, I mean. Those guys took photos of me, so they all know I'm pregnant. I need to have this baby. And Red needs to go to school.'

'People have babies in the Outback. They must do.'

'I've been through this. You can't do that. You can't just take off and leave all certain medical care behind. In Renmark the care we'd get would be world class. If we took off, it would be up in the air. I'm already more than seven months pregnant, and I'd have no plans for delivery. It would be completely irresponsible.'

'So we can go to New Zealand.'

'I can't fly. Plus, they'd find me in a trice. I don't know, Beth. I can't really work it out. Why don't you talk to Tony?'

Someone is knocking softly on my door. I know I can't stay in bed all day. I put my hand over the receiver and tell them to come in. It's Rachelle, with a cup of tea. I remember, in the nick of time, not to say her name. Beth was entertained and incredulous when I recounted exactly how unhappy Andy was with the bed he'd made for himself, but I still don't think she'd appreciate my accepting tea from the pregnant enemy.

'Beth, I have to go. I'll call you back later.'

'Cool. I'll go over to see Tony now. You look after yourself. Remember, you can come down here today.'

'I know. And Beth, give Red a huge hug from me.'

'On its way. Do you want me to try to tell him what's going on?'

'Please. I'll talk to you later.'

I turn to Rachelle. She has lost weight, despite, or no doubt because of, her pregnancy. Her face is a ghostly white, and she has, probably temporarily, lost her sharp edge.

'Talking to Andy's ex?' she says listlessly. 'Anyway, we thought you might want a cup of tea.'

I take it. It's much too strong, but I appreciate the surprising thought. I manage to sip it without wincing, and I put it down next to the bed.

'I should come and join the party,' I tell her, 'but I'd much rather hide out all day long.'

She sits next to me, and looks a bit awkward. 'So, stay here. Mrs P, you're the only other pregnant person I know. When you were two months, did you feel like shit, yeah, like you couldn't be arsed to do anything? Did you throw up all the time, you know?'

'I felt terrible. We didn't tell anyone till I was three months.' Those days seem so innocent now. 'So I was pretending to be normal. Teaching and everything, and I was sick, and tired, and miserable. But it does lift. How many weeks are you?'

'Nine.'

'So you haven't got much longer till you start feeling better again.'

'You promise?'

'I promise. Honestly. It gets a lot better. I loved it when I started showing. Around four or five months I was euphoric all the time. People treat you very differently once you've got a bump, believe me. They look after you. If there were any strangers in Craggy, they'd come and talk to you.'

'But then I'll have to have a baby at the end of it, yeah? And that's like a scary thing. It's OK for you, you've already got Red.'

'Well, that's a whole different matter. You are very young to be having a child, Rachelle.' Despite everything, I feel myself drifting back into teacher mode. 'But you're in a stable relationship. You're married. This pregnancy wasn't an accident. You have everything going for you. Having a child isn't the worst thing that can happen. I think it's one of the most rewarding things in the world. You hear stories about sleepless nights and constant crying, but the fact is, once you've got a baby, those things don't matter. So you're tired for a while. You're not going to be any more tired than you are now, I can promise you that. And you cope at the moment. It's a good thing, Rachelle, not a bad one.' I think that what I mean is, it's a good thing for me. It's not necessarily a good thing for a teenager, but, in the long run, I know she's going to be fine. In fact, Rachelle's baby will almost certainly have a more stable home environment than mine. This is a chilling thought.

'Thanks, Miss,' she says meekly. 'I mean, Lina. I didn't expect it to be like this.'

'I know. Is Andy supporting you?'

'He says nice things sometimes, but I don't think he's into the idea so much, you know? And he always talks about when he was married to your friend, like that was a good thing.'

'I'll have a word with him.'

'Will you do that? Thanks. And, look, I don't understand what's going on out there and with those English people – I mean, what's that girl doing here, yeah? She was staying at the motel with the bloke. I don't really get it, but are you all right, yeah?'

'I don't know. Not really. I'm worried about Red and the baby more than anything else. You'll see, it is a huge responsibility, and you feel so guilty if you do anything to hurt your children. This one is entirely my own fault. I don't know what's going to happen.'

'Good luck. You'll be fine, Mrs Pritchett.'

'Thanks for the tea, Rachelle.'

She leaves, and I consider getting up to follow her. Instead, I lie on the bed, and curl up. I'm staying here just as long as I can.

I wish I knew what had happened to Leila. Until our friendship was abruptly ruptured, I adored her. I dyed my hair blonde because I wanted to look like her. It didn't work, of course, because of my eyebrows. I was continually plucking them away so they didn't reveal my natural darkness. The Academy disapproved of my Marilyn campaign, but nobody ever told me to stop it.

I wish I knew whether she'd done it; whether she'd put that one disastrous night behind her, and had a dancing career. In a way, I hope she did. She betrayed me, when I thought I was going to be all right, but I hope she's happy now. I imagine she was intimidated into telling the truth. That would never have happened to me. I would never have confessed.

I suppose the press will track her down. I'll find out what's become of her soon enough. I know I'll never see her again.

Mentally, I line up the best friends I've had over the years. There's Sophie, lost and found; Leila, lost; Nina, lost; and Beth, so far still around. It's not a great record. Leila and I were always bad for each other. We encouraged each other from the very beginning. Together, we would climb down the fire escape and make our way on the District Line into London. We discovered, when we were out, that men appreciated our toned physiques and our strange balletic grace. We started meeting friends of Leila's brother, and going clubbing. The men were eligible public schoolboys. The women were beautifully dressed socialites. Underage ballerinas were a novelty, and we never had to buy our own champagne. We rarely paid for our ecstasy or speed. As the years passed, we found ourselves going out every weekend. Part of the comfort of the institution was the breaking out of it.

By our last year at school, Leila had a boyfriend called Freddie who sent her bouquets at the Academy, and I was embroiled in a liaison with an aristocrat called Giles. Both of them were in their late twenties, and both were riotously entertained by the idea of their teenage paramours studying listlessly for a couple of token A levels before prancing around in leotards.

By and large, we managed, with some pharmaceutical help, to keep us in ballet classes, but it wasn't the same. We didn't have the edge we needed. We fell behind, while keeping up. You can't sustain that kind of regime. By the Christmas of our last year, I'd been told by Jonathan, the ballet master, that my career within the company was on the rocks before it had even begun.

He kept me behind after class one afternoon. I knew I'd danced atrociously. I'd lost my balance completely and unforgiveably on a pirouette because my head was spinning faster than I was. I'd stopped turning and stepped out of line to catch my breath. Everyone noticed. 'So, you've decided to take the social life over and above the ballet,' he said quietly.

'What makes you say that?' I asked, smiling and executing a perfect double pirouette to prove that I could do it really.

'You're not outstanding. You're good, sure, and I'm sure you could do all right in the corps de ballet for a few years, but you haven't got that fire that we all loved at the beginning. You used to be something really special, and now you're not. You're normal, Daisy, and you've brought that upon yourself. A screw-up like today's, that kind of thing can't happen to you any more. You're old enough to be in the company now. No one's going to take you on if you piss about on the stage. Nobody's interested in dancers who come to class off their faces on speed. You had the option to be something fabulous, and you blew it.'

'You're just trying to scare me.'

'We've tried everything we could think of to scare you already. You remember, two years ago, I said you were fast-tracking yourself to being a run-of-the-mill dancer. Sure, the envy of other dancers in less exalted circles, but I think I told you that you weren't going to be exceptional, and I was right. It's happened. You haven't taken care of yourself, or your dancing. You know that you need to be disciplined about this. You're not. That's fine. But I wouldn't expect much more input from the Academy.'

'Are you just saying this to wind me up?'

He turned away. 'No,' he said, and he put on his sweatshirt, and left me in the studio without a backward glance.

That shattered my dreams of becoming a world-renowned prima ballerina. Those, however, are the dreams that every young girl harbours for a while. Mine were just shattered later than usual. It felt devastating at the time; but it was nothing.

That particular night, on the other hand, tore apart the lives of everyone it touched. The popular version, following Leila's betrayal, had me cast firmly as the villain. I was a precocious, streetwise drug peddlar, and, it was implied, I had done it on purpose. I took poisoned speed to Giles's flat, but I didn't take any myself. I just sat and watched four of my friends die. The mythical version would never have stood up to scrutiny, but nobody scrutinised it closely, because people wanted it to be true.

It was my turn to buy the drugs. Freddie had done it last week, and Leila the week before, and Giles the week before that. It was bad luck. The whole evening hinged around luck. It was luck that I happened to be Marjorie's first punter after that batch arrived. It was pure chance that Leila and I preferred ecstasy for a night out. We hoarded our speed for the next day, to get us through school.

It seemed so banal at the time. I would give up everything I've ever had, including my children, to go back. I would stay at school and learn my French verbs. When I'd made a token effort with them, I'd stretch and dance a little. Then, perhaps, I'd watch some television and have an early night. I'd rescue my whole life, and I wouldn't even know it. In a parallel universe, I hope that happened. In this one, I dashed up Marjorie's stairs, two at a time, with no sense of foreboding whatsoever. I have a dim memory of swinging my hips, though no one was there to see, and knowing I looked good in my little skirt, with my bare legs. My hair was scraped back from my face, out of habit, and I was wearing a little eye make-up, and some lip gloss.

We used to love Marjorie, although, in retrospect, she was a pathetic figure. I didn't know any better. She epitomised the world outside boarding school, and all our narcotics came from her. She was a parody of a Kensington dealer: a fifty-year-old woman with a ravaged face, who lounged in her apartment, perpetually stoned on heroin. I wonder whether the law ever caught up with Marjorie. I hope not. It was Marjorie who located Noeline, so the least I can give her is my good wishes.

Marjorie's heroin haze belied a sharp business sense. No one fucked with her. That is, no one had fucked with her before.

She knew what I wanted, because our order rarely changed, and she had it ready.

'My darling!' she exclaimed, from her chaise longue. She was wearing a kimono, as usual. 'How is the bal*let*?'

'Fine, thanks.' I was in a hurry to get back to the others.

'I've got something you're going to adore. It's just arrived. You are the first to sample it. Shall we have a sneak preview?'

'I would, thanks, but everyone's waiting. Is it good?'

'So I'm told.' She was slurring her words. Marjorie levered herself to her feet for long enough to open her safe and take out a bag of pills, and another bag of speed, and to replace them with the cash I handed her.

'After this, you'll be dancing *Swan Lake* backwards to a speeded up tape. Inject it.'

'And the pills?'

'Have they ever been anything but superb?'

'Of course not.'

She slumped back, and waved me away. 'Enjoy!' she called huskily. I fully intended to. It never occurred to me that this transaction qualified me as a dealer.

Now that I allow myself to look back on Marjorie from an adult perspective, I wonder how she got to where she was. Could she have been happy, sitting alone in her expensive apartment and selling narcotics to well-heeled clients? What did she want from her life? Then I wonder whether, if that night hadn't gone so dramatically wrong, I could have ended up like her. I've never thought of that before, but it is perfectly possible.

Six people were draped around Giles's living room. Giles welcomed me with a snog. He was one of the notoriously louche members of the aristocracy, and just by hanging out with him I'd become a staple feature in various gossip magazines. Even at eighteen, I was still labelled a 'wild child'. These days, Miss Mary wasn't so keen to catch up with her former star pupil when I went home, and Sophie was baffled by my tales of drunken sex. Several shots in magazines had almost had me thrown out of school.

Giles had brown hair in the Merchant Ivory flop that was all the rage. He looked a bit like Hugh Grant who, back then, was known only for his part in *Maurice*. He had good genes.

I lay on the white sofa, interlocked my legs with his, and handed him my treasure. On the floor, at our feet, Leila and Freddie were entwined. Red-haired Mary, who, by now, was black-haired Maria, was curled gracefully in an armchair. She was a year older than us, and already a member of the ballet company. Giles's younger brother, George, poured me a glass of white wine, and put our favourite tune of the moment, by Black Box, on the hi-fi.

'What d'you get us, Daise?' demanded Giles, raising his voice above the music. His cheeks were pink and white and wholesome. I'd slept with Giles, curled up next to his naked body, while his face was grey and his heart pumped with artificial stimulation, but he always recovered his looks, and at the beginning of any evening, he was invariably cherubic. It probably wouldn't have lasted.

I kissed his mouth. 'The usual. Marjorie says the billy is some fantastic new thing she's just got in. She said we should inject it.' I always felt self-conscious when I called drugs by their nicknames, but no one laughed at me for saying 'billy'.

'Cool. I'm doing that then,' pronounced Mary, who had been amazed when she'd discovered the rebellion that had been going on for years without her knowledge. As soon as she'd realised we went out snorting, injecting, and just plain swallowing almost every week, she'd demanded to join us. Her career would have been hampered, inevitably, as a result.

'Me too,' agreed Giles, and George and Freddie nodded their assent. Marjorie was their guru. I looked at Leila, who shook her head.

'I would, but I don't want to inject. It might show in class.'

'Me neither.' Leila and I were among ecstasy's most fervent admirers. We took up to seven in a night, and Leila, like me, had spotted an opportunity. If the rest of them were having speed, we would get all the pills. We'd take some of the speed back with us to get us through the next day.

Giles, as the host, assembled the equipment. I try to remember exactly what everybody else looked like that evening. These were the last moments of their lives.

I watched my friends injecting. Mary, dressed in red jeans and a black body, tried to insist on a clean needle, because she, if no one else, was scared of HIV. There was a chorus of complaint, and in the end she was told to go first.

If the poison had acted quickly on her, at least the others would have been all right. But Mary just lay back in her chair, and sighed, and then Freddie injected himself, gesturing to ask Leila, wordlessly, whether she'd changed her mind. Leila and I took our pills while the others passed the syringe.

It took us for ever to notice that something was wrong. For minute after minute, the two of us grinned inanely at each other, anticipating the high, oblivious to everyone else. '*Hot* temptation!' shrieked the tape. Then I leaned back against Giles, and wondered why he didn't respond. Leila turned to Freddie.

'Fred, are you all right?' she asked him.

'Have they gone to sleep?'

'We'd better wake them.' By now, we must have had an idea. It was too much to contemplate. I saw Mary, still curled in her chair. I imagined that she moved her hand. Relieved, I stood over her and shook her shoulders.

'Mary!' I said, loudly, over the music. 'Mary, are you OK?'

Leila was bending over Freddie.

'He's not saying anything,' she said.

'Nor's Mary. Giles neither.'

We looked at each other. This was confusing.

'Oh, fuck.' I could feel myself bubbling with ecstasy, and yet all our friends were, at the very least, unconscious. I wasn't sure what was really happening. 'Shall we call an ambulance?'

'What about George?'

George was still and clammy. I took his wrist, like they did on television. I couldn't feel anything.

'It must have been the speed,' I said slowly.

The ecstasy enhanced every feeling, every sight, every texture. I felt the pores in his skin, and I knew that, if his heart had been beating, I would have felt its thump.

'What shall we do, Leila?' I said, quietly. 'We can't leave them. If we're here when the ambulance comes we're going to be in such trouble. If we're not, they might find us and then we'll be in even more trouble.'

Leila was shivering. 'Can we just go back to school? It's not our fault. Nobody will know we were here.'

'They will. They know these are our friends. They'll find our fingerprints. That's what they do. But we have to get an ambulance to make sure they're going to be OK.'

And so we did. First Leila phoned 999, and then, panicking, I called Marjorie, and screamed at her. She jerked out of her stoned slumbers as soon as she heard my voice.

'The fucker!' she yelled. 'It was a new guy, darling. I trusted him! The absolute fucker. Don't say a word to the police about me, and I won't say anything about you if they come calling. Right? We've never seen each other in our lives. Call me when it calms down. Now fuck off.'

I put my shoes on, and waited. The ambulance and the police were there within five minutes. We let them assume control. In a way, it was a relief.

chapter twenty-two

16 January

The front page inches, slowly, through the fax machine.

Christie reaches for my hand, and squeezes it. We watch it creep out together.

They have given us the entire front page. 'SUICIDE GIRL'S NEW LIFE', reads the headline. The capitals scream out. I'm so glad I work for a tabloid. The understatement of the broadsheet press would have undermined this story. Its shock value is everything. This front page looks as excited as I feel.

Below the headline is Christie's photo of Daisy at the door, looking at once sexy and scared in her pink dress, and beneath that is my story. I turn sideways to skim it as it emerges. The subs have barely changed a word. My favourite part is the byline: 'Exclusive,' it says. 'Lawrence Golchin,' reads the second line. 'In Craggy Rock,' reads the third. It's the *exclusive* I like best. And it is exclusive. This is my exclusive story.

'She was declared dead three years ago,' reads my first sentence. 'For ten years, her family, friends and the authorities believed her suicide notes. Yesterday we found Daisy Fraser living a new life in the Australian Outback. Daisy apparently committed suicide at the Severn Bridge when a drugs party went horribly wrong. Today, she is a heavily pregnant schoolteacher and a respected member of the community. She calls herself Lina Pritchett and she is married – to a man who has no idea of his wife's deception . . .' It is a fabulous story. I am exhilarated. This is better than drugs. This is worldwide renown.

'Well done,' says Christie, generously. 'You did it.'

'Well done yourself.' I start trying to assemble the page, which is coming through in A4 tiles. Christie's pieces are trailed for pages two and three. One of them is a colour piece about Craggy and its people. It was supposed to be a litany of shocked reaction as we broke the news to the good and trusting burghers of the town, but nobody would speak to us (clearly Daisy still has some clout around here. I blame the cantankerous mother-in-law). Poor Christie struggled, and ended up turning in a rushed account of the 'close-knit community' into which Daisy had insinuated herself. In other words, everyone likes her more than they like us and that isn't fair. Normally people who suddenly find they have a notorious neighbour are eager for their ten minutes of fame, but these people really pretended they weren't bothered. They'll come round.

'Do you think anyone here has any idea that more of us are going to turn up?' I ask idly, hoping that I'm not overestimating my story's appeal.

'Not the foggiest. They're all focused on rallying around and cutting us dead. They can't have stopped to imagine it.'

'But more journalists will come, won't they?' I'm anxious about this. I have to bring someone here. If all else fails, I can always say I brought Christie, but that is different. That is personal.

'Of course they will, you wanker. Everyone's going to want to buy her up. Have we offered anything yet? Because we should exploit our advantage while we're here. As for the townsfolk, as I think we're obliged to call them on our pages, they haven't seen anything yet.'

'This might be beyond anything they've experienced. Even beyond what they've seen on telly.'

'Wow! Real life in "more exciting than telly" shocker. What shall we do today?' Christie looks bored. She's twiddling her hair. Sophie used to do that.

'Wait for the calls to start?'

'While we do that?'

'Don't we have to stay at the motel? If only the fucking mobile worked, it would be different.'

'Well, you can see why the networks don't bother to spread their coverage across the whole of the dead red centre of Australia. By and large it wouldn't be worth their money.'

'So we have to stay here. This place is starting to do my head in.' It smells. We were up almost all night in my room, putting the story together, and answering calls from London. Christie had to go and man the reception desk, because both Nora and Rachelle declined to stay up all night purely to connect calls to our bedrooms.

'The Dugout Motel, may I help yew?' she said the first time, in an Australian accent. It wasn't a very good accent, but it clearly fooled Patricia. 'Certainly, ma'am, I'll just put you through,' and we both legged it across the courtyard to pick up the ringing phone in my room.

'That Pat is fucking rude!' Christie said later. 'No wonder Nora didn't fancy working the night. *Yes, Lawrence Golchin or Christie Baxter.* She didn't say either hello or please. Let alone, *can I speak to.* Or *thank you.*'

My first call to London is my career highlight to date. I got through to one of the newsdesk assistants. I taped the call for posterity.

'Hello, Kim,' I said, 'it's Lawrence Golchin here. Is Pat there?' I had toyed with the idea of calling straight through to the editor's office, but I knew that was the sort of behaviour that makes enemies.

'Hello, Lawrence. I'll see if I can find her.'

Pat came on the line, eventually. 'Larry,' she said. 'I thought you were on your hols?'

'I was, I am, but I've stumbled upon a story that I think you might like. In fact, I think you're really going to like it quite a lot.' All my veins were bulging with excitement. My heart was going like a hammer. This was the moment it became real.

'Fire ahead. I've got a conference in a minute.'

'OK, I'll get to the point. I'm in a place called Craggy Rock, which is north of Adelaide, in the desert in Australia.'

'Mmm?' I could hear her typing as we spoke.

'You remember that girl, Daisy Fraser?' I knew she would. 'Well, I've discovered that she's living here. I've got photos. I've got her fingerprints and her handwriting. Obviously that all needs analysing, but without a doubt it's her. She didn't even deny it.'

'Did she confirm it? This isn't the first time we've been offered this type of story. They never stand up.'

'No, she wouldn't really say anything. Pat, you might think I'm mad, but it is definitely her. As soon as you see the picture, you'll see that.'

'How did you track her down?' Pat's scepticism was insulting, but I didn't care.

'It's a long story. You remember I used to go out with her best friend? Well, it was through her. Through Sophie.'

'Fine. You'd better scan those photos first and send them over. We'll get the fingerprints and handwriting done in Australia, it'll be quicker. You'll have to courier them to Jack Vine in Sydney, OK? Then when we've got the evidence we'll take it from there.' She broke off for a second. I heard her speak to someone else. 'Yeah, be there in a minute. Larry, be honest, how likely is this to be a looky-likey?'

'Not at all likely. I have some independent corroboration you might be interested in. Christie's here with me.'

'Christie Baxter? My God, Lawrence, people will talk.'

'Let them. Now, I'm going to pass you over. I'll get on the case and give you a call back. Christie can get Jack Vine's details off you or Kim.'

While Christie was beaming down the phone, I thought things through, and hoped I wasn't banned from the cybercafe, and that they had a scanner. There was definitely no courier service. I took the phone back, and explained.

'Leave it to us. Give us your number, and start working up that splash. No guarantees.'

A few hours later, a courier arrived from nowhere and took it all from us. He was a small, ferrety man from Alice Springs. We'd had no idea that Craggy had an airport until he told us. With a few misgivings, I handed him the bag containing all the proof that our story was true. He looked to me like one of Pete's mates, tricking us into handing over our most precious goods. However, everything was in Sydney a few hours later, and soon after that our story was officially true.

And now it's in the paper.

'We can't just hang around here all day,' I say, taking Christie's hand. 'At the very least, we owe ourselves – each other – a drink.'

'We need to sleep. It's ten o'clock now. We barely slept at all last night. We haven't had a shower since yesterday morning and we've been rushing around quite a lot. You look dreadful, Larry, if I may speak frankly, as a friend. So why don't we clean ourselves up, nip out for some breakfast, and then come back and sleep. It's not as if anyone in London's going to be ringing us during their night. The story will be on the streets by about half five this afternoon, our time, and we need to save some energy for then. Come on. Even the Watergate guys needed a kip from time to time.'

I nod my head. Suddenly I feel very tired indeed.

chapter twenty-three

'Bloody hell, Lina! What have you done?'

I open one eye, reluctantly. I was sleeping soundly for the first time in days. I recognise the voice but I have no idea whose it is. I was dreaming of the sea. Nothing was happening. I was just sitting on a sandy beach, with my baby girl in my arms. We were both looking out at the ocean. The water was calm. I was happy.

My eyes do not want to open. They are glued shut, and only one of them unsticks itself. I see part of Red's room. It's not tidy any more. My clothes are all over the place. I glimpse yesterday's knickers, screwed up and inside out on the floor. I begin to remember the earlier part of the night. I lost my senses. I couldn't cope. I threw things around. I wanted to destroy everything. It was all I could do to prevent myself trying to abort the baby, for its own sake. I looked for a knitting needle for a while, before I stopped, looked at myself, and felt sick.

I roll over onto my other side. My arms hurt. I feel my left forearm with my right hand. I cut it last night. The cuts are tender, but they seem not to have bled much. I can't believe I'm doing that again. I never believed I would regress that far. This morning I am staring straight back into Daisy's life.

'Lina, wake up.' It's my friend's voice. Sophie? But Sophie wouldn't call me Lina. The voice takes on a new sense of urgency. 'Lina, there's blood on your sheets. Is it the baby? Wake up!' She sits on the edge of the bed and shakes my shoulder. I slide, slightly, down the depression she makes, and I open my eyes. She has beaten me. She's forced me to return to the world I hate. The world that hates me.

I frown. 'Beth?'

'Lina, is the baby all right?'

'What are you doing here?'

'Came to see you. Look at that blood. Shall I take you to hospital?'

'No. It's fine. It's not the baby. I hurt my arms.' I hold one out to show her.

'Fucking hell, Lina. Why?'

'Was sad. Used to do it.'

'Well, you need to pull yourself together now.'

I shake my head and turn away from her.

'Sorry,' Beth says, 'normally I'd indulge you, but this time I can't. Look. Someone else came to visit.'

She's pointing to the door. I look around blearily. Standing on the threshold, with tears in his eyes and looking as though he hates me, is Red.

Beth perches on the loo, and talks to me while I'm showering.

'Of course I'd never have barged in with him if I'd known what a state you were in. You sounded together before.'

'I'm not together now. It's not your fault. Just gives me one more thing to be guilty about.' I know I should wash my hair, but I can't be bothered. What I look like seems entirely irrelevant. I soap my bump instead.

'Lina, the paper's come out. You are extremely famous. Margot's fending people off left, right and centre. There's a crowd outside the door, and so far that's just the local journos. The others haven't had time to get here, but they will. You can't do this. You need to be sane and sensible and strong if we're going to get through it.'

'Easy for you to say.'

Beth stands up and flings back the curtain. I am wet and naked, cut and bruised, and I don't care. She's glaring at me.

'Not that easy, as it happens. I've just driven for most of the night with your frightened child in the back of my car and your angry husband next to me, asking me, all the way, whether I had any idea and why you hadn't told him and what your marriage vows were all about. Now, excuse me, but I do happen to have a job, and a home, and a relationship, and these people are feeling completely abandoned by you, especially Red, because Red's an innocent pawn in all this. 'Everyone you know has just discovered that everything you ever said to them was a pack of lies. I've gone out of my way not to criticise you for that, and to look after your family since you're not capable of doing it. So don't you tell me that anything at all is *easy for me*, thank you very much.'

Tears are running down my cheeks. I try to soap them away, and step out of the shower. 'Sorry, Beth. I don't know what's happening to me.'

'Here, have a towel. Have you washed your hair? Then get back under that shower and do it.'

'Tony's here, then?' I shout over the running water. 'Where is he?'

'With his family. He'd like a word with you, when you're up to it.'

'He's going to leave me, isn't he?'

'Who knows?' She sounds weary.

Neither of us speaks for a while. I wonder where Red has gone. He turned and ran when I tried talking to him. Beth puts a hand on my shoulder, and leads me to the basin. She puts a comb into my hand.

'I'll find you something to wear. You haven't cut up all your lovely clothes, have you?'

I shake my head. 'Just crumpled them.'

'You'll still be the smartest woman in Craggy.'

'The most creased. Actually, not even that.'

As she leaves the room, I silently thank Margot for her anxiety to have a better house than her neighbours. The guest room and Red's old room were carved up by plywood partitions so they could share this windowless 'guest bathroom', with its avocado suite. No one else comes to this part of the house, ever. I can make myself a little bit presentable before I have to face anyone. I switch on the light above the basin, and examine myself.

I've never looked worse. My eyes are almost hidden in the saggy skin that surrounds them. The whites, insofar as they are visible, are bloodshot. While I was asleep, someone has come along with a cosmic marker pen and drawn in huge black bags that extend halfway down my cheeks. The rest of my skin is pale, and a few spots, as a perfect finishing touch, are breaking out on my chin. I comb through my hair and reach for some moisturiser. It's my special pregnancy moisturiser, though I'm sure the only way it differs from its run of the mill counterparts is in its price.

When Tony got used to the idea of fatherhood, he embraced it. He loved the early months, when I was feeling like death. We both felt that the baby was a miraculous, positive and remarkable thing. I remember Tony picking me up, one day, when Red was out. 'We're going to have a baby!' he shouted. 'Half you, and half made of me.' Then he hooked my legs over his arms, and carried me through to the sitting room, where he sat me down and switched the telly on.

'I'll get you a cup of tea,' he promised, and was back with it in two minutes. He had never done that before. Pregnancy seemed, on that day, as though it was going to be a perfectly happy, contented interlude in my life, when nothing else could possibly be as important as nurturing our foetus, as it grew its fingers and toes and tooth buds. Nothing should be more important than that. For the first time in ten years, I stopped worrying. I know it can only be coincidence that, at that point, Sophie appeared, but it doesn't feel like it. It feels as if fate, or even God, is letting me know that I cannot have everything. I bought myself endless mail order pregnancy products in those carefree early days. Things like that seemed to matter, then. Now, I scrub roughly at my face with some moisturiser on a piece of loo paper, as though, through some new form of science, this process might make me pretty and self-possessed. I realise that it's going to be hours before my puffy face returns to its former state, and I don't think I've got hours. I can't begin to imagine what's going on in the rest of the house, or outside it. I can barely imagine how I'm going to get dressed, let alone walk through my bedroom door and face people. But I know I can't hide in here for ever. At the very least, I have to face Margot and Tony and Red. From the sound of the voices coming through the walls, there are a lot more people here than just my former nearest and dearest.

I don't want to face them. I don't want to see any of them. I want to smash the stupid mirror, and my stupid face with it. I pick up a posh glass bottle filled with special 'pregnancy' bubble bath, and swing it back. I can do this. I can smash myself. Beth grips my arm. I hadn't realised she was there.

'Seven years' bad luck,' she cautions.

'That's going to make a difference when I'm in prison.'

'OK. Different tack called for. Margot's sheltering you in her house. She doesn't have to. She could turn against you if she wanted, and then everyone else would too, and then you'd have nowhere to go. Don't vandalise her house. It'll make things much worse for you.'

I look at her in the mirror. Then I drop my arm. 'OK.'

'Here.' She holds out a dress that used to be my favourite. It's made from floaty chiffon, and is patterned with roses. 'Wear this. It wasn't easy to work out what was clean, underwear-wise, but I think these ones are.'

'They are. Thanks.'

I get dressed, as slowly as I possibly can.

chapter twenty-four

17 January

The story stands up. The bloody story actually stands up. Not only does it stand up, but everyone is going mental about it. Christie and I lie together on her bed, and watch the news. Our story is at the top of every bulletin. The local news – the South Australian news, that is – is as obsessed as I am. As we lie in the dark and musty room, we watch a brittle blonde doing a piece to camera.

'The town of Craggy Rock was previously known as a hard yakka opal mining town,' she says. 'Little did these residents realise that there was an escaped prisoner living in their midst.' She turns, and the camera swings to a woman standing next to her. 'Rachelle Fisher works in the local motel. She was taught by Daisy Fraser at the local school. Rachelle, did you ever suspect that there was anything out of the ordinary about this woman?'

Rachelle, who is skinny and pale, shakes her head emphatically. 'No,' she says, wide-eyed. 'I mean, like, she was my teacher, yeah? You don't expect a teacher to lie to you, do you? Mrs Pritchett – Fraser I mean – used to tell us *not* to lie, if you can believe that.'

'Do you know her well?'

'I mean, me and my husband, that's Andy, we moved into her old house when they moved away. She's, like, a nice lady. I mean, she really is.'

'And Rachelle, you've very kindly agreed to let us have a look around that house, haven't you?'

'Yes, that's not a problem.'

Christie squeezes my hand. 'Bitch,' she says lethargically. 'I asked

Rachelle to talk to me hundreds of times yesterday, and she wouldn't do it. In fact she said I was scum and told me to go fuck myself. Why's SATV getting the tour around the old family home?'

'She's been told that you and I are scum and she goes along with that, but as soon as some fellow peroxide bimbo invites her to be on telly, she forgets everything she's meant to be doing. You know, she's probably so thick that she hasn't noticed that talking to this woman is exactly the same as talking to you.'

'But less classy.'

'Naturally.'

'Because if she'd spoken to me she could have been in the actual story as it was broken. She would have had a place in history.'

'You know what I really like about you, Chris? Your modesty.'

'I'm being immodest on your behalf.'

We look at each other. We smile, and then Christie breaks the eye contact and flicks through the channels.

'Don't you want to see what her house is like?'

'It hasn't got her stuff in it, has it? Boring. It's just going to look like this place, all dark and smelly. I wish this fucking dump had cable.'

Neither of us imagined the story taking off like this. Our phones have been ringing constantly, to Nora's disgust. We've done countless tele-phone interviews about the way I stumbled upon Lina when I was on holiday with my girlfriend. That story has to be airbrushed a little, but then again, doesn't everything? I know that, somewhere above Asia, a jumbo jet is heading this way, bearing the British press en masse.

Our paper isn't dispatching any more writers, but, as proof of our status, they've already sent along an agency photographer from Sydney. He's a bit too camp for me. The man has highlights, for God's sake, and he dresses far too trendily. In my experience, snappers are grizzled, cynical old men who guzzle a couple of pints of stout for breakfast and reminisce bitterly about the good old days when they were photographing Vietnam. They are emphatically not young, not handsome, and not articulate.

We were waiting outside the bungalow, this morning, when he turned up.

'G'day,' he said with a smile. I sensed Christie tensing beside me, expecting, as I was, to be told to fuck right off and not show our mongrel faces again if we knew what was good for us.

'Would you guys happen to be Lawrence and Christie?' he continued, beaming. I realised that none of the Craggy Rock residents who abuse us for sport wear purple, skin-tight T-shirts, and white combat pants.

'Yes, we would,' Christie told him nervously. 'And you would be . . . ?'

He extended a hand cheerfully. 'I'd be Patrick, mate, and I'm here to help you guys. The paper's sent me from Sydney, so you can put that camera away if you like. Leave that side of things to me.'

Christie shook his hand enthusiastically. 'Welcome to Craggy Rock! I'm so glad not to have to bother with the photos any more. I'm crap at it! I mean, you wouldn't write a story, would you? So why am I here taking photos?'

'As it happens I do some writing as well – obviously not when I'm on assignment for a British paper! Was that shot of her in the doorway yours?' He started unpacking his large shoulder bag.

She smiled coyly. 'Yes. It came out OK, didn't it?'

He punched her on the arm. 'Listen to her! It was superb, and you know it. I was reading everything on the plane, and I think it's going to become one of those iconic images. Every single Australian paper in the land is carrying it today. Don't suppose you get fees when it's used do you? Because if you do, you'll be a very rich lady.'

'You mean an iconic shot like that one of Christine Keeler?' smiled Christie. He looked blank, so she tried again. 'Or Diana and the landmines?' At this he grinned.

'*Exactly* like that.'

I felt a little left out. I'd never thought of Christie as a fag hag, but, watching her in action, I realised she was exactly the type. Gays always seem to go for women who are a little bit troubled, and who trowel on their make-up. Christie fits the bill on both counts.

Patrick looked over at me. 'Lawrence! I hear it was you who found this little lady in the first place. I must say, when I spoke to Michael in London he was raving about you. I mean, really raving. It was all, can you go and help out Lawrence, this is Lawrence's story, we want to take the pressure off them. I'd say you were next in line for the editorship if you wanted it! Pulitzer Prize, here we come. Has anyone else interviewed you yet?'

I was bursting with pride. 'Some of the local papers have asked for quotes,' I told him as casually as I could. 'And the local TV. Nothing major.'

'Fabulous.'

'I'm going to my room,' I tell Christie. 'I'll have a shower and get back out there. We shouldn't really be leaving the house unattended. We might miss her.'

'It's hardly unattended. Every journalist in Australia is there.'

'So what if she comes out and says something and every journalist in Australia gets it, and we have to call Pat and say, sorry, we were watching telly and we missed it.'

'If she comes out we'll see it on telly and we can run over there. Anyway, Patrick's there.'

'Patrick is not having a byline.'

'I'm going to take him a sandwich later. And a couple of cans of Coke.'

'Christie, I hate to break this to you, but he still won't fancy you.'

'Larry, Larry, funny old Larry. I do not fancy Patrick. I am completely aware of the fact that he'll never fancy me. That doesn't matter in the least. I like him. He's fun to be with and he makes me laugh. That's all.'

I don't say anything.

'You're not jealous, are you?'

'Of course I'm not bloody jealous.'

'I think he quite likes you.'

'Shut the fuck up!'

She bursts out laughing. I leave the room.

When I put the key in my own door, all I succeed in doing is locking it. It must have been open already. Yet I always lock it.

I open it gingerly. I imagine someone breaking in, possibly with the help of a spare key from Nora, and going through my things, searching for clues. I don't know what clues they could be after. Now that the story is in the public domain, I have no secrets left. It could, I suppose, have been the woman who comes to make the beds, but she came this morning, and I've been back in the room, and out again, since then.

Somebody's sitting on the bed. I gasp, and then try to pretend I didn't.

'Hi, Larry,' she says, stony-faced.

'Sophie,' I say guardedly. 'What are you doing here?'

'Came to visit.'

'That's nice.'

I walk in, and close the door behind me. Sophie looks the same as she always did, apart from the fact that she never used to hate me. She looks exactly like she looked yesterday. I expected her to look different now, to dress differently, to have grown up in some way and moved away from me. She should have changed, even though we only just split up. But she is as sweet and as petite as ever, and she's wearing her little strappy sundress. It's yellow, and she looks adorable. Her hair is down. She shakes it back.

'You look nice,' I say, and instantly wish I hadn't.

'I didn't come here to be complimented. Lawrence, what are you doing? Have you seen what you've done?'

I try not to show my excitement. 'I've done what I told you I was going to do. It's all come together, that's all.'

'You've done what you told me? You mean in your parents' garden, and countless other times afterwards, when I said, you won't write about Daisy, will you, you must absolutely promise me that, and you said, of course I won't, my darling, I'm taking you to Australia because I love you and I want you to find your friend, and I said do you promise, and you said, yes, you did promise. Is that what you have in mind?'

'Not then. Afterwards.'

'You're a pig, Lawrence Golchin. I came to see you partly because you've got off so lightly. I wanted us to split up properly. Acrimoniously. I wanted to tell you that you betrayed me in the most treacherous way possible, and also that I knew all along about you and that Christie tart. It couldn't possibly have been any more obvious. It was like you wanted me to know. You go to the office lunch, you phone me with a woman nagging at you in the background, you stay at yours and then you get all shifty the next day and ask me to marry you. Was that when you told her? Did you arrange with her to come out here and meet you, so you could move seamlessly from the chick who led you to the story to the next one who would help you destroy a few lives with it?'

She can't really have known about Christie. She must be bluffing. 'It wasn't like that at all, Soph. I did love you, I mean I do. I really do.' I have no idea whether I'm telling the truth. I haven't had time to think about Sophie in all the excitement. I realise, though, that one day this story will die down, and I'll be back in London on my own. I don't think I want to go out with Christie. I wonder, for a second, what my brothers will say about my treatment of Sophie. I don't suppose I'll be able to dress it up to make it look reasonable.

She doesn't look at me while she talks. 'Oh, shut up, you stupid prick. Look at yourself. I can't believe I was taken in by you for so long. I just want to tell you a few things. One is that the only reason I went out with you was because of low self-esteem. I didn't think I was worth anything better. Your career is pathetic and laughable. Sometimes when you were talking about it I had to pretend to cough because you made me laugh with your desperation. As for Luke and Matt, they're worth ten of you, and they know it and I think they're both going to be very happy. You, on the other hand, are going to end up as a sad, lonely middle-aged man, falling asleep in his armchair and spilling whisky over his trousers. Fucking the work experience girls.'

'This isn't the Sophie I know.'

'That's because you never noticed the real Sophie. You were too busy thinking of me as sweet and vulnerable. I can be tough, you know. I've been talking to Daisy and we've both decided that I should sell my side of the story. I'm going to tell the world every single detail about how you got your story, and I mean all of it. Christie will, of course, have a walk-on role.'

Her face is hard, and she's been looking at the wall. I know she's serious.

'You can't do that.'

'You see, you can dish it out but you can't take it. I can do it, and you know that very well.'

My heart is leaden. She can do whatever she likes. She has every right to sell a first-person account of what's happened. There will be intense interest in it, and Patricia will probably like me a little less. It will be embarrassing.

'Please don't.'

She smiles. 'Sex with you was never anything special. I'm not surprised you've never had a serious girlfriend before. Sex isn't really your thing, is it? You're pathetic. In every way. I'm only sorry I ever got involved with you. Anyway, that doesn't matter any more. All that matters is that you know what I think of you, you know what you've done to my friend, and you know that your days in Craggy Rock should be numbered.'

'What do you mean by that?'

'I just mean, well, exactly what I say. You shouldn't stay around here too long. Lots of people don't want you here. It's not like London, Larry.'

I feign astonishment. 'Not like London? Really? I hadn't noticed.'

'Shut up. People here hate you. You should leave the story to someone else, and get out.' She stands up and walks out of the room without even looking back.

As soon as she's left, I think of some remarks I could have made. It doesn't matter. She just wants me to leave for her own reasons. I'm sure of that. She was trying to scare me away, because she doesn't like the fact that she led me to the story. She hates to be reminded of her own naivety, and that, I suppose, is fair enough.

chapter twenty-five

I can hear Sophie talking to the woman. Sophie knows I'm standing in the hallway, listening, but the journalist doesn't. As I hoped, they're talking about Lawrence.

'And you really didn't have any idea, then, what he was planning?' asks the woman from the liberal British broadsheet. She sounds sceptical.

I imagine the expression on Sophie's face. 'I didn't!' she protests. 'So OK, I know that looks naive, but that's because all you guys are here now. It's hard for you to imagine things the way they used to be. You know, all I wanted was to find my friend again. I was completely fixated on that. Larry offered to help me. I didn't question his motives because he was my boyfriend. I feel stupid about that now, but he did ask me to marry him, you know.'

'He never mentioned that! Should I congratulate you? I guess not.'

'No, but thanks for the thought. You know when you spend all this time with someone, and then you look at them and wake up and wonder what the fuck you thought you were playing at? I never kidded myself that I was swept off my feet, but I thought Lawrence was as good as it gets. I thought that by the time you reach thirty, you have to settle for whatever's available. I thought he'd do. I never actually agreed to marry him, but I probably would have done. At which point, I now realise, he would have run a mile.'

'Did he buy you a ring?'

'Yes. Hey, I like yours. That's beautiful. Far nicer than the one Larry got. I never wore it, anyway. When are you getting married?'

'In May. It seems like it's years away.'

They both giggle. Sophie and Gemma, the journalist, are getting on rather well. I feel a stab of jealousy. Sometimes I forget that Sophie isn't as tangled up in this as I am. She could go off and have a normal life any time she wanted. The fact that the woman she's talking to is a journalist doesn't preclude Sophie's making friends with her. She insisted on doing the interview with a reputable paper, without any payment. If I was her, I'd have taken the money. That could be why I'm in this mess, and she isn't.

Someone hammers on the front door. This happens about four times an hour, apparently in the hope that I might suddenly have changed my entire personality and be ready to let them all in and make tea. Every time, I think it's the police. I assume that, if it was, they'd shout, 'Open up! Police!' or something similar. Then I'd know to let them in. I haven't looked outside since seven this morning, and even then there was a small crowd.

I gallumph from the hallway into my bedroom. I've moved out of Red's room, so he can sleep in his rightful place. I'm sharing the guest room with Sophie, while Tony camps out in the lounge, and Beth sleeps at Jen and Tabitha's.

I shift on the bed, unable to get comfortable. In the end I stretch my legs right out in front of me and lean on a cushion. I am longing to get out of here. I have been inside for two days, and I want to see the sun. I want to walk. I want to sit on the lawn in Renmark, in the shade, and drink a glass of mango juice with that pregnant woman, Jess. God only knows what she makes off all this. I want, at the very least, to feel reasonably capable, to be able to relate to my family. I appear, however, to have run out of all physical and mental energy. I can't speak to anyone apart from Sophie, and sometimes Beth. I can't look Tony or Red in the eye. Our family life was a sham all along, and I was the only one who knew it. I am wretched with hate.

The street outside has been colonised by people who want to know all about me. For them, it's a job. For the people of Craggy, it's a distraction. For everyone who reads about me in the papers or who follows the television news, it's a soap opera. I can name the people who are really affected by what's going on here. Me, Tony, Red and the baby. The four members of the Fraser family. Giles and George's parents. Freddie's parents. Mary's mother. Everybody else is just involved through their own choice, for entertainment.

They've arrived yesterday, and overnight. There are more people here than Craggy can support. Beth says half of them are staying at Clarrie's. She's going over there later, just to laugh at people with masses of money and generous expense accounts sleeping on bunk beds, sixteen to a room. Apparently they've been asking Merv to run a taxi service, although you can walk from one end of town to the other in fifteen minutes. Prices in the pizzeria, and even the kebab shop, are trebling when they step through the door, because they're happy to pay any amount of money. Mick told Beth that they actually seem happy to spend more, because none of it comes out of their own pockets. Margot says more water's arriving because of the extra demand, and that the whole town's going to be charged for it. I'm glad. It keeps my neighbours on my side.

I press down hard on my poor bump. I'm waiting for something to happen, but I have no idea what it is. Perhaps the police will arrive, or my baby will appear. I haven't watched the television or looked at a newspaper for days. Red has kept away from me. Tony has barely acknowledged I'm here. Even Beth doesn't seem to want much to do with me any more. I just sit, alone, on the bed or in Brian's chair, and I emit my toxic vibes. Everyone else congregates in the kitchen. They use the back door, so I needn't see them at all. Once again, my meals are brought to me on a tray.

I lived like this before, when I was waiting for my trial to start. Then, too, the only person I could see was Sophie. I was in Kingsbridge, for the total lack of anywhere else to go. My Daisy-family then, like my Lina-family now, hovered on the edge of my life, not knowing what to say. I stayed in my bedroom, making the occasional trip to the bathroom when I didn't think anyone was about. At eight o'clock, one o'clock, and half past six, Mum would tap on the door and vanish, leaving a tray of food. With the breakfast, she'd leave the post. Most letters were from nutters. None of them were supportive, unless you count Marjorie's.

Sophie came to see me most days. Sometimes I'd suddenly notice her, sitting on my bed. 'Where did you come from?' I'd ask her.

'I've been here for twenty minutes,' she'd say calmly.

'Got any chocolate?'

'Sure.' After a while, Sophie knew she had to bring me fatty food. I was changing my appearance in the only way I could.

I have butterflies in my stomach all the time now. For most people who are caught up in press scandals (and my heart goes out to all of them, even the corrupt politicians), this would be as bad as it could get. I am trapped, indoors, with the terrifying pack ready to beam absolutely anything I say around the world in an instant. I hate feeling like a victim, but it's hard to know how else to see myself.

For me, this is just a prelude. It is almost certainly a mere foretaste of the incarceration to come.

The door opens, and I tense up. Sophie comes in, and I relax.

'How'd it go?' I ask, not really caring.

'Well, I think. She was nice. I didn't talk about anything I shouldn't have.'

'I heard some of it. Sounded fine.'

'Why don't you come into the living room? Gemma's gone. There's some things for you in there.'

The prospect of 'things' doesn't excite me. Particularly not when they turn out to be newspapers.

'Beth pinched them from outside,' Sophie explains.

'It was hardly stealing,' says Beth, who is sitting nonchalantly in Brian's chair. She's in my place. I fix her with a hard stare, but can't be bothered to complain. 'They were just sitting there with a stone on top. Everyone looked at me when I picked them up, but no one said anything.'

'I bet they said something,' says Sophie, with a grimace.

'Oh yeah, sure, they said, "How's Daisy today," and all that crap. I assumed we all knew that. They didn't say, "What are you doing taking our papers?" which is what we were talking about.'

They glare at each other. I hadn't noticed the friction between my only friends before.

'Tell me about your love life,' I say to Beth, to distract the women from each other, and to distract me from my fate.

'Oh, Jim. He's fantastic. Gorgeous, witty, caring. I thought you'd never ask.'

'Where did you meet him?'

'On the river. He moored next to me.'

'That's so romantic!'

'I know. He runs a vineyard. He's perfect.'

Sophie joins in. 'He sounds too good to be true. What's the catch?'

'No catch. And Andy's calling me every couple of days to see if we can work things out together. I am feeling very popular right now.'

There is a moment's silence while Sophie and I try to contain our jealousy.

'To be honest, Beth,' I tell her, 'you may as well take these papers back. I can't tell you how much I don't want to see them.'

Then, in spite of myself, I lean forward and peer at the front pages. It is a horrible compulsion and I want to resist it, but I can't. These are Tuesday's British and American papers, and I see the same photograph of myself, in my pink dress, on the front of all of them. I don't look bad, considering I'm about to have a baby. My hair is a bit straggly. I am flushed and I look angry. I was angry, then. Now I'm just incapacitated with terror and foreboding.

Sophie picks up the remote, and switches on the television. I lunge to grab the controls.

'Come on,' she says, standing on her chair and holding it above her head. 'You've got to face it. It won't be as bad as you imagine.'

'Oh, leave her alone,' says Beth lazily.

Margot has satellite television. She likes MTV to play in the background, 'so I understand what the young people are talking about, and besides, love, it's more fun than the news'. Three teenage girls are pouting to camera. CNN is in the middle of *World Business Today*. On Sky, however, is a picture of the house in which we are sitting. A skinny, blonde woman in full make-up is apparently outside the front door, talking to a presenter in London. She is quite clearly extremely uncomfortable – the sun is shining straight onto the top of her head and she isn't wearing a hat – but is trying to act the slick professional.

'Thank you, Alison,' says the studio anchor, a middle-aged man with bouffant hair. He might have had a transplant, or it could be a wig. 'Tell us what's going on now. Have there been any developments?'

'No, Matt,' says Alison, with a desperate smile. A drop of sweat slides down her face. 'In fact, today's main development has been the arrival of yet more representatives of the media. As many as thirty journalists have come from Great Britain. You can see, to my right, how hectic it has become. One thing is for certain: the town of Craggy Rock has never seen anything like it.' The camera swings around, to show a cluster of uncomfortable looking men and women. 'With the arrival of more tourists than usual, all of them keen to see the town where this woman has been living, accommodation is now at a premium. However, no one has caught a glimpse of Daisy Fraser herself for nearly two days. We are sure that she is in this house, the home of her mother-in-law, but she has shown no signs of emerging. Certainly, someone is in there. The air-conditioning units have been working nonstop, and various people have been coming and going via the back door.'

This is surreal. I feel strangely calm. It is too much to take in.

'We should paint this house,' I say. 'Then they could watch it dry. Give them something to do.'

'They'd accidentally make an art film,' says Sophie with a tense smile.

She stands by the window, and flicks the curtain, which has been closed for days. As she pulls it, she stands back, and I huddle down on the sofa. I study the picture on the screen, and watch a minor commotion starting. Some of the crumpled hacks reach for their notebooks. Photographers jump up and focus their huge lenses. Alison looks around. 'Matt, it seems that we do have some movement. I think there are signs that someone might be about to emerge.'

'Fucking hell,' says Beth, whose profile, in my chair, might be visible to a prying lens.

'This is too weird to be true.' Sophie laughs uneasily. 'I mean, this is Sky News. I know it's not the best telly in the world, but people do watch it. People on step machines are watching it at my gym.'

If I think about this for too long, I'm going to break down. 'Is everyone else in the kitchen?' I ask instead.

'Course they are,' Beth tells me. 'Even though we keep telling them to come and see you. If they won't come to you, you have to go to them. This is the most fucked-up fucking household I've ever seen in my life.'

'No one wants to see me,' I complain. 'Only the people out-side.'

Sophie takes over. 'Lina, you married Tony. You have to talk to him. You can't do everything through me and Beth just because you're scared.'

'If Tony wanted to talk to me, then he'd come in here. Red hates me.'

'Red is ten. He doesn't hate anyone. He's confused, and the longer you let him stay away, the worse it's going to be in the long run. He's getting fed up of being bossed around by Beth.'

'At least I try to impose some order on his screw-up of an excuse for a life.'

I look from one to the other. 'I just haven't got the strength. I used to talk to this bump all the time, but now I'm just pretending it isn't there. Sophie, I wish we'd run away, the other night, even with nowhere to go. I can't face it, staying behind. Plus, I know, really, that those pricks out there aren't going to leave until I talk to them. And I'm surprised I haven't been arrested yet.'

The girls look at each other, and leave the room. I had forgotten how entirely ill-equipped I am for this sort of attention. I thought I had escaped it. I thought I'd achieved a life of obscurity. I'll never be free, now. I'll go to prison, and the moment I come out, it will start again.

I could take Red and walk away from my marriage and everything else. I could do my best to shake everyone off. There is a chance that, a long way from here, we might be able to start again. I cannot, however, do that while I'm seven months pregnant. I can't run for ever. This time everyone will be looking for me. Britain was densely populated enough for a disappearance into smoggy air to be possible. Australia is not.

I look back at the television, then flick through the channels. I am perversely aggrieved to see that my story is not, by any means, on every channel. I see cartoons, Japanese news and dubbed films, before the outside of this house reappears. When I see it on TV, I appreciate just how ugly it really is. This time it is on CNN, and a statuesque woman with enormous hair and flawless make-up is talking to Lawrence. If they're resorting to interviewing each other, they must be desperate.

'It was a movement, Cyndi, in the window of the left-hand side of the house,' he's saying. 'For myself, I had a very clear view of Daisy Fraser looking out at us, and it will be interesting to see whether anyone's caught that on camera.' Lawrence gives the viewers a bright grin. His face is so uniformly purple that it's impossible to tell to what extent he's red from exertion and how far he's sunburnt. His eyes betray some desperation, although I'm sure he would be astonished to know it.

'And what do you think this might mean?' smiles Cyndi, through gritted teeth.

'Obviously she's getting restless. I wouldn't be surprised if we saw her within the next few hours. Nobody can stay cooped up for that long.' He has a point, I think. 'Her new family and her few friends have been reluctant to give us any ideas as to her wellbeing.'

Cyndi turns back to the camera and clasps her microphone to her chest. 'I'm here with Lawrence Golchin, the British reporter who found Daisy Fraser living in this most remote of locations. Lawrence, what was it that led you here?' She holds the mike to him, with her head on one side and her hair swinging down across her face.

I press the off button.

I'm on my own, with a pile of newspapers. Last time, it was the papers that messed with my head and stopped me functioning as a normal girl. A normal girl would have grieved for her friends. She would have talked to Leila about that night, and tried to make sense of it all with Sophie. She would have let herself recover.

Instead, I was suddenly famous. Even before anyone knew about my shameful role, I was tainted by drugs and death. They never traced exactly what the lethal ingredient was in the speed, but according to the coroner, if they hadn't injected, they'd almost certainly have been fine. It turned out that injecting amphetamines turns them into a class A drug, and turns the maximum penalty for supplying into life imprisonment. The de Montforts were one of the most famous society families in Britain, and they hated me and Leila. They hated the fact that we'd survived. If Giles and George had been the lucky ones, they'd have hushed the whole thing up. As it was, they complained to all the eager journalists outside their door. They made sure that everyone knew that, in their book, 'dancers' were synonymous with whores.

The tabloids lapped it up. They were thrilled that we were the ones who'd walked away. They loved the fact that we were young, lithe and photogenic. They loved the hundreds of file photos of us. I didn't realise, at the time, that they were being gentle.

Mary's mother was sympathetic, and told me, falteringly, that she didn't blame us for what had happened. She blamed, she said, the dealers and the pushers and the importers. Freddie's parents said the same to Leila.

Leila and I huddled on the phones at our respective parents' houses, and whispered to each other, late at night. We agreed that we'd say the boys had bought the drugs. I trusted her. I knew I had no choice.

She changed her mind, and told the police the truth. Journalists found out in no time. Suddenly, I became that evil pusher, and the newspapers went ballistic.

The world changed. Every time I went out, they followed me. My own face stared, grimly, from every newspaper. I officially dropped out of the Academy before their bureaucracy processed my expulsion. I stopped thinking about becoming any kind of dancer. Then I stopped thinking about anything. I would go into newsagents, and flick through the tabloids, compulsively seeking my own face.

Perversely, part of me was fascinated by my transformation from innocent ballerina to murderous tart. Raunchy photos emerged. I saw myself dancing topless at nightclubs with Giles and other men, a glass of champagne in my underaged hand. I was sixteen, seventeen, eighteen. These pictures would be contrasted with shots of Mary looking pious in the company. I wanted to stop the newspaper-buying public and tell them: I have been demure and gracious too. And Mary has been clubbing. This is not as black and white as it looks.

Then I was charged, and the stories almost stopped. It was a hiatus. The press were waiting for the trial, and so was I. So were my parents, and the bereaved parents. We were all waiting for the same thing.

Wanting to die was the basis of my life for those weeks. I couldn't go through with a court case. I didn't have the courage. The thought of standing in the dock made me tremble. I didn't think I'd be able to stay upright. There was no doubt that I would be found guilty, and I knew I'd be sent to prison. Even though I was not the real dealer (Marjorie still scared me so much that I hadn't mentioned her name), I was going to get the harshest punishment available, because of the publicity. It didn't matter that Giles had frequently bought drugs for me, that he'd introduced me to the delights of amphetamines in the first place. Somewhere along the line, Giles, who was twenty-six, had become the victim of a scheming eighteen-year-old vixen. I was barely able to register the fact that my boyfriend had died.

Ten years have elapsed, and I'm still defensive. I wish I could throw my hands up and say: I committed the crime, so I'll take what's coming to me. I don't dare. I read a few newspapers after my suicide, and by then, when I was putatively dead, the gloves were truly off. You cannot, after all, libel the dead, and anyway I had no reputation left to besmirch. I was officially a cowardly, murderous whore. One columnist, a woman called Amanda Ratchett, wrote with such vitriol that I fantasised about taking *her* to court. I also dreamed about cutting her into pieces and feeding her to the vultures. I can still recall parts of her outpourings. 'Despite her innocent name,' she wrote, 'Daisy is no flower. This is the girl who, at the tender age of 18, poisoned five of her closest friends with illegal drugs. Now she appears to have taken her own life, leaving just one survivor from that terrible night. What went through her head as she jumped, only Daisy and God can know. But all parents can sleep a little easier in their beds tonight. It is not often that we see a manifestation of pure evil. This is what Daisy was, and now she has sent herself to Hell, where she will rot.'

I am crying tears of frustration. I haven't thought about that bitch for years. I hope she's died a vile and lingering death, on her own. I hope she's been sacked. I hope she's been sued. I hope she's got cancer.

Above all, I hope she isn't writing sanctimonious, knee-jerk bollocks about me today. I gingerly locate the *Courier* in my pile of papers, and flick through it, looking at the bylines and attempting to ignore everything else. She doesn't seem to be there. Then I skim the words. I don't want to read about myself. They'll have it all wrong, and what is factually correct will be misinterpreted. Everything is twisted. Everything is fucked. This is my life, my private life. If the police want to talk to me, then they will come and get me. It has nothing to do with the people who write the papers, who read the papers, who want to follow my life as though it were any of their business. I'm not hiding in this house to sell newspapers. If the public thinks I'm immoral, then everyone else involved in the process is every bit as bad by association.

I lean back, and stretch across the sofa. At the moment, the thing that pisses me off more than anything else is the array of weaselly notes that comes through the door. Everybody wants to interview me. They think I'm too dizzy to remember that after I get arrested, I won't be allowed to talk to the press. They know they've got a tiny window to get their story. They insult my intelligence. I am no longer a stupid druggy dancer who doesn't know how the world works. I am a teacher and a mother. I am a survivor.

The tone of the notes infuriates me. I pick one up from the table. It's written in Biro on a page torn out of a notebook.

'Daisy,' it reads, 'would it not be more sensible to carry out an interview with me on a "pool" basis?' At this point, the Biro ran out. He carries on in black. 'We all want to give you a chance to put your side of what has happened, and then we'll be happy to leave you in peace. I think you'll be surprised at the sympathy people feel for you out there. Please give me a call at the motel. Best, Graham Ward.'

As far as I'm aware, no one else *has* a side to this story. Lawrence is making a valiant effort to market his 'side', and Sophie is retaliating with hers, but that is just a subplot. This is not about anyone except me. No one knows how I got here. Everybody wants to know, because they're nosy. It really is that simple.

I know that the 'pool' angle is a lie. He would never share my interview. He'd keep it for himself. And nobody mentions the fact that if I tell, or sell, my story to one publication, then all the rest will slag me off even more.

The door creaks open. To my surprise, it's Tony.

'Hi,' I say listlessly.

'Hello,' he replies shyly. 'Hello, bubba,' he adds.

'You might as well say it properly.'

Gingerly, he approaches me. He leans down and puts his face next to, but not touching, my stomach.

'Hello there, bubs,' he says loudly. 'This is your daddy speaking. We can't wait to meet you. Don't ever forget how much we love you.' He looks up, questioningly. I nod to him to carry on. 'I hope you've not been upset, mate. It's got nothing to do with you, all right, and I'm your daddy and I'm going to take care of you.' Hurriedly, he adds, 'Me and your mummy, we both are.'

He sits next to me, heavily.

'Look,' he says abruptly. 'Sophie and Beth have been telling me to speak to you. If not, I may as well have stayed in Renmark.'

'I do understand, you know. If this was, I don't know, a film, you'd accept it all and we'd carry on with an enhanced family life with no secrets, but—'

'It isn't like the movies.'

'I know.'

'The trouble is, I never knew we had a secret to start with. Now I sit down and I think about it, and I wonder how I was so stupid not to guess. Not to guess even that there was anything wrong.'

'You knew I didn't want to talk about my life in England because it was too difficult for me. We fought about it recently, didn't we? So it did disturb you. You did have an idea.'

'But you told me that your family died in a crash. And I believed that. I mean, a bloke doesn't question a thing like that. What kind of a bloke wouldn't believe that? And it turns out all your family are still about.'

'Are they?'

'That's what it says in the paper.'

'All of them?'

'You've got a brother and sister, yeah?'

'Yeah. Mum and Dad?'

'Back from the dead. It said they were going to come out to see you, all of them. With some newspaper.'

'Excellent. Exactly what's needed.' I look at him. 'You know,' I tell him, speaking without thinking because I know that if I thought I wouldn't say anything, 'you were my salvation. You gave me a life again. I thought Red and I were going to be wandering around, looking over our shoulders, for ever.'

'Only trouble is, I didn't know I was doing it.'

'Is that an insurmountable problem? Does it necessarily matter? I know what a betrayal it seems, but it doesn't change our relationship. I didn't tell you because I couldn't tell anybody. These are incredibly serious charges I'm looking at.'

'I don't think they're that bad, you know. We've been reading about it. Seems people all know that, if it hadn't been Daisy, it would have been one of the others would have done the buying. The worst you'd be looking at is running off when you were on bail.'

'Maybe in normal circumstances that would be true, but you have to factor in the pressure from the press. If it had been a group of normal people on a council estate, that would be one thing. But it wasn't just any old people, was it? I remember how the de Montforts felt about me at the time. And look out of the window. Do you think they're going to be happy unless I get banged up for life?'

'They'll move on to the next thing soon enough, love.'

He called me love. I try not to react. I know he only did it out of habit.

'Have you seen anything about Leila?'

'Was that the blonde one?'

'Yes. Do you know what happened to her?'

'The mongrels are trying to hunt her down. I think she was last seen teaching ballet in America.'

So Leila escaped, too. She got off with a token fine for the speed and E that were still in the flat, and then she was free. Still, that drugs offence should have kept her out of America. I wonder how she got round that one.

Tony's still speaking. 'How come youse two got off without a scratch? They said those amphetamines were deadly. No chance of surviving if you injected. Did you not inject? I don't know how these things work. Feel like a right prawn.'

'We didn't take it at all. I was saving some to get us through school the next day, but for a night out, me and Leila always liked ecstasy better.'

'Lina, you haven't been out of it all this time, since I've known you, I mean? I know people hide it. And since you've been pregnant?'

'Tony, I haven't touched any drug, of any kind, since that night. I vowed that I wouldn't, and I haven't. It's the last thing I'd want to do.'

'Except the booze.'

'And the occasional fag. Cigarette, I mean.'

I want to lean on his shoulder. Sophie and Beth have offered several shoulders between them, but they haven't been the same. Sophie is too tiny and fragile, and I can't avoid the conclusion that Beth doesn't really like me any more. I try it, tentatively. I just want to feel, for a few seconds, that I'm not alone. Even if he pushes me off, it will be worth it.

He puts an arm round my shoulders. I feel my eyes pricking with tears, and I close them. I sniff the familiar smell of his shirt. It's Tony's smell, mixed in with deodorant, washing powder, and sweat.

'It's still our baby,' he says, nuzzling my hair and touching my stomach. 'And I'm always going to be mates with Red. So you know

I'm not going to leave you and never see you again. I still want to be there when it's born.'

'What about after?'

'I think about us going back to some sort of marriage, darl, but I can't picture how it could be. I would always be thinking there were other secrets. I don't know if there are or not, but I wouldn't be able to sleep for thinking I was a mug.'

'What about if we sat down for an afternoon, or a day or a week or however long it took, and I told you everything that's ever happened to me, in the tiniest detail?'

'It couldn't work. Because it was coming from you. I couldn't trust it.'

'How about if you talked to Sophie about everything that happened to me before I left England?'

'Too many gaps.'

'If I'm hiding anything else, the wankers outside will unearth it. You know they will. That's what they're here for. They're digging around for dirt, and if it's there, believe me, they'll find it.'

'No. It took them more than ten years to find you here, and that was only because of Sophie.'

I snuggle in closer to him. This is bleak. 'So what will we do? What about Red, and the baby? Will you look after Red for me if I go to prison?'

'Of course. Don't even think about that. I've been talking to Mum.'

'Does she hate me?'

'Not at all. Sure, she used to think you were the greatest thing that ever happened to the Pritchetts, but she's all right. You've got the baby on your side. So she says we need to know what you want to do. I mean, are you going back to England?'

'No, of course I'm not. I don't want to go back there ever. Unless I'm extradited. No way. Apart from anything else, I couldn't take my baby away from her father, and I don't think Red would thank me either.'

'You really don't care about your real family, do you?'

'The Pritchetts are my real family. Red and the baby are my real family. You are. Even Pete. I don't care about the Frasers. I don't even dare think about them.'

'So would you be staying in Renmark?'

'If the good people of Renmark would have me, yes, I would.'

'Then we don't have a problem.'

I grin, despite everything. I am suddenly supremely confident that, with the passage of time, Tony and I could forge some new kind of relationship. The baby will draw him back to me. We won't have any secrets. The idea of being completely honest scares me, but I'm sure I can do it. It opens up new vistas. Anything might be possible. This could, eventually, become a cathartic force for good.

I am, of course, glossing over the inconvenient fact that I'm a fugitive from justice, and that Tony will probably have to bring up both children on his own.

Someone bangs on the door, again. We both ignore it. At least they can't ring the house any more, because both phones have been pulled out of the wall.

'I wish they'd fucking bugger off.' I burrow further into Tony's arm. This time, he gently pulls me out.

'Only one person can make that happen,' he says, looking me in the eye. I look away, because I know what he's going to say. 'And that's you. The only reason they're here is because they want to talk to you. Why don't you get yourself washed and sorted, and go and see them? Show them that no one fucks with Lina P.'

The sitting room door creaks open, and Sophie, Beth and Red appear. Sophie has a plate of sandwiches. Beth is carrying a large bottle of Coke and a jug of water, and Red has plates and a stack of paper cups. I watch him. I've never seen him shrink away from me before.

'Hello, Red,' I say, as normally as I can. 'Are we having a picnic?'

'Yes,' he replies, staying close to Beth. 'An indoor one. You have to eat, you see. It's for the baby.'

'You are absolutely right. Do you want to come and sit over here, with me and Tony?'

Tony shifts over, opening up a space for Red between us. He looks reluctant, but lowers himself anyway.

'Talk to the baby,' I urge him. If he remembers that there are two people in my body, his ambivalence might be dissipated a little.

'Hi there, little baby,' he says, rubbing my stomach. 'It's your brother here. I'm back, to look after you.' I feel a timely shift in my womb. Red's eyes are wide.

'It kicked me!' he exclaims. 'It didn't just kick me; it moved all around. I think I felt its hand.' His face is lit up with excitement.

'It's reaching out for you,' I tell him. 'It's saying it needs you around.'

For a brief moment, everyone in the room is happy.

I take a sandwich. Even though it's made with sliced white bread of the type I despise, and although the cheese inside it is processed and tastes of chemicals, I like it. Beth passes me a cup of Coke. I take a sip, despite the fact that, early in my pregnancy, I would never have touched caffeine. The baby's going to be dealing with an awful lot more than caffeine. I know I have to pull myself together. It's the only way I might be able to salvage something with Tony. People are depending on me.

'After lunch,' I tell my assembled friends, 'I'd better have a shower and put on some clean clothes. Then I'm going outside to meet my public.'

chapter twenty-six

19 January

'When they said Australia,' spits Graham, who works for the *Courier*, and is thus my arch rival on this story, 'I thought, great. I thought, your luck's in here. I thought, beaches, sand, barbies.' He looks around. It is the middle of the morning, and Craggy Rock looks bleaker even than usual. When the sun's really strong, it drains everything. It is intensely depressing. 'And here I am on fucking Mars. Cheers, Larry, for digging up this one. We're going to fucking crucify her for this.'

'You're welcome, Graham,' I tell him graciously. I am sitting in the midday sun, with no shade for miles around, and I have been looking intently at a nondescript house for three hours. When I did this two days ago, I was a deluded fool, wasting my time but bothering no one. I do it today, and I've arrived.

I've been interviewed on camera for some of the world's strangest TV stations. Editors of rival newspapers ask me to write pieces for them, and every time I turn one down, I make a point of telling the newsdesk at home. People are going crazy for this story. I could go and work for anyone I chose, and unless the guys in London review my salary, I will.

This town has changed beyond all recognition. Every single bed in Craggy Rock is now occupied. Journalists are sleeping at 'Clarrie's Backpackers' Lodge', sixteen to a dormitory. Hacks with limitless expense accounts are speechless with rage because there's nothing to spend money on. There isn't even a cab service, although the bloke from the garage said he'd start one if we were really intending to pay him good money to drive us from one end of the street to the other.

'Course we'll pay,' I heard one of my colleagues tell him earlier, before rounding on him triumphantly. 'But only if you give us receipts!'

There are no expensive restaurants, and the only accommodation available by the time the third wave of Brits arrived – me and Sophie being the first, and Christie the second – was a ten dollar bed in a fleapit.

I sit and watch the front door serenely. There has been very little movement today. Ratty little Pete came and went. Then Margot left. They both swore at us in passing, but there's strength in numbers, and I don't take it personally any more. From time to time, neighbours arrive to watch us watching the house. Graham collared a woman earlier as she left the house opposite. It's an equally offensive bungalow.

'How do you fancy a holiday, madam?' he asked her. 'This could be your lucky day.'

'What do you mean, how do I fancy a holiday?' she demanded.

'I'm offering you cash, love. Money for you to go away, so I can rent your house off you while you're gone.'

'Rent my house? So you can spy on poor Lina?'

I wished I'd thought of it. It was a brilliant idea. With a good pair of binoculars, you'd never have to go outside.

'A thousand dollars for the week,' Graham offered. 'Plus, I'll buy you a ticket on the next bus to . . . I don't know. To Hanging Rock.'

'And make me miss all the excitement? My house has been on the television, you know. Who would look after the shop while I was gone?'

She wasn't budging. I was glad. Graham would be unbearable if he pulled that one off.

So even the locals, who profess to hate us because that's what Margot's told them to do, can't drag themselves away from my story. A tale of someone coming back from the dead is irresistible, and all over the world, punters want to know about it. The fact that she is young, attractive and heavily pregnant makes it even better. On top of that, she's still wanted for involuntary manslaughter, possession of class A drugs, and skipping bail. Her husband, meanwhile, has done time for GBH. The story has tension. It has children, death, narcotics. It has everything. If they wanted to, I'm sure they could add a few more charges to that lot. Impersonation, use of a false passport, something like that.

I am at the centre of the Daisy Fraser universe. When anyone wants to complain about something, they sidle up to me. Today, I am in the middle of a disgruntled group, and I'm serenely batting away their complaints.

'Cunts,' adds Graham. I think he's talking about everything and everyone.

Professionals who take a reasonable amount of care over the way they look are struggling with Clarrie's showers, which don't even work unless you put a coin in. Yesterday evening, I was with a crowd in the bar, trying to hide the fact that I don't get served there, when a woman called Cyndi came storming to our table. Cyndi works for CNN, and she's disgusted that no amount of money can buy her the luxury she considers essential. 'Don't laugh,' she said sharply, and we looked up and tried to control it. Normally, she has enormous hair. It is an independent entity that sits magisterially at the summit of her being. The laws of gravity do not apply. It is a huge, yellowy nest that could house a family of rare ostriches. Last night, however, it was limp around her face, and covered with suds. Her face was red and damp. Even her lips weren't shiny.

'Cyndi!' exclaimed Graham, smarmily. 'Or should I say, Cindy *Crawford*?'

'Screw you. The fucking water ran out. I need sixty cents. Someone. Yes?'

We all fumbled in our pockets, none of us daring to take the piss any further.

There are about fifty journalists here, and we are, for the most part, reasonably friendly with each other. Everyone knows that, one day, any one of us might need a favour or a job from any of the others, so a fierce amount of networking is going on. The British seem to be sticking together. We rather look down on the Australians except when we need something. The smattering of hacks from other countries are less inclined to stay up drinking, late into the night, and more inclined to take their duties with ostentatious gravity.

The backbiting has started, but it isn't as bad as I expected. This morning, I listened with pleasure while a bloke called Harry, who I recognised from his byline picture, laid into Gemma from the *Liberal*. Gemma, although pretty, trim and otherwise inoffensive, has emerged as my unlikely enemy. Harry is a grey-haired hack from the old school, who's been working for the same, nominally left-wing tabloid for hundreds of years. Like many others, he's taken exception to Gemma's modus operandi. She arrived yesterday, and this morning she strolled into that house to interview my ex-girlfriend. I'm glad I'm not the only one who feels put out. Everyone, it seems, recognises this as a tabloid story, and everybody sees it as an inversion of the proper order of things when the broadsheets twist it so it's about the journalists.

Harry intercepted her as she left the house. A crowd immediately gathered.

'Not so fast, young lady,' he said as she increased her pace to avoid him. 'Would you like to tell us all what that was about?'

She stopped and looked him steadily in the eye. 'No,' she said, clearly. She actually looks younger than me. Her face is tanning gently, as though we were under the kinder Provençal sun. I don't like that.

'It's just that Larry here was saying his wee girl was threatening to talk about how he got his story. We don't do that. You know we don't do that. No one here should touch that story with a bargepole.'

'Oh, don't be ridiculous. You know you'd have jumped at it.'

'I would not. But that's typical of the fucking *Liberal*. A story like this, there's always someone from the fucking *Liberal*. They come over so holy, and at the same bloody time, 'scuse the language, at the same fucking time they slag us off and they repeat every single detail we unearth for them. You can't have it both ways. I'm telling you, I'm going to read every piece you write. If you get sanctimonious about so-called tabloid intrusion, I'm going to write a leader with your name in it. You're intruding too, lassie. You're part of it. Remember that.'

She stuck her chin out at him. 'Please,' she said. 'Be my guest. I'd love to read your thoughts. Now, if you'll excuse me, I've got a piece to write.'

Harry watched her leave, with his head on one side.

'Sexy lass,' he said.

I'm disappointed in Gemma. I had high hopes for her; so much so that Christie and I moved into my room so we could sublet Christie's room at a profit, and I handpicked Gemma to increase my chances with her. Depending on what sort of piece she comes out with, I can see that I'll have to give it to someone else, and leave her homeless. It's the least she deserves. The Backpackers' is full, so she'd be fending for herself in the desert. She'd have to see whether Sophie and Daisy would let her into their happy household.

It looks like I'm stuck with Christie. We have shagged once, and it was all right. To be honest, I'd rather have the freedom. I didn't end one relationship just to get embroiled in another. Besides, I've had advances from interesting places, and I'd like at least the theoretical chance to act upon them.

It's baking today. I look positively at home sweltering in the desert, compared to some of my colleagues. I glance around. You can spot the Australians. They are the people, like Patrick, who saunter around effortlessly. My favourites are the middle-aged porky men like Harry and Graham, who can't take a step without buckets of sweat pouring off their white bodies. They make me look suave.

'Cheer up, Graham,' I tell him as condescendingly as I can. Graham is much older than me, as well as bigger, stronger, and more established. I've seen him out on stories before, and it feels wonderful to be able to patronise him at last. 'You'll get used to it,' I add. 'After all, Daisy Fraser did.'

'Thank you for that, Lawrence. Looks like your lady friend's settling in pretty well, too. That's what Gemma said. She said she's doing just fine.'

The key thing is the interview. Daisy's going to have to do one, and it needs to be with me. I admit that my chances, on this score, are not striking at the moment. Daisy hates me, and Sophie really hates me, and they are in that house together. They are hardly going to be mellowing each other's attitudes. But this is still my story. I have to talk to Daisy. I want her to tell me everything, so I can tell the world. She owes me that much.

Nothing's happening today. As a result, I get to be the subplot. I am constantly being asked for quotes by other hacks, for sidebars explaining how we tracked her down. I gloss over my relationship with Sophie, because I know that anything I say about her will come back to haunt me when her story (the truth, presumably) hits the streets. Sometimes I cut her out of the tale altogether.

The comprehensive three-page interview will complete my triumph. It will be syndicated everywhere, and it will confirm me as the world's top journalist. Having a chat with Cyndi on CNN from time to time is one thing. I suppose that puts me in the league, but the exclusive, the 'My new life, by Daisy Fraser', would make my world complete. It has to happen within the next couple of days. Some guy from the *Sydney Morning Herald* said they wouldn't extradite her until she'd had her baby, but I suppose they could still take her into custody if they wanted. I think they're leaving her alone for now because, with her house under this dedicated guard, she's effectively a prisoner as it is.

Apart from anything else, in my quiet moments – and I have now got used to the fact that, until she breaks her silence, there will be many of them – I discover that I want to talk to her. I want to get close to her, to know her. I want her to realise that she doesn't have to hate me. I want to be her friend like I was Sophie's friend, only much, much better. I want to know how she got here from rural Devon. I want to know it for myself, and not just for my readers. I am not someone who watches soap operas or reads trashy books. If I am curious, then I can't begin to imagine how iconic her story will become with my fellow countrypeople. My fellow people. There's a journalist here from India, for Christ's sake.

As I ponder, the woman in question wanders over.

'Hi there, Gita,' I say with a smile.

'Hello, Larry,' she responds. I like her big brown eyes. I'm sure she fancies me. Gita wears shocking pink lipstick, shorts and a T-shirt. In a way, it's a shame, as she'd be stunning in a sari, or one of those trousers and tunic things that Muslim women wear. Having said that, though, it's nice to see her legs.

'How can I help?'

'A few questions, I'm afraid,' she says apologetically. 'In the absence of anything else to report on. Could you tell me, first of all, why you came to Craggy Rock?'

'I came because a friend had been here last September,' I begin, and we run through the usual routine. When all bases are covered, she apologises again.

'It must be very galling for you to answer these same few questions every time,' she says, looking at me and twiddling her hair.

'You know, I don't mind at all,' I confide. 'I suppose it could get boring in the end but so far I like talking about it.'

'You have all the facts at your fingertips. Thank you. It must be your finest hour.' She smiles.

'It is. How about you? Are you enjoying it? Have you left India before?'

'Oh, very much so. I am South Pacific correspondent for my paper, which is a national newspaper, so I am very rarely in India these days. In fact I am based in Sydney.'

I am warming to Gita. She is a little older than me, but I like that. If she lives in Sydney then the chances are she's one of India's more emancipated women, and doesn't have an arranged marriage lurking in the background. There is nothing to say she's single, but she isn't wearing a ring, and she's flirting with me. I remember, with a rush, that I can have any woman I want. I can tell that Cyndi, from CNN, has a soft spot for me, but she's too old. I already have Christie on tap. Gemma's out of the frame, thanks to Sophie's meddling, but there are a few other sexy young reporters I haven't spoken to yet. That only leaves Daisy and that blonde woman who comes in and out of the house with the boy. They would probably not be impressed with my credentials, but you never know. It's a question of getting close enough to Daisy for her to realise that she can trust me. It's going to be an uphill struggle. In fact, I shouldn't mention the word 'trust'. That can come later. She's been shut in that house for days, and she's going to have to come out soon. I don't trust her not to do a runner at night, so I've organised a round-the-clock-watch for this evening. We have to get to her.

I decide to jot some notes in my book. I have been more circumspect since the discovery that it was my trusty notebook that led Christie out here. Of course, with hindsight I'm glad it did, but it might not have worked out that way.

IDEAL COURSE OF EVENTS
- Sophie to go home at once with no further interference.
- Daisy to realise most hacks will leave if she gives an interview.
- Daisy to pick me as her interviewer.
- My interview to be syndicated and me to be as famous as Bernstein and Woodward.
- Me to fly home with Daisy? Maybe as she's extradited. Then I can move on to big and richly remunerated job with any tabloid and get flat, car etc. as per previous lists.

There is a mass movement, and I spring to my feet, along with the other bored hacks. This happens whenever someone enters or leaves the house. Normally they sneak out round the back so we get worse photos. This is the first time the front door has opened since the last time Daisy came out.

And it is her. She's wearing trousers this time, which is a shame for the world's front pages. Her trousers are cream, and her T-shirt's red. Her hair is scraped off her face, and she's put on some red lipstick to match her top. Her bump protrudes proudly. Once again, I admire her pregnant physique, but this time I must admit that she doesn't look healthy. She doesn't look happy. She's tried to hide it with make-up, but she is fucked. Momentarily, I feel sorry for her.

'Daisy!' I shout, among the mêlée. 'Daisy, how are you feeling?'

She doesn't hear me, because everyone else is shouting too. She stands, silently, watching us with something that looks like contempt. Eventually the shouting dies down. I remember that she used to be a teacher, and feel a bit silly.

'I'd like to make a statement,' she says calmly. Normally people read their statements from pieces of paper, but this one appears to be improvised. Her voice is shaking just a little. 'I realise that you have mostly been sent here by your employers to cover a story and that you're just doing your jobs, but we need to be left alone. You've got your story now, all right? I'm here. My family are here. I'm due to give birth in six weeks. I can confirm what you already know, that I used to be known as Daisy Fraser. That is all I am prepared to say. If you leave us in peace today, then I'll come out and answer some questions tomorrow.' She turns to go inside.

'Daisy!' shouts a man from a tabloid, next to me. 'Will you be doing an interview?'

She turns back. 'No,' she says, over her shoulder.

Everyone erupts. 'What do your family think of what's happened? Are you still with your husband? Will you be staying in Craggy Rock? How do you feel about seeing your parents?'

She closes the door firmly behind her.

I sit down again to try to formulate a more detailed strategy. I have no advantage any more.

THINGS TO DO
Get a one-to-one conversation with her (how??).
Talk to her. Remember to call her Lina. Point out that no one will

leave her alone, for years if necessary, till she gives interview.
Don't mention the police.
Promise copy approval.
Also promise enough money to give baby an enviable start in life,
get it to uni, and so on.

I cover the page with my hand as Patrick sits next to me. He seems
to have given up worrying about the dust stains on his white trousers in
the same way that I have. Short of buying a folding chair, there's nothing
to be done about it. No one sells folding chairs. I asked Patricia to send
one out, but she laughed, and when I tried to take a normal chair from
the motel, Nora caught me.

We nod at each other, and I close the book.

'Didn't mean to interrupt,' he says. 'Carry on, mate.'

'No, it's all right. It was nothing important.'

'Larry, can I ask you something?'

'Sure.'

'Do you feel good about all this?'

'Do I feel good about it? Of course I feel good. I mean, I'm too hot
and she's being a bit stubborn, but yes, I think it's all going fine.' That's
not what he meant, and I know it.

'I just, like, can't help thinking about what she's suffering in there. She
went through heaps when she was a teenager – she saw her friends die
in front of her, and she had all that guilt to deal with, and now she's
living here, with children and a new life. She is obviously a fantastic,
strong, wonderful woman. Now she looks dreadful. It's like, who are
we to take it all away from her? No offence to you personally, mate.'

I smile, wounded. 'That's just the way these things go, Patch. I know,
if you stop and think about it, as if she was your sister or something, then
it all looks different, and OK, she is someone's sister – in fact her family
have wasted no time selling their stories – but she's also someone who sold
dodgy drugs to her friends, and they died because of her. How would you
feel if Mary Futter was your sister? She was nineteen when she dropped
down dead from injecting poison. Which Daisy gave her. If you look at
it from that perspective, you'll see she's not so innocent.' I wish I could
manage to talk about this without sounding pompous. It even comes out
pompous in my pieces. The subs always rewrite those bits.

'But, mate, I'm not saying she's innocent. I'm just saying she's suffered enough, don't you think? Have you never ingested an illegal substance? Because you'd be unusual, to say the least, if you hadn't.'

'Sure I have.'

'Ever bought anything for yourself and your mates, for convenience, and taken some money off them?'

'That's different.'

'Only because of luck. And she dealt with it. Faking a suicide, and then somehow pitching up in Australia, and having a kid, and starting a new life. It's not exactly taking the easy way out, is it? If it was up to me, we'd go away today and leave her to it, like she said.'

'We can't do that. The police will be here soon – we can't miss that. I know she's the kind of woman that people like you admire – in fact, she's a classic, isn't she? – but if you look at it through the eyes of the law, you can't let someone off the hook because they're good-looking and admirable and have strength of character. You can't only prosecute unsavoury old men.'

Patrick lies on his back, with no thought for the consequences for his beige T-shirt. I lie down next to him. The sky is completely, utterly blue.

'I've had enough,' he says, without turning his head towards me. 'I don't think I want to do this any more.'

'What do you want to do instead?'

'Mate, I haven't got that far. Hey, and when you say she's the sort of woman that people like me admire, you might want to hold your horses a minute. We can't be stereotyped like that. It's not all Judy Garland, you know.'

'You love Judy Garland, I heard you say so to Christie. Plus, you like Christie, and she's that type.'

'That type?' He reaches over and punches me on the arm. 'Christie is not a fag hag, mister. She's a strong and independent woman. Yeah, sure, she's great company. But just because you might see me as a stereotype, that doesn't mean I am. We come in all shapes and sizes, you know.'

'I know that. I'm not prejudiced.'

'Bloody right you shouldn't be. You'll be surprised.'

'What do you mean by that?'

He props himself up on his elbows and looks at me, with a little smile.

'Nothing,' he grins. 'Come for a walk?'

chapter twenty-seven

They leave in the middle of the night. I can't sleep anyway, not with my life in suspended animation. I am only too happy to get up and waddle around, saying goodbye to my only family. In fact, it's a treat. Normally I spend the night looking into the blackness, trying not to disturb Sophie, and waiting for morning.

I wish I was in my house. We should never have moved away. If we hadn't, then at least I'd get to be imprisoned among my own things. I wouldn't be stuck living out of a suitcase, and I'd get to amuse myself by tidying my own kitchen rather than suffering Margot's. Perhaps, now that she's going, I'll be able to sort it out for her, insofar as brown, beige and orange are sortable.

I don't want to see the Frasers again. I want to be one of the Pritchetts. I can't believe the Frasers have come all the way here. Surely even they could have taken a hint that strong. My birth family will probably turn up at this house tomorrow, while my adoptive family, including my little boy, will be on the other side of the state. I know it's the best place for Red to be, but I hate to see him leave me.

I wish I could think of an escape route, but I am paralysed with indecision. Last time, I made a meticulous plan, and I followed it to the letter. This time I seem to have lost all that sharpness. Perhaps it's because I'm so pregnant. Maybe it's because I'm older. It could be that I'm not so desperate, although I don't know why. I have far more to fight for this time round.

'Mum,' whispers Red, climbing into bed next to me. Sophie shifts sleepily on the camp bed. 'Margot says it's time to go.'

He is all tousled in his pyjamas, and he smells of sleep. I cuddle him. I don't want him to go, and, despite the many charms Renmark has to offer, he doesn't want to go. My ten-year-old would rather stay cooped up with me in a house that is now a famous eyesore, in the desert, at the height of the summer, than live in a big, airy home by the river, with freedom to do as he likes, and a friend next door. And yet, for a while, I doubted that he loved me.

He clings to me.

'Come on, baby,' I tell him. 'Up we get.'

'Margot says some of the mongrels are waiting outside, so we mustn't switch any lights on. She said to use your torch and she's got some candles.'

'OK, pickle.' I pull him in closer.

They never spent the night outside the house ten years ago. If they had, I might not have made my exit as flawlessly as I did.

Getting away without being spotted was crucial. I had all the documents I needed, thanks to Marjorie and her contacts. I didn't betray her to the police (neither, surprisingly, did Leila), and she was so grateful that she bought a passport and had it doctored for me. For all I know she's still out there, still selling her dodgy substances. Still lounging in her flat in a heroin-induced haze.

As soon as I was given the dead girl's identity and knew that I had to be Australian, I dedicated as much time as possible to watching lunchtime soaps and learning the accent. 'See you this arvo,' I'd say, copying Scott from *Neighbours*. 'I'm taking a sicky,' I'd repeat after Bobbi from *Home and Away*. I was still lurking indoors, but now I had a project.

Sophie tried to make me leave my room, even just to go downstairs, but I wouldn't do it.

When my dark roots were long enough, I cut all the blonde off the end of my hair. The day before I left, I took some of Mum's frumpy clothes from the back of her wardrobe and put them in my wardrobe. Then I got drunk with Sophie. Early in the morning, I dressed in them. Mum never had any sense of style and I doubt she's developed one since I last saw her. At three in the morning, I applied heavy make-up, with a clumsiness enhanced by alcohol, and my transformation was complete. I was Noeline.

Leaving was surprisingly easy. My biggest handicap was my hangover. The car was parked on the street outside, and not in the driveway, so there was never much chance of my waking Mum or Dad. The Maxi had long been traded in: I was stealing my parents' chunky Volvo. I drove north, on the M5 and then west on the M4, where I stopped at some services to post the suicide letters I had written to Mum and Dad, Rosie and Ed, Sophie, Leila, Giles and George's parents, Mary's mother, Freddie's parents, the Director of the Academy, and (I agonised over this one, but did it for emphasis) the editor of the *Courier*. Then I reached the bridge. It was five o'clock in the morning, and the only vehicles around were lorries trundling through the night. It was cold, and I huddled in my coat. I was ready to go.

I pulled off the motorway at the roundabout, just before the bridge. Down the side road marked 'works access only' there was a motorbike. Marjorie had promised it would be there, and I'd had no choice but to believe her. The key had arrived in the post the previous week. I had ridden one before, with Giles, and although he'd taught me the basics, I was not confident. If Giles had survived those amphetamines, he would probably have died on his bike. I didn't want that fate to befall me.

On the middle of the bridge, I stopped to throw the car keys into the water. I looked down, and considered, briefly, throwing myself after them. I could do it. I had already announced my demise to the world.

I was sorely tempted. The prospect of the life that awaited me, as Noeline, was exhausting. I couldn't imagine where I would go, what I would do, and whether I could get away with it. The water below would be black and velvety. It would be so easy. No one knew I was here. All I needed to do was to climb on the barrier and then slide down. I could have done it in a few seconds.

Nobody would ever have known about the baby. It would have died with me, as soon as I hit the water. My body, with its improbable embryo, would have been washed away. No prison, no family, and, above all, no more guilt. I would join Giles and George, Freddie and Mary. It would be right.

I could do that, or I could try for something different. It was a dilemma I had faced for weeks, and I had already made up my mind.

I had to give it a go. I would go and live somewhere sunny, and I would be someone else. If I was caught, at least I would have tried.

Most people who have committed an offence, and been caught, end up facing their trial. They plead guilty or not guilty, but, either way, they stand up in court in front of twelve good citizens and whichever members of the public have chosen to come and watch. The fact that more journalists than usual would have come to see me didn't make any difference at all. I knew that if I lived in a society, I had to abide by its rules. So I elected not to live in this particular society. I was going to give myself a chance to try again. With one last look down into darkness, I turned my back. I climbed onto the bike, and went to Wales, under the cover of darkness. At the toll booth, I threw the correct change into a coin bin. I had crossed my first border.

By the time I got to Newport, I was shaking with excitement and I felt sick. Although the wind wasn't in my hair, because I was wearing a helmet, I felt it was there metaphorically. I was free. I didn't want to enjoy it too much, because I knew it wouldn't last. Nonetheless, it was time I had clawed back for myself, and, even if I got caught straightaway, I was glad I'd done it.

I locked the bike, and caught a National Express bus to Fishguard, and a ferry to Rosslare. Another bus took me to Dublin, and Noeline already had a plane ticket that would take her from Dublin, via Amsterdam, to New Delhi. The first words I ever said as Noeline were, 'Yeah, g'day, can I have a ticket to Fishguard please?' The assembled cast of *Neighbours* couldn't have pronounced it more professionally. The cashier didn't bat an eyelid. I was away. And, astonishingly, it worked.

My first few weeks in India were the most intense time of my life. I was no longer the person I had been from birth. I didn't even have the same nationality. I had to be somebody new. I was Noeline, and sometimes I wished I knew what the real Noeline had been like, to give me some guidance. I started off doing everything the opposite way from my old self. As my confidence built, I came to realise I could be whoever I wanted. I could go where I chose, as long as I stayed away from tourist haunts. I never saw the Taj Mahal. Instead, I skulked around low-grade hotels, bought loose Indian clothes, did my washing under a cold tap and hung it out to dry on the hotel roof. I ate from stalls on the street and kept myself as healthy as possible, mainly by sticking to vegetables. On trains, I travelled in the 'ladies' carriage' (a stipulation routinely ignored by various men), and I crisscrossed the country at random, getting off at stops in the middle of nowhere and locating a bed for the night. I fought off groping hands, and bought myself a wedding ring that soon brought my finger out in a rash. I read books, and tried not to think of home, of Giles, of Sophie. My face lost its chubbiness in no time, but my natural hair colour, my bushy eyebrows, and my growing belly provided enough of a disguise. I directed all my thoughts towards my future, my baby. Soon, I had Red in my arms, and he was the best disguise of all.

I read about my disappearance anxiously. *The Times* of India lifted a story directly from a British paper. From this, I learned that my parents hadn't actually opened my bedroom door until the early afternoon, when Mum delivered my lunch and noticed that I had not yet touched my breakfast. Occasionally, I've tried to imagine how she felt when she looked nervously round the door, and found that I wasn't there. Did she smile, happy that at last I had left my self-imposed imprisonment? Or did she immediately realise I'd done something terrible? She must have known I wasn't anywhere else in the house. Perhaps, for a moment, she thought I was in the bathroom. Maybe she called my name. I don't know. I suppose I could ask her.

Everyone seemed to accept that it was suicide, although there was a little speculation that I might have escaped. Over the months, I read about sightings of myself in Russia, China, South America and, worryingly, South India. I wondered whether the Indian one really had been me. There was no mention of Red. That was when I moved to Bombay. A big city seemed safer than anywhere else. People get lost in Bombay all the time. I loved the city. One day, perhaps, we'll go back.

Margot appears in the doorway. I was half asleep, and am not pleased to see her.

'Aren't youse ready yet?' she demands, in a stage whisper. She looks at Sophie's semi-conscious body on the floor. 'It's time to go. Come on, Red, get your clothes on. Lina.' This last word is said with a curt nod in my direction. Margot has spoken to me as little as possible recently. She must be pleased to be going away, but I'm sure she's less delighted that I'm remaining in her house. I would hate to leave her in my lovely kitchen.

Margot leaves us a torch, and walks out. I hold it under my chin, and shine it up on my face, trying to look frightening. Then I shine it on Red. His lip is quivering. He reaches out and hugs me.

'I don't want to go,' he sniffs, and buries his wet face in my shoulder.

I try to be brave. I would be dead if it wasn't for Red.

'But, baby, Renmark is the best place for you to be. You need to get back to school, and you'll be able to go out, and play with Daniel, and hang out with Beth on her boat. I'll be back as soon as these people have gone away.'

'It's not fair. The baby's allowed to stay.'

'If the baby had been born, then it would go to Renmark too, with Tony and you. It's only because it's still in my tummy that it has to stay with me. Look, shine the torch on it.'

He puts the light up to my skin, and we both feel the baby turn away. Red laughs, and I haul him out of bed.

'Come on, tinker,' says Margot, briskly, when he's had half a bowl of Coco Pops. 'We've got a lot of driving.'

Red moves closer to my chair, and hangs on to my arm.

'We'll play car games,' says Tony. 'We'll look for kangaroos.'

'I do not want to go. If you try and make me I'll scream so all the journalists come.'

'Oh Red,' snaps Beth. 'For Christ's sake! The rest of us can't wait to get away.'

In no time, he is sobbing uncontrollably. I lead him to a quiet corner of the living room, and sit him on my knee. He fits himself round the bump.

'Come on, Red,' I tell him. 'What about school?'

'We used to go to school together.' He is looking at me accusingly.

'I know. And we will do again, I'm sure. For now, you'll have to leave me to get rid of these people, because it's no good having them annoying us, is it? You're going with Tony and Beth and Margot, all squeezed into Beth's car. It'll be fun. You'll have a good time. And before you know it, I'll be home too and everything will be fine.'

I wonder if my words sound as hollow to him as they do to me. I'm haunted by the knowledge that the police could come for me at any time, and that I might not see my son for years. He is the baby boy I gave birth to, as Noeline. He's the child who gave me a new life. My heart is breaking. I hope he doesn't know it. I want him here, with me.

'Mum, when you come back, will Sophie come with you?'

'I expect so. Why, do you like her?'

'I *really* like her. She's so funny and nice. Not as cross as Beth.'

'Good.'

'So I think I should stay here with you and her. You need a man to look after you.'

I pull him close. He puts his arms round my sturdy bosom, and hugs me tightly. He's not going anywhere, and we both know it.

No sooner have I gone back to bed, than I hear a nervous tapping on the back door. I look down at Sophie, but she doesn't stir. I'd forgotten what a sound sleeper she is. Although I ignore the knocking, it persists. Eventually, I get up, baffled. It must be a friend, or at least a neighbour. Even Lawrence wouldn't get me out of bed at – I check the clock – twenty past five.

I stand in the kitchen, and hesitate over whether or not to switch on the light.

'Who is it?' I say quietly, in the dark.

'Is that you, Daisy?' comes the whispered reply.

I know the voice. This is the last thing I need.

I open the door. She looks scared, and immeasurably older. Her hair is long, almost to her waist, and she's wearing a T-shirt and pyjama trousers. She tries to smile at me, and I try to return it.

'Come in, Rosie,' I tell her, weakly. 'It's nice to see you.'

chapter twenty-eight

20 January

In the middle of the night, I am suddenly wide awake. I stayed outside Daisy's until two o'clock, when Christie came to relieve me. Whenever our target emerges, day or night, we'll be on hand to yell for an interview.

I sit up in bed. The human mind is an amazing organ. My subconscious has been mulling something over. It has now reached a conclusion, and it is ready to communicate it to the real me.

It is blindingly obvious. Red is Daisy's child. Giles is his father. She must have been waiting for somebody to wake up to it. She must be hoping that we won't. This is my next story. It would be perfect if I got the interview. I could throw it in as a casual question.

The trouble is, she'd deny it. And I will not be able to prove it, unless I begin some extremely careful preparations.

It is half past four. I decide to go and visit Christie on night duty. She's on my side. Together, we'll make this one stand up.

Christie and I are indulging in some routine snogging when they come out. She might not be the girl for me, but she's pretty good to be going on with. She certainly knows how to use her tongue. I would guess that she's had plenty of practice.

'How old were you when you first got off with someone?' I asked her, yesterday. We were in bed, indulging in some post-coital pillow talk.

'Why?'

'Just curious.'

'Twelve. You?'

I was on the spot. Naturally, I couldn't tell her the truth, so I made something up.

'Fourteen.' I smiled. 'Bit of a late developer.'

She laughed. 'I might have guessed. Who was the lucky girl?'

'Her name was Jess Smith,' I replied, truthfully. Christie's never going to meet Jess. She's not going to discover that I was eighteen, and Jess was twenty-one and lying, unconscious, on the floor at a houseparty at the time. In fact, to this day, Jess almost certainly doesn't know that I snogged her. She tasted of vomit, but it was worth it. 'What about you?'

She grinned, a faraway look in her eyes. 'Paul Cooke.'

'Do you know what he does now?'

'I do, actually. He plays in the reserve team for West Ham.'

I punched her arm. 'A footballer? Good work, girl!'

'It's a result, isn't it?'

The strange thing is that while we chat happily about our various exes (or, more accurately, Christie's various exes and Sophie), neither of us has mentioned Christie's current boyfriend. I don't even know whether or not she's still seeing him. The truth is, I couldn't care less whether she's got someone at home or not. I don't want our relationship to continue. I'm just having fun and so is she, and that's fine. It passes the time. We're not the only hacks indulging ourselves, and I imagine that the vast majority of the liaisons that are hastily being formed to pass the time are illicit.

We jump apart when a car door slams. We haven't noticed any light or movement inside (though admittedly we haven't been concentrating). It's only one slam. That means only one person has got into the car, unless they've all got in by the same door to make less noise.

'Someone's off,' says Christie, walking briskly towards the driveway.

'They certainly are,' I reply. 'Nice try, Mrs Pritchett, but we've caught you once again.'

The ignition starts up, and the car inches away from the house. I run towards it, with my torch.

'I knew we should have got a bloody hire car,' Christie complains. 'How are we going to follow?'

I shout back over my shoulder, 'It's OK. She's not there.'

I run beside the car, looking in, until, just before it speeds away, the driver's window winds down, and, before I realise what's happening, a juicy lump of phlegm lands squarely in my face.

Through the passenger window, a woman is yelling at Christie. 'You just fuck right off,' she shouts, 'you parasite scum, you rotten mongrels, you fucking tossing dicks!'

'Morning, Margot,' Christie yells back. 'Just doing our jobs!'

The car is gone, and I turn back. I try to wipe the phlegm off my face before Christie sees it, but am hampered by the fact that it makes me want to spew.

'That's gross!' she laughs. 'My God, it's the worst thing I've ever seen. Hang on. Let me get the camera. We'll capture it for your new byline shot.' She is doubled up with laughter. I wipe it off with my sleeve, and rub my sleeve in the dust of the road.

'It's not that funny,' I tell her. 'I might go back to bed. These people are the scum, behaving like that, not us. We don't go round spitting at them, do we?'

'Ah, but they'd say we spit on them metaphorically.'

'Well, they're a bunch of cunts.'

She puts her arm round my shoulders. 'It's all right, Lazza. Sorry I laughed. I didn't mean to. I was just surprised.' She pauses to stop herself from giggling again. 'Who was in the car?'

'Well, as you heard, that hag of a mother-in-law, and the cunt of a husband and in the back I think it was the blonde woman.' I suppose I should cross her off my list of fantasy shags. That only leaves Daisy in the subset marked 'desirable yet unattainable'. 'I'm sure if we got this gob analysed we'd find that wanker's DNA.'

'Tony Pritchett, you mean? Bound to be. So, there was no one on the floor?'

'I'm pretty sure there wasn't. No piles of blankets.'

'And you wouldn't get a pregnant woman in that boot, so she's still here, with little elfin Sophie, and the boy. Our friend Red. Wonder why they didn't take him?'

'Thank God they didn't. We don't need to go anywhere.' The thought of running around Craggy Rock looking for a car to borrow at this time of night is not appealing. Merv's cab service probably wouldn't offer the dedicated level of service we need. In the absence of a car hire outlet, let alone a twenty-four-hour one, we would certainly have ended up stealing a vehicle, and that might have been difficult to explain to the newsdesk.

'We should ring London,' Christie says, 'in case they want to get a stringer to wherever these guys live now. What was it called?'

'Renmark. Like Denmark, but different.'

'Let's call them. Then they can have someone waiting, a reception committee for the happy band of runaways.'

'It's the least we can do.' No one has ever spat at me before. I've always been a respectable, desk-bound journalist, or else I've been one of the pack on someone's doorstep, hassling a victim who deserves it. Because they always deserve it. Me and my friends and my family, we don't end up plastered all over the papers. That is not through chance. We don't behave in a way that would shock the general public. We don't shag the wrong people, we don't commit adultery, we're not mixed up with drugs, and there are no love children.

For a moment, I pause to consider my own family. I suppose there was my night with Christie, and then our fumble on Christmas Day. That was infidelity, though not, technically, adultery. The hours my dad spends looking at his gay porn on the internet might not look good if they were made public, and I have no idea whether he takes his urges any further. I know there is a stash of dope in Luke's room, and another in Matt's, and there might even be some in my old room as well. That still leaves Mum clean. Although I have had the occasional fleeting suspicion even of her, based on the fact that Luke looks nothing like Dad, and uncannily similar to 'Uncle' Raymond, who is supposedly no blood relation at all.

If anyone was interested in us, I suppose they could dig around and find a story. But we're not charismatic, and we're not public figures. We're just ordinary people leading ordinary lives. If we were public figures, or consorting, as Daisy did, with people who routinely appear in papers and magazines, we'd know that we had to be whiter than white. It's a fair price to pay for all the benefits. I abhor the idea of a society where celebrity comes free, where people can use the press to promote themselves, without the danger of a comeback. Britain's tabloid press is the best in the world, and people should be proud of it. It plays a vital role. If it didn't exist, if it wasn't independent, then totalitarianism or fascism wouldn't be far behind.

'Christie?' I say. She's settled back down outside the house, and she looks up at me.

'Mmm?'

'I'm really proud of what we do. I am. Even when we get spat on, I think we're doing the right thing. Don't you?'

'What? I don't know about you, but I'm doing my job, and I'm doing it because I enjoy it, and to secure myself a good future.'

'You don't think about it any more deeply than that?'

'What am I now, too shallow for you? No, I don't. What's brought this on?'

'Just something Patrick said. I've been thinking about it and I disagree with him.'

'I'm so pleased for you, Larry. Now, what are we going to do tomorrow? You have to assume you're not getting your famous interview, so how are we going to play it? People are going to start drifting off after the weekend. Your Red angle's going to keep it hot, so we have to decide whether we can rush into print without any confirmation of any kind. Ideally, we should run some DNA. The de Montforts would go with that, surely? And apart from anything else, we need a photo.'

'We need to put it to her. Otherwise she can deny, *and* put out a statement saying we didn't even give her the opportunity to comment. So we have to get to her somehow. So we shout it out, or write it down, and put it through the door?'

'Last resort.' She holds out her thermos. 'Have some coffee? Or are you going back to bed?'

'Don't suppose you're coming?' The thought of cuddling up to Christie, with her comfy tits, suddenly pleases me immensely.

'I'll join you when Patch arrives.' She presses the light on her watch. 'Fifteen minutes.'

'Deal.'

I stumble back, feeling pleased with myself.

Outside the motel, a female figure is wandering around apparently aimlessly. When I get closer, I see she's wearing pyjamas, and that she looks like a taller, slightly older version of Daisy. I know exactly who she is.

'Hi,' I say, and she jumps.

'God, you scared me. What are you doing out at this time of night?'

'My job. What about you?'

'Couldn't sleep. Jet-lagged. What's that on your face?'

I put up my hand, and find that I've missed a bit of phlegm. Hastily, I wipe it off with my sleeve.

'Nothing,' I tell her. 'You must be Rosie.'

'And you are?'

I offer her my hand. 'Lawrence. Friend of Sophie's.'

'Ex friend, surely? Lawrence, can you point me in the right direction? I want to go and call on my sister without that tosser from the *Courier* breathing down my neck.'

My heart leaps. 'Sure I can, Rosie. I'll take you there.'

I lead her to the house. The stories keep landing in my lap.

chapter twenty-nine

Breakfast time feels like a holiday, which is perverse. It's ten o'clock, and, unlike Red and me, Sophie has been up for hours. Later this morning I'll clear up Margot's kitchen. I've been longing to rearrange it for years. She's got all her mugs in a cupboard above her head, and she, like me, has to stretch up on tiptoes to reach them. She uses mugs far more than she uses, say, the posh glasses that are at shoulder height. I've offered before to arrange it all more logically, but she's always turned me down. Today I have my chance. I know she won't bother to move everything back.

Because I still have Red, I am less agitated than I have been since this whole nightmare began. The fact that Tony and his mother are speeding further away from us every second cheers me up immeasurably. I'll try to sort things out with Tony later. For now, I am with my little boy, and my best friend. That's all the company I can handle.

I've seen one of the Frasers. I know they'll be around later, but it seems they're not the ogres I imagined. Rosie says I'll be able to deal with them, and so I'll have to.

This morning, I even had a shower. I've put a load of my clothes in the washing machine, and I'm reasonably ready to face another day trapped indoors. I'm as ready for the parental visit as I could ever be. We know what to talk about, and what to avoid. I have an ally, and that makes me feel surprisingly confident. Part of me is still twelve years old, still longing for Rosie to notice me. That part is triumphant.

'I've been watching the news,' says Sophie, beaming as she sits down with her bowl and a mug of coffee.

I look at her. 'Oh,' I say.

'No. It's good news. You'll want to hear this. It seems your friend Leila has resurfaced – she's written to the *New York Times* about you.'

'Saying?'

'Saying everyone should leave you alone, that the two of you were young and silly and that you didn't deserve anything that happened to you.'

'Did she mention the fact that she dobbed me in?'

'She said she's always felt bad that you ended up taking all the blame when it wasn't your fault any more than anyone else's.'

This cheers me. 'No one'll take any notice of that, but it's sweet of her. Is she teaching dancing?'

'Yep. They had a picture of her now. She's stunning. I know she always was, but she looks fantastic.'

'Maybe I will see her again one day, after all.'

'You never know. Hey, we're running low on supplies. No more proper coffee, and this is the last of the bread and the butter. I'd better go to the shop.'

'What day is it?'

'Friday.'

'So how long have they been here? Since Tuesday? It feels like for ever.'

'Three days. Amazing, isn't it? I must say, I feel great without Beth here. She hates me.'

I can't think of anything to say to that. She hates me, too. 'Hey, Red,' I say instead, 'how do you fancy getting your social life going again? You don't need to stay cooped up like I do.'

He studies my face. 'Do you mean go and play with Eric and Tabitha?'

'Exactly. Sophie can take you.'

'Or they could come here.'

'Much more fun for you to go to Tabitha's.' I can't imagine Eric's father dealing with the straggling hacks who might be sad enough to follow Red around. Jen, on the other hand, would give as good as she got. 'Why don't you call them? Give Tabs a ring now. You'll have to plug the phone back in, and if it rings, don't answer it, just pull it out of the wall again. And remember to tell her that she can't call you. If she says she'll ring you back, ask what time you should ring her instead.'

'He is absolutely adorable, you know,' says Sophie when he's gone.

'Isn't he just? Do you think he's going to be all right?'

'Well, yes, in broad terms. Kids are resilient. It does all rather depend on what happens to you.'

'Every time someone bangs on the door I expect the police. I can't imagine why they haven't been yet.'

'Pete checked it out with the local guys. Says no one's told them to do anything, so they haven't. Hey, guess what, my interview came out!' Her eyes are shining.

'Have you got it?' I ask, excited.

'No, but they talked about it on Sky. It sounds like she's done a superb job. Shame Margot hasn't got a computer, or we could look it up online. I'll get a copy of it off Gemma later.'

I butter a second piece of toast. 'Sophie, that's wonderful. I'd love to see Lawrence's face.' I think about it. 'Not enough to actually go out there and look at him, of course.'

Red returns, excitedly, with an immediate invitation to Tabitha's, and, as we know the Frasers will be pitching up this morning, Sophie takes him straight out. I hope they don't get too much hassle on the way.

Abruptly, there is a loud rap at the door.

I don't answer.

'Daisy!' shouts a vaguely familiar English voice through the letter box. 'Open up! We need to talk to you. You said you'd answer questions today.'

It's Lawrence. I wait, standing in the hall and looking at the letter box. As I stand there, I remember that Beth and Tony should have taken the cot to Renmark. The bloody thing will stay here for ever, now.

'It's important,' he continues, with an anxious edge to his voice. 'For one thing, Lina, you already know that your family are here. They're going to be visiting you very shortly. Just thought you might like some advance warning. The other thing is, I need to ask you something about your son.'

I walk straight up to the door. 'What about my son?'

'Lina! Hi! How are things?'

'Could be worse. I enjoyed Gemma's piece today, and I'm sure plenty of others did too.'

'How did you see that? It was very unfair, actually. I'm thinking of suing.'

I laugh. 'Now, that I'd like to see. Anyway, you're not really dragging Red into this, are you? It's got nothing to do with him. I thought even you guys might respect the privacy of a pre-pubescent boy. Is he all right?'

'Yeah, I'm sure he's fine at his mate's house. Nice kid, Tabitha. That's why I thought I'd come and talk to you now, while he's away. We're interested in his adoption. Was it legal?'

'Yes, it was legal. As I'm sure you already know. You can get a copy of the adoption certificate. You've probably got one. Where are you going with this? Can't you leave him out of it?'

'So, you categorically deny that he's your natural child?'

'Yes. My natural child is in my womb.'

'OK, fine, sorry to have bothered you. Now, how about an interview? Give you a chance to put your side of what's happened? I'd give you copy approval, and we'd certainly be offering enough of a financial inducement to see both your children comfortably through university.'

I walk away. He calls both my names a couple of times, before he gives up.

When Sophie comes back, I share my fears with her. If I wasn't concerned for the health of my unborn baby, I would be an alcoholic by now. Every single time I have a cup of tea, I wish it had the propensity to knock me out.

'Daisy, I can't tell you, again, how sorry I am,' says Sophie. We both ignore some loud banging on the door. 'That interview with Gemma brought it home to me just how much this is my fault. I just saw her outside. She says the other hacks are ostracising her but that her paper is delighted with the piece. Lawrence pretended not to notice me. But one interview isn't going to make a difference. The fact is, I brought Lawrence here, and if we hadn't come, then you, and Tony, and Red and Margot would all be absolutely fine. Your marriage would be fine, Red would be fine, and the biggest thing going on would be that you'd be waiting for your baby to be born. Instead, you're about to meet the family you ran away from, and every time anyone comes to the door you think it's the police. And it's all my fault. I wish I'd never come to Craggy in the first place. I wish I'd never gone travelling. Then I wouldn't have seen you, I wouldn't have told Lawrence, and everyone would have been all right.' She's crying. I feel slightly detached. If, unimaginably, the roles had been reversed, I'm sure I'd have done what Sophie did.

'I'm just hoping something good's going to come out of it,' I tell her, more optimistically than I feel. 'Don't beat yourself up.' I put an arm round her shoulder. 'It's my fault. It is. Everyone knows that. I knew, all along, that I was living on borrowed time. Part of me never expected to get this far. Part of me was overjoyed to see you in September. It was going to happen sooner or later. It's exhausting. It's a cliché when they call it living a lie, but that's what it is. It's your whole life. You're living it day in and day out. In lots of ways, I'm glad to be able to tell the truth at last.'

I'm saying this to make her feel better. I wish it was true.

The door knocking hasn't stopped. Someone has been battering it. Now he, like Lawrence, begins yelling through the letter box. These journalists are not particularly chivalrous.

'Daisy, this is Graham Ward from the *Courier*. I'm here with your mother and father, and your brother and sister. Can we come in?'

'Do you want me to go?' asks Sophie quietly.

'Maybe just check Red's all right. I don't want him here while they are. Go out the back.'

I go to the letter box.

'Graham,' I say loudly. 'Of course I'm very happy for them to come in. But it has to be them alone. I don't want you in the house.'

'Sorry, love, but it's all or nothing.'

'What do you mean?' I know exactly what he means, but Rosie and I agreed that we'd make a fuss.

'I mean, they're signed up with us. They did that before they left London. We flew them out. The contract clearly states that *Courier* representatives are to be present for the first meeting between them and you. I can post a copy through if you like.'

'No thanks. I didn't sign any contract.' I hate these people. Who the fuck do they think they are? There is some slight excitement in the background, which is presumably caused by Sophie's exit. I try to hear what's being said to her, but it's over too quickly. 'I didn't sign it, so I don't have to abide by it. I want to see my parents, and Edmund and Rosie, but I don't have any particular yearning to see you. I'm sure you understand.'

'Of course I do. But they are now contractually forbidden from seeing you unless I'm present.'

'Can one of them come and talk to me like you're doing?'

'Rosie's standing right next to me, love. Here she is. You know, all this bollocks would be much easier face to face.'

'Don't push it.' I know he'll have a tape recorder shoved into Rosie's face, so I have to watch what I'm saying.

'Daisy?' she says. 'Is that you?'

'Hello, Rosie. How are you?'

'We're all a bit confused. Can't we come in?'

'I'm worried about this journalist. Wouldn't you rather see me without him being there?' We are both acting, and we know it.

'Sorry, but it was the only way we could afford to come here, to see if it was really you. So Mum and Dad just signed whatever it took.'

'There's no way round it?'

'No.'

'I guess you'd better come in, in that case. All of you.'

I open the door with a heavy heart, and see my blood family for the first time in nearly eleven years.

Rosie and I exchange tentative smiles. The rest of them gaze at me as though I were an alien, and I can understand that. I have come back from the dead. I was so convinced by my own cover story, that it's almost the same for me. Mother and Father, bewildered and sad, have come back to life after the fatal car crash that propelled Lina to Australia. Edmund looks like a sad middle-aged man, as Rosie warned me he would. Only Rosie looks normal, and I concentrate my attentions on her. It's the only way I'll get through this.

chapter thirty

20 January

Christie and Patrick are looking at me expectantly.

'I asked her,' I tell them in triumph. 'You were right, Patch. As soon as I said it was about her boy, she was there in a flash.'

'You went in?' asks Christie innocently.

I glare at her. 'You know perfectly well that I didn't.'

'Did you get what Daisy said on tape? And is she going to be on her guard now?'

'Yes, and probably. But now we've got her denial we can run a story, so it doesn't really matter. Patch, did you get a shot of the boy when he came out with Sophie?'

Patrick nods glumly. He's having another conscience attack. 'Are we actually going with this?' he asks. 'Because I must say I think the ethics of involving a kid are pretty bloody questionable.'

'We're going to keep away from him.'

Christie interrupts. 'But if we could prove he was Giles's son, that would be better, wouldn't it? Because otherwise they could just carry on denying it. I think it would be fantastic if we could prove it.' She catches Patrick's eye and tails off. 'Somehow.'

Tactless she may be, but she's also right. I resolve to keep Christie and Patch apart until the piece is filed.

'Chris,' I say to her, 'why don't you call Giles's folks and get some reaction off them? See if we can buy them up?'

'Because it's the middle of the night where they are. I'll do it this evening.'

'Fine. Well, I'm going back to the room to make a start on this piece. I'll see you later.'

'OK,' says Christie. 'I think I'll go to that house where your treacherous elfin one took Red, to keep an eye on him.' She looks at us both. 'Oh, for Christ's sake! I'm going to stand outside, cultivating my tan. It's what we've been doing all week.'

That bitch Gemma hasn't even got the decency to stay out of the way. She's gossiping with Gita, who doesn't appear to realise that we're meant to be ostracising her. Gemma made me sound like a bastard. The whole piece was about me. The words 'treachery', 'operator' and 'liar' featured heavily, all in direct quotes from Sophie. Despite the full frontal attack by the liberals – or, more likely, because of it – I still seem to be something of a hero. I'm enjoying the attention.

Meanwhile, that twat Graham is making a show of parading the poor, jaded and jet-lagged Frasers in front of everyone. Rosie looks exhausted, but so do the rest of them. We've all read through the old cuttings and seen their stories. I know some of the front pages by heart, after my researches before we came here. 'My anguish, by Daisy's mum, cont. page 2, 3, Amanda Ratchett page 14, comment page 20.' Today, the mother is shrunken and lost, and she looks a bit mad. Her hair is completely white, and she seems to be wearing the same outfit she'd have worn on holiday twenty years ago. Maybe that was the last time she came to a hot place. She's wearing an elasticated skirt with big flowers on it, and a straw hat that she's clutching constantly in case it blows off. I know she's in her late fifties, but she could be seventy. Mr Fraser looks relatively normal. A bit jowly, a bit saggy faced, but no different, really, from anybody else's father. Not so very different from my own. His shoulders are square, and he stands up straight. He doesn't look happy, but most men of his age have an air of disappointment.

I try to imagine what I'll be like when I'm approaching sixty. I'm sure I won't have that pathetic aura. I'll have triumphs to look back upon. I'll have this story, for one thing. I am now virtually guaranteed professional success. What was the next item on my wish list? The career is in the bag, and, presumably, the salary likewise. The car and flat shouldn't be a problem. I'm aware that my ambitions of a couple of months ago included winning the tennis league, which doesn't seem like much of a goal from here, and acquiring more friends (I have them!), more respect from my family (I imagine it will be forthcoming; in fact, I'm going to call them) and finally, domestic stability. And that, I think, is where I'm going to fall down. Domestic stability used to be last on the list because I thought I had it in the bag. Now the closest thing I've got is my fling with Christie, and suddenly the professional success looks pale and easy, and the love of a soulmate represents the holy grail.

I have given up on Sophie. There are plenty of others out there. I sleep with one of them, when we manage to be in bed at the same time. I've flirted with all the women in Craggy Rock, and while that might not normally be an impressive boast, it is at the moment. Admittedly, my female admirers will begin to drift off towards other stories after the weekend, and the native women of Craggy are less drawn towards me than are their journalistic sisters, but I've enjoyed it while it's lasted. I've enjoyed it, but I haven't followed through on it. Somehow, I haven't wanted to.

The only woman who seriously interests me right now is Daisy, and that, of course, is not going to happen. Being with Christie means so little that it's an effort just to remember that it would be impolite to lie naked next to her and complain about the way Sophie's being so rude to me. I know I sacrificed my relationship with Soph on the altar of the story, and it has been worth it, but soon the story will be over. Daisy will be locked up. Red will be a de Montfort. My work will be done. What, I wonder, will I have then?

The strange thing is that, although I miss having Sophie around, I don't miss *her*. I should miss her physicality – when I see her, I recognise, in a disconnected way, how sexy she is – and I ought to miss the sex. In a strange way, I'm glad she gave that interview about me. Now I don't feel so guilty, and I have an excuse to hate her. Christie is a distraction, a way of releasing my tension. Yet I feel a desperate longing for something, and I have no idea what it is.

From a distance, I try to catch Rosie's eye, to acknowledge our complicity, but she has her back to me. Her brother's close by her side. She and Graham independently agree that he's the weird one. He certainly looks it. He moves in a shy, jerky way, and Rosie says he still lives with their parents, at the grand old age of thirty-four. His hair is brushed forwards, and he wears spoddy glasses. He'd make a classic paedophile. In fact, angry parents could easily burn his house on the off chance. Perhaps that's why he's living with Mummy and Daddy.

Rosie, on the other hand, is a glorious woman, and not just because she's given me her story to spite Graham. She is every inch Daisy's sister. The Fraser girls together must make a force to be reckoned with. It's unbelievable that they haven't been aware of each other for the past ten years. Rosie's taller and, if Daisy wasn't pregnant, Rosie would be much curvier. She's never had children. I asked if she had a boyfriend, and she said yes, and I decided she really is a little bit old for me. Still, she's gorgeous. I've never seen anyone with such luscious sexy hair. She's kind of graceful and confident. More than that, she represents survival, whereas her brother, weird Edmund, is the control experiment, demonstrating what she could have become. She didn't succumb. She got on with her life, in Daisy's absence.

I'd love to know exactly what they said to each other last night. I sat outside the back door for over an hour before she came out and gave me her quotes. We chatted for a while. She spoke to me as if I were a friend.

'Did you tell Daisy I was out here?' I asked warily.

She laughed. 'No. Funnily enough you weren't at the top of our agenda. Why?'

'She doesn't much like me.'

'I can imagine. Don't worry., I'm not Daisy. I like you, because you're not Graham Ward. My criteria are basic at the moment.'

I got Patrick to do some photos just as it was getting light, and went back to the room to write up my account.

'They're going in! How do you like that?' Patrick is behind me, touching my shoulder.

'It's a fair cop. What can we do?'

'Is this the ruthless Lawrence Golchin we've all come to love? If I didn't know why you were so laissez-faire about this, I'd be worried.'

I twist round, and smile up at him. 'Obviously I would kill Graham and trample his filthy body into the dust if I thought that would get me into the house, but it wouldn't work.'

'It's just a trashy little bungalow. In a week, all these people will be gone, and that house will be of no more interest to you than, say, that one over there.' I follow his finger. That one over there is the house Graham tried to rent the other day. Like Daisy's abode, it's a ramshackle Outback dwelling with unsightly air-conditioning units stuck to the outside. Patch is right. It's the dullest house I've ever seen.

We both pause to watch Sophie coming round from the back of the house. A few among our number get up and follow her languidly. I make a show of pretending not to see her, even though I'm aware of her looking in my direction.

'It's not the house itself,' I tell Patrick, to take my mind off her. 'It's what's inside it. Sorry to state the obvious. Hey, you will protect me from Graham later, won't you?'

'Course I will, though a poof like me's not much of a match, I'm afraid.'

'Rosie hates him. She was desperate to talk to Daisy without "the irritating tosser from the paper".'

'A woman after our own hearts,' notes Patrick. 'She's fabulous, Rosie, isn't she?'

'Very. She's *furious* with her parents for signing the *Courier* contract without reading it. Imagine signing away your right to a private reconciliation in order to get free air fares.'

'Talk about selling your soul.'

'They even made them fly economy.'

Patrick leans across and gives me a kiss on the cheek. 'It's exploits like that that make you a star.' I feel myself blushing. I've been kissed by a gay man! I know it's just what they do but it feels a bit strange. I can smell his moisturiser. 'Why don't you go and have a sleep?' he adds. 'You must be shattered. I can look after things here, and Christie, I don't doubt, is practising her own brand of tabloid intrusion elsewhere.'

Wherever Christie is, she'd never look after me like this. She's jealous that I met Rosie without her, and sneaked past without involving her in the story. 'You said you'd be waiting for me in bed!' she shouted when I came back to the room at seven and set up my laptop.

'Sorry,' I told her. 'Something brilliant came up.'

She didn't even ask what it was. She only cares about herself.

A sleep would, theoretically, be just the thing for me right now. It would keep me away from Graham. He's bound to hear a rumour soon. On the other hand, I feel strung out, and I don't think I'd be able to relax for wondering what was going on without me. As well as talking to Rosie and her family, I need to confer with Christie about the boy. She has taken that on board as her own story, and I'm glad. It's a bit hardcore for me. You don't really want to involve children. I've done my bit with the questions, and the next stage Christie has in mind is beyond anything I'd do. I need to keep an eye on it, and wait for the British papers to arrive by fax.

'Cheers, Patch,' I say, 'but I've had so much coffee, I think I'm better off awake at the moment. I'll knock off early tonight, and catch up a bit. Maybe make an exit before Graham gets on my case. Anyway, Christie seems to have done a vanishing act and you'll need someone to keep you company.'

He shrugs. 'Up to you.' Then he leans his head on my shoulder, and gives my knee a little stroke. I flinch away, but this is, I realise, more for show than because he repels me.

chapter thirty-one

'Tea?' I say brightly, looking around Margot's sitting room and trying not to think about the absurdity of what's happening.

'Please,' says Graham straightaway. 'Milk, two sugars.'

'I didn't mean you. Mum, Dad, tea?' I didn't want to address them this way, but apparently it will make them happy. 'Edmund? Rosie?'

No one says anything. I try to read Mum's face. I don't want to consider Dad, for the moment.

'Yes, why not? A cup of tea,' she says quietly. She looks different from the capable mum of my childhood. I now know, from Rosie, that even then she was quietly dosing herself on tranquillisers. Apparently it got much worse after her youngest child disappeared. 'Daisy, you always used to drink it black. Do you still do that?'

'No I don't. That was only because of the ballet, because I didn't want to put on any extra weight. Stupid really, because I needed the calcium. And I still do, for the baby.' I'm hoping that the extremely noticeable baby might make this a bit easier, but no one responds. 'I'll make a pot,' I say eventually, doubting that Margot possesses a teapot. 'Unless anyone wants coffee?'

'I'll have coffee,' says Ed, avoiding my eyes. 'White, thanks.'

'No problem. Dad?'

'Coffee.'

'Fine.' I get up. This would be bad enough without some vile piece of journalistic flotsam witnessing it all. It is excruciating.

'I'll help you.' Rosie jumps up. Graham frowns. 'Graham, chill out,' she says. 'We won't tell each other any secrets. We'll only talk about tea and coffee and where the milk is. OK? I mean, she's pretty heavily pregnant, and it wouldn't be very gentlemanly of you to make her do it on her own.'

I smile a watery smile at Rosie. Last night I resented this strange woman who looked like me, and had a claim over my life. I knew she was entitled to come into my house during the night, and to look at me with that shocked expression, but I didn't like it. Then I remembered that if it was odd for me, it was a hundred million times worse for her. I remember how I used to long for her to treat me like a sister. Now, perhaps, we'll have a chance to be real sisters. Red, innocent of all my hangups, will love her.

Graham nods tersely. 'Go on.'

I turn to him. 'Oh Graham, that is so big of you. Thank you *so much*.' He's in his late forties. His features are mean. I remember his face and his byline from the first time around.

Our breakfast things are still in the sink. My household management skills have gone to pieces this week. When I was Daisy, I was always the messiest girl in the dorm. As soon as I became Lina, I was preoccupied with details, through necessity. Over the years, the obsession became a genuine part of my personality. Now I seem to have lost it. Amongst the breakfast things are last night's glasses: a tumbler with a trace of whisky, and my wine glass. I felt sure the baby wouldn't mind, as it was a unique occasion.

Rosie puts the kettle on, and under cover of its noise, we begin to whisper.

'I thought Ed was going to grow up handsome and suave,' I tell her. 'I can't believe how different he is. This is killing me. Look at what I've done to the family.'

'I know I said this last night, and I did promise to get over it, I am aware of that, but I cannot credit the fact that you're alive. It really is a resurrection. Christ.' She stares at the wall for a minute, clearly trying to maintain her composure. Today, she's wearing her hair up, and she's applied full make-up. She looks competent and calm, but she isn't. Then she takes a deep breath.

'All these years I've been saying to people, my sister died. I try not to say she committed suicide, but if they don't already know, they always ask. And then I have to tell them. In some ways this is the thing you hope for, all along. It's classic, isn't it? Maybe she's not dead, they never found her body, maybe she's living happily somewhere else.

You think that if that did happen, you'd be over the moon. In fact, it's so unbelievably hard to contain the anger.'

'Sophie said the same thing. Is that why Edmund won't look at me?'

'Partly, yes. And then not only are you alive, and married—'

'Probably not for long.'

'I know. But you are, and here you are expecting a bloody baby. Do you know how long Paul and I have been trying for a baby? Of course you don't. How could you? It just doesn't seem to be happening for us. And you've got everything, and you got it without us.'

I put my arms round her, but she pushes me away. 'Sorry, Daise, it was all quite positive last night, but now I need to keep going. I can't lose control. We agreed on how to handle this.'

'OK. Friends, for now?'

'Friends. No issues until that wanker's left us alone.'

I find a tray, and assemble four cups of tea and two mugs, and the cafetiere containing some of the replenished coffee supply. Rosie carries it, while I follow with milk and sugar. My stomach is curling up, the baby is kicking in rebellion, and I would rather be anywhere else – even outside with the world's press – than here.

'Excuse me for one moment.' I smile, and head to the loo. I stroke the baby, grateful that its incursion into my bladder space has given me a few extra minutes. As I piss, I wonder whether I could leave through the back door. Of course I couldn't. The woman who gave birth to me is sitting in Margot's living room. I can't run from those ties for ever. I thought about Mum a bit, despite my better intentions, when I was travelling with baby Red, and again since I've been pregnant. The whole experience of raising a child must make anyone re-evaluate their own upbringing. I wonder whether I'll have to break the news, soon, that they've had a grandson for the past ten years.

I lurk on the toilet, feeling like a child skiving a lesson. I have to face the music now. I've been found out.

'Whatever possessed you to call yourself *Lina*?' demands Dad. 'What was wrong with the name we gave you? We thought it was pretty, didn't we, Lucy?'

Mum nods. She is watching me closely. 'You look just the same,' she remarks. 'No wonder Sophie recognised you. I'd have known you anywhere.'

'I took on someone else's identity,' I tell Dad, avoiding his eyes. 'I had to, to get away without being caught. The girl's name was Noeline, and that's what it says on my passport now. I hate the name, so I adapted it to Lina. It was the best I could do with it. I've become quite attached to it now. It's strange to be called Daisy again.' I cringe. I shouldn't have said that. I should have said I loved their name and hated my new one. Rosie said they need reassurance that I didn't run away because I hated them. The trouble is that, in some ways, I did.

'I always loved the name Daisy, though,' I lie. I loathed it. It's fey and girlish. If your parents call you Daisy, you can be sure they don't think you're ever going to become Prime Minister. Lina was a stronger name. Lina can do anything. 'I was sad to give it up,' I add. At least all this might comfort them a little when it's in the paper.

'So what, if one might inquire, happened to the original Noeline?' says Ed, looking into the corner of the room. 'If you became her, whom did she become?'

I falter. 'She died.'

'She really died, or did she just pretend? Can we ever be sure?' He hates me.

'Really. She was in London, working and travelling, and she was killed crossing the road. Through some process, her passport became available. So I became her.'

Mum is white. 'Her poor parents. How old was she?'

'At the time, seventeen. In fact, she was seven months younger than me, so I lost a bit of life experience when I became her.'

'You must have two birthdays,' smiles Rosie. 'Like royalty.'

'My Daisy birthday has been a secret one. I've celebrated it alone. I was talking to Sophie about it the other day. I used to be older than her, and now I'm younger. She's thirty, and I'm twenty-nine.'

'You're not,' says Dad. 'You're thirty as well.'

'Yes, I suppose so. I guess I've missed a party.'

We sit quietly, waiting for someone else to say something. Eventually, Rosie breaks the silence, as I knew she would.

'So, Mum, you're going to be a grandmother after all. Just when you were despairing of it ever happening.'

'Yes. Perhaps I should be excited, but I can't get over the fact that Daisy's still with us, not yet. An Australian grandchild is simply too much to contemplate, on top of everything else. I hope it's a boy.'

Rosie looks at me. 'I think we're all expecting to wake up at any minute.'

I smile back, weakly. 'Me too.'

'When's the baby due?' she adds.

'Seventh of March. Not long now.'

'And where are you going to have it?'

'That rather depends. Ideally, I'd like it to be born in the town where we moved recently – quite a distance from here.'

Graham, who has been concentrating avidly, butts in. 'You're all right, love, you can say Renmark. We all know where it is.'

'Fine. In Renmark, I hope.'

Encouraged, Graham intrudes further. 'Mrs Fraser, how do you find it, seeing your daughter again after all this time? Can you tell us how you're feeling?'

'I'm feeling fine, thank you. She makes a nice cup of tea, don't you think?'

'Is it good to see her?'

My father answers. 'Naturally it's good to see her. She's our daughter.'

'Will you be staying in touch?'

'If she will stay in touch with us, then yes, of course, I'm sure we will,' Dad says sharply. 'Mr Ward, you said you were purely a silent observer.'

'You did,' confirms Rosie.

Graham grimaces. 'Fine,' he says with a shrug, and he leans back in his chair.

I can't think of anything else to say. I am acutely aware that I am the bad guy, and I don't want either to be flippant or to give Graham any interesting quotes. He's already got a good story on his hands – he has the first thing that even approaches an interview since I've been discovered, and he's only the second hack to walk through the front door. Rosie told me he's encouraged them all to ask me about the mechanics of my escape, but that they've agreed amongst themselves not to go into it. Ed has, admittedly, broken ranks, and I hope he's not going to do it again by asking what happened after I got the passport. I promised Rosie I'd tell them all about it another time, when everything I said wasn't going to be relayed, word for word, to the rest of the world. She agreed that this was probably the better idea.

'Tell me what's going on in England,' I say brightly, aiming my question towards my female relatives. 'How is . . . everyone?' This sounds a little lame but I have no idea whom I should be inquiring after. The Queen, perhaps.

Rosie takes up the challenge. 'Well, Mum and Dad moved away from the house, partly because after what happened to you, it didn't feel private any more. People were always turning up, even members of the public.'

'Christ, that's foul, isn't it?'

'It's not a situation they could live with, really. So they moved to the south coast, oh, years ago.'

'How is it there?'

Mum looks at me and smiles. 'Oh, Daisy, you'll love it. It's a beautiful location. It's a thatched cottage, with trees and flowers and a little stream at the end of the garden. It's quite idyllic. We'll have to keep the baby away from the water, of course. But they found us there very easily as soon as they wanted to. It's not easy to hide. In a way I can understand why you came so far.'

Graham sighs. We manage to prolong the conversation, as dully as possible, until an hour has gone by, and he gives up hope of a thrilling story or an exciting clash between estranged family members, and takes them all away.

As they are standing by the door, Sophie rushes in. She runs straight into Dad, and jumps back from him.

'Hello, Mr Fraser, sorry about that,' she pants. She is out of breath, and flushed, and she looks scared. He steadies her, with his hands on her shoulders.

'Sophie, are you all right? What's happened?'

My mother is overjoyed to see her. I'm sure she wishes Sophie was her daughter, instead of me. 'Sophie, love,' she smiles. 'How wonderful to see you. How *are* you? And what a strange place to meet you after so many years!'

'I'm fine thanks, Mrs Fraser,' she says quickly. 'Lovely to see you. Sorry to have led the press here.' She turns to me, not even waiting for Graham to get out of earshot. 'Lina,' she says. 'It's Red. He's gone.

I was inside with Jen, and he just vanished from the garden, and no one knows where he is.'

'I know you've got him.' I stare him in the face, and he looks back shiftily.

'I have not,' he says, his face twisted. I notice that his teeth are surprisingly white. 'I promise I haven't. I wouldn't do a thing like that. Covering a story is one thing. Kidnapping a child is something completely different and you don't have the right to make those kind of accusations.'

'Fuck rights. I don't give a shit about anyone's rights. I just care about my son's right to play without being fucking abducted.'

'Has he really vanished?'

'Lawrence.' I am at the end of my tether. 'Stop playing games. Do you have any idea where he could be? He's ten years old, for Christ's sake. He's missing. If you've got him, tell me. If you haven't, get your friends to help look for him. This town is full of mineshafts. If he's on his own . . .'

Sophie puts an arm round my waist. 'Leave this to me, Lina,' she says softly. 'I'll find out what Larry knows. You need to go home. You're not in any condition to go running around the desert.'

I don't even look at her. 'Fine, you sort out this tosser, and I'll get on the phone.' I go back in, pursued as far as the door by a handful of crumpled Europeans. They shout questions, and I pause on the doorstep and turn back to face them. Five cameras click in my face.

'My son is missing,' I tell them. 'He was playing at his friend's house, and he disappeared from the garden. His friend said she went inside to fetch drinks and when she came back he had gone. Now, I am frantic with worry. I need to find him. If any of you can tear yourselves away from looking at the outside of this house, please, please, go with Sophie and help us look for him. And if anyone knows where he is, just tell me.' I look at them for a moment.

'That's dreadful,' says a woman, but nobody volunteers any information, so I slam the door behind me.

As soon as I tell Pete what's happened, he says, 'Leave it to me, darl,' and slams down the receiver. If anyone can locate Red, it should be Pete. I know he'll mobilise everyone else. For good measure, I phone our old number as well.

'Hi, Rachelle,' I say, 'it's Lina. Is Andy there? I need people to help us find Red.'

'Hi there, Lina, how's it going?'

'Well, OK until Red disappeared. We need Andy's help. Do you know where he is?'

'Yeah, you only just missed him. Pete called a minute ago and Andy just left. What's happened to Red? Is he all right?'

'That's fine. No, I don't know if he's all right. He was playing at Tabitha's, and then he disappeared. I think one of the journalists took him. They've been asking questions about him. I'm so worried, Rachelle. I'm out of my mind. If you see any of the other guys, can you get them to help? Pete's rounding people up.'

'Sure I can. Pete and Andy'll sort it out, you know they will. Hey. Red's not stupid, yeah? He knows his way around. He'll be all right.'

I think about it. 'He'll be all right as long as it's light.'

'Oh, they'll find him by then. These are the guys you're talking about. How's your baby doing?'

'Oh, fine. Yours?'

She sounds weary, and older. 'I can't wait to feel better. I'm just chundering three times a day.'

The house is still. I should phone Tony, but I'm scared of what he might say. I am, quite obviously, an unfit mother. It's the kind of thing they bring up when you're having a custody battle. I'll only tell Tony after Red's been found, or when it gets dark.

I am being pulled apart. I know it was those journalists. He wouldn't go off on his own. He's never done that in his life. He likes playing with Tabitha and Eric. He's a good boy. On the other hand he must have been disturbed by everything that's happened, and when he saw the open desert, he might have run into it. Perhaps it represented freedom. Maybe he needed to get away from me and all the constrictions on his movement. I can sympathise with the idea of running off for a few hours alone.

I won't be angry with him. Just let him come back.

I wonder whether that's what my own mother said about me.

I sit on one of the bar stools. If he's alone, he can't have gone far from Tabitha's house. Pete and the others will find him easily if they go out on their bikes. He would have aimed for the ridge. That was always our favourite place. But it would take him hours to get there, and that's assuming no one else is involved. No one with access to a car. Which seems, in the light of Lawrence's questions, like a big assumption.

I don't care that I'm nearly eight months pregnant. I don't care about the midsummer, midday heat. I don't care about the press outside. I have to go and find him myself.

Brian's old bicycle is round the back, and I wobble and struggle to balance. My centre of gravity has completely shifted, and even without that complication, I can barely ride this rusty contraption because my feet only reach the ground if I tip it right over. I lean it against the house, and run in to get a hat. I'll still be quicker on the bike than on foot. I won't get very far if I collapse from sunstroke, and that is a very real possibility. I find one of Margot's baseball caps and set off.

Naturally, I had forgotten that my comical cycling image was going to be syndicated the world over, as if anyone really cares. It means nothing. It has no connection with me. They must be wetting themselves over the fact that, finally, something is happening. Her boy's gone! Hurrah! They probably snatched him purely to make me come out of the house. As I wobble unsteadily past my disciples, I notice Graham and Lawrence yelling at each other. Graham has Lawrence by the collar, and they look as if they are about to come to blows. Graham would win. It couldn't happen to two nicer guys. Maybe by some form of natural selection, they'll wipe each other out.

More of them are hanging around Tabitha's house. Her mother is outside, talking to someone's tape recorder. Eric and Tabs are nowhere to be seen. I hope they're inside, sheltered from it all. I scan the crowds, discounting the familiar British figures that lurch in my direction as soon as they recognise me.

'Jen!' I call, approaching Tabs's mother. 'Any news?'

She stops, mid-sentence, and squints at me. 'You on Brian's bike? Watch out on that thing. Pete and the boys are looking for him. Haven't heard anything. He'll be right.'

I see a figure appearing from around the back of the house, but as it comes closer, I realise it's only that Christie woman. I don't like her. She slept with Sophie's boyfriend, and quite apart from that, she seems particularly aggressive, and frighteningly single-minded. I haven't come face to face with her since she took my photo, in the doorway on Tuesday. I don't want to now. I examine her face. It's closed. She's not giving anything away. Would she hurt my boy? He doesn't know anything that could help her, the whole trick would only rebound on her, and she must know that. I give her a wide berth as I cycle past.

The air is perfectly still. There is no breeze. I should have eaten something before I came out. It's stupid to cycle around like this. It won't do anybody any good if I get lost too, yet I have no idea where I am. The desert all looks the same, now. The earth is brown dust. The dust is in my eyes, up my nose. The sun is so strong. I can feel my arms and my legs burning. It hits the back of my neck, where I am exposed and unprotected by the cap. I remember why I make Red wear hats with a cotton flap down the back. My head is pounding. I can't go much further. The baby is still. I hope it's all right. I know I'm getting dehydrated, and I know that's bad for the baby. I don't know how to balance the needs of my two children, one vanished, the other unborn.

There's a big rock. I wobble, half fall from the bike, and let gravity pull me down into the shade. This is violent weather. It is not weather for a little boy to survive on his own. He had a better hat than mine but, like me, he won't have water.

In every direction, there is nothing but heat. There are rocks, and there is dust. This is the way Australia is. It's the ancient land of the Aborigines. Anything else – any settlement – is an illusion. This land should not be populated by frivolous runaways like me. I check myself. In fact, it is as apt a place as any for a runaway. It certainly isn't the place for hordes of sophisticated Londoners. I try to focus my mind. The journalists dissolve. My little boy is lost, and it's my fault. Everything that happens to him is my fault. I should have given him a stable home, but I couldn't. I should be looking after my baby, but I can't. Now he's lost, and I know, he knows, everyone knows what happens to people who get lost in the desert in this heat.

I remember the times I rammed the point home to the children at school. I never imagined, then, that the only child to forget the advice would be my own son. And that the only adult would be me.

Time passes, and nothing happens. My head is feeling bad. My abdomen aches, and becomes rock hard. This must be a Braxton

Hicks contraction. I hope, at least, that it's not the beginning of the real thing. I must get back to Craggy. They might have found him by now, and if I was heading the right way for the ridge, I'd be there by now, so I must be somewhere else. All I have to do is find the town. There's nobody to ask, and I don't have the strength to get up. There isn't even a wallaby who might point me in the right direction. It all looks the bloody same, that's the trouble with the desert. If I go the wrong way, they'll never find me. I could ride in a straight line for a month and not see a single person.

If I die, if they don't find me, they'll think I've done it again. Everybody in the whole world will assume that I've run away to start a new life somewhere else. Even Sophie and Tony will wonder whether I've left them behind. Instead, I'm ending a new life before it's even begun. In a detached way, part of me likes the idea of Lawrence and Graham and Christie combing the airports for anyone who could be Daisy in a new guise. They'll get into trouble, surely, for letting me escape from under their noses. If no one finds Red, they'll think his disappearance was part of the grand plan, that he is with me. Nobody will believe, for one moment, that Red ran away, and I went looking for him, and we both got lost in the desert and died of thrist. It is a time-honoured, almost a romantic way to go.

I don't want to die, with my baby, under a rock. By the time anyone finds my body, we'll just be bones. I breathe deeply, and summon enough strength to get onto the bike and point it back in the direction I came from.

I start pedalling. I know I'm not going far.

chapter thirty-two

20 January

It is a struggle to try to make journalists work together. We all know that anyone who stumbles across a lead is not going to share it. I wouldn't. Essentially, every man or woman is out for him or herself, but that stark truth is obscured by a gloss of pseudo solidarity.

Despite Daisy's disappearing act, there are fewer people here than there were on Wednesday. I know I should be thinking about my own return home. The story has a new lease of life for now, but it won't last for ever. This morning, I noticed that I'm sunburnt, a bit skinnier than usual, and looking haggard. My hair is turning to straw. I have a bloody nose and a bruised face. I am not healthy, and I'm probably going to get skin cancer. Sophie packed sun cream when we came out here, but she inconsiderately took it with her when she left me. I've had no protection at all against the famously toxic Australian sun.

We are all working in the motel and the Backpackers' today. It's the first time I've noticed the logistical problems borne by those less fortunate than myself, i.e. everyone who's sleeping in the dormitories. I never asked them how they managed to file stories when they didn't have their own phone line to plug in a laptop. It turns out that anyone who's not quick enough to bag one of the three computers in the 'internet annexe' is forced to make a reverse charge call to London from the phones on the street, and dictate their copy straight from their notebook, like people used to do in the olden days.

I am lounging in our room, calling airlines and getting passenger lists faxed through. There's absolutely no point in doing this whatsoever, because she won't be travelling under her own name. The only way we're going to catch her leaving Australia is by being at the airport, and spotting her. I allocated myself this task because it was easy and it kept me out of the sun for a while. For some reason, despite Sophie's harsh words and Graham's punches, most people still seem to think I'm in charge here. I have the television on, although I'm not watching it, and I'm lying on the bed with a can of Coke. My head hurts. Sometimes, when I stop for a moment, I realise I'm in a bad way. I'm tired and strung out, and formless things are nagging at me.

I know, for instance, that my editors have seen Sophie's interview, and yet they haven't contacted me about it. I won't ask Christie if Pat mentioned anything. I'll just see if she says it herself.

I am going to hunt Daisy down, wherever she is. Gita and Cyndi and Gemma, and all the other women bar Christie, think she got lost looking for Red, but I know, and so do all the blokes, that she's simply taken advantage of everyone's distraction to put a plan, a long established plan, into action. The women say she couldn't have left her son. I say she left her family once before and now she's done it again. Different family, same girl.

The door opens abruptly, and Christie comes in. She doesn't look me in the eye.

'Where's lover boy?' she demands.

'I thought I was your lover boy.'

'Not mine. Your lover boy, I meant. Aka Patrick.'

'Patrick is not my lover. You're the one that fancies him.'

'Oh, shut up.'

'He's in his room, I guess. Packing to go back to Sydney because he's so disgusted by your behaviour. And your precious blood is in the minibar.'

'I know.'

I doubt that Christie and I will be enjoying spiritual and physical communion ever again. She's been driven madder by Craggy even than I have. I'm still reeling over what she did. She's put us completely into the wrong, and made the absent Daisy look wholesome and slighted. Today she looks slightly demented. Her clothes are dirty and she seems to have thrown random garments on together, without any thought for the resulting effect. She's got no make-up on, and her face is red and raw. She looks like a backpacker.

'Chris, can I just ask you something?'

She looks at me suspiciously. 'What?'

I can't hold it back any longer, and find myself shouting. 'What in fuck's name did you think you were doing, assaulting a little boy with a syringe? If you really, really felt it was essential to have his DNA, you could have got some cells off the inside of his cheek. You didn't actually need to puncture his skin with a needle.'

'We've been through this before, Larry. I didn't know how to store cheek cells. I'm hardly going to get a second chance at this, am I?'

'You're just a nutter. I never realised before.'

'He signed a consent form.'

'But he didn't mean it. That was just a crappy little form you knocked up yourself. This is *so* going to come back to haunt us.'

'At least I don't nick people's stories and get beaten up in front of everyone.'

It's fair to say that Graham was unimpressed by my piece about Rosie. In fact, as soon as he heard, he grabbed me outside her house. The only possible saviour I could think of was my mother, and it seemed unlikely that she would materialise and scare away the big bully. She did that for me once, but I was six, and in the long run it only made things worse. 'What?' I demanded of him, with unconvincing indignation.

'You fucking know what.' His eyes bulged. 'You little prick,' he added.

'You still got the interview,' I said, in a voice that was supposed to be strong and uncompromising, but which came out pathetic and squeaky. 'I didn't take anything that was yours. Rosie just wanted to talk.'

'She can refund those bloody air fares. But I don't care about fucking Rosie. You little tosser, you knew exactly what you were doing. What's my piece worth now? They said fuck all, anyway. The interview was a pile of crap.'

'Sorry. I still haven't got anywhere near Daisy.'

'Yeah, well, Daisy was as interesting as a turnip on Valium. Same goes for all that fucking family. No wonder she ran away – they must have bored her suicidal. What did Rosie say?'

'Well . . . it was all quite interesting.'

'Cunt!' He had gripped my collar throughout our exchange, and now he lifted his fist. I couldn't even think about punching him back.

I couldn't think about anything except getting away. I turned my head and looked around, desperate to distract him.

'Look!' I squeaked. 'Daisy, on a bicycle!'

'I don't give a flying fuck if it's the fucking Pope on a tandem. With the Spice Girls.' And he punched me squarely on the nose. It really hurts. Initially, I assigned myself the task of finding out whether the local doctor, some Greek bloke, had given Daisy a letter allowing her to fly. I thought that while I was there, I could get him to check out my face, which feels as though it's falling apart. Then I decided I'd rather stay indoors, away from Graham.

'You going to let me use the phone then?' Christie demands, switching the television off and taking a swig from my Coke.

'Sure,' I tell her, and get up. 'I was just leaving anyway.'

'Good.'

It's almost dark when I get there. For once, as soon as I bang on the door, I hear footsteps, and a light goes on. Sophie flings the door open, with Red standing just behind her, holding her hand.

She looks at me, and in a fraction of a second her expression changes from anticipation to disappointment.

'Is that the one who used to be your boyfriend?' asks Red, in a stage whisper.

'I'm afraid it is,' she tells him, narrowing her eyes at me. 'What?' she adds. 'Haven't you and Christie done enough damage? We're calling the police, by the way.'

'Soph, it was nothing to do with me, I swear. He's all right, isn't he? Is there any word from Lina?' I congratulate myself, as I always do when I remember to use the preferred name.

'Do you think we'd be answering the door if there was? Leave us alone. I can't believe you're still doorstepping people at a time like this. Red's been very upset indeed today, which is your fault, and now his mother is missing. Haven't you got better things to do?'

'I just wanted to check that you were OK. I mean, despite everything that's happened between us, I'm still concerned about you. I realised that there'd be no one here to look after Red apart from you. I thought maybe I could bring you anything you needed from the shops, or something.'

'In exchange for what?'

301

'Nothing!'

Her face softens for a moment. 'No, Larry. We don't want anything you could get us. You've got your thing to do, no doubt, and we've got ours. And by the way, I know what you guys will be thinking, and there is absolutely no way Lina's done this on purpose. She didn't have a grand plan. I know that for a fact.'

'Can I quote you?'

'Be my guest.'

As she closes the door in my face, Red blows me a loud raspberry. I won't, under the circumstances, hold it against him.

I sit outside for a while, and then turn to go. I don't fancy spending another night looking at a dark bungalow. It suddenly seems like a sad way to behave. Anyway, I've got a quote. I can phone that through, even though it's morning in England, and the paper, with news of Daisy's second disappearing act, is already out. In many ways, this new disappearance is a fabulous development. It's only the memory of that little boy's face that stops me embracing it joyfully.

I suppose I'll have to go home sooner or later. I walk around Craggy for a while, and think about what I'll do. My job is assured, and I've had a few advances from other employers. I'll be able to do the rounds of radio and TV when I get back, no doubt, but then again so will Sophie. I shouldn't have to defend myself against her scorned fury. If I paint her as a rejected harpy, I'm sure that the nation's menfolk, at least, will side with me.

Yet, despite the rosiness (the English winter looks more inviting than ever), I can't face going back. I want that interview. I want to be wherever she is, and ask her every day until she finally gives in to me. She must know that, otherwise, she's going to be hassled for the rest of her life. Just as soon as we find her. We all wanted the police to come for her, so there could be a court case and she would have to explain how she skipped bail. I suppose there could still be one. Journalists ask the police every day why they haven't done anything yet, but apparently they're not going to extradite her until she's had the baby. The Australian cops should get her for the false identity thing, and the immigration fraud, but they don't seem bothered. I know it's been public for less than a week and they're still getting their act together, but I can't believe they haven't done a single thing. It would make fabulous television. They hint that this is why they're waiting. I think they feel sorry for the woman. 'We know where she is,' said a laconic press officer in Canberra last time I phoned. 'That'll do us for now.'

She's melted into thin air. They're going to look ridiculous.

It will be my life's work to track her down, and make this happen all over again. She's clever, but I'm clever too, and this time I know she's got a baby. It might be a game of cat and mouse, but in the end the cat will win. Just like I did this time.

Christie, thank God, has left the room when I get back. It's so much like home now that it occasionally surprises me when the bed's been made. I lie down and open a can of Fosters. At least they'll serve me in the offy – the 'bottle shop' – if nowhere else. I decide to call home, to tell Mum I was thinking of her today, without mentioning that I was being battered at the time.

'Hi, Dad!' I exclaim when, eventually, I don't get an engaged tone. I expect him to manage a few words in recognition of my international renown.

'Lawrence, is that you?' he says grumpily.

'Yes!'

'I'll get your mother.'

'But Dad . . .' I say desperately, into thin air. I shift uncomfortably on my bed. He didn't even want to speak to me.

'Hello, love,' says Mum. 'Are you back?'

'No, I'm still in Australia,' I tell her breezily. 'It's very hot. So, what did you think? Did you like my story?'

'Your story, Larry? Did I like it? Well, not really. How could you treat Sophie like that? She was such a lovely girl. We thought you two were going to get married.'

'I had to, Mum, because of my career. It was the only way I could get the story.' It isn't coming out right. 'Don't you think it's good to catch a criminal?'

'A pregnant woman, Lawrence? What has she ever done to you? Your fiancée's best friend? To be honest with you, I don't like to say so, but I think it's disgusting. I never imagined a son of mine could behave in such a way. Your brothers weren't overly impressed either.'

'You don't understand the way these things work, Mum. None of you do. It's not as clear-cut as you think. Wasn't someone impressed, because I can tell you a hell of a lot of people here were.'

'Luke and Matthew are very fond of Sophie. We all read the article about her and we all feel very sorry for her.'

'But you don't read the *Liberal*.'

'Luke saw her on the front and he bought it.'

'So none of you are even slightly pleased for me at the greatest professional success I've ever had? You're all just sad on Sophie's behalf instead? You didn't even feel a little bit proud when all your friends were talking about her?'

'Of course we're pleased for you, darling, if it makes you happy.'

I slam the receiver down. She doesn't understand anything.

Someone knocks on the door.

'Come in!' I call angrily. It's Patrick, and he's smiling.

'She's back,' he says, and bounces on the end of my bed. I force myself into a sitting position.

'What, Daisy?'

'Who else is missing? Yeah, mate, she appeared an hour or so ago. Lost in the desert all along. Dehydrated, but fine.'

'Bitch.' I can't help myself. Patch looks surprised.

'What do you mean?' he asks. 'I thought you'd be glad. She's still here. And alive, and she hasn't pulled off another disappearing act beneath your nose.'

'Yeah, it's good. I know. Sorry. I'd just got myself hyped up for chasing her all over the world some more, and now I don't have to. Did she say anything?'

'No. We think that guy Pete found her, riding her bike in the desert. She looked in one hell of a state, and I don't think anyone even tried to talk to her. They just went off to amend their stories. She went into the house and I guess she's staying there.'

'It makes us look a bit silly.'

'I'm sure she won't be grieving over that. And it's so good for that little boy.' He puts a hand to his chest and looks at me. 'I'm so relieved,' he adds.

'You, Patrick, are far too good a person to be mixed up in something as sleazy as journalism. You know that?'

'True. I'm just a living saint, really.'

Before I know what's happening, he's sitting next to me, and a fraction of a second after that, his arm is round my shoulders. Then he's turning his face towards me, and I seem to be turning mine towards him. I'm not recoiling. He's kissing my bruised lips. I'm kissing him. It's strange to kiss someone who isn't a girl. His mouth is like my mouth. It's bigger than a girl's mouth. Vaguely, I wonder why this is happening, but I do nothing to stop it. In fact, it seems to me that I'm positively loving it.

I'm not gay, though.

chapter thirty-three

The moment I see Red, all the tears I have been holding back burst forth. I didn't want him to see me cry, but I can't help myself. He runs to me, and I close the door firmly before I let him rush into my arms and hang round my neck.

I hold him so tight that I wonder whether he can breathe properly. He is gripping me just as hard.

'You're all right, darling!' I whisper. 'I thought something terrible had happened. I thought you were lost out there. I'm so sorry.'

'I thought you were dead,' he says quietly. 'Like Nina. And the baby too. Me and Sophie . . . we were scared. It was just the two of us and we didn't know where you were.'

'I tried to be upbeat,' says Sophie, apologetically, from somewhere behind him, 'but obviously it didn't work. What on earth happened?'

'I was just stupid,' I tell them, disengaging Red's reluctant arms from my neck, and walking to the sitting room. That cot, I notice, is still sitting there. Nobody can be bothered with it now. It seems like a relic of a quaint and innocent era.

'Sit down,' says Sophie, 'and put your feet up. Do you want a drink?'

I'm dying of thirst. Almost literally. 'Loads of water, thanks, Soph. I'm so glad you were here with him. Well, I just went out looking for you, Red, honey, and I got lost very, very quickly, and I got too hot, and I remembered I hadn't got any water, and I realised that that was a very silly thing to have done. I was on Brian's bicycle, and when I started trying to go back, I found that I didn't really know the way I'd come. I was so hot, I had such a headache . . . I thought I'd had it, but I forced myself to keep going just on the remotest chance of stumbling across anything or anyone that might help. Then I gave up. I couldn't go any further, and it was beginning to get dark, so I stopped, but then I realised I was near the ridge. I thought you might have gone there, sweetie, so I tried to walk up it, to look for you. I couldn't do it, so I just sort of fell over. But, luckily for me, Pete thought you might be there too, so he'd whizzed over on his bike, and when he came down, there I was. We left Brian's bike out there, and Pete brought me back to town on his. So here I am.'

Red's eyes are wide. 'Mummy, you were so lucky.'

'I know. You must never do anything like that, promise?'

'Of course I wouldn't. It's a silly thing to do.'

'So where were you all that time?'

Red looks away. His face clouds over, and he rubs the inside of his elbow. Sophie has come back into the room with a jug of iced water and some glasses, and she winces.

'You're not going to like this one little bit,' she warns me. 'I think that, in spite of everything, we need to call the police.'

I lie awake, trying to work out what to do. I lost myself in the desert and managed to survive. The desert is massive, and my being found was utterly unlikely. I've been given a second chance.

When Pete appeared next to me, he didn't seem real. I was almost beyond caring. I was scared that Red would read the papers, or listen to the gossip, and that he'd go through the rest of his life thinking that I was alive, somewhere, living a life that didn't include him. I didn't think of it at the time, but all the tourist trips out into the desert go to the ridge. If I'd died there, they'd have found me, and speculation would have been quashed. He would have been OK. Motherless, siblingless, but all right.

I nearly killed my second child. That is torturing me. That, and what Christie did. I know for a fact that she now has a vial of my boy's blood. She assaulted him, and Sophie's right: we have to call the police. I hate her, and I'm going to make her pay for what she's done; but the worst of my venom is reserved for myself. If I hadn't done what I've done, with the potential to shatter so many lives, Christie would never have gone anywhere near my little boy. If I hadn't lied to him for his entire life, there wouldn't be a story.

I don't know what she's going to do with the blood. I try to imagine

Giles's parents, after all these years. I can only speculate about what this week has been like for them. They'll probably embrace the idea of a young grandson, after the loss of their two boys. I've known, since the day I discovered I was pregnant, that they would want Red. That was why I had to run away. If I'd stayed and had the baby in England, they would have got him. I don't want them to have him. Red would hate that. Red belongs with me. If Giles's family team up with Christie, we'll all be in trouble. My little Australian skater boy will find himself shoehorned into English public school life. He will be cosseted and overprotected. He will never know the baby. He will miss me, for ever.

I remember Lawrence shouting through the letter box yesterday. 'Who is Red's father?' That's the kind of headline they could run. It says nothing, but people love it. The soap opera goes one stage further. 'Daisy Fraser last night categorically denied that her son, Red, was the child of Giles de Montfort, the young man she killed with a drugs overdose.' They'll run with that. I know they will.

The Indian adoption won't stand up for a second, although I've always been deliberately vague about it. And how is a little boy meant to deal with the most unusual discovery that he isn't adopted, after all? Would it seem like rejection? Nobody else's mother pretends they're not their mother. It is an extraordinary predicament for a child. I always assumed he'd find out one day, but at a time when we would be friends, rather than mother and son; when he knew all about my past and when, as an adult, he'd understand that life is not black and white, and that his birth was the most joyous thing that ever happened to me. He saved my life. If he hadn't been growing, silently, inside me, then without a doubt I would really have jumped off the bridge. One day I hope he'll understand.

I wanted to tell him myself. I didn't want him to find out from some distortion cooked up by Christie and Lawrence. I try to think of a way to buy some more time.

Sophie and I attempt to make breakfast as normal for Red as possible. After her shopping expedition yesterday, we now have Weetbix, Cheerios, and slightly stale croissants warmed up in the microwave. Sophie's drinking coffee. She looks shattered. I try to imagine being in her position.

'Sophie, do you want to go home?' I ask, pouring inordinate amounts of UHT milk onto my cereal, in an effort to build up the baby's bones after yesterday's battering.

'What do you mean? Do you want me to leave?'

Red looks shocked. 'Sophie, you can't leave. We need you until we move back to Renmark. And when we go to Renmark you can come with us too, and if you like you can live in our house, or else you can live with Beth on the houseboat.'

'Just as long as you know that you don't have any obligation to be here with us,' I remind her. 'You look like you could do with a break. That's all. I thought you might need to get away on your own for a while.'

She is annoyed. 'Well, I don't, all right? I want to be with you two. Christ knows, you need somebody. You don't do such a fabulous job, left to your own devices.' She turns away from me and then stands up and walks away. I hear her door slamming. I don't know what to say. I was only trying to remind her of her options. I didn't mean to upset her.

'For fuck's sake, now look what you've done!'

'Red Pritchett!' I am genuinely shocked. 'Where did you learn that? You must never say things like that. It's extremely rude.'

He looks at me pityingly. 'Oh, Mum. Me and Tabs and Eric say fuck all the time. And so does Tony. I taught it to Daniel. Everyone says it, except not Sophie, and not you, normally.'

'But it's still rude.' I smile at my own hypocrisy, although I feel anything but happy. 'Why don't you go and give Sophie a hug and tell her we know we need her?'

They come back a few minutes later.

'She's staying,' proclaims Red.

'Only for as long as you want me,' Sophie adds, 'and I have to draw the line at living on Beth's boat. I'd end up pushing her overboard. Sorry to fly off the handle. I really don't want to go home. I hate the thought that you might want me to. I plan to stay around till long after the baby's born, if that's all right.'

'All right? It's wonderful.' I know, and she knows, but Red doesn't, that she might end up looking after Red and the baby while I'm in prison; that I will very likely be extradited after it's born, and that Red and the baby will either have to come to England and face the press during the trial, or stay in Australia with Tony, motherless. That is without the complication of Red's paternal family. It would be neatest of all if Sophie, as a single, attractive woman, could take up with Tony, and become the new me, while I languished behind bars. Sophie would then be my alter ego, the good girl I could have been, if I hadn't gone to the Academy and plummeted off the rails. But I know it would have happened even if I'd stayed in Kingsbridge. The Academy did its best to impose a rigid discipline on my life. No one would have succeeded.

'You must hate Craggy, though,' I add. 'God knows, I do, but I have to be here, and you don't. That was all I was thinking. I was feeling bad about making you live in this horrible artificial situation.'

'And why are you in this horrible artificial situation?' she demands, and doesn't leave me time to answer. 'Because I saw you here last summer, winter, whichever way you look at it. And I came back with Lawrence. This is only happening because I made it happen. It's my fault. I feel bad. You shouldn't. Well, you should a bit, but I should even more. Look what's happened to Red. I feel responsible.'

'Me too.'

Red is watching us, quietly. 'I don't,' he says. 'Why did she want my blood, anyway? It was so red. Like me.'

'She just wanted to play a trick,' I tell him, wondering whether he'll believe me. 'She's a horrible woman. Now, if you've finished your cereal, why don't you go and get dressed? We need to get some order back into this house.'

''Kay.'

The moment Red's gone, Sophie starts writing on the back of one of the hacks' notes. I crane to see what she's doing.

'I'm going out there, to talk to them,' she says. 'If one of us goes out and tells them we're calling the police, they'll have to write it up. 'Specially if it's me, because there's nothing else to say about me. Then they'll know we mean business. We can't look as though we're going to let Christie and Lawrence get away with this.'

I listen from behind the curtains as she reads the statement. Her voice is clear, and she sounds deadly serious. 'This is a gross infringement of his legal and moral rights,' she says, 'and as such we have informed the police of the assault. The story which we expect to appear in this afternoon's British papers contains no truth whatsoever. Mrs Pritchett has nothing to hide. We will be instructing our lawyers to seek a payment of damages to Red, to compensate for the extreme distress he suffered in the disgraceful incident.'

I wish I could see their faces. For once, no one's shouting any questions. She comes straight back in.

I hug her. 'Well done. Now I'd better get down to the doctor's and get this baby looked at.'

chapter thirty-four

21 January

I don't know why I bothered to walk to the edge of town. I knew what I'd find: nothing. I should be used to the heat by now, but I'm not. I am weighed down by it every moment of every day. On the way up here, I walked past the house where Daisy used to live, with her family. I looked at it curiously, but I didn't stop. It's a funny little place. I can't get used to these silly houses that look like two windows and a door in the earth. There's something animal about living like that. It reminds me of the Wombles.

Now I'm sitting on a small hill, with the fax of tomorrow's front page in front of me. The dusty earth stretches away in every direction. Craggy looks pathetic from here. It looks freaky. It's just plonked down in the middle of absolutely nowhere. No wonder everyone who lives here is a nutter. You'd have to be.

I'm not wearing a hat. All those fussy things people tell you – it's all mind control. I don't want to wear sun cream, or drink water. I drink coffee and lager, and I'm doing all right. Water's for girls. I'm surviving.

They've run with our paternity story. After yesterday's fiasco, it makes us look like twats. I hope everyone else copied it in their late editions. The peg of the story is Daisy's denial, hotly followed by our own speculation, dressed up by Christie as: 'Last night, the worried de Montfort family was asking itself about the implications . . .'

It would all be fine if it didn't come hot on the heels of yesterday's mass hysteria. We all got sucked into believing she'd vanished again, and we all came out looking like twats. Everyone painted it as 'Daisy pulls it off . . . again'. It was a huge misjudgement. News of what Christie did to the boy is bound to leak out, especially if Sophie really has called the police. Gemma will probably splash on it.

I felt better about myself than I have for ages when she read out that statement. I stood, with Patrick's arm surreptitiously round my waist, and I felt my power. I have made Sophie the woman she is today. I've embittered her. I already knew from the way she insulted me in that piece that she'd become hard-nosed and capable of standing up for herself. 'Cynical manipulation of my vulnerability' indeed! I will always remember the sweet Sophie who waited for me on Paddington station, huddled into her thick coat and looking at the teddies.

She's come a long way. I'm delighted that she's slagged me off in public. She's descended to my level. I've corrupted her with my betrayal. I am powerful, like the Marquis de Sade. I am a destroyer of trust. I leave women reinventing themselves in my wake. I am attractive. I am a sexual being. I have no preconceptions about myself. Today, for a while, I felt indomitable.

The woman who stood up in front of the hastily reconvened world's press evinced no love for me or any of my kind. You'd think there might be a bit of residual affection there, but when I tried to catch her eye, she looked straight through me.

She sounded professional. She was hard, and efficient, and for those few moments, she was definitely in charge. I could see she was scaring Christie. We hadn't expected them to call in the police. She must have been bluffing. It would be suicidal of Daisy to summon the law to her house, whatever we've done.

I look at the blurred story on my knee, and thank my own judgement for making me hand control of the paternity issue to Christie. If anything's going to rebound on us, this is it. Patrick's said so all along.

People seem to know about Patrick and me. It seems I'm the only person in Craggy who doesn't think I'm gay. Even Patrick misses some of the subtleties of my situation. All the journalists I pass in the street smirk at me. I know I'm not imagining it, because some broadsheet tosser asked whether it was true that Patrick and I had a room we weren't using, and, if so, whether he could have it. As if I'm going to shack up with Patrick and Christie, both at once. Last night I spent some time with Patch in his room (which was in many ways extremely bizarre) and then tiptoed back to sleep with Chris. By that point I quite fancied staying the night with him, but Christie wouldn't have taken that well.

When I stop and think about it, I'm astonished at myself. I spent the evening almost naked with someone who has hairs on his chest and bulging pectoral muscles. He shaves, like I do. He has hairy toes. He's just like me, and somehow he's alien with it. It felt right at the time. It felt like a dream.

It doesn't matter what people think, that's what Patrick tells me. Of course it matters. If I believed that what people think has no importance, I wouldn't be doing this job. My whole life is dedicated to directing what people think. I know that everyone in the world has been talking about Daisy this week – I also know that Craggy's tourism numbers have swelled many times over, with people desperate to look at her – and that's because of me. I have controlled their minds. I have embedded Daisy Fraser in the brains of every producer of every daytime talk show, every newspaper columnist, every person who has ever wondered what it would be like to leave their life behind. Every hairdresser thrashing around for something to say to her client, every sixth former chatting in the common room, every mother waiting at the school gates. They're all talking about her, and it was me. I did that.

'Larry,' I tell myself, 'gossip doesn't matter. Look at the bigger picture.' I try, but, apart from the heady excitement of the fact that I have dented the international consciousness, the bigger picture is confusing, not consoling. Sooner or later, I'll have to go home. If I go home, I'll have to leave Patrick in Sydney. He lives on the other side of the world from me. I think that's a good thing. It takes away any danger of my staying around him longer and officially becoming a faggot. I will have a certain degree of fame, and, thanks to Sophie, some notoriety. There will be potential new jobs everywhere I look, and yet I won't have a partner, of either gender. I wouldn't want a male one, of course.

I still haven't got the interview with Daisy, and so I have to hang around until she gives in. I hope Patrick stays here. He's the only person who's on my side. He is, in fact, the only one who likes me. When I get back to London I'm sure I'll go back to rampant laddish heterosexuality, but for now, I'd rather hang out with him. It was OK for the Romans to hang out with men, wasn't it? No one called them queer.

I was on my two-week holiday when I broke this story. I spent the first week chasing it, and the second week writing and updating it. My holiday only actually comes to an end today. That means I can take another two weeks off, and that's what I'm going to do. I'm going to send Patricia an email. I don't want to ask her on the phone, not even with the entire mass of planet Earth between us.

I try to find a comfortable position on the rock. It's baking. If yesterday had been like this, Daisy wouldn't have survived long enough to be found. I hate this heat. Patch says it's much better in Sydney. He says the climate there is 'positively temperate', and that I should go back with him. He lives somewhere called Balmain which he says is 'utterly gorgeous, darling'. I'm tempted to go, just for a break. Nobody would give us weird looks in Sydney. This place is stifling me.

I'd like to see Ayer's Rock and the Great Barrier Reef. When we got here, I assumed we wouldn't find Daisy, and that Sophie and I would have a holiday travelling around Australia instead. I almost wish that had happened. If it had, I'd still have a girlfriend. I wouldn't have any sexuality related issues. Nor would I have a bloody nose, and I wouldn't have been spat upon. I'd still be a normal person.

I wouldn't be famous. Daisy would still be living her giant lie. I wouldn't have experienced that once-in-a-lifetime buzz. I said I wanted to bring someone else to Craggy Rock, and in all I must have brought over a hundred people, when you factor in the tourists as well. Whatever happens next, I wouldn't change a thing.

There's just one thing that would make this complete. I have to speak to her. I walk slowly back into town, and head towards Margot's familiar shack, to sit in my usual spot, and wait.

'Coming for lunch, Laz? We do need to talk.'

'I don't want any.' Lunch is unnecessary. 'You go. I'll just wait here.'

'You have to eat something. You didn't have any breakfast either. You're looking weird.'

'Oh, cheers. Thanks, Chris. I'm a big boy now. Can look after myself.'

'Well, that is precisely my point. You obviously can't, because if you could you wouldn't be like you are now.'

'Go on then, tell me. What am I like now, O wise woman?'

'OK, fine. You're skinny. You're a strange colour, sort of purple. Your skin's covered in spots. Your mouth is bruised. Your nose is swollen and scabby. You've got two black eyes, and I could be wrong here but I could have sworn that you used to be heterosexual. You're quite a catch, that's for sure. I'm the envy of Craggy Rock.'

I look at her, and wonder whether I should be angry. I can't find it in myself to resent her pettiness.

'I'm fine, Christie. It's a well-known fact that everyone's a bit bisexual. It's the logical way to be. All I want is this interview. I'm going to get it. Tell you what, here's ten dollars. Bring me something if you like.'

'Don't fucking patronise me. You're not doing me a favour by allowing me to get your lunch, you know. This is for your benefit. Seriously, Larry, I'm going to call Pat and tell her to take you off the story.'

'Well, you can't because I'm officially on my holiday. All I'm doing is getting this interview, and as soon as that's done I'm going to Sydney.'

'To shack up with your gentleman friend.'

'Jealousy, Christie, is an ugly thing.'

'I'm not fucking jealous. Just a bit, well, aggrieved. I got dumped the other day because of you, because of my role in that piece Sophie and Gemma did, and I never even complained once. Now I seem to have been dumped again, by you, in favour of some queer.'

'I thought you liked Patch.'

'I do. It's you that's fucked me about.'

'So go home.'

'I'm booked on the Adelaide plane tomorrow morning, and it cannot take off a moment too soon. The rest of the story's going to be done from London. The de Montforts are doing a big interview about their fight to get their grandchild, and it'll all kick off from there.'

'When I get the Daisy interview, we'll have a wicked double whammy.'

Christie sighs exaggeratedly, and walks off. I look at my hand. The money is still there. I wonder whether she'll bring me any lunch. Probably not. I seem to have upset her. The strange thing is, I am upsetting everyone. I'm not doing anybody any harm. I'm not interested in them. All I want is to wait for Daisy. I'm glad Christie's going home. I'm glad most of the others are too. I don't want to go. This is my story, and if there's no one else here, then she'll have to talk to me. I will wait for as long as it takes. I'll tell her I'm sorry to have ruined her life and everything and that we'll try to put it back together. That's a good line.

You see, there's nothing else I can do. I don't want to move on to another story, because my work is not done on this one. The next story won't be my story. It will belong to everyone.

London is a world away, and suddenly everyone I care about is in Australia. Patrick's here. Daisy's here. Red is here, and even Sophie's here.

I am the only one who wants to stay. The fact that the story has a new lease of life has enthused no hacks at all. Quite the opposite. Everyone was about to go home, and then it turned out they've got to stay after all. There has been no movement, and we don't like to knock on the door any more. There was never any point.

When Daisy, Sophie and Red emerge, I struggle to my feet. As I stand up, black spots float before my eyes. Most of the disgruntled hacks follow them down the road. I think about it, but it turns out that I don't have the energy, so I stay where I am instead. I become gradually more agitated as to where they might have gone. Even though they have no bags, they might be leaving town. Only four of us have stayed behind, and two of them are asleep. I shuffle over to Gita.

'Do you know where they went?'

'No.'

'Oh. Right.'

There doesn't seem to be anything else to say.

'When are you going back to India?' I ask eventually. She looks at me strangely.

'I don't live in India, Larry, remember? I live in Sydney.'

'Do you? Right. Well, when are you going back to Sydney? I might go there, you know.'

'I know. I can keep track of the story just as well from home so I think I'll leave tomorrow morning.'

'Will you be sorry to go?'

'Sorry? Sorry, Larry? No, I will never have been so glad to leave a place, and a story, in all my professional life. Sydney is a stunning city, and I miss it. Do you know the city? No? Well, I live in Manly, which is across the harbour, and every morning I take the ferry to work. It takes thirty minutes and it is breathtaking. It is uplifting every single day. I cannot wait to get back home.'

This offends me – after all, Gita and everyone else was only too happy to fawn over me a few days ago – but I bite it back. Gita's nice enough. I shouldn't alienate her as well. At least she speaks to me without smirking.

We hear the car before we see it. A dirty beige station wagon draws up to the gate in a cloud of dust, and stops right beside us. Inside it is a nondescript man who's losing his hair. At first I dismiss him as a ghoulish tourist, but a closer inspection reveals that he's wearing police uniform.

'Good afternoon,' I say obsequiously. 'Officer,' I add. Gita looks up and smiles.

'Afternoon,' he says curtly. 'Mrs Pritchett and her son around?'

'I'm afraid you've just missed them. They're not going to be far away.'

'Then I'll wait. You would be?'

I extend a hand to him. 'Lawrence Golchin, the London *Herald*.'

He shakes it. He looks bored. 'The *Herald*, eh? I'll be needing a word with your lady colleague. Jason Gibbon. Alice Springs police force.'

'Jason Gibbon?' I mock, despite my better judgement. He glares, Gita widens her eyes at me and shakes her head, and someone else takes his photo. He ignores everything else I say. I hope Officer Gibbon might invite us to wait in his car, but he doesn't. He just sits there by himself, with the passenger door open.

When the party of three trails back, I shout a token question before he can say anything. 'Hello, Lina, how about an interview? How do you feel now that the police have turned up?'

She ignores me, naturally, and walks straight to the car to talk to him. Then they all go inside.

chapter thirty-five

When we get back from Dr Angelos' surgery, relieved that everything's fine, the journalists on the doorstep are taking photos of a policeman, who is waiting for us. He has a balding head, and a pleasant face, a bit like Tony's, and he's sitting implacably in his car with the door open. He appears to be ignoring the fact that he is at the centre of a huge commotion, and is pretending to read a paper.

When I see him, I clasp Red's hand tighter and try to quell my panic. He is here because Sophie asked for someone to come over. Craggy Rock only has two policemen, and he is not one of them. I wonder where he's come from. On the one hand, I know that his immediate mission is probably to investigate the assault on Red, but on the other, he won't be able to avoid dealing with me in some way. Perhaps I should have skulked at the surgery until he'd gone, encouraging him to overlook me entirely.

'Shall I go back to the doctor's?' I whisper to Sophie.

'No!' she hisses back. 'Don't be ridiculous.'

We walk up to him, ignoring Lawrence's questions, smile, and invite him in. The reinvigorated members of the press surge up behind us, yelling questions. I locate Gemma from the *Liberal* and give her a watery smile, grateful for the piece she wrote. We ignore everyone else. Lawrence looks strange. Someone has clearly punched him in the face, and I can only assume it was Graham. Christie seems to have gone to ground. I wish she was here. Then we'd be able to turn our law enforcement officer around, and point her out.

'Can we get you a drink?' I ask as soon as we've closed the front door.

'Thanks, mate.' He grins. 'Don't know how you do it, with this bunch. Every bloody day, I mean. Got a lager?'

I look at Sophie. Alcohol is off my radar again now, and will, I hope, remain there until the baby's safely out. She nods.

'There's some of Pete's left. I'll go and get it.'

'And I'll have a glass of water, thanks, Soph,' I call after her. Red jumps up to follow her, and I am alone with the law. It is happening at last.

'Sorry,' he says suddenly. 'Didn't introduce myself, in all the confusion. Jason Gibbon, Alice Springs police.'

'I'm Lina Pritchett,' I tell him unnecessarily. 'Why did they send you all the way from Alice? We expected one of the local guys.'

'Thought it was better this way. As you'll know, we've had an eye on matters here in Craggy for the past week, and it seemed a good chance to come along and check up on you. Figured we'd wait till you were left in peace, but then this happened and I said to myself, why send one of the goons along when you can go yourself? So I did.'

'Thanks.' I think so, anyway.

'This boy of yours, then, how's he doing?'

'Oh, he's going to be all right,' I say, as Sophie and Red come back into the room with drinks and snacks. 'He's bearing up, considering.' Red sits firmly beside me. He'd be on my lap if he wasn't trying to make a good impression. 'Red, this is Officer Gibbon. He's come to talk about what happened in the desert, OK?'

'How are you doing, Red? Call me Jason. We're all mates round here, aren't we?'

Red nods, and I feel a sense of foreboding. I am on the wrong side of the law. This man is the law. Therefore we are not all mates.

'Can you tell me what happened yesterday? I hear you got into a bit of trouble, mate?'

Red stares into his glass of juice, and doesn't say anything.

'It's OK, darling,' I tell him. 'You can tell Jason all about it. He's here to help us.'

Red looks at me anxiously. I nod. Then he looks to Sophie, and she nods encouragingly as well.

'Would it help if we left you to it?' she asks, and Jason mutters that it might, so we take our drinks into the kitchen. I try not to dwell on the fact that my little boy is being questioned by the police.

*   *   *

'All done,' says the affable officer, standing in the kitchen doorway. My heart has been thumping and I've been occupying myself with my longed-for rearrangement of the crockery as a pathetic distraction from everything else. When Margot returns, I hope she'll come to appreciate the fact that she now has the cups in the easiest cupboard for her to reach, and that the dust-encrusted utensils that she never uses are cleaned, disinfected, and stored on the top shelf. Amid many protests from Soph, I had to stand on a kitchen stool to put them there. It made me pant. I was planning to stay as fit as I could throughout this pregnancy, and I was going to be particularly active and healthy towards the end. Renmark, after all, has seductive walks, a pool and a gym. Instead, I am a gigantic blob of a woman, trapped in a house that isn't mine.

'Is everything OK?' I ask him. 'Did he tell you everything you needed to know?'

'Reckon. We sorted out exactly what happened. In my humble opinion, ladies, it's an outrage and there's no way someone can be allowed to get away with that, even if she is a sheila.'

'So are you going to arrest her?'

'For sure. I might need to talk to you two as well, to corroborate what young Red says. Not that we don't believe him, just for the files.'

Sophie beams at him. 'Of course! Do you want to do that now?'

'If it's no trouble.'

An hour later, we think Officer Gibbon is about to leave, when he turns back.

'There was one more thing,' he says awkwardly, leaning on the cot in the hallway. He looks at me. 'Mrs P, I'm afraid I'm going to have to ask you a few questions, by yourself.'

'That's OK. I thought you might. Do you want to do it now?'

'No. Sorry, I really am, but I'm going to have to ask you to come to the precinct.'

'What do you mean? Here, in Craggy?'

'No. That's not a precinct at all, is it, just someone's bloody lounge. I mean, will you come back to Alice with me? You understand I have to do this? I can't come into your bloody house after all this and then walk out and arrest a journalist. I have to take you along, even if it's just for show.'

'Will I stay in a cell?'

'No. You're coming with me of your own free will.'

'Do I need bail money?'

'I sure as hell won't keep you in, not in your condition. No chance.'

'Where's Red going to go?'

'I assume that Red and Sophie will be able to stay here, but if they want to come with us they'd be welcome. However, it will involve riding in the car with Miss Baxter.'

'Alice is miles away. It'll take us the rest of the day.'

'I know. I was thinking about that. How about this. I didn't want to spring it on you, so I'll find myself a bed for the night, and we'll all go to Alice in the morning. Whoever wants to, that is. But you'll have to come. I would tell you not to do a vanishing act, but I know you're not going anywhere in that condition. When's it due, anyway?'

'Early in March.'

'We won't keep you long. I'll get one of the blokes to bring you back. If this all goes somewhere, and I'm afraid it's going to have to, then we'll make sure nothing happens before the little one's born.'

I watch him leave. I cannot speak.

'There's absolutely no way that Red and I are coming to Alice. I would, but Red isn't.' Sophie is firm on this point. I've never seen her so unmoving about anything.

'Why not? Red needs to be near me. We agreed that. He needs to be with me while he still can.'

'The last thing he needs is to go to Alice Springs in a car with Christie bloody Baxter. It's in completely the wrong direction. It's taking him further away from all the other people in his life, and he's not sitting in an enclosed space with that woman for hours and hours. You know how upset he still is. It would finish him off.'

'Maybe you and he could come on a bus?'

'Actually, I think we should go on a bus to Renmark.'

'Sophie! You can't do that! I might never see him again!' I hate this. I knew it would happen. Red's going in one direction, and I'm going in the other, and I haven't even explained to him, yet, about his father. Not to mention his mother.

I am a completely crap parent. He'll be in therapy for years to come because of me. After tomorrow morning, the next time I see him will be when he visits me in prison. I have to fight Sophie on this, even though I know she's right. I was going to send Red to Renmark a few days ago. If I hadn't given in to his wailing, and my own longing to have him near me, then Christie's assault would never have happened.

It would. She would have found him, wherever he was.

'But I'm not staying in the police station overnight. What am I meant to do when they let me out? I'm nearly eight months pregnant, Soph,' I complain. Even though I'm essentially being arrested, in the politest possible way, part of me is excited. At least I'm leaving Margot's foul bungalow. Something is going to happen, and even if it's a bad thing, at least I get to travel.

'You can fly from Alice to Renmark, if you like.'

'No I can't. You know I can't. I'm not allowed to fly. Plus they'll probably want me to stay in the area. Once this is going to the courts, the papers can hardly write a thing about me any more. It's going to be over. All I need is some time with my little boy.'

We fight about it late into the night. Red is supposed to be asleep, but I'm sure he's listening. The unborn baby is shifting around and kicking my bladder. I wish I could keep it in my womb for longer. Maybe I could have a two-year pregnancy like Macbeth's mother did. Was it Macbeth? I think so.

For a while, when we were in India, I used to buy cheap editions of the British classics from the bookshops, and force myself to read them. I'd read all the notes as I went along, and after I finished, I'd read the introduction. I wanted the education I'd squandered. I knew, then, that I was going to have to work somehow, and I was certainly never going to be a ballerina. I assumed I'd give private English language tuition. I never thought I'd end up as a teacher of literature. The schoolchildren of Craggy never appreciated my detailed textual knowledge of the tragedies.

This baby, though, is going to be born. In many ways, I can't wait to meet it. We know each other. I recognise what food and drink will make it kick, and I'm sure it knows far more about me than I'd like it to. I was going to kid it into believing that it had a stable, normal mother with a stable, normal background. Now it's found me out.

I hate Craggy Rock. I hate Margot's house. It's beginning to smell in here, despite the air conditioning. I should leave her some money when we go, for the electricity. But I won't. She's hardly going to come after me for it.

I like the fact that no one's been able to phone us. I've spoken to Tony and Margot only when I've wanted to, which hasn't been often. I've forgotten all about Beth. I don't care about them any more. Even my sister has vanished from my radar for now. I'm not actually sure that the Frasers are still in Craggy, though I think they'd have said goodbye if they weren't. The world has shrunk, again. Now it only contains me and the baby, Red and Sophie. My marriage has dissolved and vanished in smoke. That's irrelevant. A month ago, when Tony and I were fighting, it was the most important thing in my world. Now I have to make an effort to remember that I am married at all. Daisy isn't married. Only Lina is married.

It is time to move on. Even if I'm moving on to Alice Springs, with an embarrassed policeman, I'm getting out of here. Leaving Craggy the first time was exciting. Leaving for the second time makes me realise how much I hate it.

'You know when you leave something,' I say to Sophie abruptly, forgetting that we were arguing, 'and it makes you realise that all the time you forced yourself to put up with it, you were only pretending?'

She looks at me and laughs. 'Yes, of course I do. That's the way it is with me and Lawrence.'

'And me and Craggy Rock. I tell you, right now I hardly even care if they lock me up, or if they send me back to England. As long as I get away, and stay away, that's pretty much good enough. I mean, it's a dump, isn't it? That lad, Huw, the one who started all this by taking my photo, he actually had the right idea when he said you should only stay here one night.'

'I'm glad you've realised at last. I suppose it has certain things going for it, but frankly I'm astonished that you stuck it out for three years. Didn't you go crazy?'

'I wasn't allowed to go crazy. I was Lina, and this was where Lina lived.'

'Are you still Lina?'

'I don't know. Maybe I need to be someone new now. I'm neither person.'

She takes my hand. 'Daisy, you stupid girl, you don't need to reinvent yourself every time things change. You're still Daisy. Go back to being yourself. It's OK, now. Whatever's going to happen, will happen. You'll still be you.'

'I wasn't last time.'

'You were young last time. And . . . pregnant?'

I look at her. Then I walk through to the sitting room, to be as far away from Red's bedroom, and earshot, as possible, and sit in Brian's chair. Sophie sits next to me, and looks expectant.

'Of course I was,' I tell her. 'That's why I ran away.'

'You poor thing! Why didn't you say? You could have trusted me.'

'I couldn't have trusted anyone. I couldn't even trust myself. Dancers don't even *get* pregnant. They are notoriously infertile.'

'I feel terrible about causing all this. I know I keep on about it. I mean, here I am saying you could trust me, when patently obviously you couldn't. Look at what I did. You couldn't trust me for a moment.'

'I didn't find out until after Giles had died. It was a complete accident, needless to say. At first I thought I was just late because of all the stress. In fact I don't think I noticed for ages. Then I suddenly realised. It was when I was at my parents' place, not coming out of the room. Until then I'd been vaguely planning to take an overdose or something, and I think I really meant to do it. I couldn't have faced the trial. When I realised I was actually pregnant, my first instinct was to have an abortion. To abort Red, in fact.'

I remember that day so clearly. Some details have faded with time, but others will stay with me for ever. As soon as I found I was pregnant this time around, the memory tried to force itself into my head. At the time I didn't let it. Now I do.

Getting a pregnancy test had been the first hurdle, although as soon as I thought of it, I knew without a doubt that I was having a baby. It seemed important to confirm it, in secret. I couldn't ask Sophie or Mum to get me one. I couldn't ask anyone. I had to do it myself. The trouble was, in Kingsbridge, I couldn't have gone to the chemist without whoever was behind the counter shopping me to the press. That didn't bear thinking about.

I was in a state, but I began to formulate a plan. The next time Mum and Dad left me alone in the house, I went straight to Rosie's room and searched through her things. I was sure I'd caught her on the phone last time we were all home, muttering something about how 'it was negative, thank God'. I went through everything, glancing at her diary while I was there. She didn't even mention me, I discovered, and she had an older boyfriend called Mitch. In earlier, more innocent days, I would have tried on her clothes and underwear, but that day I threw it all aside. Eventually, in the bottom of a cupboard, next to a half full box of tampons, I found a small box called 'Clear blue', and, in it, one white plastic stick. Thank God, she'd bought a packet of two.

I wasn't surprised that it was positive, but it made me tremble. I'll have an abortion, I decided, first of all. I was eighteen, and I was going to go to prison because I'd killed my friends. Having a baby was completely out of my orbit. I sat on the loo in the peach bathroom that was, these days, all my own, and I cursed Giles for his carelessness. I was wearing the white satin pyjamas I always wore, and a huge pair of woollen socks. My hair was longer than usual, and unkempt. I was a mess, and I knew it.

It had happened the week before the drugs. We'd gone to Giles's flat, as we always did before a night out, and, while Leila and Freddie snogged on the sofa, Giles and I repaired to his bedroom. It was not the first time we'd had sex, not by a long way, but it was the first time he'd messed up.

'Daise,' he muttered, with the intense look on his face that I loved. He was moving inside me. We never used condoms because Giles didn't like them, and although we both knew about Aids, we didn't seriously think it could affect us, not least because he always pulled out at the last minute, and came over my stomach.

'Giles,' I responded, looking fondly at him. He was my fourth lover, but the first who'd made me enjoy it. I did feel a bit silly saying his name.

'You're so fucking sexy,' he continued, and I writhed underneath him. Then, suddenly, his face changed, and he groaned, then let out a cry.

'Sorry,' he said a minute later, with a smile. 'I'm sure it'll be all right.'

I wasn't bothered. 'Me too. What are the chances? Dancers don't get pregnant.'

We got up and dressed, and I wiped myself with a tissue and thought no more of it.

I couldn't believe it when Tony and I took so long to conceive. It didn't seem right, after Giles and I had done it so easily.

I didn't know how to have an abortion without the general public finding out about it. I couldn't have done it on the NHS, because then I'd have ended up in a public ward and my cover would have been blown instantly. I had no idea how to go about it privately, and no money. I began to wonder whether I had an alternative. At first, I saw a bump as a potential disguise, and nothing more. I phoned Marjorie.

'Sweetie.' She sounded tetchy. I was sure she didn't want to hear from me. 'What can I do? Surely you're not shopping again?'

'Of course not. Marjorie, I need to get away. Can you help me?'

'How far away?'

'Completely. I need to vanish.'

'So you need a passport and money?'

'And a plan.'

'And then you'd never stand up in court and say my name?'

'Never, ever, ever.'

'I can probably help. I'll call you back. What's your number?'

She called back. She sorted it out for me, to save her own skin. I was nearly three months pregnant when I left. Noeline saw a doctor as soon as she got to India. She found the care there was superb, even though she never saw the same doctor twice. Luckily, Marjorie had given her enough money for private health care, and the baby boy was born, amid considerable agony, while Noeline was strapped to a hospital bed, with her feet up in stirrups, screaming obscenities.

The midwife smiled as she handed her the baby for the first time.

'Red!' she observed. He was the staff's favourite baby, because he was big and burly and he cried the place down. They loved him.

And he *was* red. The other babies in the hospital were brown and sweet. This one was crumpled and cross. Noeline liked the name, and she kept it, because now she could do whatever she liked. If she'd had the baby at home, Daisy's parents would have insisted she name him 'Jeremy Giles' or something similar. They weren't here. They had no idea that either she or the baby existed. She was free.

The image she'd had of herself strolling barefoot around India with a gurgling baby tied to her back turned out not to be grounded in reality, and for the first few months of Red's life, Noeline was at a loss. They stayed in cheap hotels, until she decided to settle in Bombay.

He cried for half the night, and upset the other guests. She struggled with him, struggled without her sleep, but she managed, and so did Red. She took him out during the day and let him see everything that was going on around them. It amused her that he thought India was where they lived, he and his mother. It was his whole world. He had no idea.

At first, Noeline pretended she was married, and that, wherever they were, she and Red were on their way to meet her husband. Then she started going back to places where they'd already been, and trapping herself with her lies. She changed her story. She was a young widow. Her husband had recently died, and she and the baby were travelling while she tried to find herself. No one questioned that story. People befriended her, and helped her. She wore a wedding ring. Her husband's name, she said, had been Michael. That was Giles's middle name.

'It wasn't easy,' I tell Sophie. I don't really want to talk about it, even now. 'In fact, it was terribly hard but that was good. It gave me something to concentrate on. Everything was immediate. I had to think about how we were going to get through the day. That was it. He was part of Giles, so it seemed that Giles wasn't completely dead after all. Red looks a little bit like him, don't you think? I began to get over what had happened. I was looking after someone so I had less time to feel guilty. People were absolutely wonderful towards us. They made such a fuss of him. Red is the best thing that's ever happened to me.'

'And so will this baby be,' she says, leaning forwards and stroking my stomach. 'Red saved you last time. You should tell him that. And this little one's going to do the same this time round. You're lucky.'

'In a weird way, I think you're right.'

chapter thirty-six

22 January

He took them away, in his car. All that time when he was sitting there looking nonchalant, he knew he was going to take Daisy, and Christie, away from me. But he didn't say anything. I wish he'd taken me instead of Christie. I wish something would happen to me.

Now I really am alone. I can't decide where to go. I feel strangely comfortable in this hellhole. Anywhere else would be scary. I've never been to Sydney. I don't want to go to London. Patrick's in Sydney. I should go to him.

Lucky, lucky Christie. I should have assaulted the boy. Then I would have been arrested, and I'd be in the car with Daisy right now. I'd be there. I would be a bigger part of the story than I've ever been. I would have crossed sides. I would, like Daisy, have become a transgressor. I'd have been reported upon. Together, we would be the proponents of the action.

Instead, it's Christie and Daisy who are in it together. I wonder whether they're talking in the car. I hope Chris has got her tape recorder on.

When Patrick was drunk last night, just before he left this morning, he became maudlin. Part of me wanted to cheer him up, but I couldn't. I mean, I'm sure I could have if I'd wanted to, but somehow I couldn't be bothered. I haven't got it in me to comfort someone else. I want comfort myself.

'You won't come to Sydney,' he said, looking glum. 'You say you will but I know you won't. As soon as I'm out of here you'll forget about me. I know you will because it's happened before.'

'What do you mean,' I asked him, 'it's happened before? You've never asked me to come to Sydney before. For Christ's sake, I've only known you a week.'

Patrick sighed. 'Not you, Larry. For once, we're not talking about you. A year or so ago, I met Mark. I fell for him big time. Thought he was everything I wanted. He'd been engaged to a girl not long before, like you, Larry, but like you he said he was happy with me and that to be with me was what he wanted. Then he got scared and changed his mind. He went back to the woman. Just like you're going to do.'

'I'm not!' I was annoyed with him for manipulating me. He'd forced me to say that. 'For one thing, Sophie wouldn't be up for it.'

'That is *so* not the point.'

'And for another thing I want to be with you. We've had a good time together, haven't we, and that's in these fraught circumstances where everything else comes second to the story. I'm sure we could have a great time if we were free to concentrate on each other.'

He looked at me in a funny way. 'That really is how you see it, isn't it? Everything else really is a distraction. For you. In a week you've gone from being engaged to Sophie to shagging Christie, to re-evaluating your sexuality with me, and now you're wondering whether to come to Sydney and try the old queer lifestyle, and all the time you've barely noticed it because you've been so obsessed with what's going on with one poor pregnant woman who's got into trouble. Don't you think that's even a little bit odd? For fuck's sake, Larry, it's only work.'

'Only work! It's a good thing we don't all think like that.'

He looked seriously pissed off by now. We were lying in bed together, naked. I was trying not to feel self-conscious, but it's hard to get used to the fact that our bodies are essentially the same. From habit, I would occasionally stroke his flat chest, then hope he didn't realise what I'd been doing.

He spun around to face me. 'Not only is it only work, but it's also not particularly noble work. Joe Public hates journalists, and have you ever wondered why? It's because we hound people like we've been hounding Lina and her family. We stir things up. We do terrible things to people's lives, and then we give ourselves a good pat on the back and move on. And we don't actually do anything. All we do is report on what other people do. We're cowardly.

'You know why I went into photojournalism? It was because I saw it as a potential force for good, and even as an art form. I thought I could get out there and report on things, and people, that nobody knew about, and maybe help make things better. I could be a subjective filter for the world, and bring new ideas, and places, and people, into Australians' living rooms. I saw myself, eventually, working for *National Geographic*, that sort of thing. Then you end up doing agency work to pay the rent, and before you know it you're in Craggy bloody Rock screaming at a pregnant woman who was living her life perfectly harmlessly, teaching little kids and having babies, before we came along. This is not a good story, Larry, whatever you might think, and I am not in any way proud to be associated with it.'

I got out of bed, forgetting to be embarrassed about my nudity.

'At least you've let me know how you feel,' I told him coldly. 'I wonder why you're so keen to be associated with *me*, in that case.'

He put his arms round my waist and tried to pull me back. Taken by surprise, I sat down abruptly. Then I stood up again, and put on my pants.

'Don't take it personally! I dislike your brand of journalism, your British tabloid mentality, which is the same as the Australian tabloids I suppose. I like *you*. You're attractive, Larry. You're a good person at heart. I admire your single-mindedness. I love the way you set your mind to something and don't stop until it's done. We're good together, aren't we, sexually? Considering you've never done this before, you're actually awesome. It's just this story that makes me uncomfortable. And that's almost over now. Come to Sydney with me. Leave all this behind. See what else the world has to offer. We can sit by the harbour and drink white wine in the afternoon, and eat oysters and shrimps. We can go to bars where no one's going to stare at us and laugh and whisper, and everywhere we go, you're going to get served. And I don't mind telling you, I want some of that famous Golchin single-mindedness focused on me.'

He was too intense. We didn't part on particularly good terms. Sometimes I think we talked at cross purposes. He had no idea how much he wounded me with what he said about my story, and when I looked at him, when I took in what he was saying, I wondered whether I was hurting him as well.

So he went. He caught one of the small flights that everyone's queuing up for these days. Suddenly, no one can wait to leave. Well, I can wait a little while longer.

Then Daisy and Christie were taken away, and now there's practically nobody left at all. Even Sophie and Red have gone. They got on a bus to Adelaide, and I couldn't be bothered to go after them. I'd only get spat on by that vicious thug. I followed them to the bus stop, because I thought the de Montforts would like to know the whereabouts of their grandson.

'Sophie,' I panted, running up next to her. 'Did that Gibbon bloke take Daisy to Alice?'

'Lawrence, fuck off. Surely you've done enough now? You've screwed things up for everybody. Even you should be satisfied with this. Your work is done. Congratulations. Go away. We're not talking to you.'

'Because he told Christie he was taking her to Alice, so I guess that's where Lina is too.'

She didn't reply. Red turned his head to look at me. I held his glance. He looked all right. He wasn't crying, at least. For a moment, I considered comforting him with the news that he might be going to have a luxurious new life in London, but the moment seemed wrong.

'Are you going to Renmark?' I asked him instead.

'Not telling,' he replied calmly. 'Sophie, you've never said fuck before.'

'She has. Are you going to Alice?'

Now neither of them was talking to me. If only I'd contrived to run the story while staying friendly with Sophie. Then I'd have the kind of access I'd have needed. If Sophie hadn't told Daisy, the first time she met her, early in the morning, that I was a journalist, then I would at least have met her socially before they all turned me into the big bad ogre. Then I could have written about that. We could have spent the evening together, and at the end I could have started asking her about being Daisy. It would have been a legendary article.

'This is all your fault,' I told Sophie bitterly.

'I know,' she said, through gritted teeth. 'Now go away.'

There's nobody here. I don't know what to do with myself. The sun is beginning to set, and for the first time there is no point whatsoever in sitting outside the bungalow. It's empty now. It's meaningless. People always told me that it was, essentially, just another eyesore, but I couldn't believe it. I still feel some kind of reverence. I wonder whether I should break in and take some photos. I'm not sure there's much appetite now for pictures of the hiding place. I might as well. One day, someone will write a book about her, and at the very least I'll be able to make some money from the shots. They'll be like the photos of Anne Frank's hiding place. A postmodern version.

I walk back towards the motel. If Daisy was Anne Frank, I realise, I would have to be a Nazi. I scrub the simile from my mind, and try to think up a better one. Daisy Fraser hid in this unprepossessing house like a mole in a hole, like a rabbit in a warren. That doesn't work at all. It's crap. The house was her unlikely haven, the Brazil to her Ronnie Biggs. That doesn't work either. The only thing that comes to mind is a victim sheltering from a despot, and that does not serve my purposes at all. I don't even know why I'm trying to turn a phrase. I don't know if they're even going to have a Daisy Fraser story in the paper tomorrow.

I go back to my room. It's just mine, now. All Christie's stuff has gone to Alice, and I'm glad.

Suddenly, there are vacancies here. I watch a large blond couple letting themselves into Patrick's room. I want to stop them, to touch the woman on the arm and say, politely, excuse me, but I had anal sex on your bed this morning. I'd love to know what she'd say. They look up, and smile vaguely at me.

'Afternoon,' I say.

'Good afternoon.' They're European in some way. Dutch, I think, or something.

'You just passing through?'

'We have come out of our way, in fact,' confesses the woman. 'To see this woman we have read about, where she lives.'

'Daisy Fraser, you mean.'

'Yes, of course.'

'I actually know her a bit.'

They are agog. 'You do? And is she in Craggy Rock today?'

I smile. 'Actually, I'm afraid you just missed her. She went to Alice Springs this morning. But I'll show you her house, if you like.'

It isn't over yet, I tell myself, as I take my torch and my Swiss Army knife from my bag. People are still interested in my story. I've influenced these people's holiday. I feel a surge of energy. I will write the book myself. Now that Daisy's gone to Alice, and Red and Sophie are in Renmark, I'll bow out of the day-to-day reporting. What I'll do instead is, I'll go to Sydney. I'll show Patrick that he was wrong to have so little faith in me. I'll take one of the light aircraft, and then I'll sit in the sun by the harbour, and catch the ferry to Manly like Gita, and I'll drink cold white wine and eat oysters, and I'll write a compelling synopsis for my true life crime story. Everyone'll want to read it. Everyone in Britain, and everyone in Australia, for a start. Once I've got a publishing deal, I'll go back home and get back to the office, and I'll write my book in my free time – in all those early mornings and late evenings when I used to go to work. Once it's published I will be the acknowledged expert on everything pertaining to Daisy Fraser. I'll probably get to go on TV from time to time to talk about her. By then, too, she will have been tried so the mechanics of her escape ought to be in the public domain, at last. I'll write an appendix to deal with that.

I arrange with the Dutch people that I'll show them both her houses first thing in the morning, and I go round there on my own to break in. I pass familiar looking people in the street, and, since I've been living in this small community for over a fortnight, I try smiling at them and saying hello. Nobody acknowledges me. Even Nora didn't speak to me today. I think it's because of the arrest. They hold me responsible, for some reason. I don't care. Let them say what they like about me. It wasn't my fault. I just exposed the truth.

I walk casually to the back door of the bungalow. I don't think anyone saw me. This time, they've locked it, but it only takes a matter of seconds to pick the lock. I feel fantastic as I do it. I am capable. I have a skill. It is ludicrously easy. I think if I shook the door, it would probably come open.

It is weird inside. All the curtains are closed, and the air is perfectly still. The air conditioning is, not surprisingly, switched off. I move around in the darkness. I have been in here once before, also in the dark, and I remember roughly where things are. I'm going to have to let some daylight in, however, for my photographs. I wish Patch was still with me. He could have taken some brilliant shots, although I'm sure he wouldn't have. Instead, I'm left with my Canon Sureshot, trying to do the best job I can.

It's not difficult. I stand in the doorway of each room, and fit as much of it into the viewfinder as I can, press the button a few times, and then close the curtains again. I've almost finished when the telephone rings. It pierces the stillness, and I look round, scared. My heart starts pumping, and I walk towards the phone, desperate to silence it. I've called this number myself, numerous times, but it just rang and rang. I'm sure it was unplugged. No one can live with a ringing phone.

My hand is on the receiver before I realise I shouldn't answer it. But it might be Daisy. I need to speak to her. In fact, it's almost certainly her. She left before Sophie and Red. She'll think they're still here.

Fuck it. I pick it up.

'G'day,' I say, trying to disguise my voice with a poor Australian accent.

'Who is this?' demands a male voice, and I don't know what to say, so I hang up. Then I finish my photos as quickly as I can. It's surprisingly spacious in here. I've got every bedroom, including the one where I know she slept. I've got both bathrooms. I'm in the living room, which I notice has a satellite television connection, when the ringing starts up again. I wonder whether Daisy used to sit in here and watch her house on the screen. She must have done. Three shots, and I'm finished.

I hurry to the back door, pursued by the ringing phone, but as I go, I trip over a cot in the hallway. I should have remembered it. It catches my ankle, and sends me sprawling. Before I can get up, I hear a key in the front door. I struggle to my feet, and head for the kitchen. If I can get out of the back before whoever this is gets in, I'll be all right.

He catches me with my hand on the handle.

'Hold it right there,' he says, and I turn around to see Pete. Pete, whose brother is Daisy's husband. Pete who fancies Sophie. Pete who hates me. If I didn't already know that he hated me, I'd certainly know it now. He's staring at me with venom. His face is twisted and ratty. His cheeks are pinched, and I don't like his expression. I don't like it at all.

I keep going. Once I'm outside I'll have a better chance of bolting. He wouldn't harm me in the open air. People would stop him. Except there's no one here now who would care. My closest allies in town are the Dutch couple.

He grabs my shoulder. I wince. He's got my sunburn. I wait for the punch, but it never comes. I try to wriggle away, but his fingers dig into me. Then someone comes up behind him. I wonder whether they're going to stop him, but when I open my eyes, I see the big thug, Andy. He's not on my side. Nobody is on my side.

Andy takes me by the top of my arm. I use all my strength to push them off me, but it doesn't work. I try to punch Pete, but he just laughs.

They escort me outside. I try to work out what's going on, but it's not easy to think straight. What went wrong? I know I need somebody to save me. If they were still here, Daisy or Sophie might stop them. I know Christie and Patrick would try to do something. I try to run, but I can't get away. They're leading me to a battered van.

'Let me go,' I manage to say. 'I'm sorry.'

'Oh, we're going to let you go, mate,' laughs Pete, as they throw me into the back. I scream at them. I wish I'd carried on with karate when I was a boy. Then I'd have surprised them.

The engine starts and I feel it underneath me. I open my eyes. We're driving. They can't be taking me far, because there isn't anywhere to go. I try to stand up, but I'm too tall, and besides, there isn't much point.

'Where are we going?' I call, but nobody answers. I bang on the partition, but they ignore me. They are making no concessions to the bumpy ground, and the suspension is shot to pieces. I struggle to my feet and look through the back window. We're in the desert. Craggy has already disappeared. I can see stones, and rocks, and dust. A huge cloud of dust behind us. I try the door. Jumping out would be a stupid thing to do. I'd be better off staying on board. I know they're just doing this to frighten me. It has worked. As soon as we get back to the motel, I'll pack my bags, and I'll get myself to Sydney straightaway. I'll leave the story for a while, and use this episode when I come to write the book.

Abruptly, the van stops. I am thrown right back, and hurt my back on the partition. I lie on the floor, in a foetal position, and wait. Pete and Andy open the back doors, and pull me out by the feet. I kick at them.

'Right, mate,' says Pete, with a smile. 'This is your stop. Seeya.'

'When are you coming to get me?'

'Get you, mate? Why would we come and get you?'

Andy looks over his shoulder. He's already halfway to the van. 'This is the way we let you know, in Craggy, that we don't want to see your mongrel face any more,' he says.

'I know! And I'll go! I'm going to Sydney as soon as I can. I'll go today!'

'Bloody right you'll go today.'

I shout, and beg, and whisper and swear, and tell them I'm sorry, but they ignore me, and get back into their van, and drive off in a huge cloud of dust.

The sun is beginning to soften, but it's still hardly bearable. I pull myself up so I'm leaning against a rock, but the rock is too hot. The shade, at least, should be lengthening soon. I wish I hadn't done this story at all. I wish I'd left with Patrick. I could be sitting next to Sydney Harbour, right now. He must be back there. He was flying to Adelaide, and changing planes, and going home from there. Patrick is at home, in Balmain. Christie is in police custody, and that seems, to me, a remarkably safe place to be. I wish I was Christie. Daisy's with the police as well. She'll be all right too.

They've done this to scare me. They might not like me, but they're hardly actually going to leave me here. If they did that, I'd die.

I wish I had some water. They could have given me just one bottle, to keep me going. The landscape here all looks the same. Nobody's going to chance upon me here. All I can see, in every direction, is the desert. It's like being on the moon. This is what it was like for Daisy, the other day. Suddenly, I feel close to her. This is an experience we've shared. We can talk about it. Pete rescued her, and he'll rescue me, too.

Soon the moon will be out, and then all the stars will follow. I think I can make it through the night.

I take a stone and use it to write in the earth.

PLAN
    Seek out shade and shelter.
    Wait.
    Don't move from here otherwise they won't find me when they come back.

They'll be back for me in the morning, I know they will.

chapter thirty-seven

I was right about the baby. She is a girl.

They put her into my arms as soon as she's born, and suddenly I forget how exhausted I am. She snuggles into my breast, and I stroke her cheek. She overwhelms me. This is my daughter. This is the person I've been carrying everywhere I've been. She's been through it all with me, and yet she wasn't even born yesterday. She was born today. Today is her birthday. March the sixth, the day before she was due.

Despite all she's been through, she seems calm. From time to time, she cries a funny, squeaking little cry, but she doesn't seem upset, or angry. She doesn't seem to be disturbed by anything more than the fact that she's been squeezed through a birth canal, which must be confusing, and the pressing need for food and love. I look at her little face. She's perfect. She has deep blue eyes and long dark eyelashes. Her hair is sparse, and what there is of it is dark. She looks up into my eyes, and I smile. I can't take my eyes off her. I never want to let her go. I need to hold her for ever.

Tony has a hand on my shoulder.

'Well done, darling,' he says. 'I knew you could do it.'

I turn to give him a brief smile, before I look back to our daughter. The birth hasn't been easy, and I'm sore and bloody, but already that doesn't matter.

'Isn't she wonderful?' I say softly. 'Our little girl.'

'With all that going on, we never talked about names.'

'What do you think?'

'Oh, I don't know, love. What does she look like?'

'Can we give her Rosie as her middle name?'

'Sure we can. How about Rosemary? And I'll tell you another

name I've always liked. You might disagree. Your mother's name. Lucy.'

'Lucy Rosemary Pritchett? That's a lovely name. That's who she is.' I stroke her face. 'Hello, Lucy,' I tell her. She looks back, deep into my eyes. It's the least I can do for Mum, after all these years.

Tony breaks the silence. 'I'll call Red. Mum can bring him in, whenever you're ready.'

I look to the midwife for approval. She nods. She's not the friendliest of women, possibly because I swore at her fairly comprehensively during labour. She must, though, have heard much worse than anything I managed to come up with. I wonder whether it's my notoriety she doesn't like. She has a jaded air.

'I've got some more checks to do on you and Baby, Mrs Pritchett,' she says abruptly. 'After that we'll have you taken down to the maternity ward, and you may receive visitors whenever you feel ready.'

I hate the medical profession's habit, shared with our still-pregnant neighbour, Jess, of dropping the definite article when referring to the baby. Her name isn't 'Baby'. Her name is Lucy. She is a baby, my baby, the baby. *Baby* makes my blood boil. It's patronising.

Tony strokes the baby's hair. 'Just going to the phone,' he whispers to her. 'Back in a minute.'

As I continue cradling her, avoiding eye contact with the hatchet-faced midwife in case she takes it as a cue to snatch my darling away for more prodding, I wonder what the immediate future holds for us. If only we could go home to Renmark, and live as a family. If that were possible, I would never complain about anything again. I would be delighted to stay up all night, every night, with my little Lucy. I'd put up with anything Tony inflicted on me, whether it was internet pornography or questions about the past. Nothing Red said or did would faze me.

Red, at least, won't be going to England. As soon as Jason Gibbon realised our situation, he sorted it out. He had one of the local boys destroy the vial of blood from Christie's minibar. Then he told me with a wink that he'd arrange a blood test to confirm that Red wasn't even my child, let alone Giles's. I gave some blood, and, in Renmark, Red did the same, in a controlled and friendly atmosphere this time. When the results came back, they proved his case conclusively. The lab reports were made available to the media, and, for now, the de

Montforts have given up their claim. The adoption story has been officially accepted, which seems like a miracle.

Jason never asked me where Red came from, so I was delighted not to have to tell him. Sophie and Tony are the only ones who know. I'm sure Margot has guessed. As for Red, I'll tell him one day.

Christie, by all accounts, is back in London, merrily continuing as though the whole nightmare had never happened. Nobody prosecuted her. We let it drop, because we all preferred her on the other side of the world. Tony found a piece she'd written on the internet last week, about the burning down of a gay cinema in London. 'By Christie Baxter', said her byline. 'Head of investigations'.

For the past month, we've had a façade of normality. Officer Gibbon asked me some cursory questions in Alice, then had a policeman drive me to Renmark, which seemed, to me, to be beyond the call of duty.

'Can't have you dropping the little one on the bus,' he said dismissively when I complained that it wasn't necessary, 'and technically I'm obliged to have an officer with you at all times, to be sure you're not going to, you know, pull a vanishing act.'

He was embarrassed every time he had to remind me that he represented the law, and was not just a kindly man who had spirited me away from Craggy Rock. I wondered, for a while, why his demeanour towards me was so entirely different from his attitude to Christie. He hated her. For the interminable drive up the Stuart Highway, he chatted amiably to me over his shoulder about the pregnancy, the children I'd taught at school, and about Red. Every time Christie tried to join in the conversation, he cut her dead, and once he even turned to me, conspiratorially, and said, 'Sorry about that,' when she'd spoken.

'Children,' he said, as we drove through the endless rocky landscape. 'Best thing that can happen to you.'

'Have you got children, then?' I asked politely. He turned round, taking his eyes off the road for at least a minute, and beamed.

'Twin girls. They're seven months now, and not a day goes by when I don't wonder what we did with our time before we had them. They take up every moment, they come and see you in the night, you get used to being elbow deep in their shit, and still you love them to death!'

I was delighted to be able to indulge in some proper baby talk in this unlikely quarter.

'What are their names?' I asked him first of all.

'Sarah and Stella. Tell you what, I'll get Claire, that's my wife, to bring them down to the station later. Then you can meet them for yourself.'

Christie turned to him, clearly spotting a way to ingratiate herself. 'Have you got a photo?'

He ignored her, but fumbled in his pockets. Then he steered the car with his knees while he passed three photographs back to me. 'There you go, Lina, some photos for you. The one in the red, that's Stella.'

I looked at the chubby little girls. In the first shot, they were beaming at each other. Stella was holding a toy, while Sarah had grabbed her own toes. I thought about Rosie and Ed. The companionship of a twin must transform the world. I wished I'd had a twin. I wished I was having twins, because at least they would have been through their prenatal traumas together. They'd have been able to support each other whenever they needed it. I wondered what would become of my baby. Our family seemed likely to split into its constituent parts, and hurl itself across the world. It wasn't going to be a family at all, any more. How is a baby meant to make sense of that?

The other pictures showed the girls side by side in their high chairs, with copious amounts of sludgy food around their faces, and a small blonde woman attempting to spoon some more into one of their mouths while they were distracted by the camera. In the third, they were lying on a rug on some grass, with sunhats on their heads.

'They're absolutely beautiful,' I told him, passing them back. Christie put out her hand, but Jason intercepted them and put them firmly into the glove compartment. 'I think my baby's a girl,' I added.

'I hope you're right. You can't beat a little girl.'

By now, Christie was fuming. I knew who was going to get preferential treatment at the station, and I thanked my lucky stars for this temporary reprieve.

Because Jason was so sympathetic to my predicament – because he couldn't bear to see anything bad happen to a pregnant woman – he told me to stay in Renmark and report to the police station every day. Thus we have spent February pretending to be a normal family, despite the neighbours' curiosity. I sat outside with Jess, who was more magnificently bovine even than I was, and talked endlessly about all matters that pertain to pregnancy and birth, while parrying her tentative questions about the recent and distant past.

'So, you're all settled back here now, are you? It's so good to see you back . . . Lina?' she'd say.

'It's great to be here, Jess,' I'd reply, quickly. 'Has your baby still got its feet in your ribs?'

Edmund went back to England weeks ago, but Mum, Dad and Rosie have been staying in a hotel nearby. Mum and Dad make a fuss of Red, their 'adopted grandson'. Dad plays football in the garden with him, and tries to understand the impenetrable Aussie rules. Mum pretends to follow when he shows her how the internet works. I reminded him not to show her any naked ladies.

'Why not?' he demanded.

'She wouldn't like them, the same as I don't like them.'

'You're probably right.'

We have fished from boats on the river. We've walked along the towpath and admired the sunsets. We've had family meals together every evening, normally with Margot and Sophie as well.

It was Sophie who told us about Lawrence.

'He just disappeared,' she said. 'His mum thought he was coming home. She said when she spoke to him he was going to be home within a week or so. But he never turned up.'

'Bastard's probably still sitting outside Margot's place, waiting for Lina,' said Tony, but he looked a bit shifty.

'That'll be it, love,' added Margot, too quickly.

'He's not there, though,' Sophie insisted. 'Nora says she hasn't seen him for ages. She cleared the room so she could let it again. His stuff's still in the motel. He's just gone.'

I studied the faces of my husband and my mother-in-law.

'He must have pulled a disappearing act himself,' I said as lightly as I could, and changed the subject by taking Sophie's hand and placing it on the spot where the baby was kicking. I know that they know what's become of him. I am happy to remain in the dark.

Red has relaxed a little, and begun to enjoy school.

'I can't wait till the baby's born,' he said recently.

'Nor can I,' I lied. Tony, Beth, Sophie and I have all been painfully aware, all the time, that as soon as I've given birth, my position is going to change. Now that has happened, and even Jason Gibbon can't save me from the consequences.

Sophie brings Red to visit us. Beth will come later, because she's at work, and Tony has momentarily distracted Margot so that Red can be the first to hold the baby.

'Hi, Mum,' Red says cheerfully. 'Where's the baby?'

'Here she is.' I hold her out to him.

'That?' he exclaims. 'I thought you were just holding a blanket.'

'It's not a blanket. It's your sister. Here, you can take her if you like. Put her along your arm like this.'

He reaches out for her, and looks down at her with all the tenderness I feel. 'Hi there, sis,' he says. 'You don't look like I expected but I'm sure you'll grow up nice. You might remember me from before. I'm Red. I'm your brother and I'm going to look after you a lot. We're going to be mates. So you just learn to walk and talk, all right?'

Sophie laughs. 'Give her a chance!' She leans over and kisses me. 'Well done,' she says quietly. 'How are you feeling?'

'Sore. I had a second degree tear.' I watch her wince. 'And scared. I have no idea what's going to happen now. If only Jason was in charge round here. Every time the door opens, I expect the police.'

'They're not going to come for you now. You're not in any state to go anywhere.'

'But I will be. They say I can go home tomorrow.'

She hugs me. 'Don't worry about it. Worrying isn't going to change anything. Let's concentrate on your gorgeous baby instead.'

I feel tearful. I don't know how long I can control myself. 'She's beautiful, isn't she, she's just perfect, and that makes it worse. Don't worry. I'm not going to crack up.'

When Tony and Margot arrive, with armfuls of flowers and a bottle of wine, I have to put on a brave face. Lucy stands up astonishingly well to the ordeal of being passed around between all her doting friends and relatives. She doesn't cry at all, not even when Margot puts her face frighteningly close to her, and bellows, 'It's your gran here, darl! You'll be seeing a lot of me!' I suppose she's got used to Margot, in utero.

From time to time, I catch Tony's eye, and we smile at each other.

In spite of everything, we've got a beautiful daughter. We've been getting closer, recently. If we had the opportunity, I think we might be able to make a go of things.

He pours some Chardonnay into a hospital beaker, and hands it to me. I drink it gratefully. Margot looks up sharply. Now that the baby's physically evident, she seems to have changed her attitude to my alcohol consumption.

'Not too much of that,' she says. 'Little Lucy isn't going to want to be drunk.'

'Don't worry, Margot,' I tell her. 'Just this one small glass, I promise. You guys can have the rest.'

I stay awake for most of the night, watching the pattern the electric light from the corridor makes on my floor. Lucy wakes from time to time, and I feed her. She seems to have taken to it, mostly because I've breastfed before. I know that she has to get the whole areola into her mouth, and pump it properly to get her supplies. It's nice not to have to lie to Tony any more, that I can admit to being an old hand at all this. I'm amazed that anyone ever believed the story about Red's adoption, and am even more astonished that, as far as I can tell, they still do. It always seemed ludicrously far-fetched to me, but it just seemed the best way to avoid unwelcome questions. I never wanted him to know the truth about his paternity. Perhaps I should have told him the bare bones of it – that his real dad died before he was born – and answered his questions when he was older as truthfully as I could.

In the morning, I eat breakfast and gaze, infatuated, at my little girl. I could look at her for ever. When someone stops in the doorway, I don't look up. Then he clears his throat.

'Hello, Daisy,' says a voice I know well.

'What are you doing here, Dad?' I ask, without smiling. I can't imagine why he's come on his own.

'Sophie called us.'

'Where's Mum and Rosie?'

'They're on their way. Stopped off to get some goodies for you and the little one.'

He walks in, and stands awkwardly by Lucy's cot. I am struck again by how old and wretched he looks. The Frasers seem determined to stay back in our lives, and so I'm going to have to get over the guilt that stabs me every time I look at them.

'You can pick her up if you like,' I tell him. 'Say hello.'

'Will that be all right?'

He lifts her gingerly, and rocks her in the crook of his elbow. Then he sits on the edge of my bed.

'When you ran away,' he says, 'and before that, when you were – what was it the school used to say? – off the rails, were you very unhappy at home?'

'I suppose I thought I was. But when I think about it I brought it all on myself. I mean, there was nothing concrete wrong at home, was there? I didn't have any more reason to be unhappy than anyone else. Sometimes I used to think I was actually an orphan child, that I came from a much more glamorous circus background, or that my real parents were dancers. But you didn't do anything wrong. Really.'

I've never spoken to my Dad properly before, because I was a teenager when I last stayed with my parents, and pre-pubescent when I last lived with them. When we've seen them in Renmark, Dad has been subdued. He's sat in the corner with a drink in his hand, and he's observed us. He's avoided my eye, and I thought he hated me.

I used to hate him, when I was a little girl. I can't remember exactly what he did to earn my disapproval. He didn't hit me. He didn't force himself upon me. He never interfered with me sexually. For years, I allowed myself to assume that he had, because it was the only way my messed up head made sense. In fact, he just embarrassed me. He embarrassed me, and he bored me. I'll probably embarrass and bore my children, before too long. Everything that happened came from me. I wasn't a victim.

Mum and Rosie rush into the room. Mum sits next to Dad and takes the baby. I am exhausted. I want to go home, and yet I don't, because I have no idea what will become of us.

'Well done,' says Rosie quietly. 'Was it OK?'

'It was fine,' I tell her, without thinking about it. 'I mean, it was fine insofar as childbirth can be fine. As soon as you see the baby, you forget all about it. Do you like your niece, then?'

'She looks adorable. Hey, you've done the right thing by Mum. We had to rush into the ladies on the way in, because she was overcome, yet again, by the Lucy aspect of things.'

'It's not too weird for you, is it, seeing a baby?'

'Of course not! It's still too weird for me seeing you. The baby's fine. We're going for IVF when all this is sorted out.'

'Paul must be missing you.'

'I'm going back next week.'

There is a long silence as I contemplate next week and what it might bring. I can't bear to think about it. I know I'm not getting out of this one. I'm just going to have to face it.

It is an officer, in uniform.

'Morning, Mrs Pritchett,' he says. I recognise him from my trips to the station. 'I'm Detective Inspector Smithers. We've met before. I'm afraid I need to ask you a few questions.'

'I'm sure you do.'

'When are they letting you go home?'

'Maybe this afternoon.'

'So we'll give you a day or two at home, as long as you don't go anywhere. Can you come and see us on Thursday?'

I look at him. I try to think of the right thing to say.

'Sure,' I tell him. 'Is the afternoon all right?'

'We'd prefer morning. And don't worry. We're not too harsh on a lady in your situation.'

He leaves without looking at the baby. I pick her up and hold her close.

I have no idea what will become of us.